In The Salt

Hays T. Blinckmann

In The Salt

For my husband, Jan-Marten
and my sons, Hugo & Max

"April is the cruelest month, breeding lilacs out of dead land, mixing memory with desire, stirring dull roots with a spring rain."

T.S. Eliot

ONE

Maggie sat staring at her nails. She ground her teeth together to help her focus. It was coming again, the wave of nausea and fear. Fighting the panic attack, she looked up at CNN playing on the TV monitor in the airport lounge. The words *focus, focus, focus* kept running through her mind. And then it came, *my mother is dead.* The one resounding thought that had been echoing in her head for the past twenty-four hours. Maggie could see those letters in typewriter font flashing across the front of her mind. My mother, my mother is dead. Each time emphasis on a different word, MY mother is dead. My MOTHER is dead. IS DEAD.

"Now boarding flight 82 nonstop from New Orleans to Boston. First class passengers and people needing special assistance may proceed through gate 4," the anonymous voice from the loudspeaker roared. Maggie just sat there forgetting she was a first class passenger. She was more the special assistance type, she thought sardonically. Maggie gathered her one leather carryon and dropped her sunglasses from the top of her head down over her eyes. She did not have patience for Miss Mary Sunshine Stewardess greeting everyone at gate 4 with the neatly pressed white polyester blouse, red scarf and platinum hairdo. She hated it when they purposely paused to read her name. Why? Who cares what our names are?

"Thank you, Miss Atwood," the perky stewardess said.

Maggie managed a smirk and bolted through the gate door. The only real thought compelling her was the Bloody Mary she was about to have with her second Valium.

Maggie had booked the first class ticket after her fourth glass of scotch. If she had to go home to Haven, she was going to go in style. She had gotten a case of the "fuck its" as she called it when your actions were above and beyond your financial or emotional means. It was the "fuck its" that lead her to New Orleans in the first place. And it was that "fuck its" that had stopped her from speaking to her mother. Maybe they weren't working out for her after all.

The call had come at exactly 12:07 p.m. yesterday from Millie, her mother's next door neighbor and closest family friend. Maggie remembered the time because she could not stop staring at the cable clock over the TV, as if she averted her eyes her entire world would melt away. When she saw Millie's caller ID, she had instinctively known it was bad news coming to bite her on the ass. In preparation, she sat on the couch and hit the talk button. She had been expecting this call for years, but Maggie could not believe it had finally picked a date and time.

"Maggie, it's Millie, hon."

Maggie could already hear it in her voice. She visualized poor Millie telling neighbors later it was the worst phone call she'd ever had to make. Maggie wanted to say, 'It's okay Millie, I know, I have been waiting for years,' but instead she sat there silent.

"Maggie, your Mom... Vivian.... She fell down the stairs last night and well... hon, she had been drinking. I guess we all knew it had to catch up with her sometime."

Millie's voice was breaking up and immediately Maggie began to panic, wishing to God her mother was not in a coma. Her mind flashed to sitting bedside in a hospital, her mother a vegetable enduring the endless idea of death.

"Her brain hemorrhaged from the hit, hon. She was gone in an instant. No pain, hon. None whatsoever."

Millie's voice faded and Maggie, just for a second, felt relief. Her mother's death was black and white, quick as a flash. No monitors beeping, no prolonged pain, no pulling the proverbial plug. But within a split second the relief was gone and Maggie realized what Millie was really saying and her heart turned to stone. The sad truth was that she always knew it would be this way. Her mother, Vivian Atwood, had been the most active and vibrant alcoholic anyone could have ever known and to have had it end any other way wasn't in the stars.

In the hours that followed, Maggie managed to call her boyfriend Marten at work, pour herself heaping tumblers of scotch, and book a first class ticket direct from New Orleans to Boston. The brown, smoky feeling that burned her chest competed with the ache that was beginning. A deep pain that she knew would take months, years to subside. By the time Marten had gotten home, she was sitting on the floor of the bathroom, crying into a towel, and clutching an empty glass.

Maggie stopped talking to her mother two years prior, prompting her move from New York City to New Orleans. Not once had she called home to tell her mother where she was or that she was in love or living with the man of her dreams. It would have been the one wish Vivian would have loved fulfilled. Hearing every detail of their relationship would have given Maggie's mother something to look forward to, perhaps a wedding and then grandchildren. Cruelly, Maggie did not spare one crumb of her happiness for her mother. She had kept all her affection and attention for Marten as punishment for her mother's many failures.

Accepting her mother's death was like choking on air itself. The vortex of her life was closing and her brain felt fuzzy and black. Marten gently wrapped her in a blanket and refilled her drink. "Maggie, breath darling . Listen to me, you will get through this. It will hurt, but you will get through this," Marten whispered over and over. "I love you. That will never change, no matter what happens next."

Maggie looked at him and felt the surge of realization hit her chest like an iceberg. Here was this gorgeous man, dedicated and devoted to her, and she had cheated on him. Maggie never talked about her family, never acknowledged more than their names. Now, she was realizing her obstinacy and silence had been an adultery all of her doing. She had withheld her past, skirted over the details of her family and made it precarious to ask. She made it seem consequential to their happiness, that her secrets remain hers. Her family was a topic not allowed in their relationship, making it capricious and ephemeral. Yet, he was still there before her, accepting of the circumstances. Why did he love her unconditionally? No one in her family did; they all had conditions, rules, the delicate balance of all their lives contingent upon the dutifulness of one another. Was she going to have that kind of relationship with Marten, exactly like her others?

Maggie had met Marten on a hot New Orleans April afternoon. For two months she had been living in the French Quarter and trying to find work. She had just left an unsuccessful job interview with a magazine and easily succumbed to the music and drinks calling to her from a local bar. She had liked the piano player, the breeze through the windows, and the fact that the bar was empty. She was deep into a paperback and halfway through a gin and tonic when Marten Klein strolled in and ordered a beer. Maggie tried not to stare but he was so attractive. At 6'3", blonde hair, blue eyes, he was the epitome of his German heritage. At 31, Maggie had given up on attractive men being unmarried, straight and normal and just assumed this was another cosmic joke. Karma was dangling the hope of love before her like a mirage in the desert.

Still, Maggie could not help but steal glances of him for the better part of an hour before he finally broke the ice. "Why do you suppose someone would put a cake out in the rain?" he had asked making direct eye contact with her. The pianist was singing Donna Summer's *MacArthur Park*.

"Wouldn't the better question be, why make a song out it?" Maggie retorted, shrugging her shoulders just a little and smiling.

"Ah, yes Americans do have a funny way of illuminating the wonders of the world." He said wryly.

"Or maybe we just have better drugs that make us see baked goods in strange places." Maggie deadpanned. Immediately, Marten burst out with a hearty laugh and moved one stool closer to Maggie.

They talked all afternoon about music, movies, books-discovering they both liked comedies, Italian food, and expensive wine; yet each disliked politics, California, and dull people. Marten was six years her elder and at 37, he seemed mature but with a boyish guile. She spent the entire night searching for what was wrong with him but, in the end, she had learned maybe there was love at first sight. And in... of all places, an empty bar.

Living in New Orleans, post Hurricane Katrina, Maggie was getting used to bleak and melancholy stories. Marten's was no different. He was from Hamburg, Germany and only moved to the States a few years back. He had already lost his parents to health problems too soon and divorced one wife back in Germany. Marten had presupposed that growing up one should have a big fancy job and a wife in order to be happy. The job, buying and selling international goods, was financially profitable but an emotional abyss. His wife was pretty and dull and valued his bank account more than his heart. So Marten left Germany and came to New Orleans to be a carpenter, rebuilding houses for the needy after Katrina. He liked the feel of a hammer, being outdoors, building something that would last, and having a drink in the middle of the day if he wanted. He had Euros in the bank from Germany and no one to answer to; he was a free man. He was happy for the most part, which not a lot of people could say. Marten told her it was not really what he wanted to be doing with his life but said that everyday he was reminded he's not the only asshole out there who has a shitty go of it.

They had been dating for six months when she moved into his apartment on the edge of the French Quarter. And now, two years later, they both knew marriage was the next step. Yet there was a wall between them, a roadblock that Maggie had carefully built and would not let their relationship pass. Marten had been open and up front about his past but Maggie had been reserved and secretive about hers. She found it difficult to explain the complexity and abnormality of her childhood. The difference between their families was that tragedy had struck Marten and his family; they were the casualties of fate and circumstance. Maggie's family had created their own misery through booze and drugs, lies and deceit. Her family was riddled with alcoholism, addiction and depression. Their pain was self-inflicted with each drink they took and each fabrication of reality they made. She found it unfathomable to even feel sorry for them or herself when the course of their lives had been by choice, designed by the drama. Maggie was sick and embarrassed by it all.

Marten, like the people of New Orleans, had felt true loss. They were the ruined amongst the ruins. Her family had not lost anything. They were criminals who robbed themselves and anyone around them of happiness. That was why she had moved to New Orleans, to distance herself from them. Now that she had met Marten, she stayed far away, scared that they would inflict the same damage on her relationship as they had on her. If she could keep her past and her present separate, she and Marten might have a chance. In the two years that Maggie had been with Marten, the man she loved more than anyone else, she had not spoken to her family.

That night, Marten sat in bed with her until her shaking and sobbing subsided. They rode out the night together; Maggie curled up staring at the night lights of the French Quarter. Although she did not say a word, he reminded her over and over that he loved her. He would get her through this. If she could have said anything without fear of breaking, she would have told him she loved him too.

And deep in the recesses of Maggie's heart, if she could have, she would have told Marten that her family had broken her in all the wrong places and that she didn't know how to mend. They had made her voiceless and shallow, and she feared her love for him was as impermanent and deceptive as their love for her. She would have confessed that she was like her family, each one of them in the worst possible ways, and despised herself for it. But worst, she could not change who she was, not even for him. And the only way to explain it was for him to meet her mother. She was the most important person in her life for all the wrong and right reasons. And now it was dawning on Maggie that the chance was gone.

Sitting on the plane, Maggie thought about her life or what she thought was the lack of one. Going home, the irony got to her, how far away from her past she had run but how she had not gotten very far. She had Marten, but what else? No marriage, no children, no real career. Maggie was either a failed writer or an aspiring one. She could not decipher the difference. Her obsession with writing started when she was a young girl when Maggie loved to dream up stories about fantasy lands and faraway princes. She wrote poems and amusing pieces for her boarding school English classes and then majored in creative writing at college. But did that make her a writer? Had she taken the notion too far? Stayed too long at a party she wasn't really invited too?

From an early age, Maggie worked hard and got into her father's alma mater, Tufts University in Boston. For four years, she focused and filled herself with twentieth century literature and creative writing classes. After graduation she travelled, seeking experiences outside of what she had known from her childhood in Haven, Massachusetts. Her twenties were a blur of tramping around Europe, staying and working were she could and scribbling in self indulgent notebooks. Eventually, tired and broke, she ended up in New York City.

She had a quick wit about her and, during her time in New York, she'd write cultural pieces for the latest hip rag around town. Maggie was known for her venomous take on society and biting remarks about 'American' culture. Once she wrote an article about how Andy Warhol was the Milli Vanilli of the seventies, a great little dance number that had everyone fooled. Her humor was what New York readers loved, but it was not exactly what Maggie had dreamed of writing all those years. Always in the back of her mind was her family and her childhood in Haven, the story she really wanted to tell. Now she was in the Big Easy, and it was not so easy. She had not made the connections or the friends like she had in New York. Instead, she dropped off old articles here and there waiting for someone to be inspired. But how could they be inspired when she, herself, was not? Words were failing her. Writing had become a chore. When Maggie was a child, she learned early to write the world in which she wished to live. When her mother would drink, Maggie would retreat to her bedroom and create fairy tales about being saved by a prince. Maggie was older now, she realized that no one was going to save her. Writing was not saving her either. The unfortunate truth in life is that you are responsible for yourself, end of story, kaput. Even people who win the lottery are not saved from themselves, even with 100 million dollars they still end up drunk or in prison.

"Miss Atwood, would you like lunch?" the flight attendant asked. Maggie, a little foggy from the Valium and Bloody Mary did the most obnoxious thing she could, she waved her little plastic cup implying she wanted another one. Normally her motto was not to treat people like servants but right now her moral compass was a bit askew. Maggie's grandmother Virginia used to say "manners are for free", meaning anyone can use them and usually Maggie respected that credo. But at the moment the Valium was mixing so nicely with the vodka that she finally could let go. Marten was always saying how wound up she was, holding her own self to impossible standards.

But wasn't that the game she was playing with herself? She knew she could commit herself to Marten, could write a novel, could hold a writing job, yet she hadn't. She let the days slip by, things unsaid, the computer untouched. Maggie couldn't figure if it was focus or purpose she lacked. It manifested in a disappointment in herself she was always trying to mask. No one would have ever described her as soft, but she tried hard to not let people see the bitterness either. Self-medicating helped a little too much.

Just like her mother, Maggie thought ironically as she watched the clouds drift past the airplane window. Her mother could never really run away from who she was and now it caught up with her at the bottom of a flight of stairs. Was it time for Maggie's demons to catch up with her, for her to free fall right into her failures? Would her life be as miserable as her mother's? Maggie brushed away the free flowing tears and stared at the racing landscape below her. She sighed and took the last swig of her drink. "Fuck it."

TWO

Exiting Logan airport, Maggie was blasted with the brisk, wet air. It was a typical April day in Massachusetts-50 degrees, overcast and rainy. This is what New Englanders called spring. Back in Boston, Maggie let the feeling of the familiar wash over her. While the mix of cultures of New Orleans excited her, here Maggie blended in. Her slim 5'7" frame, short strawberry blond hair, pale freckled skin and round green eyes matched all the other Boston Irish bustling around her. Surrounded by the Fitzpatricks and the O'Malleys, the salt air and pubs, where the accents were as thick as the sweaters, Maggie was once again home. Inhaling the salt air was like breathing life back into herself. As a child she would walk along the shores of Haven with her grandmother, and marvel at the taste of the salt in the air. Her young mind tried to comprehend how salt could be in the ocean and in the air and on the dinner table. She told her grandmother since there was table salt, the other two must be water salt and air salt. Standing there outside of Logan Airport, she felt the pull of her grandmother's hand and heard herself say it again. Air salt.

Marten had wanted to come but unable to explain why, Maggie refused. To soothe him, she said it would be better in a few days. Just give her a few days. She wanted to breathe the thick cool air and taste the sensation of being home, alone. Marten had never been to Massachusetts and, at the moment, she did not feel like playing tour guide. She wanted to re-enter her world as herself, as solitary as she had left. Maggie knew she would feel whole again like a distant traveler returning home. She had missed the vast gray sky, the salt that played on the edges of the breeze, the constant smell of the ocean close by more than she could admit.

Then she heard her name.

"Mags? Margaret Knowles Atwood, over here!"

She turned slowly to the familiar face and felt tears rush to her eyes. Looking at George Sherwood was like standing in her childhood bedroom. Nothing was more comforting. Growing up, George was Maggie's best friend, simply by circumstance of being the same age and living on the same street. Otherwise they were night and day. George was 6' 4", 275 lbs. and as a kid always had shaggy brown hair in his eyes. But now that they were getting older, he wore his hair in a buzz cut to de-emphasize the fact he was losing it all together. Ten years ago, George was briefly a running back for the New England Patriots. When he blew his knee the third season, George took the nest egg he had made and returned to their hometown of Haven to become a veterinarian. He married his high-school sweetheart, which was by no means Maggie, and moved into his parents' house after they died in a car crash. Of course George would be there, like he always had been.

Maggie felt herself choke as she said "G", and in two swift strides, was wrapped in George's arms. He had a dark blue Suburban waiting for her and shuffled her into the warm front seat. Maggie looked around at the children's car seats, and the carpet of toys, and the vet manuals and began to laugh. When he climbed in the driver's side, Maggie could see the worry in his eyes.

"G, really.. a *Suburban*? Really?" and with that George broke out in an ear to ear grin. Maggie raised her eyebrows, shaking her head from side to side. It had been the running joke between them when they were kids, George was the conformist and Maggie was the bohemian. George did every Little League sport, until high school football consumed him. He got straight A's in all the average classes, and he mowed every lawn in a one mile radius of their street after school. George had been homecoming king, and his now wife, Mitzi Moller Sherwood, had been homecoming queen. He was the perfect product of Haven, Massachusetts. Unlike George, Maggie was the quiet introspective type and hated sports. Team or group activities terrified her, so Maggie preferred spending her time alone, writing about the life she would eventually have. Although they were opposites, she and George shared their childhood. She missed him when they were apart ,and Maggie knew their friendship was the one thing that had never failed her.

Here at home George was her knight again. Although they were an unlikely duo as children, they never saw their differences. They lived on the same street and found each other free on Saturday afternoons. It was Maggie's imagination that led the way, and George was always a willing participant. They were pirates and thieves, they were knights and explorers, they were children. But it was always Maggie who lurked around George's house wanting him to play with her, take her someplace else other than her own home.

"How did you know when to get me?" Maggie eyed him.

"That boyfriend of yours, Marty?"

"Marten," Maggie corrected.

"OOh-Kay, Marten, well he called last night and asked me to. But he was reading my mind because I was about to call you anyway. I just, well, hadn't gotten to it yet."

"That's okay, G. I wasn't in any shape to be on the phone. Marten called you?" Thankfully she had at least told him about her best friend George. Maggie should not have been so surprised. It was like Marten to be errantly thoughtful. He had kept saying how he did not want her to be alone, and he usually got what he wanted.

"Yeah, he seems like a pretty nice guy, Mar-TEN. Where's he from though, a Rocky movie?" George had obviously picked up on Marten's accent.

"HA Ha, you provincial freak. Germany. Let me tell you, it is better than a Haven accent any day! Speaking of, how's the Mitzinator?" she jabbed.

Maggie sighed. It was nice to be back with George like this, giving each other shit. People usually could not stand their conversations because it always seemed like they were fighting. But you had to understand, it was no-bullshit, bullshit.

"She's great. Pregnant again."

"Jesus, George! What are you going for- a litter? Trying to get a group discount on pediatrician bills?" George and Mitzi already had three kids, all boys, all named after football players. It was George's dream to have a big family since he was an only child and had already lost his parents. Inside Maggie was truly happy for him.

"Good one. A vet joke, nice touch. Seriously, Mags, how are you?"

Now, George had his big brown bear eyes on her and Maggie turned towards the window.

"Tell me everything that happened yesterday," Maggie said in a whisper.

She knew he would have come home from work and gone to her mother's house for the police and the ambulance.

"Do you want to do this now?" George hesitated.

"I've had two Valiums and three Bloody Marys all before noon, now is the best time."

"Aw, Mags," he sighed.

"Don't lecture George, not now."

Even when George killed his knee, he rode out physical therapy on aspirin. He never drank anything stronger than a Sam Adams, being a good ole' Boston boy.

"I'm keeping an eye on you," he said.

With that Maggie leaned over and pressed her face on his arm, "And eye on you." George laughed, he never could resist a pun.

"I got the call at work around eleven from Millie. She had just found Vivian and had called 911. I called Mitzi and told her to take the kids to her parents for the day so, you know, they wouldn't see the police on the street and then I headed to your house. The police had only been there a few minutes and then, well, the ambulance came. We all talked about it for a bit and then it was over. They took her to the hospital and Millie said she'd call you. That's that. Nothing more."

Maggie sensed George was over-simplifying the situation. He had undoubtedly seen her mom lying at the foot of the stairs, bleeding and battered. But Maggie did not press him, knowing he would not tell her any details anyway.

Maggie was living in New York when she got the call from her mother that George's parents were killed. Bob and Peggy Sherwood were traveling on I95 between Boston and Haven, returning home from a musical in Boston's theater district when George's father had a heart attack while driving. Their old Volvo went spinning into oncoming traffic and neither of them survived. George took losing his football career as a chance to start a new life but losing his parents deepened him. Maggie had come home immediately but she was completely at a loss as to what to do for George. The Sherwoods had been everything to her, her spare family, the one she always imagined that she was apart of. For the two days before the funeral, she sat on the corner of Bob and Peggy Sherwood's couch immobile. She watched as Mitzi, his wife, fluttered about making arrangements, chatting with neighbors, serving food and drinks, but Maggie felt on the edge of it all. She watched helplessly as George politely accepted condolences, shook hands, and gave his own handkerchief to grieving friends and relatives.

Maggie wanted to scream at George, c'mon, get angry, tell these people to piss off! She wanted to grab him and make him drink a six pack and run into the ocean naked like when they were teenagers. But she remained mute. Maggie felt out of place amongst his high school buddies and the people of Haven, so she stayed there on the periphery in case he needed her. It was at the funeral when George reached out. Maggie was alone and seated at the back pew. Her mother would have joined her if she had not been drinking steadily since the accident and had locked herself in her bedroom that morning. But George spotted Maggie while standing alone by the altar. Moments before the ceremony started, he walked in full view of everyone down the aisle and extended his hand. She took it and followed him up to the front row. He would never say how much he needed her, but at that moment she found out. Maggie was as close to being his sister as anyone could get.

As George drove closer to Haven, Maggie firmly stared at the trees edging the highway. She focused on the specks of green dotting the branches and longed to jump out and smell the spring leaves. If she did not think about her mother, she was happy, even relieved, to finally be home.

Haven was just 45 minutes south of Boston along the Massachusetts shoreline. People often missed the little seaside town, opting to head out farther to the Cape or the islands. With few tourists, Haven had maintained its lobster village charm. Gray salt-box houses with red geraniums in the window boxes lined the streets and big Victorian houses blocked the water view. Four streets made up the central part of Haven containing small clothing stores, the old Sherwood hardware store, the bookstore, drugstore, pizza parlor, ice cream shop and a few T-shirt shops for the tourists. Haven looked like any other New England seaside town, the same pubs hawking the same clam chowder. Back towards the highway were the strip malls with the chain stores, but Haven itself was still a small town. The salt air was getting stronger as they neared, as was the nor'easter wind. Maggie rolled down her window and inhaled deeply the scent of the rosa rugosa and spring crocuses.

"Well, Mags you got me the whole day, where would you like to go first?"

Maggie could read between the lines, this was not meant to be a simple question. George wanted to know if she wanted to go to the morgue to start funeral arrangements or to her mother's house. Maggie sighed and thought of the half full bottle of Valium calling from her bag. She would not take one in front of George but was happy to know they were there.

"She wanted to be cremated."

Maggie let that hang in the air, waiting for some reaction, more from herself than George. Maggie always envisioned making her mother's funeral arrangements, but now, in the present it felt so remote. Everything was always so clear in her imagination.

"Let's roll, I can't put this off or I might disintegrate. To the hospital."

"It's okay. It is hard, but you'll do it. You will make it." George tried to comfort her since he had been through the same experience with his own parents.

When they walked up to the hospital doors, Maggie had forgotten how quaint a small town hospital was. Its gray cedar shingles blended with the coastal architecture unlike in cities where hospitals loomed large and tall, a testimony to cement. Here the one story building was suitable for emergencies, babies, and a helicopter pad for the occasional Boston airlift. Off to the side was the nursing home where Maggie's grandmother, Virginia, had stayed for nearly five years before finally passing. Maggie paused for a second and felt an ache deep in her heart for her grandmother's hand to lead her through this mess. Quickly, she shook her short red locks as if to clear her mind of the loss in her life. Now was not the time to dwell on more sorrow. As they entered the front doors, they were greeted in unison by a nurse and two doctors.

"Hey George!" they called.

"Jesus, George are you still prom king?" Maggie smirked.

George smiled and made motion with his hand mimicking fixing the crown on his head. Maggie stopped, when she saw the sign for the morgue.

"G, I need a sec." Maggie spotted a bathroom door off to the side and sprinted for it. Inside she splashed water on her face and stared into her eyes in the mirror. She was looking for herself, to make sure she was not crumbling off in little pieces. She felt like an old stone statue blowing away bit by bit in the wind. Maggie needed proof in the mirror that parts of her were not disappearing. Maggie took another valium. She knew she should not but, well, fuck it. Was feeling this really going to make her stronger or some bullshit like that? No, she was going to do this numb, and she will have the memory to refer to for the rest of her life.

Maggie reappeared to see George with the medical examiner. The small balding man was chatting with George about his pet dog when they noticed her return and stopped.

"Hi Miss Atwood. I'm Dr. Polis. Now, just a few things and we will try to get this done with quickly..."

"Cremated, she wanted to be cremated." Maggie knew she was being rude but she just wanted this over with and never see this little bald man again.

"Okay, that's easy, Miss Atwood. You just need to sign the release papers. Then your mother will be sent ..."

"Please don't tell me. I just don't want to know. Just tell me when will she be ready?"

Maggie was dancing from foot to foot, the fear of what was about to happen consuming her.

"In four to five days. Would you like a special urn?"

Dr. Polis was softly trying to work with her from his years of experience with grieving family members. But Maggie was not up for being 'handled.'

"No, just the cardboard box, or whatever, I don't care."

She was about to lose it if he did not ask.

"Okay. I will get the right paperwork together. Now...would you like to see her?"

There it was finally hanging in the air, the last time Maggie would ever see her mother. George broke the silence.

"Mags, you have to. I know from experience, you just have to."

"Dammit G, I know *you know*. I would regret it if I didn't go in there blah blah blah, but it was different for you," Maggie said through clenched teeth.

There she said it, the question that had been aching in the center of it all. How did she really feel about her mother? For George, he had loved his parents unquestionably and they had loved him. George never felt guilt, the guilt that she had been trying to push away for twenty-four hours because part of what she felt was relief. Relief that all the anger and suffering would end. But whose suffering, her mother's or her own?

"Maggie, you did love her despite it all, okay? I know that and don't, especially right now, talk yourself into something else. Right now, go in there and make peace. Take all the time you need, but get your ass in there and say goodbye to your mother," George demanded.

"Peace. There's a word she never knew. " And with that Maggie walked through the swinging doors.

Vivian Murphy Atwood lay there on a gurney covered to her neck in a white sheet. With her strawberry blond bob lying flat and her eyes closed, she looked almost asleep. Maggie could feel her heart beat slowly, booming. Thank God for drugs. As Maggie moved closer, she focused on her breathing and let herself shut down. The gash on the side of Vivian's head was stitched and dry. It looked smaller than Maggie imagined, it was deep. Her head had hit a corner. Hard. Vivian's face was calm but an ashen gray. Her spirit was gone, her stillness was its own life. One of her mother's arms was exposed, so Maggie could see the stitches and bruises on her wrist. Vivian had held out her arms to stop the fall, and both wrists were left broken and twisted. Seeing the physical evidence, Maggie's breath caught in her throat. It just was not her mother lying battered on a cold table without her thick painted eyelashes and red lipstick. Vivian was never without her 'face' as she always used to say. No matter what happened the night before Vivian always did her eyes and lips the next morning. Never let them see the inside, she always told Maggie. Ironically, every time Vivian drank that is exactly what she did. She showed everyone everything inside and out.

Maggie pulled up a chair next to her mother.

"Hi Mom."

As soon as she said it, she felt the tidal wave hit her heart. Anger welled up inside her.

"You finally did it didn't you?" Maggie almost screamed.

The angry child was coming out. "It didn't have to be this way. YOU chose this, okay, do you understand? I tried to help you, dammit. But you made it so hard to help you. You made it so hard to love you. I'm sorry, I just couldn't save you. I didn't know how." Choking to take a breath, Maggie's voice became soft as the tears fell fast from her. "I loved you, Mom, I always did. That was never in question, but you made it impossible. Your drinking was the darkness in every room. I'm sorry, but I couldn't find the light..that's why I left." Maggie could feel her throat swell. She tried to swallow back the guilt. Staring at her mother, she tried not to think, *this is the last time. I cannot fix it anymore.* For a few moments, Maggie just sat very still staring at her mother's face, letting the quiet of the room calm her. She desperately wanted to leave, but that moment carried such a finality Maggie was not sure she could face. After all these years, Vivian could still break her heart one last time. Maggie willed herself to stand and brushed the hair back from her mother's ears. She struggled to speak, sobs breaking her words.

"Goodbye, Mom. I love you. I always did." It was all she could manage and, with that, Maggie ran from the room.

Maggie kept going until she reached the outside. The thick, wet air hit her, and she breathed so deeply her lungs hurt. Walking in circles, she just inhaled and focused on the sky, the trees, anything but inside her own head. George came bursting through the doors.

"It's okay, Mags," He said waving his hands in a downward motion, like she a suicide walker on a ledge.

"I know you've been through this, George, but don't give me a pep talk. Just let me feel this, okay? I can't, I just can't." Maggie paced.

"Yes, yes, you can Maggie, and you already are. The hard part is over. You did it. I promise you that was the worst."

George stood there looking her in the eye. And Maggie let go with what she was really feeling.

"Ah, Jesus Christ, George, what the fuck?! I thought I could handle this. Me, of all people. I've been expecting this for twenty years. I mean, seriously how many car accidents, how many nights did she drink herself so close but it never happened? I mean, the suicide attempts, just everything had prepared me. But now, I want to run, George. I can't do this. I can't do a funeral and people telling me... about my loss. Jesus, half the town knows I almost went insane living with her. What loss? She never did anything...she was rich and miserable and she took me to hell and back with her. I don't want pity, George. I want this all to go away. I want to go to the airport, and I just want to get the fuck away."

"Sorry, Mags, you can't run from this. Not this time," George's voice became stern.

"You have to do all of it - the funeral, cleaning out the house, just like the rest of us. Running ain't gonna cut it this time, kiddo."

His voice softened again, as he grabbed Maggie by both her arms. He stared hard into her glistening green eyes.

"The story between you and Vivian, well, it's like a puzzle. First you have to put all the pieces together to see the real picture and then you have to take them all apart to put them back in the box. You need to do this Maggie. You won't get on with your life until you work through this. You have to come to terms with what it was. You need to really see it, and then you can put it away for good."

George was reading her mind. Maggie kept thinking that George had it differently because he was close to his parents. They ate dinner together, went on vacations, and attended his wedding. But even he, with the perfect family, had to go through the boxes and sort their lives out. After a few moments of silence, George said, "Besides, Millie bakes apple crumb cake for funerals and everyone will show up an hour early if you have a yard sale. Oh, and the liquor store gives you ten percent off for the funeral, twenty for me, you know, cuz' I lost two." George winked at her.

Maggie felt the blood rush back to her face.

"Yeah, yeah, you're a funny guy, George Sherwood. All right, let's get this shit over with," Maggie said as she went back in to finish the paperwork.

"That's the spirit!" George held the hospital door open for her.

It was 5:30 p.m. when George dropped Maggie off at her house. He insisted she should come to his house for dinner. But refusing, Maggie just wanted to be alone. She could not bear the thought of George's happy home. Mitzi plump and pregnant, scurrying after three adorable round-faced boys. And Maggie was not up for seeing Mitzi's floral redecorating of the aging seventies look Peggy Sherwood had always loved. Maggie could only take so much change in one day. She had to beg George to stop at the liquor store on the way home so she at least could have a bottle of wine. She did not tell George she spent $55.00 on it and bought two bottles–another case of the fuck its. Also, Maggie knew she would drink good wine slower and the hangover would throb less.

Grove Avenue, where George and Maggie grew up, was literally a drive downward. Haven was on a steep hill and getting to the water was always a decline from wherever you were. Since the wealthy could afford the water view, the majority of the larger houses were along the shoreline. Like all the streets leading to the water, the modest size houses were at the top of the hill. George lived in a modest sized one and Maggie lived in the grand one at the end of the street. But Haven never coveted the rich. Everyone lived together as neighbors. There were never fences or gates, just boxwood hedges and hy-drangea bushes.

The Murphy house was the 'big one' on the water. Typical of a New England shoreline house, it evolved from Colonial architecture. The house was grand, boxy, and cedar shingled, and it had two vast wrap-around porches for ocean views on both the first and second floors. The green shutters, white trim, and grand porches gave a regal backdrop to the flowering hydrangeas, pe-onies, irises and poppies that bloomed every summer. People who boated by dreamed and wondered what it would be like to stand on the manicured lawn on a sum-mer's eve. The whole property had a magical aura that entranced onlookers and, only on occasion, gave its resi-dents peace.

At the end of the street was a small beach the size of a single lane road. To one side was a pier, where anyone along Grove could swim or sit and dangle their feet in the water. The beach was used for putting small sailboats or kayaks in and out of the water or letting dogs splash and swim. Off to the left was considered Murphy beach, public access allowed people to walk along the wa-ter's edge, but most respected the owners' invisible boundary. Maggie could remember hours of her life along that shoreline, either by herself or walking with her grandmother. As a child, it was the first place she could go to get out of the house. Sitting on the beach, hearing only the wind and the gentle lapping of the waves, calmed her. During the summers, her and George were either putting in or taking out sailboats, kayaks, or rafts. Some nights they would light a little fire and camp on the beach if their parents allowed. Then they would stare back up at Maggie's well-lit and watch people walk from room to room. Maggie loved that feeling of being outside and looking in, not being a physical part of her family but an outsider, a bystander. George and her would make up funny conversations if they saw two people talking, and Maggie would laugh like everything in the world was normal.

Maggie loved the house as if it were a part of her. In the winter when the trees were bare and the flowers were gone, it was visible at every angle. Maggie could see its grandness naked. Without green grass or the summer porch chairs, the house stood unadorned against the winter wind without complaint. And then six months later, in the blink of an eye, it was trimmed in columbines and bleeding hearts as soft as the summer. The house had been Maggie's ally all these years and she sought refuge in its corners and familiar smells. Every time she returned, it was the house she could count on to look the same, be the same, give her the same love in return.

Maggie said goodbye, and told G not to worry, and headed up the path to the her childhood home. Millie had left the front door unlocked, so Maggie stormed in and dropped her bag, just like she used to do everyday after school. But this time, the house was quiet. The air hung in the bluish gray light of the fading day. The stillness reminded her of the life that had left her mother. It had been over two years since she had been home, the Christmas before she went to New Orleans, but she was not going to stroll down nostalgia lane. Instead she realized that not a painting, a curtain, a knick knack had changed in the house in years. It was exactly as she had left it, as she had grown up in, and she was grateful. Maggie's gaze instinctively swung to the bottom of the stairs. Her mind tried to replay what happened here the day before, but she refused to oblige. Quickly, turning on a light, Maggie grabbed her bag and reached for her cell phone. She had not talked to Marten yet and, right now, she regretted not having him there.

Her cell phone had been turned off since the plane. She had five missed calls from Marten and several unexplained numbers. She did not listen to the messages but pressed a button to speed dial home. Marten answered in one ring.

"I'm sorry, my phone was turned off."

"It's okay, it's okay, are you okay?" he said in his accented English.

"Thanks for calling George. Really, it meant a lot."

"I don't always listen to you, you know, and that is not always such a bad thing."

"Yeah, okay you were right," she paused, "I went straight to the hospital."

Like George, Maggie knew Marten would understand. Funny how George and Marten had death in common. Both their parents gone, unfortunately, were turning into her benefit.

"How did you do?" Marten asked.

"It sucked. George said that would be the worst of it, tell me he didn't lie. Or just lie to me, because I feel like I am crumbling. It's like one minute rolls into the next and I can't figure out how got there. How am I here in my house? How am I without you?"

Maggie choked back the tears. Rummaging through the kitchen drawers, she found a corkscrew and began attacking a bottle of wine.

"That's exactly how it goes. Then one day you wake up from it all and it will be more of a memory than a reality. But right now, life will be this seamless fog that you just have to keep pushing through, but you will. Trust me, you will. Do you want me to come tomorrow?"

Maggie wanted Marten to hold her, crawl into bed with her, and watch bad sitcoms on TV. But no, she did not want him here just yet. There were too many things she had to face by herself.

"Honey, I just...it's just you are one world, and this is a whole other one. I just have to get used to this one again before I-"

"-let me in," Marten finished the sentence.

They both let that hang there understanding its implication.

"No... honey, " Maggie faltered.

"Yes, Maggie. I'm not judging you. I love you. So you do what you need to do. But understand, eventually you will have to let me all the way in...for us."

Maggie imagined the three words after that, *to go on*. And Maggie wanted to spend forever with Marten. There was no other man she could imagine loving. But George was right, she had to put this puzzle together first before putting it away.

"Maggie, I'm coming on Friday. I have already made the plane reservations." Maggie felt relieved. She realized she did not want to be in control and make that decision. It was Monday so that gave her five days, perfect. God, she really did love this man.

"Actually, honey, that's great. It will give me enough time to readjust and miss you absolute loads. "

"That's my girl. Now, I hate to tell you this but your sister called."

"Aw, fuck," Maggie thought about the missed messages.

THREE

In 1966, Vivian Murphy was not only the prettiest but one of the brightest girls at The Westlake School. With her strawberry blond hair, slender frame and piercing green eyes, Vivian stood out at the all-girls boarding school. Westlake was situated in a remote part of Connecticut far from the highway, and even farther from Haven. Jack and Virginia Murphy had chosen the school for its charm and seclusion thinking it best for the young daughter Vivi to finally separate from home. The Murphy's could afford the prestigious boarding school because Jack Murphy owned a well established insurance company in Boston. He insured large corporations for health and worker's compensation, amassing his wealth with lucrative University contracts. Boston is home to more than forty colleges and with very little reason for people to sue universities and few accident related job injuries, Jack Murphy acquired quite an insurance fortune. But Virginia had preferred a seaside home to the bustle of Boston and moved the family to Haven when Vivian was just four.

Shortly after they settled in Haven, Vivian's younger sister, Esther was born. Esther, or Essie, was born with terrible asthma and a fragility about her that demanded her parents' full attention. Delicate due to her constant ailing health, Essie was treated like a princess. Soon after, John Jr. arrived as the youngest Murphy. As the only male heir, Johnny stole the spotlight. Even in his adult years, Johnny never changed his name to John or Jack but remained Johnny, clinging to his childhood persona. Vivian resented the attention her parents bestowed upon her siblings, thus was neither the doting older sister or daughter. Instead, Vivian preferred to be on the fringe of the family, aloof and independent. When the option came to go to boarding school, she eagerly agreed.

Vivian acclimated easily to Westlake, enjoying the sisterhood of girls confined to one space. It was a place for her to finally speak her mind and be comfortable around peers who enjoyed her humor and vivaciousness. Vivian not only became a leader in her classes but in the general campus society. She maintained straight A's but, unlike other girls, a rebellious streak came naturally to her. Once nearly the entire freshmen class was expelled for smoking cigarettes in the woods behind the auditorium. Unbeknownst to the head of school, Vivian had not only organized the event but bought the cigarettes. When the Seniors dominated the dorm vending machine, she hid it in her closet and only allowed other freshmen to use it. And it was Vivian who discovered the telephone number of St. Barlow's, the boys school, two miles away.

By October of her senior year, Vivian was pregnant. The father was just a boy, Thomas Atwood, a Boston senior at St. Barlow's. Without telling anyone, they drove to South Carolina and eloped on Thanksgiving. When they returned home for Christmas holiday from school, they broke the news to their parents. Back in

Boston, Molly and David Atwood were heartbroken. The Atwoods were quiet, kind natured people like Thomas and were determined to make the best of the situation. They chose to support Thomas and Vivian and their future grandchild, even though they believed the timing was too soon.

Vivian's parents had a different reaction. Enraged, Jack Murphy drank for two days. Vivian's mother demanded that the marriage be annulled and implied that Vivian should 'take care of the situation.' She announced she would not support or publicly acknowledge her daughter's indiscretion. But Vivian, as stubborn as her mother, fled to Thomas's family in Boston for the holidays. It was an awkward yet warm welcome.

The day before Thomas and Vivian were to return to their boarding schools from Christmas break in order to finish and graduate, Virginia Murphy arrived at the Atwoods. Wearing her most pleasant face and exhibiting all the grace of her upper class standing, Virginia gushed with kindness. She complimented Molly and Dave Atwood on their home and said how much she admired Dr. Atwood for being a hospital physician. Virginia was overcompensating for her true feelings. To her, businessmen and lawyers were the "right" career choices but doctors were equivalent to teachers, public servants. After tea, Virginia asked if she may speak to Thomas alone. Thinking Virginia had come to make amends with their son, the Atwoods confidently left the room. Minutes later, Thomas burst through the doors red faced and with tears in his eyes. Molly went back in the parlor and the graceful, smiling Virginia was gone. Instead there sat a stone-faced woman putting on her white gloves one at time.

"Mrs. Murphy, why have you really come?" Molly said with clenched teeth. Thomas was her son and she would not allow someone to hurt him in her own home.

"Mrs. Atwood, I think we can come to an understanding. I agree, Thomas should finish his schooling. Then Mr. Murphy and I hope he will return here to Boston to begin a university. We are fully prepared to financially help Thomas and Vivian get on their feet. I say Boston, because I would like to be close to my grandchild. That way Jack and I are better able to help the two children." She emphasized the word 'children' as if they had just made a mess in her kitchen, not adults starting their lives. Molly heard the catch in her demand. Thomas was not going to be allowed to make any of his own choices when it came to Vivian.

Virginia continued. "Now, Vivian will not be returning to school, we have withdrawn her tuition. Mr. Murphy and I do not feel it is right for her to stay with you either. I will be taking her back with me today and she will be with us until the baby is born. By then, we shall have arranged for a home for our new family, again here in Boston."

Molly noticed the faintest twitch in Virginia's eye as if it took all her restraint to say these words. Unfortunately, Molly could not object just because she distrusted this woman. Vivian was not her daughter, despite the fact, she had grown quite fond of the girl over the past two weeks. Molly thought Vivian had spirit, and she could see her son's attraction to her. Although Molly agreed Thomas and Vivian were too young to be married, she did see the spark between them and hoped the years would nurture that spark. Molly was an optimist, this woman on her chintz sofa was a sadist.

When Molly went upstairs, she heard Vivian comforting Thomas. Somehow, Molly thought it would be the other way around. She saw Vivian gently kiss Thomas on the lips and brush the hair out of his eyes, she whispered for him not to worry. What Molly heard next made her have great compassion for her daughter-in-law. Vivian said, "I've never had a chance to love anyone before, so nothing will stop me from loving you." With that Vivian quietly went back to her parents' house in Haven, the one place she had waited so long to leave.

Excerpts from the Diary of Vivian Murphy Atwood
April 1970

I am starting a diary because all the great tragic women have diaries. That's how people fall in love with them and then they are famous and movies are made. So now, while I am young, I will write about how horrible my parents are by keeping me imprisoned here in dreadful Haven. Like Anne Frank, not really, but you get what I mean. It is not fair!! They won't even let me graduate from high school. All my friends are going to do exciting, adventurous stuff and I'm pregnant and married. I don't feel married. Thomas calls almost every other day but we just talk about classes and his friends. He is so super sweet about the baby. He wants to know everything I am feeling, but what can I say? I feel bumps in my stomach, I have heartburn, I pee every five minutes. Even though the doctor has heard the heartbeat, it is not real to me. I don't feel like a mother. I know it is a girl though, I can feel that, I don't know why. I know Thomas wants a boy but he would be great with a girl. I don't think my parents care what he or she is, just that she is not like me.

May 1970

Daddy has been drunk for two days, and Momma just threw the good china at him. Bits of Wedgewood are all over the den floor, and Daddy is just laughing in his old leather chair. Thomas and I won't be like that. He will be sweet and bring me flowers, and I will make him dinner. He is talking about being a doctor, and we will be this fabulous Boston couple invited to all the parties with our beautiful baby. Momma says I should focus on keeping my head on the ground, whatever that means. She says having a baby is serious business and to stop my nonsense. So sorry, Momma, that I have dreams. I don't think that woman had a dream in her life and that's what makes her yell at everybody all the time. Be this, be that, no wonder Daddy can't stand her. Essie and Johnny are her beloved ones. Me, I don't need her to love me, I have my whole life ahead of me.

June 1970

I am moving to Boston in a few days. Thomas is setting up the apartment Daddy got for us. I am so scared but so excited. Living on my own, bye bye Haven! No more answering to Momma. I get to do things MY way. I am going to be different from her. Just wait. Yeah, Boston!

August 1970

She's here! Sarah looks like Thomas with fine dark hair and large eyes. I wished she looked a bit more like me. I feel like I am going to break her, and everyday I fear something will happen to her. Thomas says not to worry but I have to constantly get up and check to see if she is breathing. I never thought I would be this scared all the time. I am so exhausted. No one told me she would eat every two hours. And my stomach is so ugly, it still looks like I am pregnant. Thomas is so happy, how? I am so tired.

Vivian gave birth to Sarah Atwood during the summer of 1970 in a Boston hospital surrounded by her parents, her husband, and her in-laws. Vivian's parents had secured them an apartment in Boston on Commonwealth Avenue, and Thomas would be attending Tufts

University in the fall. But long hours of medical residency and the years of hospital hours did not seem so appealing once he held Sarah in his arms. So instead, Thomas set his sights on becoming a lawyer. He wanted to take as little of the Murphy money as possible.

There was a secret that motivated him, one that he never shared with Vivian. The night Virginia asked to speak to Thomas alone in the Atwood house, she had offered him $20,000 to run away and abandon Vivian and their child. Virginia Murphy was clear. Her intentions were to thoroughly rid Thomas from their lives. While Thomas believed he loved Vivian in a way that would last them a lifetime, it was more the pull of his unborn child that he could not abandon. In exchange for his freedom and quite a sum of money, the condition was never to see his unborn son or daughter. Thomas, having had such a strong relationship with his own parents, could never imagine not seeing his own child. He felt humiliated when Virginia Murphy stared him down in the parlor that day. He simply stood before her and said a resounding 'no' before he fled the room. But an embarrassment lived inside him, knowing that she thought he could be paid off. Admittedly, for the briefest of moments, so did he.

In the beginning, Vivian seemed genuinely happy with her new husband and daughter. She kept the house, tended to Sarah, and grew to know her new neighborhood in Boston. They all felt the beginnings of a secure little family when Thomas began school in the fall. But in order to avoid taking advantage of the Murphy money, Thomas worked around his classes and was gone twelve hours a day. And when he was not working, he was studying. Vivian became lonely and irritable. It did not help that Sarah was a colicky baby and cried most days. Vivian never considered herself helpless, her parents were tough on her, yet she felt alone without Thomas home. She was barely eighteen and missed her time at school when she was surrounded by friends and had the freedom to come and go. Vivian loved Sarah but she began to resent her as well. For crying, for taking Thomas's attention, for needing her so much all the time. When Vivian starting drinking, it began quietly that time on Commonwealth Avenue. In the afternoon she would take sips of leftover wine from dinner the night before. Just a few swallows to take the edge off, then she would have a cigarette. It was her "treat" before Thomas came home, but these indulgences became a daily routine.

Still a child herself, Vivian found it hard to emotionally connect with Sarah. She kept her clean and fed but interacted very little with her. When Sarah become old enough to go into day care, her mother happily took her. Then Vivian discovered modeling. Although she was not extremely tall, Vivian had an enviable petite figure and bird-like legs that fit designer clothing. She would get jobs either modeling in the designer stores on Newberry Street or for their catalogs. Instead of focusing on Sarah, Vivian was re-invigorated meeting new people through work and hosting parties for her new friends. Too tired, Thomas said little when he came home to an apartment full of people smoking, drinking and the loud music. He felt guilty leaving Vivian alone everyday and thought it was good that she was creating her own life. It energized their marriage now that Vivian was happy, then their lives turned the same corner again. Vivian became pregnant.

Vivian's resentment returned knowing what pregnancy entailed and losing her newfound freedom to another child. For six weeks, she brooded and turned down modeling jobs. She drank more than she should. Thomas and Sarah stayed away from her as much as they could, hoping she would change her attitude. Then Vivian miscarried.

Excerpts from the Diary of Vivian Murphy Atwood
September 1973

I cannot believe how selfish I am. I am such a horrible person. There was a life inside me and I didn't want it. What? So I could wear pretty clothes? Why was I so angry to be pregnant again? Thomas was excited-of course- and I turned into such a bitch. Women can have children and work, I could have done it. Instead I am such a pathetic, hateful, selfish person. Just like Momma. Maybe I thought I was turning into Momma and that scared me, having another child. But I can be different, I know I can!

I should pay attention to Sarah more, she needs me. But she seems so distant. I feel like she doesn't love me or at least doesn't like me. But I can change that. I will stay at home with her more and, the next time I get pregnant, I will be happy. Lord, I promise I will be a better wife and mother, just give me another chance again. I will also write in my diary more!

By the way Vivian had been acting, Thomas thought she would have been relieved to lose the baby. But it was quite the opposite. Vivian was racked with guilt and felt her own selfishness that caused the miscarriage. She may not have planned for the baby, but she did not want to lose it. When Vivian was back on her feet an older, more mature woman emerged. She threw herself at Sarah like she had just discovered her. Sarah was three and a half and relished her mother's full attention. Vivian cut back on the parties and work so that Thomas could come home to a quiet house for his final year of university. Everyone noticed the change within Vivian and thought that maybe the tragedy had been a blessing, curing her of her restlessness.

But people never really change. They just grow more into who they are and who they long to be. Not having been the center of attention in her parents house, Vivian thrived on it in her adult world. People were attracted to her beauty and wit, and it thrilled her. The happiest times in her life were when she was in boarding school and modeling, not when she was playing good wife and mother. Vivian needed accolades for her efforts not the martyrdom of motherhood. So a year later, Vivian was back modeling again, Sarah was back in day care, and Thomas was preparing to go to Harvard law school. Everything appeared in order, but Vivian was spending less and less time at home and coming home later and later. Unfortunately, Thomas was more of a thinker than a fighter. When Vivian was happy, she was loving and pleasant to be around, so Thomas rarely questioned her mothering or her lifestyle. He took the passenger seat in their marriage as Vivian's modeling was helping their financial independence from the Murphys.

A year flew by and Sarah was four years old. She began attending school but had difficulty as she had become a shy, introverted child. Sarah had grown so accustomed to playing alone at home that she had problems interacting with the other children. In daycare people dismissed Sarah's insecurity as a "phase". But once she started school, there was nowhere for her to hide. Sarah clung to her teachers as if they were mother figures. Sarah did her school work to please everyone, but she showed no natural ability or talent in any subject. She desperately needed her mother to pay attention to her, but Vivian had thrown herself into the Boston city life- attending art openings, concerts, and lavish parties for painters, poets, writers and musicians. It was the 1970s, and the world seemed on the verge of exploding. Gone were Vivian's mother's days of tea and little white gloves. Women were wearing their hair long and as straight as their blue jeans.

Vivian took to the women's movement with a personal sense of purpose. Eventually modeling bored her, so she began to write articles for alternative newspapers summarizing events and happenings. She thought of herself as having a career equal to Thomas's, as a writer. They would both work to achieve their dreams. But again, Vivian became pregnant.

Excerpts from the Diary of Vivian Murphy Atwood
October 1974

Yes! I am pregnant again. It feels so right this time. I love being in my twenties. I love my job, yes, yes, yes, all is good. I am due in April, cosmically a better month. Children born in April are artists, and I feel again this time it will be a girl. I love Sarah, but she is not like me, she doesn't see the positive in life. She is always so sullen, I should involve her more in work and she will see how the world is changing. But this time is so different. I won't be so young. God, I was such a baby when I had Sarah. I was so lost, how did I ever do it! Lately, I have fallen in love again with Thomas too. He is so solid and always happy for me/us. He will make a great lawyer. At first, I thought he would be another suit like my father. I thought he would never understand the revolution going on in the world, but he loves the challenge. T' wants to fight big corporations and bring down the man! He believes women should get equal pay for equal work and isn't afraid to fight for the gays. I do wish this little one inside me has my looks and T's smarts. See Momma, take that. T' and I have done it after all.

This time really was different and Vivian thought the pregnancy was a blessing. Now, Vivian felt she had her own life she wanted to share with this child. To her, Sarah had become distant and in-comprehensive. She was moody and overly sensitive to Vivian, constantly causing friction between them. Instead of mending their relationship, Vivian focused on the new baby. She was convinced this unborn child would follow her and be her partner as she discovered herself as a poet, a writer, a free thinker. This was the child she could teach to be like her.

When Margaret Atwood was born in 1975, Vivian instantly felt connected to her. Maggie was two pounds bigger than Sarah at birth. Rarely crying, Vivian felt instantly at ease with her. Maggie also looked like Vivian with the same round green eyes and soft strawberry blonde hair. Seeing herself in Maggie, Vivian knew she wanted to give her the world. Surprisingly, Sarah too was excited and lively about the new baby. Everyone expected jealousy but Sarah was honestly thrilled to have a baby sister in the house to play with. She had given up on winning Vivian's affection, so now she focused on giving all her devotion to baby Maggie. With both Vivian and Sarah happy and present again, Thomas could start his new job with a prestigious Boston law firm feeling hopeful. They would now officially be financially free from Vivian's parents. He and Vivian both had careers, two beautiful daughters and were lulled into a sense of completeness.

Maggie was sitting on the couch breathing in the familiar smells of her house when she heard, "Hello, HON? Ya in here?" She recognized the voice with its faint southern drawl, the last remnant from Millie's childhood. Millie and Archie McCullough had always been on

Grove Avenue, long before the Murphys moved to Haven. Archie and Millie were the epitome of Haven, revered and loved by everyone in town. Archie, locally born and bred, owned two local fishing companies and did well for himself. He met Millie in South Carolina when he did a stint on a shrimp boat and convinced her the snow on New England waters was worth seeing. Surprisingly, Millie did fall in love with New England. Haven was a place where she could wear her pearls everyday, and her southern charm worked easily on people.

"Well, what are you sittin' in the dark for, sweetie?" Millie bustled around the living room turning on all the lights. "Now, come on here and give me a hug, hon." Maggie rose and put her arms around the aging plump woman. Her soft blond helmut of hair and her blue eyes were comforting. Maggie could feel the dangling reading glasses crush into her chest and smell the Joy perfume. She held on for a second or two longer. Millie was as much apart of her as the old curtains in the house.

"Well, sugar, why you sittin' in here drinkin' in the dark? Not, good," Millie said waving her finger at her implying the similarity to her mother.

"It's been a pretty shitty day, Mill."

"I know, sweetheart, I know. You been breathing this drama since you was a babe, and good news is you are at the finish line. But I don't want you starting a whole other race with yourself."

"Millie," Maggie held up her hand to stop the lecture. Millie switched gears.

"So you went to the hospital?"

"Wow, Grove Avenue "telegraph" still works, huh? I suppose George told you how graceful I was."

"Maggie, honey, those situations don't require grace, they require steel boots. And you got a pair on you that could climb Mt. Everest." Maggie laughed.

"Don't feel like that Millie. You know what the funny part is?, I could never really rely on Mom for anything, and right now all I want is her to be here to take care of everything."

"She was your mother, hon. Everyone needs their mama when times get tough. And this is just about the toughest, losing your mama...regardless of how she was. Your mother loved you more than you realize, sweetheart."

"Actually, that was never the hard part, knowing she loved me. But it was how she used it to hurt me." Maggie and Millie both let that hang in the air, the truth weighing high above them.

"Your mama had her problems."

"God, I am so sick of Vivian's problems," Maggie lashed out. "She was a rich, spoiled woman who lived on Grandpa's money and had men throwing themselves at her. I mean seriously, all I ever saw was her screwing up her own life, blaming everyone else, and for some unearthly reason, everyone making so many goddamn excuses for it. She's sad, she's in pain..from WHAT goddamn it? Sitting on her ass all day and making our lives miserable? Yeah, my father died, okay? But really, it's not like she was left destitute! Grandma and Grandpa took care of everything. Then she had other husbands. Sure, they didn't die…, but they left her because she was so impossible."

Tears were flowing down Maggie's cheeks. She wanted to stop talking, stop saying all these horrible things about her dead mother, but the anger and exhaustion were taking over while the wine loosened her.

Millie stayed calm and let Maggie scream. She understood everything Maggie felt because she had watched all it unfold for thirty years out her kitchen window. When Maggie stopped and sat down trying to stifle her own sobs, Millie put her arms around her. "It's okay hon. I know, I know. I won't tell you to go easy on her, but try and go easy on yourself, okay?"

"I don't hate her, but dammit, Millie. It just could have been so different." This broke Millie's heart because Archie and Millie could never have kids. There was something wrong with Millie's ovaries and, back in the seventies, words like surrogacy, in-vitro and overseas adoption were not as common as today. So Millie always looked after Maggie with the love she had reserved for her own. When Maggie and Sarah were young, Millie baked them cookies and let them watch TV at her house. And the nights when Vivian's drinking was worse than usual, Millie had slumber parties with ice cream and bedtime stories. Millie, with her Southern grace, would never confront or question Vivian as a mother, but she did try to make up with extra love for the girls.

Maggie dried her tears, and Millie begged her to come have dinner with Archie and her. But Maggie pleaded to let her have the night to herself knowing the next few days were going to be beyond chaotic. Maggie needed time to listen to the messages from her sister and figure out in her head how in the hell she was going to handle everyone in the coming days. There was Sarah to deal with but also Uncle Johnny and Aunt Essie. And where were Peter and Mac, Vivian's two ex-husbands? Also, Maggie needed to talk to her mother's lawyer, Bill Getty, about the house. And a funeral at Grace Episcopal Church, Maggie remembered the priest had said the church would not marry her mother again, but they would bury her. Apparently three marriages is their limit. With so much to think about, Maggie poured herself another glass of wine and hit voicemail on her cell phone.

Excerpts from the Diary of Vivian Murphy Atwood
March 1978

My dear Thomas, today I watched you disappear from my life. I sit here and wish I had loved you more, told you more, been more for you. You were my rock, my anchor in the constant North wind. I don't know how I will do without you, I am terrified. Sarah looks at me with anger, blaming me for this pain she is in. I deserve it, she always had you from the beginning and now she is left with me, not even her second choice. Maggie, so young, cries because we cry. I wish Sarah knew that if I could, I would swallow her pain and take it with my own. How do I reach her? I realize all this time I had been afraid, afraid I would have been demanding like Momma so I retreated and let her do it on her own. I was so selfish. I thought Momma didn't have a life, so that is why she was always so miserable. So I was going to have a life, a career, but now what do I have without you?

I keep trying to get to something but I don't know what it is. I feel like everything is my fault and I just keep screwing it up. I should have never gotten pregnant in high school. If I hadn't had that party when we got drunk and made Sarah, ifs ... And then I made you marry me? Why? We were too young. How often did you regret doing the honorable thing? I know about Momma offering you the money, I found out that Spring. Because you didn't take it, I thought it meant you loved me. I was such a child! It just meant you wouldn't hate yourself! You had such a short life in this world, I should have let you be free. T' you will always be in my heart, my love. I can never love another. I am so, so sorry. I will never forgive myself. I love you T'. I'm sorry.

It was 1978, and Thomas Atwood was sitting behind his desk at his new law firm Colby, Kirchner, and Schmitt when he felt short of breath. He had landed his dream job with a firm that had a reputation for representing lawsuits of the David v. Goliath nature, and always on the side of David. Thomas was excited to be working with clients and aimed for spending more time in courtrooms than law libraries. At age 27, Thomas saw no reason to go to the doctor for a little shortness of breath. A few days later, he was walking home from work on Bolyston Street when he felt his left arm tingle and a sharp jab of pain in his chest. Able to flag down someone passing by, he was taken by ambulance to Massachusetts General Hospital. Vivian arrived and was relieved to see Thomas sitting up and chatting with the nurses. She burst into tears. He comforted her, said there was nothing to worry about and gave the girls the chocolate pudding off his dinner cart. Vivian and the girls left around 8:30 that night without waiting for the doctor's diagnoses because their husband and father had so assured them it was just a case of heartburn and he needed to start exercising.

Vivian had just gotten the kids to sleep when the hospital called. Thomas had had a second heart attack, and this time it was fatal. His aortic valve had failed. The science of heart surgery was too new, and hospitals were not equipped to handle Thomas's rare condition. Vivian was now a young widow and mother of two.

At eight years old, Sarah took Thomas's death the hardest. She stopped speaking and blamed Vivian for her father's 'disappearance'. Too young to understand, Maggie watched as her sister removed herself, almost violently, from the family while her mother quietly escaped amongst bottles of wine night after night. Molly and Dave Atwood begged Vivian to move into the suburbs of Boston so they could watch after the girls. But Vivian wanted no reminders of Thomas, not his childhood home nor his parents. The Atwoods finally stopped fighting with Vivian and retreated to Florida. They saw the girls on occasion over the years, but being together without Thomas was just a reminder of their broken hearts.

Vivian, desperate to ignore the tragedy, wanted to stay in the city and be amongst her bohemian friends. She believed she could get back to the fun days of parties and people in her life. But she was barely managing to keep up with her column writing for a city magazine. Her drinking started too early in the day, and too often she would forget to pick the girls up at school and daycare. Concerned teachers brought them home while Sarah quickly made up lies and excuses saying her mother was still at work. The reality was, Sarah and Maggie would find her passed out, dinner burning on the stove. Vivian had retreated from everyone, including the girls.

Sarah dutifully cleaned up the messes but found it harder and harder to face her mother, so she focused on Maggie. She dressed and fed Maggie for daycare and genuinely loved her, trying to compensate for her own feelings of loss. While Maggie, at three years old, was the opposite and cried over her mother. Maggie was always trying to wake her and pretend like nothing had ever happened. This went on for about a year, until the night Vivian would change everything.

Excerpts from the Diary of Vivian Murphy Atwood
February 1979

Fuck this world, I can't stand it. The horrible little creatures that wander around me, just go away! I can't do anything for them. I am horrible. I have pills. See Momma, you always hated me. Well, you win. I hate myself more. S hates me too, and M will be fine on her own...she is such a good girl. I am going to find Thomas! He is the only one who believed in me, loved me. I am a shell, a pretty little shell to everyone. I am smart, dammit. Smarter than you all. I win. Ha Ha. I have the pills. Goodbye, be good girls. I love you but I wasn't good enough for you , T was..I am going to be with him and we will wait for you! Be a family again! I loved you just the way you were, not like my parents. They didn't love me the way I was. I was a disappointment. But you girls, you are free. Go, be free. I am.

Vivian's life did not perish that evening as she had hoped, but something deeper and far more essential to Sarah and Maggie, was lost instead…their trust.

FOUR

Maggie deleted the messages from Marten and waited for Sarah's voice. But there were other messages from Vivian's lawyer, Bill Getty--s*o sorry, have to meet, etc.*, and Aunt Essie wheezing and crying. She had terrible asthma. Then Mac, Vivian's second ex-husband, saying he would stop by the house soon, and lastly, there was Sarah.

"Hey Kiddo," her voice broke into a sob. "I'm sorry, I'm so so sorry."

The message ended and Maggie rolled her eyes. And the oscar goes to...Sarah Atwood. Next message, "Sorry, I'm sorry. I know you don't want to hear from me, but I can't believe Mom is gone. This is so terrible. I knew it would always be terrible, but oooh, ooh."

The hysterical wailing began and a man's voice came on the phone. "Hi Maggie, my name's David, and I'm your sister's sponsor." Maggie could hear him whisper off to the side, 'Is it okay that I say that?' Maggie could just imagine Sarah nodding.

"Well, I'm here with your sister, and we have made arrangements to fly into Boston from Cincinnati tomorrow morning. She says Haven is only about an hour away. So that should put us to you around say one? Maggie, your sister really loves you, and she wants you to know she is sober and wants to do the right thing. Okay, I look forward to meeting you. See you tomorrow."

Maggie put down the phone and laughed to herself. She did not even know Sarah was in Cincinnati.

Had she expected anything less from her dear sister? Sarah had grown from the quiet, sullen child into an over dramatic, hysterical 38 year old child. David? Why would her sponsor come... oh yes, she must be sleeping with him. Fantastic, the new guy who is going to *save* Sarah is coming to her mother's funeral. The fact Sarah was in Alcoholics Anonymous had no effect on Maggie. Sarah had been in three rehabs since she was seventeen and threw the twelve steps around like little weapons. Sarah used A.A. as an excuse for every bad behavior she ever committed. Giving up her life to a higher power meant Sarah never had to take direct responsibility for any of her actions. And whenever she really screwed up, there was a nice group of strangers somewhere to hug her and say it was okay because she showed up in a church basement. Maggie thought the best form of therapy for Sarah was to strip her of everything, especially money, and send her to work in a labor camp for a year.

Unable to dwell anymore about her mother or Sarah, Maggie finished her wine and decided to go to bed. She could not tell if she was too exhausted or too drunk to care as she walked up the stairs that ended her mother's life. She knew they should have some affect on her, the vision of her mother's arms flailing or imagining the gentle thud of her head on the wall. But Maggie had sufficiently numbed herself and instead felt comforted by the worn hand rail and the slope of the old wood flooring. Climbing those stairs was as familiar and as normal as anything Maggie could imagine. She let her mind drift on one, sole comforting word: home. She repeated softly to herself, *I'm home, I'm home*, as she fell into her old bed.

When Maggie woke the next morning, she stared at the same cedar tree branch out her bedroom window that had been there since childhood. She smelled the dust in her sheets and inhaled the warm softness of a bygone time. Maggie had fallen asleep at eight o'clock the night before from exhaustion and consequently, woke up with the sun. Maggie was never good at sleeping through the night but somehow she always did when she was home. Again, the word "home" struck Maggie, and she began to softly cry. She expected her mother to be downstairs in the kitchen making coffee. She expected her mother to be there, period. Maggie let herself sob for a while as she saw the sun rising over the ocean. She had missed the sight and was comforted by the fresh salt air that wafted through the crack in the window. Maggie forced herself to get up. She knew the day was going to happen with or without her mother.

After a quick phone call to Marten, Maggie made coffee and toast. Her mother never got a morning newspaper delivered and Maggie hated having nothing to read. So she stared quietly out at the ocean trying to gather herself. As predicted, the peace was broken soon enough by the crunch of the gravel drive. First to arrive was Millie with fresh muffins and juice, bustling with intentions. Then George stopped by on his way to work to say he could stay if she needed, and Maggie said only if he would stick around with a tranquilizer gun for when her family arrived. George and Millie couldn't help but let out a little laugh knowing what Maggie meant.

At nine a.m., Bill Getty called and asked when would be a good time to meet, and Maggie told him that Sarah would not be there until after one. Bill explained he was in his car and actually could be there in thirty minutes if Maggie wanted. Smart man, Maggie thought, he had already planned to get there before Sarah. Bill Getty was not just her mother's estate lawyer but her grandmother, Virginia's, as well. Five years ago, when her grandmother passed, Bill executed the will which gave Vivian the house on Grove. Uncle Johnny and Aunt Essie were furious even though each child and grandchild got a sizable inheritance. With waterfront real estate prices escalating, Johnny and Essie felt they had somehow been duped. Bill Getty not only had to take a constant barrage of lawsuit threats from Uncle Johnny, but Virginia also put him in charge of Sarah's inheritance. Because of Sarah's well documented drug addiction and her ability to run through money like wine, Virginia made Sarah's inheritance a trust that could only be used for health and well being - not fancy cars, vacations or cocaine. And yes, rehabs did count. Unfortunately, that put Bill in the constant line of fire because Sarah eternally wanted money. From the family, Vivian and Maggie were his only allies and his favorite clients. That was why it was poor Bill who helped Maggie get Sarah into the limo after she passed out the in church pew at her grandmother's funeral service.

"Okay, Bill, you should be in the clear, thirty minutes." Maggie spent the morning making arrangements with Millie. There would be a church service and some flowers. After, a reception at the house. The funeral would be Saturday and it was already Tuesday, but Maggie did not want to prolong anything. As much as she loved being home, she wanted to get back to Marten and her life away from the past.

Bill Getty arrived in his brand new $90,000 Sl coupe Mercedes and crisp shirt cuffs rolled up in a semi-casual style. Looking younger than his 60 years, Maggie figured he must dye his hair chestnut and leave a few streaks of gray for affect. He had a stout posture but one that enjoyed a good steak and cigar and still got on the treadmill thrice a week. Maggie knew the car and the suit were courtesy of handling the Murphy/Atwood estate for years. Although Bill hated dealing with Sarah and the others, he was well compensated for it. Still without a doubt, he did genuinely care for the family.

"You look well, Maggie." He shook her hand and kissed her cheek at the same time.

"Horse shit, Bill," but Maggie smiled anyway and tilted her head for him to come in the door, "Welcome to the Big Top, the circus should begin any minute now."

"Maggie, have I ever told you how you are exactly like your grandmother? Virginia could slice ham with her sarcasm."

"Everyday Bill, and don't forget it." They both laughed.

"No, seriously, Maggie. How you holding up?" If anyone knew the skeletons in the closet, it was the family lawyer.

"Is everyone going to ask me that? I don't know Bill. Honestly, you know how long I expected this but, now that it's here, you're here, frankly its like a bad acid trip left over from college."

"Maggie, Vivian loved you very much, despite her demons."

"Save it, Bill, let's not go there right now. Let's talk business. I can handle business." Maggie sighed and poured them coffee. Maggie really was not expecting any surprises from the will. She assumed it would be fifty fifty between her and Sarah, but she never really knew how much her mother was actually worth. Bill opened his briefcase and began unloading stacks of paper.

"You want me to cut to the chase?" he asked. Maggie replied, "Please do."

"First, we know when Virginia died, she left you and your sister each $250,000." That was how Maggie was fronting her failing writing career, but she was always careful never to squander. Maggie was conscious about keeping her nest egg safe for emergencies and never over indulged herself with luxuries. She did not even own a car.

"Well, your grandmother felt it would be too much responsibility for you or Sarah- especially Sarah- to handle more of the estate. Not that she didn't trust you Maggie, she spoke quite fondly of you, but she felt you could do just fine without a large bank account to fall back on." *Because that is what ruined the rest of the family*, Maggie thought.

"She split everything three ways when she died between your mother, uncle, and aunt. She left your mother not only this house but five million dollars as well, in a trust. But by putting the money in trusts, it only gave your mom, aunt, and uncle limited access to the estate. Vivian was only allowed to live on a very large allowance every year. The reason for all this was, let's be honest, Johnny and Essie have not been known for their pru-dence. So your grandmother really was strict about the purse strings. But Vivian planned her estate very differ-ently than Virginia. Vivian, although she did not have en-tire access to her money, she could distribute it however she liked upon her passing, without strings, ties or lawyers. Vivian assumed Sarah and you would be old enough to do with it as you pleased.

"So you have inherited roughly, let's see, " Bill shuffled some papers, "Yes, $2,353,000 give or take a few cents. And, Maggie, Vivian left you the house."

Maggie stared at him speechless. She kept thinking how surreal it seemed, she had lost her mother and now she was rich? It was the first painless emotion Maggie had felt in 48 hours. But it was not the joy you'd imagine $2.5 million dollars would bring. Instead Maggie was simply relieved that she would be able to keep the house. For the past two days she had presumed her mother would have left it to both her and Sarah. And Maggie did not want to share anything let alone a house with Sarah, so she assumed she would be cleaning out their childhood home and selling it. The thought was breaking her heart just as much as losing her mother. The house felt like family, the worn floorboards and faded bathroom wallpaper comforted her, gave her the security that Vivian and her sister never could. Although her worst memories existed in the mirrors shining back at her, there in the windows was the ocean that calmed and soothed her. Maggie had longed her whole life to get away from her family, but there amongst the photographs felt like the only place she belonged.

The amount of her inheritance was a slight shock to Maggie; like many Boston bloods, her family never discussed money. Richness was the air about you not necessarily what you wore. Maggie learned early on to earn her own money and quietly keep it to herself. At her mother's encouragement, she'd had summer jobs starting at age 14, through college. Her family's affluence never affected her work ethic. No one could deny the money they had with the large house tended by maids and gardeners or the Mercedes in the garage, or the yearly trips to the Caribbean. But her grandparents' display of wealth and prosperity was always subtle. Virginia gave quietly to many Haven charities and often refused to be honored for a new wing at the hospital and scholarships at the school. And Vivian, like Virginia never flaunted designer clothes or wore ostentatious jewels. Both women avoided using cash or influence to garner attention.

Now, Maggie sat with it all in her hands. She thought about Sarah, and how all these years Sarah had suspected a gold mine, and she was right. Maggie knew Sarah would not be able to contain her excitement because Sarah was always broke. For Maggie it was the security money provides that comforted her. Maggie began to chuckle, she thought about all the times she made Marten go to cheap restaurants and would not let him squander money on gifts for her. All her prudence was for not.

Bill cocked his head and eyed her, "Maggie?"

Maggie was hysterically laughing now. She leaned over as the tears flowed from her eyes and clutched her chest. It was a deep uncontrollable laugh where every time she breathed in, the fit would start again. It was the tragic irony of the situation that made Maggie feel like the cosmic joke was on her.

The money created this chasm of loneliness, that one by one each generation of her family fell into. She remembered what happened to her grandfather when he sold his company, without work, he lost his purpose. In his later years he turned more to bourbon than his family for solace. Maggie felt their wealth created a wall between her family and the people around them. Jack died from liver disease at 68 and Virginia remarried a bottle of gin soon after. Vivian, Essie, and Johnny spent years waiting for Virginia to follow so they could have their share of the money. But when their mother left them bits of the estate tethered with conditions, they became mired in their own isolation and greed. And poor Sarah, who'd found alcohol by the age of twelve and drugs by fifteen always thought the money would save her. Maggie resented it, resented all of it. Maggie had always blamed the money for ruining her family.

Worse was Virginia fueled her children with the wealth she could bestow upon them. She used the family money like a gun, withholding it for attention. She'd promise Vivian a house of her own and then recant her offer at the last minute. Often Virginia would make grand verbal gestures to her children, promises of cars, vacations, et cetera, and then find one excuse or another to deny them. So Vivian did the opposite with her children. When she sobered from a particularly hurtful drinking binge, there would be shopping excursions, presents and cash given unconditionally to Sarah and Maggie. While Maggie mostly refused such white flags, Sarah relished them and the guilt they admitted. Maggie always swore to stay away from all those behaviors, money was neither a justification nor an alias for affection.

Maggie stopped laughing.

"Sorry Bill, I'm so sorry. It's just too much. Honestly, I just did not know there was that much left. Somehow I just never thought, well, I don't know what I thought. It is weird, Mom gone, the money, it's just the craziness never ends."

"Well, Maggie, you did exactly what your grandmother wanted you to do. You didn't build your life around the family money all these years. I know it seems bittersweet that it comes with Vivian passing but you, of all, will know how to handle it. And how are you going to handle it?"

She had no idea but Maggie went over the logistics with Bill and gave him the number of the man in New York who invested her money. Maggie chuckled realizing she just moved up from the D-list to the A-list of clients. Maybe now her banker would come from New York to meet *her* instead of the other way around.

Bill finished his coffee and made excuses for getting back to the office. Maggie knew he was avoiding encountering any family members, and she let him off the hook. She would explain everything to Sarah and give her the paperwork. Maggie would also be the one to tell her about the house. Sarah had no attachment to it, and most likely would have sold it for the cash. For both of them, it was a symbol of Vivian's preference of Maggie over Sarah. Maggie prayed showing Sarah all those other zeros would shut her up.

Maggie said goodbye to Bill and would see him on Saturday for the services. He choked up and hugged her on his way out, he really was fond of Vivian. Then Maggie took a blanket off the chair and wrapped it around her shoulders. Digging through the table behind the couch, she found her mother's cigarette stash. She always had a hidden box of Parliament Lights. Taking the cigarettes and a lighter, she headed out onto the porch overlooking the ocean. The old wicker furniture was still there, but she noticed her mother had new pin-striped cushions made. If she were visiting, Maggie would have told her mother how nice they were. Instead, a few tears welled up in her eyes as she curled up on the couch and lit a smoke. It dawned on her that all this was now hers, but really she wondered how it ever could be as long as she could hear the ghosts crying.

FIVE

     After Bill left, Maggie sat on the porch and watched the morning fog lift off the water. Most likely, the sun would burn through by early afternoon, but Maggie liked the gray stillness of the moment. When George and she were little, they liked to play hide and seek in the mist. That is what her memory felt like now, a fine mist. Maggie couldn't help but drift back to when she was four, the first time her mother tried to kill herself. That is what Sarah told her years later, otherwise Maggie would have never known. Images of her grandmother, Virginia, standing at the apartment door, Virginia's thick fur coat soft and brown. Maggie loved to hug it like a bear. Virginia promised to take the girls for ice cream if they came right away. Excited, Sarah and Maggie quickly got their coats, not bothering to tell their mother. She was passed out.

Maggie remembered saying hello to Grandpa Jack out in the hallway smoking cigarettes with two men. Maggie asked if he was coming for ice cream too. 'No,' he said, 'I'll be here when you get back.' Maggie can recall nothing else, but after that they moved to Haven. Her mother disappeared for awhile, and when she returned, they all settled into the house on the water and no one discussed going back to Boston again.

That distant night so many years ago, the course of Maggie's life had been altered for the second time. First, she had lost her father, and then that night, subtly, her mother. There it would be for the rest of Maggie's life, a fleeting feeling about her mother. A dark shadow hovering between the two of them threatening to take Vivian away forever. It was like Maggie had lost part of her mother but not all, and she would forever live in fear of losing the rest.

As Maggie stubbed out her cigarette, she heard a faint wheeze, "Margaret, dear, where are you?" Aunt Essie had arrived.

Maggie heard Essie's thick old shoes climbing the porch stairs and saw her staring through the side windows from the front. "Essie, I'm out here on the porch!" Maggie threw down the blanket and walked around the corner to see her well-rounded aging Aunt Esther.

Essie and Vivian resembled nothing like each other. Essie looked fifteen years older than Vivian, although she was the younger sister. Her hair had gone completely gray and wrinkles abounded on all her features. Unlike Vivian, she had allowed her middle to go soft and cared very little for make-up. Essie had inherited Grandpa Jack's hard features and deep set eyes that after her twenties were no longer considered handsome but manly. Her most noticeable feature was her asthma and the oxygen tank bumping behind her..

"Hi, Essie, here let me help." Maggie rushed to get her tank and hoped to avoid hugging her.

Essie always had this lingering medicinal odor about her that Maggie and Sarah used to laugh about when they were kids. Her house looked like a mini ER complete with hospital bed and tables adorned with prescription bottles. Aunt Essie loved her pills even more than she loved alcohol. Oh, she drank and was secretly in and out A.A. like the rest of the family, but it was the prescriptions that Essie could not give up. Aunt Essie invented "doctor shopping". When one of her many doctors would not prescribe her something she wanted, Aunt Essie simply took a cruise. Cruise ship doctors were like stewardesses in first class, they gave you whatever you wanted without judgement.

Not much of Essie's life had changed since her childhood on Grove Avenue. Her childhood asthma perpetuated into an adulthood of dependance. Without her parents, she become reliant on doctors and nurses to nurture rather than cure her ailments. She had accepted her sickness as a characteristic rather than a condition. Essie never was a fighter. 'It is what it is,' she would always say.

Jack and Virginia's constant enabling took away any ambition Essie may have had early on. She found it easy to fall back on her parents financially and emotionally and had little motivation to improve her life. She never excelled at school like Vivian and often withdrew socially. At eighteen, she went to a local community college not far from home and while attending, she met Roger Walsh, her one and only husband. He easily took advantage of the shy, sickly rich girl who had never had a boyfriend.

It was no surprise Virginia disliked Roger immediately, dismissing him as beneath their family. He was studying business in order to own car dealerships and/or retail stores, which disturbed Virginia on so many levels. He was short, unrefined, and constantly swearing but Essie was determined to marry Roger knowing he might be her only chance. Essie ignored her mother's quips that something did not add up about him, especially the few dollars in his pocket.

At first, life was good for Essie and Roger. He finished school while Essie quit to give birth to their only child, a daughter named Samantha. Pregnancy was hard on Essie's health, so there would be no chance for a second child. But Roger and Essie were both pleased to have Samantha. Roger started a dry cleaning business, then a deli, and then a gym, and all failed under his ownership. So they had to turn to Jack Murphy to bail them out each time. Embarrassed by Roger's continued failings and coupled with the inability to cope with motherhood at age 27, Essie's prescription drug problem crossed the line between necessity to problematic. The difficulty of childbirth and the actual reality of having a child took its toll on Essie, who was unused to taking care of others and embarrassed by Roger's failings. As Roger schemed for ways to get the Murphy money, Essie dealt with her insecurities by increasing her dosages.

Eventually, things came to a head when Essie drove her station wagon into the side of Samantha's elementary school. Essie was okay, even laughed about the incident, but the embarrassment to Virginia was unbearable. Jack and Virginia stepped in and took control again. Roger moved out without a word, happy to have a fifty thousand dollar check in his hand, and Essie visited the same rehab Vivian had in Connecticut years before. Roger and she shared custody of Samantha and raised her separately but together in Haven. Eventually, Roger re-married a stripper who he met after becoming a cop. A fact that entertained Virginia to no end.

Essie choked up with tears.

"Oh, dear, Margaret how are you? I just can't believe your mother." Essie and Vivian never exactly were best of friends, but Maggie knew Essie was being sincere.

"Yes, you can Essie, we all saw this coming. Please, don't try to sugar coat it." Maggie waved dismissively like she was trying to ward off emotions. "How are you doing?"

"Seems like I am always falling down ass backwards." Essie sighed as she sat on a porch rocking chair. When Essie was not too high, she could be pretty funny.

Maggie laughed, "Yeah, well, me too."

"When does Sarah get in?"

"Around one, I guess in an hour or so."

"You talking to her yet?"

"Nope. Guess I am gonna have to now."

"Sarah is your sister, love, and you need each other."

"Oh please, like you and Mom held hands through life." Maggie shook her head in disbelief.

"I know, but when Momma died, Vivian and I had each other and it turned out that was a good thing. Losing your grandmother was harder for the both of us than we expected, although it was for different reasons. Now, listen, try to remember the old Sarah."

What old Sarah? Maggie thought. She wanted to get off the subject of her sister.

"Have you talked to Uncle Johnny?" Maggie asked.

"Yes, he says he is going to stop by later to see you."

"To see me or sue me?" Essie lifted up her finger and waggled it back and forth meaning Maggie was being inappropriate, but she also chuckled a little out loud. Uncle Johnny had a reputation for suing most of the family lawyers over his assumed inheritance, which did nothing but tie everyone up in useless litigation. No matter who Uncle Johnny sued, he lost, every time. He sued the Haven police department for giving him a DUI. He claimed he had a yeast imbalance that made him seem drunk and that is why he blew a .12 at 2 a.m. after leaving the local bar. It certainly was not the actual copious amounts of alcohol he drank. He sued George for accepting a donation from Virginia for his animal hospital. Johnny tried to claim Virginia was not in her right mind and that George took advantage of a poor, sick old lady. Just about everyone testified in town on behalf of George including several members of the police department. Uncle Johnny was the quintessential "piece of work."

"Great. Can't wait to see him."

"That sarcasm of yours is going to get you trouble, young lady." Essie scolded.

"I don't know if you noticed Essie, but I'm getting wrinkles too, and being in this family doesn't help much." Essie laughed at her niece, knowingly. Maggie was old enough now to say what she wanted about the family, regardless of whether it was appropriate. The two true queen bees of the family were gone now, her grandmother and mother and maybe now it was time to usher in a little honesty. But Essie and Maggie didn't delve any further into family dynamics, instead, they chatted about Vivian's funeral arrangements until Millie reappeared.

Essie sat on the porch for the rest of the morning holding court until Millie helped her leave. The clock was inching toward one when Sarah and David would be arriving, making Maggie agitated to no end. *Fuck it,* she thought and snuck upstairs to take a Valium. Since she could not drink with the A.A. bible thumpers about to show up, a mother's little helper would have to do.

When she came downstairs, George was in the kitchen with questioning worry furrowing his brow. Maggie put two of Millie's blueberry muffins on a plate with extra butter on top, handed it to him, and said, "Who died?"

"Not funny, Maggie," he said biting into a muffin. Bits uncaringly crumbled on his shirt as they sat together at the wooden kitchen table.

"George, you look worse than me. Stop, I just can't take you hovering. Sarah is going to be here any minute so, if you really want to do something for me, you can invade my body, be me, and deal with her."

"First off, I am not hovering. I happen to be using you to avoid work, thank you very much. And second, not on your life. Sarah still scares the bejeezus out of me." George smirked at her with butter glistening on his lips.

"Really, George, 'bejeezus'? Who says 'bejeezus' anymore." Maggie rested her face in both her hands while leaning on the table. She felt exhausted.

"Maggie, no wonder you aren't married yet. You have to put that mouth away once in awhile. Maybe get a holster for it."

"Ha. Ha. Very funny. Marten likes it just fine, some men aren't afraid of a little verbal banter."

"Obviously, because he called me again this morning to make sure you were okay. I have to admit he seems like a pretty decent fellow. Funny too. Has you pegged pretty good. You don't realize that neat little locked house you live in is actually made of glass and some of us can see right through you." George winked at her and started his second muffin. More crumbs cascaded down his shirt, again unnoticed.

"Great, G, you finally learned how to make a metaphor. I have never been so proud. So what, you and Marten buddies now? Going to get together and reform my evil ways? Sorry, but I think they are here to stay this week. No way am I about to give up my malicious humor, sarcasm, or emotional tantrums just to make you two feel better, not with Betty Ford about to show up here to climb up on her cross, or any other of these freak shows that share my blood."

"Now there's the open and willing nature that attracts us so! So where is that book you have been meant to write your whole life since you have so much to say about everyone."

"Hard to believe but when it comes to this family, I get verbal constipation when faced with the written word. How does one describe in detail unfettered narcissism? Pharmaceutical hurricanes? Or my favorite, uninhibited greed? No your potty mouthed friend, has a pen with no ink. I think that is a metaphor men can understand. I am just living up to the family standards, completely underwhelming the world with my lack of ambition." Maggie let her head drop onto her arms on the table.

"Seriously, Maggie, c'mon, look at me," Maggie lifted her head and rolled her eyes. "It all looks like shit right now, but it is not. You have me, apparently this too good to be true boyfriend, and everyone here in Haven is behind you. There are lots of us here for you, and you will get through this no matter how your family behaves. And as for writing, it hasn't gone anywhere, it will be there when you are ready. It always has been."

"Was that my daily pep talk by George? Wow, I could get used to this," Maggie shook her head and smiled all the same. She loved George, how he always knew the right thing to say she will never understand.

"So see you tonight? Mitzi is making something to eat, but I can't promise you anything good. So just keep your mouth shut no matter how it tastes. I don't know if you have ever dealt with pregnant women before, but their sense of humor tends to develop schizophrenia." George got up, patted her on the head, and left a trail of muffin crumbs out the door.

Maggie was in the kitchen thinking about dinner with George's happy family that night, when she heard tires on the gravel drive and jumped. It was too late for another valium when she heard Sarah's voice outside. Millie bustled past her out the kitchen door, and Maggie grabbed her arm. "You can't leave me," she pleaded.

"Maggie, hon, she's your sister, your only blood. Stop being such a baby. There was a time you two were like two peas in a pod, now go work this out." Millie fled down the stairs back to her house before Maggie could say another word.

Left standing there, Maggie flashed to the night her grandparents were in New York. They had gone to see a Broadway show for their anniversary leaving her and Sarah alone with Vivian. Maggie remembered they were young enough to still play with dolls. They were babies themselves. It was winter, when the days were cold and gray and the nights long and black. Her grandmother had kissed her goodbye with worry in her eyes, a prelude to the night to come. Left unchaperoned, Vivian drank all day, and yelled at the girls to *get out of her hair*. She gave them ice cream to go away. They stayed upstairs in their room most of the night, listening to their music loudly to drown out Vivian yelling into the telephone. When Vivian had finally gone silent, Sarah told Maggie to follow her and they went hand in hand down the hall to their mother's bedroom. Sarah carefully opened the door into the darkened room, so slowly it seemed hours in Maggie's memory. Sarah pulled her into the room, and they stood next to her mother's bed, breathless like soldiers. Maggie's mind could still see the sharp slant of yellow light from the doorway cutting across the quilt. She focused intensely on the light illuminating the triangle patterns, letting her eyes zig zag with each shape, pretending not to be there. She tried desperately not to see Vivian lying motionless on the bed, fully clothed.

Sarah began tugging at her, "Mommy, Mommy, wake up Mommy."

It was common for Maggie for have holes in her memory, little black spots ripping the sequence of events like seams. It was hard for her to remember things from start to finish, always had been. Next, Maggie was being put to bed in Millie's house. Millie drew the blinds to block out the flashing red lights circling the room. Sarah was not in there with her and Maggie remembered, all she'd wanted was Sarah. It was the second time their mother had tried to commit suicide in their young lives. Unfortunately it was Sarah who saved her, sacrificing the last of her childhood innocence.

Maggie adored her older sister, she had everyday of her life. Although there was a five year age difference, Sarah never seemed to mind having her younger sister tag along. Maggie was like Sarah's pet that she needed to make sure was fed and cleaned and put to bed on time. And in turn, Maggie idolized her sister and mimicked her every move from the dresses she wore, to her favorite TV programs and music. When Sarah and Vivian would fight, which was often, Maggie would always be there to comfort her. Maggie was Sarah's shadow, her touchstone in the family. So naturally, it was Maggie who was there to see Sarah take her first drink, at only twelve years old.

When all of them came to live back to Haven after Thomas's death, Sarah was just nine years old. Virginia tried to reach the girl who was sullen and sensitive but found the task impossible. Virginia lacked patience, so it was Grandpa Jack who became Sarah's ally. He took her out fishing and golfing, appreciating her quiet nature. He allowed her to be herself and did not try to change or twist her anger into something pretty and presentable. Their misery found company in each other. But Jack wasn't enough to combat the damage caused by Vivian.

By the time Sarah was a teenager, her grief about her father's death and her mother's emotional absence had broken something deep inside her. Following the lead of her family, it was easy for Sarah to experiment with alcohol. She watched her grandfather drink himself to sleep at night in front of baseball games while Virginia sip small glasses of gin she hid in the kitchen cupboard. Her mother drank copious amounts alone in her bedroom at night. They all used it for escape, and Sarah wanted to escape too. Since they all drank in supposed secret, it was easy for Sarah to steal a glass here and there.

It was Bob Sherwood, George's father, who called the Murphy's interrupting their anniversary trip in New York. Listening to him explain the situation, Virginia's heart pounded so loudly in her chest she thought she was having a heart attack. He calmly explained that Vivian had swallowed some sleeping pills with a couple bottles of Chardonnay, and it was Sarah who had called the police when she could not wake her mother up. He, his wife, Peggy, Millie, and Archie all came to the house when they heard the sirens. He told her Vivian was at the hospital having her stomach pumped and should be okay by morning. Millie had taken the girls, and as far as he knew Maggie was fine but Sarah was quite shaken. Millie was doing her best with Peggy to calm her down.

Virginia made Jack immediately drive them back to Haven and they were home by 4 a.m.. They first went to the hospital and found Vivian stable and sleeping. The nurses said they would most likely release her the next day, and the doctor would recommend psychiatric care. By six in the morning, Virginia was waiting in her kitchen for Millie to wake, knowing she would see the lights on in the kitchen and come over.

Millie and Virginia had an odd but close friendship. Millie was younger than Virginia by five years, but they were of the same generation. Their personalities were so different; Millie was the soft grandmotherly type who embraced the world with care and love. Her sweet southern drawl drew people to her, while Virginia hardened when around others. While Virginia cared about a great many charities, she did not care for a great many people. She used her wealth to build an unspoken boundary between her and the world. Naturally, it was Millie who forged the friendship between the houses.

That morning, while Vivian was in the hospital, Millie did not bother to knock but came in the back kitchen door and put on a new pot of coffee. Virginia had been sitting there at the table watching the sun rise over the water with her arms crossed. She attempted to tell Millie she would get the coffee, but Millie just hushed her. Millie then pulled out a pack of cigarettes from her apron pocket and opened the kitchen window. It was one funny thing they both had in common. Virginia and Millie would sneak cigarettes but never smoked in public. Virginia would see Millie occasionally in her rose garden puffing away when Archie was not around, and Millie would catch Virginia by the garage trimming her hydrangeas, clippers in one hand and a smoke in the other.

Both women lit a cigarette and listened to the coffee pot gurgle before Virginia finally spoke. "How are they?" meaning the girls.

"Maggie's fine, you know she is worried about everyone else. But Sarah, I'm not sure how she will recover from this."

"I know. She is taking after Vivian, and I didn't do a very good job the first time around." Virginia exhaled and looked into Millie's eyes, who understood.

"Sometimes that is just how people are wired. Vivian has always been a handful, the girl has got a lot of spirit. But Sarah is a little different, more sensitive to what is going on around her, she internalizes it. Vivian lashes out, but Sarah has it brewing in her somewhere deep. You know, I never question what you do with your family, Virginia, but that little girl needs some help." Millie was implying a therapist for Sarah, and Virginia did not know quite what to think about that. Her whole life, if there was a problem, you just made a decision and plugged through it. Life was hard, and you had to be tough.

"I see your point Millie. I just wish it was Vivian making these decisions not me. Seems I have always been taking care of that child, and now I have two more."

"Speaking of Vivian, what are you going to do this time, same as last?" Last time meaning the reason Vivian and the girls came to live in Haven.

When Vivian first attempted suicide in Boston, when Maggie remembers eating ice cream with her grandmother, Virginia thought she was bluffing and just needed to sleep it off. Jack and Virginia had known about Vivian's drinking since Thomas's death and had been questioning whether to do something about it. Many times she and Jack discussed bringing all of them to

Haven but did not want to have a raging Vivian living in their house.

So before this incident, Jack had made arrangements with a local Boston rehab facility to take Vivian. They could not decide on the right time, knowing the fight Vivian would put up. But that night, with Vivian threatening her life with alcohol and sleeping pills, they knew it was the right decision. As Virginia and Jack raced up to Boston, two men from the rehab met them at the apartment to help collect Vivian. When Vivian woke up the next day, she had no idea where she was until the nurse told her. By then, Jack and Virginia had packed up the children and taken them back to Haven. It was too late for Vivian to fight because Virginia threatened to never let her see the girls again. Vivian resigned herself to the stay in the hospital but like all other things in her life, never took it too seriously.

Some might say it was random fortuity, or maybe it was providence itself, but Peter Moore entered rehab the same day as Vivian. He was the tall strapping type with premature graying hair and a walk of confidence. His humor was biting and he charmed all the ladies. After being with docile Thomas all those years, Vivian was immediately attracted to him and knew he was the one for her. And he her because, despite the two children and months of steady drinking, it only took a few days of sobriety for Vivian to regain her beauty and a healthy glow. So for twenty-eight days, Peter focused on becoming sober and Vivian focused on Peter. She just happened to be sober at the time.

For Sarah, this meeting would lead to the second crossroad in her life that would lead her further away from her mother, Maggie, and herself.

Excerpts from the Diary of Vivian Murphy Atwood
February 1979

I deserve these four cold walls caging me, keeping me from hurting anyone. My therapist says I need to "journal". I have to get my feelings out but I haven't a clue as to what to feel anymore. Momma was right to stick me in the hospital, I can't even bear the thought of what I have done to my girls. I love them so much yet, I hate myself more. Dr. S, my shrink, keeps asking me why I hate myself and I can't answer him. I don't know, it just always seems like Momma hated me, as did the wretched brother and sister I have. Daddy just seems to write checks but he never really notices me. I miss Thomas like crazy. I never knew how much I needed him, relied on him until he was gone. I was a horrible wife, so selfish prattling on about my modeling and my writing. Just because I like writing does not mean I am very good at it. Maybe someday I will write a book. I could do that, someday. But for right now, it is all about these four walls.

I haven't had a drink in seven days and am going out of my mind. Jesus, how these people go on and on about themselves. The only fun person is Peter, at least he knows how to laugh at all this. And so handsome too!

Peter kissed me last night in the hall. I know we shouldn't, we are here to get "better". But hey, we are sober, aren't we? We sit around all day long saying how guilty we feel for ruining our families lives, shouldn't I at least get a little reward? He is not Thomas, but I like that. He is older and more confident. Peter thinks the past should stay in the past and we just move on from one day to the next. I like that. It means when I get home to the girls, I can start new with them. Be a new Mom, make them dinner, tuck them in at night, tell stories to each other. We won't stay in Haven too long, just to the end of summer and then I will take them back to Boston so I can start working again.

Oh, Peter is so glorious! He thinks my plans are great and he is throughly interested in my writing. Who needs booze when you have love, sweet, love? Thomas would approve, I think because Peter is so smart, he will be a great influence on the girls. Even Sarah will be charmed by him!

June 1979

Peter and I are getting married. Everyone is so thrilled, except Sarah of course, but she will come around. Maggie follows him like a little puppy and even Momma approves. Daddy always seems like he wants us out of his hair so he won't mind if we go back to Boston. Momma is completely charmed by Peter, she blushes and dotes on him whenever he visits. I have never seen her this way. I am just so scared it will all come to an end. Every night I wake up with a start in the dark and think about how Thomas was here and then he was gone. I can't lose Peter.

July 1979

Married! I can't believe it but Peter and I went to City Hall and did it! I guess I was never the full wedding type of girl, two elopements in one lifetime! I do wish the girls had been there but when they are older they will understand. Peter says we can start looking for a house in Boston soon, he is just so busy working. But that is okay because I am his wife and we will be together forever anyway, right? No different from Thomas, work, work, work. I just have to practice patience. Momma was not exactly pleased we eloped but she is happy for me all the same. Can you believe Momma is happy with me? HA! I never thought I would see that day. She has been frustrated with me her whole life and now finally, well. I guess this is a fairy tale ending.

When Vivian returned to Haven from rehab she seemed a new person. She was in love. Not with herself as the clinic tried to teach her, but with Peter, and Peter was going to make her life complete. He returned to Boston, where he was a telecommunications engineer. His company was working on a telephone system that would be wireless. It would be a phone that you could carry and receive signals from various towers placed around the country, even the world. Peter loved his job and explained to Vivian how demanding it was and required him traveling quite a bit. But Vivian had not felt the stir of infatuation since high school and, at first, felt undaunted by Peter's absence. Thomas had spent most of his time away from her as well, so she understood.

After rehab, Vivian saw Peter on weekends at his apartment in Boston and left the girls at home in Haven. Eventually, Peter and Vivian were engaged. Virginia and Jack liked Peter quite a bit. They thought he was an excellent influence on Vivian because she had continued her sobriety after the clinic and seemed to be her old spirited self, with a new found kindness. But no one realized she only went to A.A. meetings with Peter, never when she was home alone in Haven.

Sarah kept her distance from Peter, still honoring her father's memory, but Maggie was another story. She followed her mother's lead and jumped in with both feet. Even though Peter had no children of his own, nor did he want any, he couldn't help but fall in love with Maggie. Maggie, in her pigtails, always had a story bubbling about what was happening in the neighborhood or one she had just made up, kept Peter captured with her infectious spirit. Maggie was an easy going child, never wanting to cause any trouble. She was polite, kind and easily made Peter laugh.

Over the next year, things became more strained. Vivian, on a whim one weekend, persuaded Peter to marry her at City Hall in Boston. Peter's long absences were making her feel insecure, so she pushed him towards marriage. They decided that they would buy a house in Boston and move the girls once they were settled. But Peter was never home long enough to find a house, and a whole summer had passed into another school year in Haven. That was when Vivian started to secretly drink again. All her old hiding spots began to fill up with bottles of wine, and Virginia and Jack turned a blind eye. They too were holding out for Peter to settle and whisk their daughter back to Boston and a proper family. But days turned into months, and when Peter did show up, he and Vivian fought terribly. He was still sober and could smell the wine on Vivian's breath, and a furious Vivian blamed him for her drinking. While Vivian did love Peter, she did not realize she knew so little about love, especially how to love. And Peter really could only ever love his work.

Peter offered a quick divorce after their five month marriage. He wanted nothing from her and they shared no property, so it was easy. But not for Vivian or Maggie. They openly lamented the end of the affair. Vivian and Maggie saw Peter as their hope for a family and a normal life. And secretly, so did Sarah. While she never particularly warmed to Peter, she did like his affect on the family. Sarah longed to get back to Boston where it promised the memory of her father. But again, Sarah was disappointed and blamed her mother. And after her mother's next incident, for Sarah there was no turning back.

Excerpts from the Diary of Vivian Murphy Atwood
August. 1979

Goddam that son of a bitch! How dare he, HOW FUCKING DARE HE! Does he know who I am? I am his wife goddamit not some whore he can visit when he feel like it. P only shows up when "he can". Fuck you P. Girls have to start school here again, everybody ruins everything for me. Stuck in Haven, isn't that ironic? Haven, a haven? Ha! I see the looks momma gives me, like I screwed up again. What did I ever do to her? She made me live here, back in her talons. For a woman who has never liked me, she never lets me go, except to rehab! Hahaha. Who cares if I drink wine. Gets the edge off, not like she isn't sipping on a gin bottle like oxygen. Fuck you Peter Moore, I am Mrs. Moore. I am somebody and should be treated like somebody.

December 1979.

Divorce, I can't believe I am a divorcee. Momma's disappointed looks are at full throttle towards me, disgraced again by her precious daughter. Maybe she hates me so much because I look like her but I am younger. She still doesn't hate Peter, calls him honorable. Please! Just because he isn't asking for anything, meaning Daddy's money. Honorable would have been to buy me a house in Boston and make good on his promises, honorable. Ha. So what I drink a little, Peter is such a saint because he doesn't? Aren't they all saints!! Sarah is even giving me smug looks. I just want to say to her if I could bring back your father I would dammit, but I can't!! Maggie breaks my heart, so stoic walking around trying to cheer everybody up. She has Thomas's heart. I have nothing but failure.

January 1980

This is it, I am done, gone, bye, curtain falls. I see the cold black light outside and I long to run into it. Twirling it around me until nothing. Goodbye everyone, I did love! I did! My girls you are better off. Be free, be wonderful. You don't need me for that, others will take care of you better than me. Sarah, dear, don't be so sad and Maggie, don't worry so much. You both are beautiful and strong! I can't shine in your light, I have no light. I did something wrong a long time ago, and learned the world was not my place. I love You!

It was the morning after Vivian's second and almost successful attempt at suicide that Millie and Virginia had sat at the kitchen table, smoked cigarettes and tried to understand what they could do to save Vivian and Sarah. Both of Vivian's breakdowns came after her marriages ended. Losing Thomas and then losing Peter devastated her. Virginia thought if she could just get Vivian to stand on her own two feet, without a man, then maybe she could pull herself together. But Sarah was another story, she was on the cusp of being a teenager with barely an ounce of innocence left.

Millie left that morning with the promise from Virginia she would seek professional help for Sarah, but Virginia never did. Vivian agreed to go to rehab again, this time in Connecticut, and Virginia was relieved to have her gone for at least two months. But soon after she left, Jack became ill. At first no one realized the seriousness of it, but it was the beginning of the end. Virginia's having to care for the girls and Jack decided that Sarah would toughen up with age. Without a father or a mother looking after her, or professional help, Sarah did toughen up. At twelve years old, when she took her first drink.

SIX

Maggie stood at the top of the porch stairs waiting for Sarah to stop crying and hugging Millie. Now that Sarah had spent roughly twenty years in therapy exploring her inner child, she was no longer the sullen brooding type. Sarah loved to openly display her affections with as much dramatic flair as possible. Maggie, who was more reserved with her emotions, found these scenes ingratiating and unnecessary.

Sarah turned towards Maggie and bounded up the porch stairs to embrace her. Unable to escape Sarah's grip, Maggie felt herself saying, "It's okay, it's alright" in between Sarah's theatrical sobs. Maggie thought, *here I am comforting her again!* The familiar irritation her sister caused crept up her spine.

Sarah began apologizing for the 'incident' four years prior that caused Maggie to stop speaking to her sister. *It was all a mistake, she was wrong, she has paid for it, she should have listened to Maggie.* Maggie bit her tongue and sarcastically thought to herself, *how could it be wrong to file a lawsuit against your sister? Gee, all sisters at some point in their lives sue each other, how natural.* Maggie pushed her sister into the house all the while saying it was okay, bygones just to get her to stop being such a spectacle. An annoyed Maggie sat Sarah down with a box of tissues and turned toward the man standing sheepishly in the door way.

"You must be *the* David." Maggie tried to say with as little acrimony as possible. Actually, David was barely a man - he looked quite young even compared to Maggie. He was tall and skinny, and wore his pants slung on his hips like it was far too much of a bother to own a belt. His curly hair flopped from one side to the other and he had dimples on his smooth round face. Maggie couldn't help but think that Sarah found him on the set of the Mickey Mouse Club. He couldn't have been older than twenty five. She was used to Marten's more mature looks given that he was a few years older than she, and she, frankly, preferred that in a man. A man should actually be a be a man. Maggie should not have been surprised her sister had found a younger guy to be with, all the easier to control naturally. And as Maggie stood between them, she could see, at thirty eight, her sister still had her twenty-something looks. Even though she had years of hard drinking and drug abuse under her skin, Sarah had the family genes. Wrinkles had yet to form on her soft, heart shaped face, and her hazel eyes were still wide and clear. But the blonde streaks in her fine, long brown hair, chipped black nail polish, and fresh tattoos betrayed her age. Sarah was trying hard to appear younger and hipper, desperately trying still to be a teenage punk rocker. But she was a woman racing towards middle age, who glaringly lacked refinement or grace. Her gestures were sharp and nervous, like a part of her never grew up, never became comfortable with herself or the world around her. So unlike her grandmother and mother.

A vague twinge of sadness pierced Maggie. Sarah and her were vastly different from when they were children. Maggie's easy nature had given way to toughness. But it also gave her a measure of capable confidence. She may yell, scream, and bitch at the world, but she was not afraid of it. Now, she was a fighter and never backed down from making her own decisions. But her sister wrestled with her demons, and it showed. Her timidity and insecurities were as glaring as her tattoos. Her bitten fingernails were like self-inflicted wounds. No one would ever mistake her for Maggie's *older* sister.

Maggie suggested David and Sarah take their bags upstairs to Sarah's room and asked Sarah to join her on the porch, alone. Maggie needed to get things straight with Sarah without hunky boy toy. While Sarah and David did as they were told, Maggie took a few minutes to puff on a cigarette and think about what the hell she was going to say.

Excerpts from the Diary of Vivian Murphy Atwood February and March 1980

Funny, only took a year for me to get back into one of these places. Guess I am good at some things. At least I have finally learned, suicide has two results ..death or rehab! I guess rehab was the luck of the draw twice. Maybe God does have a sense of humor. Have to say, Momma did a better job picking this one out than the last time. The food is good and I have my own room. I guess that is what you get the second time around! This time my shrink is a woman, Dr. M and I like her. No bullshit this time, she said . I guess she has seen people like a revolving door. I don't blame her. Listening to us whine all day that no one loves us, we are damaged, how we hurt others, blah, blah blah. On the outside, people think alcoholics must have grand stories of their defeat, bar brawls, interesting accidents and what not. But in truth, most of us are just sad and lonely and bored. We drink alone, without character or hoopla. There are only a small few who make it to the police station with a story to tell. Most of us just drown in cheap liquid until someone who loves us pulls our sorry heads above the water line.

This time no Peter, no men, just me and Dr. M. She wants to start back to my earliest memory and frankly, I can't find a first memory. It's like I woke up one day, and there I was a fully functioning child with a mother, father, sister and brother. Why do you think that is, she asks? I said, 'You're the doctor, why do you think that is?' And she asked me if I had suffered any traumas when I was a very young child. I said, 'That is the question isn't it?', because I re-iterated I don't remember! I mostly remember little Essie as a baby, so small and sickly. Momma and Daddy doting on her, not letting me near her or touch her. Momma focused all her energy on Essie, that is what happens when a baby is that small and sick, right? I can't really complain about that. I didn't really get annoyed with Essie until she was older and most definitely the princess of the family. And don't forget Johnny, who quickly became the prince. Who was I? Not either one of them. I don't think that really qualifies as a trauma, maybe I was just a bit forgotten. Left alone too long. Maybe that's why I became such a strong personality. I know I was outspoken and high strung during my teen years, hell, that is how I ended up with Sarah. But how can all those little series of events lead to this? Me sitting here, locked up like a bad girl? Because I wasn't loved enough as a child? That sounds whiny and ridiculous.

I listen to the women in my group, their fathers beat them, uncle so-and-so molested them, their mother or father died when they were young, car accidents, all of them can pinpoint the moment their life took a wrong turn. They have a memory to their misery, a single defining moment where they can say that's it! Let's analyze that! That is why I am the way I am! But I have shit. I comb through my memories like I am panning for gold in a carpet. Dr. M says to relax, but I am always so agitated and frustrated. It is like the golden ring is always just beyond my grasp. She says some people are just wired differently, she says I have a brain and I am a lot smarter than I give myself credit for. I apparently need to channel this into something. She encourages my writing, but every time I sit down to write anything besides my feelings it is like I swallowed cotton.

Dr. M wants Momma and Daddy to come to a therapy session! Ha! I spent most of the afternoon laughing over that one. I explained that Daddy's ass hasn't left his den chair in years except to get a drink and Momma will talk to you about anything but herself! If you want to know all about rare pearls, who the greatest American authors were, and how to throw a proper tea party ask Virginia. Ask her feelings, and you will get a look to melt your shoes off. It is improper to talk of such things! So Momma is closed, big deal, still doesn't explain why I am "angry," as Dr. M. says. I say I am angry because I got myself knocked up, and then I got angry because my husband died, and I am angry because I had to go back home. And now I am angry because I seem to be on this roller coaster of screwing up and I keep hurting my girls. She says we can work on that. Super.

Dr. M asked about Essie and Johnny. I am not quite sure what to say about them. They are my sister and brother but they feel like foreign objects to me. Literally, like there is Chinese written all over them. Essie was my baby sister, but she was always so fragile. I suppose I was jealous of all the attention Momma gave her but she turned into such a spoiled brat that I ceased to be jealous- just angry at her. She had the world and never seemed to do anything with it. Essie expected Daddy's money, expected a husband, expected every-thing to just happen for her. And for the most part it did but, being spoiled, it was never enough. Plus, with all the medications she takes for 'health' reasons, she really is no better off than me! Pills, please what is the difference from booze?

And Johnny, well he was always a little brat since he was a kid. He was always ratting me out. He got away with murder in the house because he was the boy. Daddy actually used to think Johnny would work for the insurance company. But by the time he was in high school, we all realized he did not have a lick of sense and he was mean hearted. Momma and Daddy tried to cover it up but I think Momma knew deep down that Johnny was a little rotten apple. I think that is another reason why she is so closed off, none of her children were perfect. Her seemingly fabulous, perfect life was broken and cracked in all the wrong places. Thus, enters her gin bottle, I suppose. Momma had her own disappointments and I guess, us children were the roots of that tree.

I know Essie and Johnny do not like me either. I was a terrible older sister, I ignored them, I did! I just wanted my own life. When I left for boarding school, I was so happy I did not have to deal with them anymore. I did not have to compete for attention anymore.

Dr. M. says I have to talk about why I tried to "take my life." I don't know, just at the time it seemed right, I suppose. How do you answer that? I mean one minute I am fixing the girls breakfast and the next I am lying in a hospital. It just happens. I really don't have a good reason. I mean the drinking doesn't help, screws me all up inside and makes me feel like dirt. But it is like I can't help it. Someone says don't look directly at the sun, what do I do? Look right at it. I told Dr. M. this time started with Peter leaving me and she says I can't blame him. Why not? Why does everyone defend Peter?! I mean Thomas left me, and then Peter. I know T' didn't mean too, not allowed to blame him for dying, but still I'm alone again. Just like when I was a child, alone in a roomful of people. Drives you crazy after a while, no one understanding, no one listening to what I have to say. I mean the girls try, but they are just girls - they could never understand what it is like to be me, nor do I ever want them too. Dr. M says I have to imagine for them how it would be to lose a mother. Frankly, I think they would be better off. I would have been better off without my mother's scouring glances and constant annoyance with me, right? Would I have been the same woman if someone sweet like Millie had raised me, or the

Atwoods? Would I have been more satisfied with life? All I can say is, I do stupid things sometime.

I have been here two months and I am terrified to go home. Maggie will smile and pretend everything is normal but I am not ready for Sarah's scorn. She will be angry. I know, how can she not be? But I am her mother whether she likes it or not. Maggie will be fine, she always has been a trooper. Maggie has Thomas's easiness to her. She adapts, but Sarah is a fighter like me. That is why we are so frustrated. I will try harder with Sarah, she needs me. But do I need her? Well, that is a strange question isn't it? I love my children but do I need them?

I have to stop all this analyzing. I have been sitting on Dr. M's couch too long.

Five years earlier when Maggie was 28 and Sarah was 33, Sarah had tried to entangle Maggie in a lawsuit over their inheritance from their grandmother. That was when Maggie officially stopped talking to her sister. Maggie had always managed to muster through Sarah's histrionics, but being legally attacked by her own sister seemed to be the final straw. Although their communication had been sporadic at best before and after their grandmother's funeral, Maggie always had a way of looking past Sarah's indiscretions. Even when at the funeral, Sarah not only passed out during the church service and had to be carried out of Grace Episcopal, but she also took the opportunity to publicly humiliate her mother during the reception afterward. Maggie expected her mother and sister to be drinking heavily that day, but her sister threw in the extra pharmaceutical element. The alcohol only exacerbated the situation. While forty or so people milled on the porch of the Murphy house dressed in their best black clothes while nibbling stuffed mushrooms, Vivian and

Sarah raged in the kitchen. They not only threw China and glasses at each other but hurtful confessions for everyone to hear through the open windows. Family secrets were being broadcast for all of Haven.

Maggie remembers Millie going inside and shutting the windows and drawing the curtains. As the argument inside built momentum, Maggie just sat there on the wicker furniture sipping her gin and tonic in honor of her grandmother. George and Mitzi sat beside her, George covering her hand with his big football paw. Mac, Vivian's third husband, sat across from her. Bill Getty and his wife drew up chairs. Archie and Millie sat too, and Bob and Peggy Sherwood were still there.

It would be the last time Maggie remembered seeing George's parents alive.

They gathered around Maggie like a palisade. None of them felt the need to interfere with the tempest in the kitchen. That opportunity had passed. Instead they circled the wagons around her and changed the subject to her grandmother where it should have been. Eventually they heard a back door slam, the squeal of tires on the gravel drive. Mac slowly got up knowing he would be able to get Vivian to bed now. The was the last time Maggie had seen Sarah until now.

The lawsuit came about nine months later. Sarah was vigorously drinking and taking whatever a doctor prescribed her when she decided she would contest her grandmother's will. Virginia had placed Maggie and Sarah's inheritance in two trusts, with Bill Getty as the trust officer, in order to safe guard the funds from either of her grandchildren from spending it all at once. Unbeknownst to Sarah, Bill eventually handed Maggie control of her own money. He knew Virginia would not have a problem because Maggie had always shown good sense when it came to money. Sarah, on the other hand, had to go through Bill to touch a single cent. Sarah, 34 at the time, naturally found this humiliating and frustrating. For years she had been banking on the cash she might receive with Virginia's passing. Sarah had no real education, no career, she floated from job to job, boyfriend to boyfriend and always managed to get by. But here was the golden ticket, just outside her grasp.

Sarah found a lawyer who worked on the promise of riches. She then barraged Maggie with phone calls telling how she needed her to file suit against Bill Getty. Maggie refused and wanted no part in Sarah's useless tirade, plus Sarah wanted Maggie to pay the lawyer a deposit. It was increasingly hard to reason with Sarah because of the various medications she was taking. So the day Maggie received court documents claiming that Sarah had included her in filing suit against Bill Getty, Maggie had had it. Sarah had lied to her for the last time. She called Bill and together they hired lawyers to represent their interests. Maggie felt Sarah had used her enough over the years and this time was it. She simply left a message on Sarah's phone saying she was done. For months, Sarah tried to reach her but Maggie went as far as to change her cell phone number and moved to New Orleans without telling her. The law suits were eventually thrown out, but Bill Getty did approve Sarah changing her trust officer to someone better suited to her needs. Now, Maggie doubted if Sarah had any of her money left at all.

Excerpts from the Diary of Vivian Murphy Atwood March 1987

I have failed Sarah so terribly. She is 17 now and miserable, nothing I have ever done is right! Why, Thomas, why! Stupidly, I watched her spiral down-hill these past couple of years doing nothing. But what was I to do? Every time I go near her she hisses and scratches at me like a cat. She just never liked me - did I like her? I love her of course, the same as Maggie, but Maggie is just easier, kinder. I watch Maggie follow Sarah from room to room, worry on her face. She knows Sarah is drinking and doing drugs, and I see the pain it causes Maggie. She does love her sister terribly, looks up to her (God knows why), and would do anything to save her. I am her mother for God's sake, it is up to me to do something. And I act numb and useless. What if Maggie goes down this road? I would never forgive myself. And pathetically, I sit here with my wine, Mother is downstairs with her gin, and Daddy isn't well at all. We know he is going to die soon. The doctor's say he can't drink but I see Momma slip it to him anyway. We are all tragic and stupid.

But Sarah, oh, I think I need to put her in rehab. My baby in rehab! And all I can think about is the shame it will cause Momma. I am a terrible clueless mother, that's what Momma will say to me. I can't stand that look she gives me, that I have somehow ruined her life again. But this I have to do for Sarah, not Momma. I have to be her mother. She will hate it but I have to put my foot down before it is too late.

When Sarah returned downstairs, she was wearing an old sweater from high school which took Maggie aback. Seeing her sister lounging on the porch, pulling a piece of peppermint gum out of a bag, looked like a picture postcard from the past. Sarah appeared ready to take the abuse Maggie was about to give, but Maggie still did not know how to proceed.

"So when was the last time you talked to Mom?" Maggie asked instead.

"Actually, just last Friday. She was headed to the garden shop to get some new roses. You know, Maggie I've been clean for seven months now and…well…I have been talking to Mom a lot. Actually, we were getting along too." Sarah was looking like child tugging at the fringes of her sweater, tears in her eyes.

"Yeah, well isn't that nice." It came out harder than Maggie wished, but her temper was starting to well up to the surface.

"Maggie, I know you are angry at me and that's okay."

"Is it now? Didn't know I needed your permission to be pissed off. So glad I have your approval," Maggie shot back.

"Mags, I did some pretty shitty things to you. I mean the money thing was a low blow. I was desperate and a drug addict and…yeah…I tried to use you. But I am so, so sorry. If I could take it back, I would. I made so many mistakes."

"Yeah, well as the one on the receiving end of those mistakes, I stopped calling them mistakes and started realizing they were choices, Sarah. Choices you made that hurt me. You want to know why we don't have a relationship? Because you made a choice with every fucked up thing you ever did."

Maggie was fuming now. She did not intend to be so indignant, but seeing her sister there, looking like her old self, sparked inside her.

"Maggie, I am so sorry. I can keep saying I'm sorry but it won't do any good until you can forgive me. You have to let it go to a higher power."

"Oh, don't higher power me. Save that holy roller crap for your boy toy upstairs. A higher power didn't make me clean up your friend's puke in the living room when I was seven, didn't drag me to parties and give me cigarettes and booze before the age of ten. A higher power didn't make you drive me to school when you were doped out on heroin. A higher power didn't steal $2000 dollars that I had saved when I was fifteen. A higher power didn't show up at my high school graduation dressed like a goddamn hooker and with a coked-out boyfriend. A higher power didn't - oh fuck it. The list goes on Sarah, you were there, if you can remember." Maggie paused for effect.

"The point is can you take responsibility? I mean, seriously, Sarah. You managed to blame the first forty years of your life on Mom, on Dad, on Grandma, and probably on me. But did you ever think, '*Hey wait a minute, maybe I did some of it too.*"

"I think about that every day, Mags, I really do."

"Really?! Really? You are taking responsibility? Then how come I was here to identify the body? How come I have made the arrangements for Mom to be cremated?How come I've planned the funeral? So far in two days, I haven't seen you exactly jump in and take *responsibility.*" Maggie sneered. Sarah stayed silent during Maggie's tirade knowing no answer was a match for her fury.

"We are sisters, Mags, I love you."

"Okay, now, what the hell does that mean? When is the last time we acted like sisters? Maybe when I was five?! Hmmm... because it certainly has not been anytime in the past couple of decades. Can you name any of my ex-boyfriends, any jobs I have held in the past ten years, or how 'bout this, what was my major in college?

"Now, I can name all three of your rehabs, and I can still remember what day you set your apartment on fire. Oh, and here's a goodie, I still remember what you were wearing when you drove my car into the water just over there." Maggie pointed off the porch to the little beach at the end of Grove Avenue.

"You were wearing my favorite jean jacket that you had convinced me a year earlier had been stolen out of my car when you borrowed it."

"I'm sorry I didn't get here sooner. I just had to process Mom being, gone, finally."

"Oh, princess had to process. So sorry to disturb you."

Maggie knew she was acting maniacal but she could not stop herself. It had been so long since she had seen Sarah and, with the stress of the past two days, she was just venting anything and everything.

"Maggie, you are so bitter, it is not good for you. You need to work through it, find some peace with yourself and with all of us. Mom didn't just hurt me, but you too. You were so little. Have you tried therapy?"

Oh God, Maggie thought. She did not want the mental health lecture from Miss Twelve Stepper. *Why can't people just let people be angry?* Because when it is directed at them, they have to reverse the tables, make the person who is angry 'crazy'. Maggie was not going to admit she had already spent twelve years of her life on two different psychiatrist's couches. She had yelled, she had cried, she had spilled every aching detail of her childhood in the requisite notebook. And after thousands of dollars and carpal tunnel from 'journaling,' guess what? Maggie was just plain pissed off. And it was not the group therapy sessions or Dr. So-and-So she needed to tell. No, Maggie needed to tell this person sitting right in front her. Maggie had waited thirty three years to inform her sister that what she did was wrong. And Maggie needed to say it to her mother too but it was too late now. So she turned all her own vengeance on Sarah, and it felt good.

"Sarah, you know what? You checked out a long time ago. Every drink you drank, every pill you popped, it was one more step on the other side of *gone*. But for those of us who were here and present and dealt with all the shittiness…yeah…we got a little bitter. I was here with Mom, day in day out. Even when I went away to school, she came crying to me not you.

"Now, I am happy you have returned from the dark side and cleaned yourself up. I have to say you look good. But don't you dare, not for one second, try to 'manage' my feelings. They are mine, okay, and you can't have them, alter them, or use them to your own advantage.

"I will make you a deal, okay? Here it is. You do not question me, you do not try to save me, you don't make one 'sunshine up your ass' comment about how I am or how I react to anything. You're processing Mom's death? Well, guess what, so the fuck am I. If you want to make the first effort at being my sister, then you let me be. You let me grieve, you let me get angry at you, at Mom, at decades' worth of this cluster fuck. You owe me that. I cleaned up your messes, now deal with mine. And then depending on how you respond, how you cope and handle everything over the next few days" -Maggie circled her arms over her head implying the the whole scenario- "then just maybe, *then* I will be able to think about a relationship with you again. But that is just a huge maybe." Maggie stared directly into Sarah's eyes.

"I accept that. Really Maggie, I will do anything."

Maggie contemplated telling Sarah about the money and the house but decided to wait. She was not up for talking anymore and maybe she still wanted to torture her sister a little more. She knew Sarah was dying to ask but would not with things so precarious between them. When David showed up on the porch, Maggie was able to escape upstairs. She needed a nap and thankful she was escaping to George's that night.

Excerpts from the Diary of Vivian Murphy Atwood April 1987

I watch Maggie and realize she knows far more than she will ever tell. She is cleaning up after Sarah. I hear her in the bathroom scrubbing in the morning, terrified Sarah will get in trouble. Is Sarah throwing up or is she spilling something? I don't want to know. But Sarah definitely is in trouble and I need to do something about it. Maggie idolizes her and I don't know why. Sarah is so zoned out, barely acknowledges her anymore. The two round-faced little girls who used to play make-believe in their bedroom are gone. One is angry and the other petrified with fear, and I am paralyzed. As their mother I should know what to do, but I don't. I am scarcely keeping myself together.

I never had that kind of sisterly relationship with Essie, the playing and adoring. When Maggie was just a baby crawling on the floor Sarah would chase after her grabbing things that might be in her way, might hurt her. Sarah was so vigilant about keeping Maggie safe. Sarah never had a problem sharing her toys, or playing for hours with her baby sister. I don't know when that stopped. When Essie came along, I certainly didn't have any of those feelings of wonder or joy about her. And did Essie ever worship me? I guess it was a different time. But Maggie and Sarah, they have that bond and I see Sarah starting to take advantage of it. Maggie would do anything for her just for a little attention. But Sarah's rage at me, at herself is taking over. I feel like it is another freight train in my life that I can't stop.

May 1987

Oh, what have I done! Why didn't I act sooner! Why do I keep making these mistakes! Years back, Dr. M. said I have to learn how to forgive myself and writing would help. So I will write it all down.

It started yesterday, Sarah came home from school and I thought she was acting a bit funny, like a teenage girl. How naive am I? We managed to get in an argument about her using the car. I have really been trying to trust her and be kinder with her lately, so I changed my mind and let her have it last night. Now I never know where she is going, but it can't be that far right? It is Haven! Well, at around eleven o'clock I get a call from the Boston police station and Sarah is there, drunk, on drugs and had smashed my Mercedes into a parked car! Thank god, no one was hurt but the state Sarah was in, it was just a miracle. I had to go to the station alone, and I had had a few drinks. I certainly didn't think I would be driving that night! Well, I managed to pull myself together, barely. I took Momma and Daddy's car and I slipped out of the house without telling Momma because she gets so livid whenever Sarah does something to shame the family. Besides, Momma has got Daddy to worry about. So when I get to the police station, an officer explained that the people with the parked car weren't going to charge Sarah (can they?), but she will have a DUI, and a drug test is pending. So the officer takes me back to see her, and oh God, it was awful. In the filthy jail cell, next to prostitutes and criminals my little girl was screaming like a caged animal. I knew immediately she was on something. We have our arguments, but it was in her eyes- she was not herself.

She was yelling and spitting at me and I did the most horrible thing I have ever done, I left her there. They said they could keep her for me until the next afternoon. I was in shock, what was I to do? The officer said it would be good for her, but I was not so sure. Damn, I wish these children had some sort of father! I was not meant to make these decisions!

I drove back to Haven, shaking the whole way, my body literally jumping out of the seat. I managed to go upstairs and sleep a few hours, then get up with the sun. Momma came down when I was making coffee and took one look at me and said, "What's wrong?"

"It's Sarah, Momma, and I don't want to hear it, not now."

"I told you that child needs a firm hand," Virginia said shaking her head disapprovingly. Well, that did it for me and I spit back at her.

"A firm hand or a cold shoulder?! Mmm, Momma isn't that your answer, just ignore it until it gets so bad and someone else has to clean up the broken pieces?! You act tough, Momma, but when it comes down to it, you taught us all to stick our heads in the sand. And now look at us, all living here miserable with ourselves, with each other. Maggie's living at the neighbors most of the time, you and I hide inside liquor bottles, Sarah is out there killing herself anyway she can, and Daddy is dying because that's the easy way out." I could not believe I was saying such things to Momma but it felt so good to get some of my anger off my chest.

"Momma, Sarah is sick, real sick, and that's not just my fault but all our faults. We didn't love her right and now what she needs is love. I left her in a jail cell last night because I didn't know what the hell to do. And that's the problem - since I was eighteen, I haven't known what the hell to do with myself, with her or with anybody. So now I have made a decision: something is going to change. If I can't save myself, I am damn well going to save my daughter, both my daughters... now, you can either help me or stand aside."

I swear Momma stood there staring at me for a full five minutes. I could not tell if I was going to get the fury from my tirade or if she really listened to what I was saying. Then she said, "Okay," and walked out of the room.

When she came back, she had her address book in her hand, the one she has literally had since 1930. Licking her thumb and turning the pages I noticed all the age spots appearing on her hands. Finally, she said softly, "Yes, here it is."

And she handed me Dr. M's office number. I was dumbfounded to see the name after all these years. Why did Momma still have the number? I just looked at her questioningly. And she said, "What? You think I just send my daughter away for two months and don't check up on her?" And instead of answering any more of my questions, she went upstairs to help Daddy.

Well, I did feel a new determination. In persuading Momma to help Sarah, I had convinced myself. I spent all morning on the phone finding the best place to send Sarah. I wanted a rehab that wouldn't be too scary or tough, just enough to set her straight.

Later, with all the arrangements made, I went to pick up Sarah in Boston. I couldn't believe it but Momma went with me. But I warned her not to say one mean word toward Sarah. And Momma said, "Child I am not a monster! I am a grandmother!" Which made us both laugh.

Sarah was so quiet and sullen in the back seat of the car, my heart just bled for her. She kept apologizing and saying she would do anything to make up for crashing my car, which was completely destroyed. But Momma had already called around to dealerships and had the exact same one being delivered to our house that afternoon. Same color and everything! I couldn't tell if that was Momma being nice or covering up another family secret. Oh well, I was too tired to think about it.

When we got home, Momma and I took Sarah upstairs to pack for the place we had found for her in Newport, Rhode Island, only an hour away. Then I watched my baby girl break down. She kept apologizing and begging for us not to make her go. I felt awful but after she calmed down and realized no one was going to change their minds, she faced the music. Poor Maggie looked the worst out of all of us. How do you explain this to a child? How do I keep it from happening to her?

The clinic specializes in teenagers, so I am placing my faith in them. Now after a long twenty-four hours, I am sitting here *writing instead of having a drink. If my daughter can do it, so can I. This morning when I talked to Dr. M. she said we could start talking by phone, and I think I will do that. Things are going to be different from now on, but haven't I said that before...*

SEVEN

When Maggie came down to go to dinner at George's house, she could not help but run into Sarah and David. She managed to avoid them for the better part of the afternoon, but here they were like needy kittens with large starving eyes staring her. The last thing she wanted was them tagging along with her.

"Hi guys," Maggie said as she opened the hall closet and began fishing out one of her mother's old fleece jackets.

"Where are you off too?" Sarah slightly whined. Maggie knew her sister wanted to hang out with her but she just was not ready yet. She could see David petting her arm on the couch like he was giving her some sort of moral support to talk to Maggie. *Gag*, Maggie thought. She never wanted Marten to 'pet' her.

"I'm just going to hang out with George for a bit, see Mitzi and the kids, you know. Shouldn't be gone too long. I think Millie loaded up the fridge with food so you guys should help yourselves." Maggie could barely look at them as she zipped up her jacket.

"Who's George?" David asked. Great, Maggie thought, he wants to be involved. Maggie rolled her eyes secretly in irritation.

"George is Maggie's best friend,." Sarah chimed in, again with hurt in her voice. Probably because she was not Maggie's best friend.

"Well, you know, George is George. You will probably see him tomorrow," Maggie said cheerfully turning towards the door.

"So he has kids?" David asked. Again with the questions. He was deliberately keeping her there and Maggie did not want to play this game.

"Yes, George lives on this street with his wife and three kids. He and I are the same age and we grew up together. Yes, George is my oldest friend and knew our mother very well." Maggie then glared at David, daring him to ask another question. She saw Sarah put her hand on his, hopefully the signal to back the fuck off. Immediately, like always Maggie felt guilty for her tone so she made a peace offering.

"Sar, listen I should be around all day tomorrow. Maybe we can go over some of the funeral plans together, okay?" Sarah looked instantly elated. Great, now Maggie felt responsible for her sister's happiness, just exactly the opposite of what she wanted. She quickly fled before seeing one last image of David smiling at his beloved like that had just won match point.

The Sherwood house had always been the dream home in Maggie's imagination. Peggy Sherwood kept a house that was amazingly clean and inviting at the same time. She baked with regularity for George and her husband Bob, so on any given day it could smell of chocolate chip cookies or peach pie. Peggy, like a TV housewife, would always be in the kitchen wrapped in an apron preparing something for her boys. Maggie relished the pleasantness of the scene, the calmness, the comfort that time and time again she could rely on. It was one of Maggie's rare refuges where she could leave everything behind.

Now, years later, the Sherwood house was a different scene and not what Maggie had expected. She was taken aback to see the change in Mitzi. Mitzi was the quintessential preppy girl always put together in matching ensembles, mostly variations on the color pink. As long as Maggie had known Mitzi Moller Sherwood, she had been pageant ready, hair in place, make up appropriately done, truly the homecoming queen. But here she was five months pregnant in one of George's old shirts and tattered jeans. Mitzi's blond curls that were usually neatly arranged, were pulled back into a messy pony tail. She looked invitingly normal. And the house, unlike the days of Peggy Sherwood, had the feeling of a hurricane. Maggie had entered through the kitchen but lingered in the doorway slightly disoriented.

"C'mon in Mags, don't be scared," George said with a chuckle. At the kitchen table were three adorable small boys with round blue eyes, ringlet hair, and chubby little fingers. But each one of them was either in the process of throwing food, punching a brother, or crying. The table, as well as the surrounding floor, looked like a war had been waged between mashed potatoes and peas.

"Oh, Maggie, I am so sorry about your mother. I really will miss her," Mitzi said rushing to put her arms around Maggie. Maggie noticed how deftly she managed to sidestep the various meat product on the floor. Maggie forgot how petite Mitzi was at 5'4", even pregnant she felt like she was hugging a flower.

"You brought wine? Oh how nice. I already opened a bottle of red, would you like some?" Mitzi then lifted a wine glass off the countertop and took a big swig. Maggie thought she was in the twilight zone, she had never seen Mitzi take a drink in her life, let alone while pregnant.

Mitzi saw the confused look on Maggie's face and giggled. "Now, Maggie, I am not such a fuddy-duddy! Listen, when you have three monsters ruining any chance of a manicure, sleep or sex then you get a glass of wine. Don't worry, one glass now and then doesn't hurt and..."she raised her voice to say this, "IT KEEPS ME FROM KILLING THEM."

"It was after Jerry that she took to the bottle," George said without looking up from the sports section. Jerry was the first born, named after Jerry Rice, then next was Joe- who could have been Montana or Nameth- and the littlest one was Elroy after Elroy Hirsch. George certainly had a flare for originality when it came to naming his boys.

"Okay, everyone in the bath and then bed!" Mitzi bellowed and immediately another round of punching, crying, and "but Mom's" began. "That's it, one more word out of you and NO PILLOWS tonight!" All three of them promptly ran upstairs. Maggie looked at George puzzled.

George put down his sports page and said over his reading glasses, "She takes away their bed pillows. Kind of mean, but I have to say effective." Maggie turned towards Mitzi and raised her eyebrows in awe. Mitzi took another swig of wine, said, "touché," and marched upstairs to deal with the children.

"Not the same Mitzi, huh?" George laughed.

"No, get out! It's like the body snatchers returned her to human form."

"Yeah, well, three kids-three boys mind you-that will bring out the best in any woman."

"Remind me never to mess with Mitzi!" George and Maggie laughed as they both began to clean the kitchen. Maggie was loading the dishwasher and George was tackling the floor when the phone rang.

It was officer Lou Mayhew on the phone, an old classmate of George's and Maggie's. Maggie had only gone to school with him through eighth grade before going to boarding school but he and George still were friends. Maggie had a bit of a crush on Lou in seventh grade, a soft spoken, kind boy who always shared his homework with her.

"Lou's on his way over. He knew you would be here tonight." Maggie was more than a little flattered thinking that after all these years maybe he carried a little torch for her too.

"He has your mother's autopsy report." Deflated, Maggie realized he was coming about her mother and not to see her. "Lou knows your sister is home and thought you might like to have the report to yourself first."

Maggie understood what George and Lou were doing-they were thinking about Sarah's drinking and wanted to avoid any confrontations. Growing up it was Lou's father, Frank Mayhew, now the chief of police, who knew their family quite well. Officer Frank Mayhew had been a part of the Murphy household since Maggie could remember. He was a short, stout man with trimmed gray hair and incredibly thick hands. As a child Maggie wondered how they could wrap around a gun. But before he was chief of police, he had forged a friendship of sorts with her grandmother, Virginia. Often he would visit for a cup of coffee while Maggie would eavesdrop from upstairs. Inevitably, the conversations were about Vivian or Sarah, and sometimes even Uncle Johnny. But as hard as Maggie strained to listen, she could never grasp what they were talking about. But her grandmother was at ease around Frank, so it seemed natural for him to sit long afternoons on their porch. Of course, now that she was older, the pieces to the puzzle fit together.

Virginia had befriended Frank Mayhew as her confidante to protect her family. Many nights Vivian or Sarah would leave by their own car and return in a squad car. Frank never arrested or charged the Atwood women for their crimes but kept a watch over them and returned them home to Virginia, thankfully unharmed. Maggie thought is was all the money Virginia donated to the police station every year, but Frank Mayhew was a pallbearer at Virginia's funeral so there must have been something more between them, a friendship of sorts.

Lou Mayhew, because he grew up with Maggie, knew the stories of their family, and naturally was sensitive to the situation.

"Sarah's sober, apparently." Maggie responded to George's masked inquisition.

"Really sober, or I just think you can't smell the bottle of vodka in my bag sober."

"No, I think she really is sober. She looks good and she brought a hunky little A.A. guy with her."

"Well, Lou was just trying to..."

"I know, it's okay. I would rather just deal with it myself anyway." Just then the front door opened. Maggie saw Lou and George were still good enough friends to walk on in to each other's houses.

Lou sheepishly stood in the doorway with one of those large yellow envelopes in his hand, and Maggie could tell he was uncomfortable. Maybe because it was about her mother's death, or maybe that they had not seen each other in so long but, either way, she could see he needed her to break the ice.

"Hi Lou, long time. Wanna beer?" He nodded with a little relief, so Maggie continued. "It's okay Lou, I don't expect anything in the report I don't already know. You can just put it over there. So how are you doing?"

"Just fine, Maggie. You look good. Guess that must be the Cajun cuisine?"

"Yep, I take jambalaya over chowder any day. How's your dad?"

"He's good, still Chief, might retire in a few years. He wanted me to tell you he is real sorry about your Mom. We are planning on going to the funeral on Saturday. You know, your Mom did a lot for us." Actually both Virginia and Vivian contributed heavily to the local police department after all the service they had given the family. And Maggie was sure the hefty donations gave them a few get out of jail free cards in return.

George switched gears and they began to catch up on old times. They sat drinking beer and wine and listened to Mitzi wrestle the boys upstairs. For just awhile, Maggie forgot about her mother and why she was home. They began reminiscing about their childhood, gossiping about old friends and teachers they knew. Then Lou started telling them what happened to old Mr. Keegan.

Carl Keegan was their 7th and 8th grade English teacher at Haven Middle School. He was a feisty old man who smelled like coffee and cigarettes and preferred to teach only Shakespeare. As kids, they were all a little afraid of Mr. Keegan because he was gruff and never accepted a single excuse for anything, be it missing class, missing homework, whatever. The whole town knew Mr. Keegan liked to drink and he was often seen at the bars and pubs a little beyond his control. As far as anyone knew, he had never been married and lived alone. Truthfully, they thought he drank because he was just lonely. Lou told them more than once he drove him home at night. Then just a couple years ago, Mr. Keegan was so intoxicated he fell down his stairs. Lou realized what he'd said and Maggie said it was okay, her mother was not the first, and wanted to know what happened next. Well, Mr. Keegan was so drunk, he'd lost all reflexes.

Mr. Keegan went down his stairs head first and never put his arms out. Luckily, it was only three in the afternoon, and he had a housekeeper cleaning in the kitchen. She found him face down at the foot of the stairs, unconscious. Without using his arms to protect himself, he had bore the full force of the fall on his head. They airlifted him to Boston and induced a coma until his brain swelling went down. Now he is home, but he has no short term memory. Lou said it was so strange because Mr. Keegan can remember Lou skipping class with George but cannot remember that he drove him home the night before. The bars know to water down his drinks now, and he doesn't notice. He just sits there reciting Shakespeare to anyone who will listen.

George and Maggie sat there feeling awful because they always made fun of "Stinky Breath," as they called him. But Lou reassured them it was kind of cool because Mr. Keegan is never bothered by anything because he cannot remember it long enough to be bothered. Actually, Lou said, Mr. Keegan is now one of the nicest, happiest people he knows. So the three of them toasted to Mr. Keegan and dubbed him 'King Lear.'

Inside Maggie was saddened, not for Mr. Keegan but for herself. Why couldn't her mother have just hit her head? Maggie could have dealt with nicer, albeit dumber, version of her mother. Maybe things would have been better between them, and she would still have her mother.

Pushing her thoughts aside, Maggie surprisingly enjoyed herself at dinner. She was never this comfortable growing up in Haven, always nervous and feeling like an outsider. Being known for her family was never easy, especially when she felt in the shadow of her mother and sister. But they were not in high school anymore and Lou and Mitzi did their best to include her in conversation. And Maggie was enjoying the more down to earth, homecoming queen. Mitzi was still the prettiest girl in the room, but neither of them no longer seemed to care. Maybe it was time Maggie gave her a chance.

Lou entertained them all with stories of his impending marriage. He told Maggie how he was engaged to a woman he had arrested. She had chained herself to a tree the city was removing and, while Lou was cutting her out, they got to talking and well, one thing led to another. Maggie laughed so hard at the thought of the upright cop and the environmental hippie. George was going to be the best man and promised to wear hemp. After such a good night of laughs and a little buzzed from the wine, Maggie dreaded walking down the street back to her house. Sarah and David hopefully had gone out or were in bed so she could be alone to call Marten. She had only been away from New Orleans for two days, but it felt like a lifetime.

EIGHT

The next morning, Maggie woke with a slight hangover as the spring light burst through the window. The sun had just risen, and the sharp, burning rays pierced the room as well as her head. She had managed to avoid her sister the night before, but she knew Sarah and David would now be in the kitchen. Maggie was never a morning person and preferred to drink her coffee alone. She always encouraged Marten to sleep in to avoid any unnecessary chatter. They had been asleep all night- what really was there to discuss? Also, that was the time of day when Maggie would try to write or, at least, think about writing. But the rhythm of her life from just a week ago felt irretrievably gone, cracked like glass. Now she was back where she started, literally, but without her childhood or adult routine. Everything felt off to her.

And there they were, Sarah and David, making toast and moon eyes at each other as they squeezed fresh orange juice. Apparently, they were headed to an early morning A.A. meeting, and Maggie was so thankful there was somewhere for them to go.

"Hi sis, how are you?" Sarah chirped.

"Mmm," Maggie barely replied, hoping they would get the hint.

"Oh, David, my sister isn't a morning person. She needs a haz-mat sign when she gets up," Sarah laughed.

"Ha ha," Maggie quipped as she poured coffee.

"Hey Mags, remember when you woke up from a nap once and you were so out of it, I told you to get ready for school and you did?! It was like five in the afternoon!"

"Hey Sar', remember when I turned all the shit in your room upside down?" Maggie deadpanned back blowing on her coffee. When Maggie was eight and bored one Saturday afternoon she thought it would be fun to turn everything in Sarah's room upside down. George helped her with the posters, the wall clock, and everything on her dresser. Even her bed sheets were turned inside out. Sarah did not return home until much later that evening after Maggie had gone to bed. But unbeknownst to Maggie, that was the first time Sarah had ever gotten high. Sarah had come home late to avoid the family, but when she slipped in her room and turned on the light, the paranoia set in. Finding her room exactly in place but upside down caused Sarah to spend most of the night sitting on her bed terrified. Stoned, she thought the devil himself was screwing with her.

Maggie did not understand the effect of her practical joke until a few years later when she learned of her timing. She laughed and laughed when she learned how freaked out Sarah had been. Now, Sarah could laugh about it too.

Sarah chuckled and told David the story. Maggie and Sarah had always played tricks on each other. Their grandmother used to say they were worse than boys. They hid each other's things and lied to each other constantly. If dinner was at 6:00, Maggie would tell Sarah it was at 6:30, and Sarah would hide Maggie's homework and watch her panic moments before school. This went on most of their childhood, but the fun stopped once Sarah began drinking and doing drugs. Well, sometimes it was funny, for Maggie at least.

Sarah promised to help with the funeral arrangements when they got back from their meeting. Millie had made most of them anyway, so Sarah lucked out again from any real responsibility. Maggie tried to focus on what she needed to do and realized she did not have anything to wear to the funeral. Using the time alone, Maggie grabbed her coffee and went up to her mother's bedroom to search her walk-in closet.

The scent of Chanel No. 5 lingered in the room. Maggie put her coffee mug down and sat on the corner of the bed breathing in her mother. It was the only room in the house that did not smell like salt air and old curtains. Vivian had kept her room up to date with fresh upholstery on the chaise lounge and new curtains every few years. She often ordered expensive bedding and never let the area rug get too old or worn. This was Vivian's sanctuary. Maggie could feel her mother wrap around her, and tears began to flow again as Maggie came back to that one word in her mind: *Mom*. Her mother would want her to get along with her sister, forgive her. Even though Vivian and Sarah fought more than laughed, Vivian could always forgive Sarah. She was her mother after all.

Maggie was twelve when she found them both sitting on Vivian's bed that horrible afternoon in her memory. She immediately sensed something terribly wrong when she saw both of them. Sarah's eyes were swollen and bloodshot and her body was shaking. Sarah was just seventeen. Vivian was holding tightly to her arms and sternly telling her, "it was fine, everything was going to be alright, *she forgave her.*" Her grandmother came out of a corner when Maggie entered and immediately pushed her out of the room telling her to go to Millie's house. Maggie hesitated, alarmed for her sister and mother and did not want to leave them. Maggie had no idea what was happening but the mixture of instinct and terror made her grab hold of the door frame and defy her grandmother's pushing. Maggie began to cry herself and screamed at the top of her lungs, "No!" Then Sarah and Vivian both became silent and all eyes went on Maggie. Vivian calmly told Maggie that it was okay, that everything was going to be okay, and that she needed to go to Millie's. Sarah sat on the bed, slowly nodded her head, and told Maggie the same thing.

Her grandmother then took her hand and led her away. While crossing the yard, Maggie peered over shoulder and saw her mother with her arms around Sarah. She watched a suitcase being loaded into the car and a sobbing Sarah climbing into the back seat. Maggie's heart broke, and she did not know why. Fear and sadness overwhelmed her as her sister drove away. As if something inside her knew then that Sarah, as a child, as her sister, was gone to her. Their childhood was over.

Three weeks later Vivian took Maggie to see Sarah at the rehab facility. The stark linoleum floor, hospital beds, and the harsh fluorescent lighting frightened Maggie. Other teenagers milled the halls with pale skin and vacant eyes. Sarah, devoid of emotion herself, sat smoking cigarettes and watching the clock throughout the visit. Maggie, unable to speak, picked at the gash in her jeans and tried desperately not to cry for the loss she had yet to understand. Maggie's memory stops there as many of the harder recollections of her childhood do. Over the years she has accepted the black holes, her swiss cheese like subconscious, as the result of traumatic events that stained her youth.

Maggie picked at the make-up on Vivian's dresser and thought about forgiveness. Holding up the expensive mascara, she brushed her eyelashes black. Then she dabbed some of her mother's red lipstick on her lips, thinking again how her mother never held Sarah and Maggie's bad behavior against them. Sure, there were vicious arguments, words thrown like daggers, but the next day Vivian inevitably forgave them. She never stormed away, never cut off communication, never ever stopped loving them. Maggie was just the opposite. When she was hurt, she retreated and with-held herself, with-held her love. She held on to her anger like a lifeline, so afraid to let it go.

Maggie walked into her mother's closet. There amongst the simple dresses and the small cashmere sweaters and loafers her mother religiously wore, Maggie started to feel the emotions that she should have felt at the morgue. She broke down. The sheer fright of her life without her mother was overwhelming. And the guilt for not forgiving her sooner, made her curl up and howl. For two years she did not return the phone calls or letters, thinking she was making a stand against her mother. Maggie just wanted her to know she would not tolerate her drinking anymore. The years of damage it had done to Maggie enraged her, and she had grown so tired of it. The roller coaster of trying to change and help her mother had been useless, and in her mind she needed a break. But in Maggie's heart, she never thought she would lose her mother all together. Always she knew anytime during the self-imposed exile, she could break the silence with a single phone call and that single word: *Mom*. Now, there was no other side, no safety net. Her mother was not out there anymore ready to love, able to forgive her. It was like Maggie fell off the precipice into a black hole, and she could not see nor feel the ground.

Two years prior, in New York, Maggie invited her mother down from Haven for a visit. Maggie's apartment, if you could call it that, was too small to have Vivian stay with her, so Vivian had the idea to get a room at the Waldorf so they could spoil themselves with room service and shopping. It was a bitter and bleak January, and Maggie was excited to have a break from her lonely winter weekends. She made plans with her friends to meet them for dinner and show Vivian a good time in the city. Maggie waited excitedly at the Waldorf for her to arrive. Vivian would have taken the train from Boston and a cab from Penn Station to get there.

Two hours went by while Maggie nervously paced the hotel's lobby, trying not to listen to her gut feeling. At four p.m. her mother staggered through the swinging doors of the hotel and saw what Maggie knew by intuition and experience. The bellman was carrying her handbag and holding her up on one side. Maggie's heart fell instantly when she confirmed her mother was drunk. Now it was up to her to get them checked in and up to their room with as little attention as possible. Maggie was incredibly embarrassed as the hotel clerk tried her best to be sympathetic. While she held her mother up against the elevator wall, Maggie swallowed every urge to cry. The disappointment she felt threatened to swallow her whole. How could Vivian do this to her? In the room, Maggie struggled to pretend nothing was wrong and urged her mother to shower and change. Maggie thought a walk in the cold air would clear her mother's head and maybe they could salvage the evening. The ever hopeful Maggie.

Everything went from bad to worse as soon as they left the hotel. Vivian became irritable and argumentative wanting another drink. Since it was frigid, it was hard to persuade her mother to stay out in the cold. Eventually Maggie gave up, and they ducked into a bar. It only took one drink to get her mother tipsy and unmanageable again. Maggie decided to still keep her dinner engagement with her friends because she had given up hopes of getting her mother back to the hotel. While her friends overlooked her mother's drunkenness, Maggie sat at the table and seethed. Watching her mother poke food around her plate, with her eyes half closed and slurring her words, inflamed Maggie. She could barely look at her let alone tolerate her. Her mother was a child, and Maggie was sick and tired of it. Vivian had knowingly ruined their weekend, and Maggie's soul was silently screaming. After dinner, Maggie made her mother walk back to the hotel although Vivian was slipping on the sidewalk and whining about the cold. Then Maggie thought to herself, she could not do it, she could not be Vivian's handmaid any longer. She began screaming at Vivian to walk and grabbed her arm and, with all her force, began pulling her like a child. Then Vivian tumbled and fell but Maggie kept shouting for her to get up and walk. Vivian, now furious with Maggie, did get up and began calling her an ungrateful bitch. Vivian made the mistake of pushing Maggie, and Maggie swung back hard. With all the rage and anger Maggie felt towards her mother's drinking, Maggie struck her mother across the face.

The horror both women felt was colder than the icy air surrounding them. Maggie did not say a word as the venom and hatred in her mother's drunken eyes spoke volumes. Paralyzed by her mother's contempt, she just watched as Vivian fled down the street and disappeared. After the shock wore off, Maggie began to feel her familiar fear. She had let her mother get away, she was not keeping her safe. Regardless of what her mother said or did, it was Maggie's job to keep her protected. Vivian knew nothing about New York and, in this condition, God knows what could happen. It felt like Maggie had watched a plane crash, and it would be hours before she knew whether Vivian was on it or not.

Fruitlessly, Maggie searched every street corner, and then went up to their room to wait. She paced and argued with herself. Her mother never bothered to own a cell phone, and there was no conceivable way to find her in the city. After two hours, Maggie could not take it anymore. Furious and terrified, she went back to her apartment in the lower east side. As her therapist had always taught her, she had to let it go, let the chips fall where they may. There was nothing Maggie could do but wait.

Later that night Maggie fell asleep in her living room chair next to the phone. At 7:15 a.m. it finally rang, and Maggie opened her eyes to the acrid winter light. It had snowed some the night before, and the walls in her apartment reflected a steel cold blue. Trembling, Maggie picked up the receiver and closed her eyes, dreading which voice would be on the other end. It was Vivian.

The flood of relief washed over Maggie, and she asked Vivian if she was alright. Vivian was crying, kept saying she was fine and so so sorry. Vivian said she knew Maggie could never forgive her for what she had done and pleaded with her to come back the hotel room so they could finish their weekend. Maggie began to cry again and said, "No, Mom. Just leave me alone." She hung up the phone and did not answer it as it rang over and over again.

Striking her mother changed Maggie. Jarred by resorting to physical violence, Maggie felt disconcerted and ashamed of herself. She had become full of rage just like all the women in her family. She was becoming a disappointment, a failure and and it made her resentful. She was thirty-one and no better than the rest of them. She had yet to have a steady relationship, and true love seemed inconceivable. Her career was so-so, just enough to keep her busy but nothing that would warrant attention or satisfaction. Nothing about her contradicted the other women in her family and that was the one character trait Maggie prided herself on, she was not like them. It was Maggie's driving force, and she had stalled. Maggie needed to escape from her mother, her past, literal a change of scene.

Post-Katrina New Orleans felt just as damaged and angry as she, but with a thin vein of hope. Maggie figured that amongst the people rebuilding their city and their lives, she could find a way to rebuild herself too. Whenever Maggie made a decision, she was stubborn enough to stick by it. Within the month, she had packed her belongings and flew to the Big Easy. She sent her mother a postcard. On it were two words: *fuck it*.

Now in Vivian's closet, Maggie cried into her mother's dresses and and kept saying "I'm sorry Mom" over and over because she knew in heart that her mother had already forgiven her. But she had not yet forgiven her mother.

Suddenly from behind, Maggie felt little sturdy arms wrapping around her and the crush of reading glasses. She smelled the Joy perfume and Millie's voice began, "Maggie, hon, your Mom would not want you to feel sorry about not talking to her. She knew you loved her and once you got on your feet about everything, you would come around. Vivian felt so bad about what happened in New York, and things, well, all the things from your past. She actually thought it was a good idea that you distance yourself from her for awhile and live your own life. She was excited for you hon', and she never thought you were a bad or mean person for not talking to her. Hell! Vivian was proud of you because she could never hold her own against her own mother. It was your strength that your mother respected and loved about you. And it is your strength that will get you through this."

Maggie wiped her eyes with a pashmina shawl.

"I was so awful, Millie."

"Hush now, child. You were angry and you had every right to be. No one could have predicted Vivian's time had come. Now what are you doing in your mother's closet?"

Maggie explained how she needed a dress, and Millie helped her pick out a Christian Dior black cocktail dress. She hovered as Maggie washed her face and pulled herself together. Millie hated it when the Atwood women had breakdowns, especially alone.

Excerpts from the Diary of Vivian Murphy Atwood
December 1988

Daddy died. I guess it is not that much of a shock, we have been watching him go downhill for what feels like forever. His liver was shot and the cancer they found in his colon had spread. But Daddy didn't want to fight it. He kept saying 'Let nature takes its course' every time the doctors offered some sort of treatment. I always felt like he gave up, on us, himself. It was like life just didn't turn out like he expected so he tossed in the towel. But whose life turns out as planned! I still never felt like I knew him. I guess I am mourning that right now. All I knew was how to make him a whiskey sour or a Tom Collins: I knew which lure he loved the most for fishing, and his favorite boat was the sloop named *Violet* in the harbor. But when he stared out the window all those lonely nights, what was he thinking? He never laughed out loud. The most you would get out him was a smirk, I guess he was too stately for such nonsense.

And Momma always made all the decisions when it came to us children. Essie was sick so it was easier to let Momma take over. He just bought her things which seemed to please her but he never truly bonded with her. And well, Johnny, he wanted to connect with him, but no one could. Johnny just came out wrong. Daddy would have been better off if he were a quieter more sweet- natured boy. A kid who loved books and fishing, not one that set fire to Millie's trash cans and hit girls for fun. But back to Daddy and me, well, he took care of me but ...well, like our relationship, I am at a loss for words. It is okay, I never say 'Oh I wish I had a Dad like on TV,' or anything. He was a good kind man and I will remember him for that.

I have not been drinking for almost seven months now. I feel good and I have been able to help Momma with Daddy. I talk to Dr. M. often and it seems like she's still digging at me trying to find the root of the problem. Why I am so dissatisfied? Why is it that nothing seems to be good enough? Why I don't have many connections with people? Hell, I don't know why, I just want to say. It is what it is. Like Johnny, going around town bemoaning Daddy's death like they were twin brothers and piece of him died. Honestly, Johnny only came around the house at the end to ask about the will. I actually heard him say something to Momma about wanting a new Porsche. What a piece of work! But it is what it is. And the doozy was, Johnny even went up to little Maggie and asked her to keep an eye out for him if there were any changes in my behavior. What a shit trying to get my daughter to rat me out if I start drinking *again. Luckily, Maggie was smart enough to see through him and tell me about it. Poor thing. She is already beyond her years living with all us crazies.*

I suspect Sarah is drinking again but she has gotten more clever about it. I have tried, really I have, but that girl is on her own path. She knows I am sober and, instead of being happy like Maggie, she is annoyed by it. I just can't please her, but she is her own woman now and well, Dr. M. says I have to do a bit of letting go. She leaves in a couple of weeks to start a junior college in Oregon. She finally finished the classes she missed last year, so I guess I have to let her go. Honestly, I am a little relieved. Sarah's tension can all be a little too much for us to handle. And since rehab, Maggie follows her around like a shadow terrified she is going to hurt herself again. I don't think Sarah realizes how much Maggie loves her. Maggie has so much love for us all, but none of us seems to know what to do with it.

NINE

After Maggie's breakdown, Millie dragged her back downstairs to eat something and tried to take her mind off her mother. They were in the kitchen having coffee and discussing the spring peonies and hydrangeas when they heard a heavy stomp on the front porch. Maggie assumed it was George checking in when the front screen door slammed in the living room. Not too many people entered without knocking, but Maggie forgot there was one person who always barged in. Realizing who it would be a second too late, she was abraded when she saw Uncle Johnny filling up the kitchen doorway.

His 6'2" frame and large upper body made him a look menacing but with long graying hair pulled back in a pony tail and his signature cowboy boots, Uncle Johnny resembled a harmless hippie. He was just another middle aged man who thought personal style should be taken from his teen years. Although Uncle Johnny's build mirrored Grandpa Jack's, he had Virginia's wide eyes and small pursed lips. The effeminacy of his features combined with a few extra pounds around his waistline made some question what team he was playing on.

"Ah, what's going on here?!" Johnny said like he had caught Millie and Maggie counting wads of counterfeit bills. Millie rolled her eyes, already irritated with him.

"Hi, Uncle Johnny. Not much." Maggie forced herself to stand and hug him.

"Maga -doodle, your Mom, I just can't believe it." A forced tear, or maybe it was real, who knew with him, streamed down his face. Maggie clenched her teeth at Uncle Johnny's contrived attempt at affection. Their relationship, while familial, was obligatory at best.

Uncle Johnny loomed in the doorway scanning the room, "So have you talked to Bill Getty?" He avoided Millie's gaze as he spoke.

Funny how everyone else asked how she was doing but not Uncle Johnny, Maggie thought. Maggie appreciated that at least he didn't dance around the issue but got straight to the heart of what this family was about: money.

"John Murphy, Jr. you have the gall to come into this child's house after her mother died and ask about the will? Remember, son, I knew you in diapers and Virginia would have tanned your hide with comments like that!" Millie roared.

Johnny was using his pinkie nail to pick at something between his back molars.

"Now, Millie just calm down, just asking is all. Didn't mean anything by it. Just a lot of family history around here that has to be taken care of."

Millie and Maggie both knew he meant whatever was left of the family's he could get his hands on.

"Poor Maggie here is going to have a lot to take care of, that's all. And I just want you to know, Maggie, I am here to help in any way possible." Johnny finally stopped picking his teeth, but his eyes were still taking inventory. Maggie knew if there was even a window of opportunity, he would come after her house claiming his right as Virginia's heir. He was like a vulture picking over the last of the goods. Good thing Bill Getty wrote iron clad wills.

"Thanks, Uncle Johnny, but I've got Sarah here to help." Maggie saw him flinch. More than once, when Sarah was drunk and high on god knows what, the chemical cocktails gave her bravado enough to give Uncle Johnny a fantastic tongue lashing or two. Fortunately, Maggie had been there to witness them and secretly relished the embarrassment it caused him. While Uncle Johnny was sneaky and untrustworthy, he was no match for the women of his family. Even Grandpa Jack thought of him as a bit of a sissy.

Billed as the golden child of the family, simply due to being male and the baby, Uncle Johnny grew to be nothing other than a spoiled malcontent. He snitched on kids at school, was cruel to his sisters, and became a tolerable annoyance throughout his childhood. He was hard to love. And Jack and Virginia always tried to look past his faults, feeling guilt for giving too many prizes rather than punishment.

Sarah and David returned from their A.A. meeting and Sarah took great delight in seeing Uncle Johnny, swatting him on the back and saying how the hell are ya, like an old drinking buddy. Johnny arched his back and lifted up his chest, immediately on guard. He continued talking while trying to ignore Sarah's presence.

"Well, I ordered two limousines for Saturday's services. You girls can take one, and I'll help Essie in the other." Johnny attempted to take charge of the room.

Maggie deflated him.

"No need. Mom was cremated, and we are just going to walk to the church and back. I don't think Mom would have wanted a big production out of the whole thing anyway."

Maggie turned to Sarah and said, "Remember that moronic limo George ordered for prom night that got stuck here on Grove?" Sarah laughed and picked up on the sarcasm.

"Yeah, did a hundred and sixty point turn in Millie's drive."

Millie caught on, "Ruined my crocuses." All three women were smugly sitting there ganging up on Johnny. They each knew the limo was more for his sake than theirs. Johnny never missed an opportunity to remind Haven the Murphy's had money.

"Guess you can cancel those limos," Maggie smirked.

"Okay, your call Maga-doodle. Just trying to help." Sarah snickered at the nick name and Maggie gave her a sisterly, shut up look.

"So my sister was cremated, huh? What, the family plot's not good enough for her?" Johnny said defensively.

"It's called resting in PEACE, Uncle J.," Sarah chimed in. They all knew Vivian would have no peace if she spent eternity next to her family.

"Well, *all-right then,*" Uncle Johnny said waving his hands in surrender. He looked at Maggie, "Let me know when Bill Getty gets here. I gotta touch base with him. You hear me?" Maggie rolled her eyes.

"Gotcha," Sarah winked, pulling her trigger finger like a pistol. She made like she was shooting him and giggled. He shook his head and walked out.

"Well, isn't he a piece of work? I tell you girls, don't turn your back on him for a second!" Millie said clearing the coffee mugs. After Millie left, Maggie turned towards Sarah. It was time. She needed to tell Sarah about the house and money before someone else did.

"David, could you give us a minute?" Maggie said. Ever obedient, David left again. Maggie couldn't quite figure him out yet.

"Sarah, Bill Getty was already here." Maggie admitted. Sarah sat down at the kitchen table and looked at her sister waiting for her to go on.

"Sorry, he wanted to avoid you."

"Totally understandable," Sarah nodded. Good. For once, Maggie thought, Sarah wasn't offended. Miracles do happen.

"He brought me the papers on Mom's estate. It was more than I ever thought. She left us each about two and a half million dollars." Maggie kept her eyes on Sarah to see her reaction. Sarah's face shifted slightly, like a smile just below the surface. Maggie did not know how she wanted her sister to react. What would have been acceptable? Did she want Sarah to jump up and down yelling "yahoo" like a monkey so she could chastise her? Or was Maggie so bitter, she needed Sarah to recreate an Amish tea party? What made Maggie so infuriated was that Sarah never valued money; she simply expected it. Because Vivian bailed Sarah out so many times, Sarah never learned the lesson of earning or losing anything of value. Her life was handed to her on a silver platter. But then again, Maggie did not "earn" her mother's money either. Really, what could Maggie say? She was benefitting just as much as Sarah, if not more. Maggie acknowledged she was being a hypocrite and needed to stop being a martyr about the money.

"Well, " Maggie probed.

"Well what, Maggie? I know you think I don't deserve it and that I am awful for being happy. Of course, I am happy. I have been in debt most of my life because of all my shitty, stupid choices and now, well, I can start clean. I screwed up Mags, and now you think I am being rewarded for it. But you know what, I went through some pretty shitty stuff. Losing Dad hurt me more because I remember him. I had the chance to love him. I'm sorry you didn't. And to Grandma, I was just Vivian's "mistake." And Mom, well, I had to clean up so many of her messes she could never look at me again. I know you have your scars too, but I just did not come out as strong as you okay?" Sarah was staring dead at her.

"I drank and fucked up because I wanted to be like them. I wanted to fit in with this family. I wanted them to love me. But you know what? You rebelled, and Little Miss Perfect was loved more."

Maggie was surprised by Sarah's anger, yet it was the Sarah she knew. And maybe Maggie deserved a little tongue lashing because, even though Sarah had hurt her, Sarah had been hurt too many times herself. Maggie resolved she had to tell her about the house, suddenly feeling incredibly guilty.

"Sarah, I am sorry. You are right, I don't have the right to judge you. It is just so surreal, Mom's gone. And now you are sober, so I hope you can handle the situation and all this money. Maybe we do deserve it after all the shit we went through, but everything happened *because of* the money, so I just don't know how to feel about it."

"Mags, don't over-think it, okay? I am trying really hard to change but if I fuck this up, then it's my own fault. Hey, just think how Uncle Johnny is going to react when he hears?" Sarah broke out into a big grin.

Maggie laughed out loud too then blurted, "Mom left me the house." Maggie expected more of a reaction from her sister but instead, Sarah was still laughing.

"I figured, Mags. I mean, I left so long ago and… well…Mom couldn't trust me. Don't worry, I'm not mad about it. You belong here. I know you won't sell it, and I think Mom made the right choice." Maggie nodded in agreement. No she would never sell it. She felt relief that Sarah had accepted the situation without a scene. Maybe her sister had changed, and maybe Maggie needed to start learning how to change, too.

Maggie spent years analyzing why her family was so screwed up. Maggie pin-pointed it to her grandmother's manipulation of others. Virginia never loosened the purse strings. It was all about control. Her love and her money was pieced and dealt like little bits of cake. It took Maggie a long time to understand why Vivian stayed in Haven and lived with her mother all those years. Vivian could have as much money as she needed as long as she lived with Virginia. Without a husband, Vivian could never support two little girls. She did not even have a high school diploma and since leaving Boston, any hopes of a career had faded. She had no other prospects for work. And for reasons Maggie never understood, her grandmother was not going to hand Vivian a blank check and let her walk away.

Maggie wanted to understand the relationship between Vivian and Virginia, but they were so different from her. They were women raised to be wives and mothers, to honor obedience. Maggie thought her mother's and grandmother's idea of duty seemed archaic, outdated. Maggie certainly personified the inability to bow down and shut her mouth. Ironically, both women in their subtle ways taught her to speak out and fight back. Maybe that is why Maggie felt so alone. She was not like them, but she was who they wanted her to be.

TEN

Later that afternoon, David and Sarah went walking the beach, and Maggie found herself slightly bored without them around to deprecate. They were all in limbo until the funeral. Here it was only Wednesday afternoon with still two more days until Marten would arrive. Thankfully, Millie had stopped shadowing Maggie and gone to one of her other charitable activities. The shock of her mother's death had worn down to a dull throb from the sharp stab it had once been. With each moment that passed, Maggie came more to terms with her mother's absence. Yet, when she was in one room of the house, she still anticipated Vivian to come strolling in from another. Vivian was always talking. She would start sentences in one room and finish them when she found you in another. But she never paused to explain what she had launched into in the first place. One just had to figure it out and keep up with her. It was one of her quirks. Vivian had a keen mind but it was never put to use properly.

Her ideas lay like paint tubes - beautiful, brilliant, enclosed-their colors never quite reaching the canvas.

Maggie always marveled at her mother's ability to retain information. One National Geographic show and Vivian could recite the statistics of the ancient pharaohs or recreate Magellan's journey. She talked about sailing the Greek islands as if she had been there and made brilliant plans for touring the Arctic, but never did she pursue the adventures. Vivian was more politically up to date than most newscasters, and no current event got past her, but she never wrote another newspaper article. Her intelligence was a rare gift, and it frustrated Maggie when Vivian spoke of the trip she would eventually take, the book she would eventually write, or the life she would eventually live. And now Maggie felt like her mother probably did, useless and undiscovered. Like she had much more to offer the world but remained locked away in her own glass house.

Maggie decided to explore the garage to escape her own thoughts since she had already searched her mother's bedroom for anything that might comfort her. She could feel her mother slipping away into the past tense and she began to crave her smell, her essence, something indefinably Vivian. She went looking for boxes of old photographs, checkbooks, yearbooks, or any other countless dust-covered pieces to the puzzle, bits of memorabilia that somehow defined her mother.

The garage not only fit two cars but had a fully separate storeroom. Maggie mused at the matching Mercedes like museum relics- one her mother's powder blue station wagon and the other her grandmother's royal blue sedan. They each had replaced the Mercedes' hood ornaments with matching silver anchors. "How 80's," Maggie thought. Maggie loved her grandmother's sedan because it was older with leather bucket seats the size of beds and with the unmistakable tick of a diesel engine. But Vivian always traded hers in every two years for a newer sleeker powder blue wagon. Maggie smiled at the sight of her grandmother's car and thought about taking it for a drive later.

Hours later, after sifting through boxes of Crayon drawings, construction paper Valentine's, and old book reports, Maggie struck gold. She found a black file box nestled on the shelf above an old desk wedged between forgotten yearbooks and scrapbooks. When she lifted the lid, beneath a clean, blue felt blanket she discovered something of incredible meaning. At first, she thought it may have been her grandmother's missing jewels but it was a much better surprise. What she did find was invaluable - her mother's diaries.

Wrapped like fine art, the diaries were like finding her mother. Four large books, crisp white pages filled with the black ink of Vivian's unmistakable handwriting. The perfectly straight lines were almost hieroglyphic, letters like boxes with strange slashes and curls. So often people would complain her mother's writing was undecipherable, but not to her. Her mother's writing was as clear and strong as Vivian's own voice once had been. Maggie, alone in the afternoon light, fell to her knees, the open box her altar, the diaries her gospel.

Realizing what she had, Maggie raced the books up to her room, and locked her bedroom door. She fingered and rubbed them like magic lamps for a long while thinking how selfish she was acting. She should share them with Sarah, but she easily convinced herself not to immediately. She had earned a little selfishness. Curiosity would never keep her from reading them, but she was terrified. One last time, she would hear her mother's words, her feelings, and perhaps she would find answers to long hidden questions. Delicately, Maggie opened the front page of each diary in order to survey the dates and put the books in the correct order. Preparing for a long night, she hustled downstairs and grabbed a bottle of red wine, a glass and cigarettes, listening for anyone in the house. *This should hold me for a while.*

Later, when it was dark, Sarah knocked on her door and asked if she wanted dinner. Maggie answered that she was exhausted just needed to catch up on her sleep. No one bothered her for the rest of the evening.

When Maggie finally put the second diary down, she felt drained. She felt like she had been reading for a lifetime yet she was only to 1980, years still to go. It was past eleven and it seemed as if the world was asleep. Sarah and David had long ago gone to bed, and Maggie could hear the house breathing. It was so soundless.

Maggie made her way to the kitchen where she opened another bottle of wine and threw open the kitchen window. She sat and smoked and sipped her wine feeling the cool April breeze come in. Spring was always such a funny time of year, warm for a few moments then cool, reminding us of the past, tantalizing us with the future. Nature sloughed its old dead skin with storm after storm until the land was shiny, new and green, like a polished apple. If you could weather the spring storms, then you earned the tender, calm days of summer.

Maggie could not even begin to wrap her mind around all she had discovered in her mother's diaries. Page after page Vivian was alive, raw, and uncensored. So honest and surprising. She could picture her mother, her red lipstick and hair perfectly done, stoic, almost unfeeling. But the diaries portrayed her as a girl again. Her thoughts were selfish, insightful, and foolish all at the same time. Who was Vivian? It was a question always too big for Maggie to ask and now, amongst book after book, was the answer. Maggie just had to put it all together.

Startled, she heard footsteps on the stairs. David appeared in the doorway and it took her second to compose herself. David was still such a stranger to her, and it was odd to see him standing in her kitchen in a pair of shorts.

"Sorry, did I bother you? I just wanted to get a drink." David went to the refrigerator and took out a bottle of water and swallowed half in one gulp. Maggie thought they must have just had sex if he is so thirsty. Funny, how she could not hear them do it in the house. Good to know.

"Sarah was worried about you tonight. She didn't think you were sleeping with your light on." David sat down opposite her. Maggie shrugged and gave him a little smirk.

Avoiding any inquiry, Maggie steered the conversation away from herself. "So what do you do David?" She sounded a little on the offensive and reminded herself he was Sarah's boyfriend, not Sarah. Just another innocent fly stuck in the family web.

"Oh, I own a bicycle shop. Bikes, I tell ya' are the next wave of the future. People are going green, getting out of their cars, ya' know? With gas prices going up and people caring more about the environment, it's pretty good for business. Plus, I can promote the health benefit of the extra exercise and-wham!-sales just keep going up. I am looking to open up two more stores in our area next year. Your sister isn't the best with finances, so I have to keep it coming in, if you know what I mean."

It took everything Maggie had not to burst out laughing, he looked so innocent sitting there! She was thinking, *she is rich you fool and you have no idea what money does to Sarah!*

"Well, that sounds fantastic, really fantastic." Maggie tried not to be smug but her mind was elsewhere. He just kept sitting there wanting to…what…*relate* with her?

"Can I have one of these?" He pointed to the smokes and Maggie pushed the pack of cigarettes toward him. *Please*, she thought, *don't let him think of this is some sort of bonding experience.* She sat there in silence as they smoked hoping he would get the hint to leave.

"You know, Maggie, I've gotten to know a lot about Sarah over the past few months." *Oh God*, Maggie thought, *he is going there. Please, please don't go there.*

"Well, your sister misses you and she has changed. I know you think I don't know shit. But here is what you don't know, I met Sarah before A.A. when she was a real mess. There was this club she used to hang out in, and I would go there every once in awhile. I saw it, Maggie, I saw it all. Sarah using is not pretty, as you know, so don't assume I am that naive, " David said.

"Okay,." Maggie conceded.

"I loved her then, and I love her now. And now she hurts because it is obvious you hurt. You need to find a way to work through your past not just for her but for yourself as well."

Maggie bit her tongue. *Well aren't you the sage*, she thought sarcastically. Instead she opted to channel her grandmother, "David, didn't anybody ever tell you to never, ever tell an Atwood woman what to do?" David leaned his head back and gave a hearty laugh that shook Maggie.

"Dude, I learned that one the hard way, and I guess I'm still learning it! Naw, I said what I had to say. I didn't mean to bother you." David stood up, gave her a devilish wink and hummed as he went meandering up stairs. Maggie could see he was one of those kids that had the world in his hands, and she could see why Sarah was attracted to him. He was not a bad guy, but still just a kid.

Maggie faced the open window again. With the spring air on her face, the barrage of thoughts about her mother resumed. Marten would be here by tomorrow night and she was genuinely missing him now. Without him, she was alone with Vivian. He at least could distract her from falling too far into the past, going back to the places she had tried to run from. But she knew she needed to get through the diaries while she had the chance. Finishing them was somewhere between her burden and her deepest desire. Her mother was calling her and Maggie was compelled to read through the night to answer back.

ELEVEN

By sunrise, Maggie sat on her bed feeling drained, having read through the night. She watched the pink light brighten the gray New England sky and felt overwhelmed. Vivian reverberated through her every pore, her words floating through Maggie's thoughts like tiny bullets. Maggie never knew how sad her mother had been, how regretful. But through her own demons, she had loved Maggie and Sarah. It was the true most honest part of Vivian's life, the love not for herself but for her children. For whatever their actions, they loved her and she them. If Maggie could find a way back to that love, then maybe she could find the peace that eluded her for so long.

Exhausted, Maggie got up and reached for her bottle of Valium. She entertained the idea of taking two and sleeping the day away. But then she thought better of it. Hadn't everyone around her, including herself, been numb long enough? Instead, she washed her face and managed to sleep until late morning.

When she awoke later that morning, Mitzi was standing over her, her belly managing to look larger than two days ago. "Maggie, you have got everyone worried sick about you," she said with her hands on her hips. Maggie laughed, thinking how Mitzi would look like a tea pot if she stood sideways.

"Mmmm, what? Why? I'm fine," Maggie said sitting up and checking the clock.

"Really? Sarah showed up at house saying you hadn't left the room in almost a day. George would have barged over here because, frankly, he has been worried too. But Mr. Abernathy's prized bull dog is giving birth, and well, now I am here because your sister is scared as shit of you."

"You know, Mitzi, I love this new dark side of yours. Drinking and swearing makes you seem like one of us."

"I could never be one of you. You guys are too screwed up. In my family, we actually talk to each other." Maggie and Mitzi both chortled. Mitzi looked at Maggie's bedspread and saw the diaries laid out.

"What are these?" she asked, eyeing the books.

"Mom kept diaries, and I found them yesterday. I have been up reading them all night." Maggie was happy to confide in someone. "I don't think anyone knew about them." Her voice trailed off not quite knowing what else to say.

Mitzi sat on the bed taking her hand, "How were they?" Maggie looked down at Mitzi's small pale hand holding hers and felt the tears welling up in her eyes.

"They were hard. Really hard, but you know, good. They answered a lot of questions. Things I thought I would never know the answer. So I'm lucky I guess. But now, I just wish Mom wasn't alone in the end." Tears fell from Maggie's eyes and Mitzi softly said, "I don't think she was as alone as you think."

"What do you mean?" asked Maggie.

"Well, I don't know what your Mom said in her diaries, but occasionally over the last few months I would see someone coming and going from the house at night. I never saw him clearly, at least I think it was a him. Stocky, like a man, and he was always on a bicycle. If I was taking out the trash or walking Ditka (George's St. Bernard, aptly named after Mike), I would see him slipping quietly in and out of the driveway. I could never tell who it was, but I am pretty sure your Mom wasn't entirely alone."

"What about the night Mom died?" Maggie said eagerly.

"Yeah, now that you mention it, I think he was there. I always take Ditka out around eleven and I thought I heard someone leaving on the gravel drive. But that damn dog had found a skunk under the house so I was wrestling him back inside. Sorry, Maggie, I don't know anymore."

"So, someone was here the night Mom died? Who? Does anyone else know about this? Does George?"

"I don't know. I mentioned the stranger once to him awhile back but George said leave well enough alone and don't be a gossip. Blah blah, Mr. High Road." Mitzi made a face like an annoyed child.

"But don't over think it Maggie. I mean, I bet it was just some friend of your Mom's. Hey, I bet whoever it was comes up to you tomorrow at the funeral and then you can find out what was going on, okay? Now I have to call George and tell him you are fine. He worries so much about you, you know."

"He thinks I am going to turn out like my Mom," Maggie sighed.

"Maybe, but you have to remember that men are a little bit stupid and overly protective too. That's why I love George so much. I hope you don't mind, but he told me some of the stories about you and your mom, the ones he was a part of anyway. I kind of made him because the way he always talks about you, with so much love. Frankly, it irritated the hell out of me. I mean, here was the love of my life going on and on about how to protect you and how he was always worried about you, et cetera. Well, of course I was jealous.

"Oh, don't give me that 'I didn't know' look. You and George have that strange bond that starts in childhood, whatever, no one can come between you two. So of course, after a while I got a little feisty about it. Especially when he had you sit up front with us at his parents funeral. Sorry, yeah I was mad. Then George explained to me about your grandmother, your Mom, and Sarah, too. And well, then I guess I got it.

"And these past few years, you haven't really been around. So now, I feel like I can get to know you on a different level. And maybe, you and I could become friends and not just you and George. I wasn't prom queen for nothing, people did like me." And Mitzi felt the relief of her confession and turned to Maggie with a big, goofy grin. Maggie immediately fell for Mitzi. She had guts and heart and Maggie could not find a reason to keep pushing her away anymore.

"Thanks, Mitzi. I like that you hated me. I do, and you admitted it. I can't say I have always been the nicest person in the world. I mean, c'mon you were prom queen. That kind of makes you an easy target," Maggie said winking at her. "But since I am your neighbor now, I suppose we can find some common ground other than George."

Maggie and Mitzi laughed, both knowing nothing more needed to be said.

Mitzi changed the subject, "So we meet Marten tomorrow?! Millie and George are more excited than they let on. They said if you ever brought a guy home, he must be superhuman. Did you know Millie has arranged a barbecue for you two?"

Maggie did not know because she had sequestered herself upstairs, but that was fine. Poor Marten having to meet her family all at once will be trial by fire. Over the past couple of years she had given Marten brief sketches of everyone. But now, how she described them seems so disconnected. Since she has come back home, the people here are her family in ways she never could understand as a child. She was sadly shallow in her description to the richness of her life on Grove Avenue. Hopefully, Marten will forget her characterizations and get to know them for himself.

Dr. Polis called and said that her mother's ashes were ready. Maggie found herself disconcerted by the idea of picking up her mother burnt and poured into a cardboard box. Not really knowing who to turn to, she asked Sarah if she wanted to go pick up the ashes with her. Sarah, giddy with Maggie's attention, grabbed her bag and ran straight for the car. Luckily David took his cue and returned to his book on the porch. So Maggie and Sarah were alone on not exactly the adventure of a lifetime.

Sarah immediately went for the driver's side door.

"Nope, no way you are driving," Maggie said in the driveway.

"What, I can drive. I'm a great driver!" Sarah whined.

"Okay, Sis, let me put it to you this way..how many cars have you totaled compared to me?"

"Fine." Sarah stewed and walked around to the passenger side. "Ya know, you don't have to be such a bitch all the time," Maggie heard her say quietly.

"I am not a bitch. I just happen to value my life, your life, and in general, the lives of other people."

"Saint Maggie."

"Damn straight, now buckle up sweetheart and let's go get Mom." Maggie pulled out a cigarette and tuned the radio to the local Haven station that never got past the 80's. Windows down, Maggie smoked and Sarah screamed the lyrics to George Michael's "Faith", sadly ironic. It was the closest thing to normal for the both of them. After Sarah had gotten her driver's license, she would drive around Haven with Maggie, two young girls singing, smoking, and escaping their mother's rants. Maggie adored her sister then, listening to Prince, Duran Duran, and The Police. She could do no wrong.

When they arrived at the hospital, Dr. Polis handed Vivian to them without fanfare as both women stood there dumbstruck. They looked like soldiers marching back to the car, holding the box like an active grenade. Once inside, Sarah broke the silence.

"Is this weird or what?" Sarah gaped at her.

"I know. It's not Mom. I mean Mom just cannot be in that box. I feel like there should be a strand of pearls or something on it." Sarah burst out laughing.

"It just needs a glass of chardonnay and some lipstick." They both sat there laughing until tears began rolling down Maggie's face. She was exhausted from staying up the night before, and sitting with her mother in her lap was all too much. Thank God Sarah just remained silent and grabbed Maggie's hand. They sat quietly for awhile like that, tears rolling down their faces, the salt air pushing through the windows. Eventually, Maggie pulled out and headed home.

Their evening was uneventful as Maggie sat mutely through dinner, not really listening to David talk about their lives back in Cincinnati. He tried to involve Maggie in the conversation, but her mind kept drifting to her mother's empty seat at the head of the table. She felt guilty about hiding the diaries from Sarah, but she was not able to part with them yet. It was as if she was watching over her mother. The diaries, just ink filled pages, felt more like her mother than the urn sitting on the side table. The urn they ironically found empty in the garage, another mystery that would never be answered. Naturally, both women made David transfer the ashes being too squeamish themselves. Soon Maggie would have to share the diaries with Sarah, but she did not want Sarah's judgement. Maggie did not quite trust Sarah yet, something felt off to her about this new persona. Sarah had a wealth of bitterness and hurt that she could use like venom, just like her mother. And Maggie knew it was down in her, just below the surface, and she needed to be careful not to scratch too deep.

Around two a.m. Maggie woke with a start. In her dream, both her mother and her sister had fallen down a deep stone well and she couldn't reach them. Maggie could just hear them crying out but there was blackness around her. This was a dream that Maggie had been having since she was a child but it still had the same affect on her. She felt the pressure in her chest and the waves of helplessness and loss that she always associated with both of them. Maggie, sweaty with a racing heart, reached for Marten not realizing where she was. But then she recognized the cedar tree swaying in the moonlight and sat back, sad to be alone. After all these years, you would think Maggie would have gotten used to that dream, the simplest manifestation of her reality. She didn't need Freud to analyze that one, but she tended to have the dream when something was wrong. Yes, granted her mother had just died, but something else felt ungrounded to her. The gnawing feeling that she had a had ever since she finished the diaries. It came in a flash, there in the quiet, *her mother did not want to die. Her mother did not want to die*, Maggie thought again. After all those years of trying to kill herself through the alcohol, she knew in her heart, this time, Vivian wanted to live. Completely convinced, Maggie asked, *so why did she die. Why did she die now?*

And then another thought struck Maggie so deep she actually lifted herself off the bed: *Mitzi.* What did Mitzi say about someone being in her Mom's life, some man being in the house the night her mother died? Now, nothing seemed right to Maggie. Now, it all seemed horribly, horribly wrong.

TWELVE

Maggie focused her attention on Marten as she backed her grandmother's sedan out of the garage and purred diesel out of Haven. It would take a little less than an hour to get to Logan airport, and Maggie was well ahead of time. Happy to be on the highway, Maggie's thoughts drifted back to her mother. She spent a restless night wondering, who was with her mother the night she died? How many more secrets did her mother have? What really happened? After reading her mother's last entries Maggie was certain that Vivian did not want to take her own life. Maggie had read the report, Vivian's blood alcohol level was .06, not even enough to be legally drunk. *So how did she fall down the stairs? Did whoever was there see the accident or cause it?* The car ride ended up making Maggie more anxious and irritated. Hopefully, Mitzi was right - whoever was there would reveal themselves at the funeral tomorrow.

Pulling into arrivals, she breathed and told herself to relax. Marten would help her figure it all out, if he did not think she was crazy. With that thought, Maggie felt a little inkling of hope again as she ran inside the airport to wait for him.

During their drive back to Haven, Maggie talked nonstop. She told Marten about the diaries and what she learned about her family. She told him about Sarah, George and Millie, about the money and the house, about Essie and Uncle Johnny, and about what Mitzi said about someone being at the house the night Vivian died.

"Maggie, do you really think your mother's death is suspicious?" Marten said skeptically. He sounded worried.

"What? You think I am over reacting don't you? I suppose murders don't happen in Germany?" Her voice had a desperate edge to it.

"Darling, people just don't just catapult down the stairs everyday." She told him the story about her English teacher, Mr. Keegan, who did go head first down the stairs and now thinks he is King Lear.

"Mom had two broken wrists when she died, so she must have tried to stop herself. Shouldn't she have just banged her head? Doesn't it seem wrong to you?" Maggie pounded her hand against the steering wheel.

"Maggie, honey, shhh, take it easy. I see where you are coming from, but don't you think you are just reacting to the stress? I think Mitzi is right, whoever came to the house will probably talk to you about it tomorrow. There will be an explanation, I promise. Now, what do you say we take some time for ourselves before we have to go out tonight..mmm?" Marten cocked his head and winked at her.

Maggie was irritated. She had wanted Marten to support her, back her up, and he was just not getting it.

The last thing on her mind was sex. Now, she just wanted him to go away again, to be alone again. But she looked sideways at him and realized this was the man she loved whether she liked it or not, and he deserved better than her tantrum.

Maggie tried sweetly, "Hon, not today. Right now I just need you to hold my hand and get me through this. Sex would be shit with me right now anyway, my head is just spinning. Okay?"

"Can't help but try." He smiled deeply at her and immediately she softened. The stress eased out of her shoulders as she began to tell him about the barbecue at Millie's.

It seemed more like a rehearsal dinner before a wedding than the night before a funeral. Millie had set a beautiful long table in the back yard, covered in her fine china and blue hydrangeas. The garden flowers were just beginning to bloom for the season, and the night was clear with a slight chill to the air. The slightest hint of summer sends New Englanders running outside. Marten was having culture shock with the temperature below eighty five, but Maggie found one of her grandfather's old fisherman's sweaters for him to wear.

When Maggie and Marten arrived, Archie and George were arguing the logistics of which to put on the grill first, the chicken or the lobster tails. Millie and Mitzi were arranging and rearranging bowls of pasta and salads. Mitzi's boys were dragging Ditka around trying to ride the poor dog like a bull. Sarah and David had already seated themselves having left the house early to give Maggie and Marten some alone time. As soon as Maggie and Marten appeared at the garden gate everyone stopped what they were doing. Maggie thought they looked exactly like a Rockwell portrait.

Millie was the first to come running up to Marten, her reading glasses bouncing on her bosom as she hurtled over the boys. Wiping her hands on her apron, she grabbed Marten's arms and squeezed him, "We are just so pleased you are here. Come in, come in!" *Oh christ,* Maggie thought, everyone was acting like Marten was her first 'beau'.

George almost shook Marten's arm off and Mitzi flirted with him. Sarah was more reserved, trying to keep her babbling to a minimum, although she did reveal in the first three minutes that Maggie did not grow any boobs until she was seventeen. Maggie had forgotten Sarah's humor had the maturity level of a thirteen year old boy. Maggie felt herself relax a bit with the idea of her family and her life coming back together. It seemed everyone, including herself, was in good humor.

Mac's arrival soon after was everyone's jolt back to reality. James 'Mac' Donald was Maggie's and Sarah's second stepfather and the last to have loved their mother. Uniquely different from Vivian's first two husbands, Thomas and Peter had been classically tall and handsome, Mac's personality enhanced his looks. It was his character that attracted everyone. But tonight he was drained, his eyes were sad, and his limbs hung loose.

Mac may have been attractive once but now in his early sixties, he was more of a winsome personality masked in wrinkles. He wore his gray hair shaggy and his clothes loose which gave him a disheveled grandfather quality. While his belly had protruded over the years, his eyes remained a welcoming, soft brown. He was not a man who strode through the room confidently but shuffled quietly, as was his nature. His calm character and assurance had attracted Vivian more so than his looks.

Mac had met Vivian in a bookstore in 1989, but they did not really date and marry until 1991. Afterward, for more than ten years, they lived on Grove Avenue as a part of the Murphy-Atwood clan. Maggie had been sixteen when she met Mac and immediately liked that he was funny and reserved. His personality was not as loud as the women in their family, but he had an inner resilience. Maggie had already been at boarding school when Mac married her mother, and their friendship developed in a casual, friendly way. There was never a need for Mac to be a father figure. Maggie was on her own doing well in school, and rarely got in trouble. Often the time between them was spent ordering pizza, playing backgammon, and fighting over who had better taste in art, literature, and movies. In his twenties, Mac wrote a novel that became semi-famous among collegiate intellectuals. Hollywood attempted to make a movie but, like many good novels, it never translated to screen. Eventually, his hopes of being the next Hemingway faded, and his writing career was dictated by practicality. Now, he wrote travel dialogues and book reviews for newspapers and the Internet. Not exactly the career he had planned, but neither was the marriage he had with Vivian.

As Mac stood at the garden wall, Maggie's eyes stung with tears. It was odd to see him standing there alone without her mother on his arm. Maggie was the first to jump up and hug Mac, but Sarah lacked the same affection for him. She awkwardly gave him a quick butterfly hug and introduced David. Maggie introduced Marten and watched the two men give each other a warm smile. It felt good to be around Mac. He was a large part of her good memories. Everyone else at the party saw Mac regularly in Haven and waved him in like the old friend and neighbor he was. Now the conversation re-centered on

Vivian, and the dinner never quite regained the frivolity it once had.

Seeing everyone gathered, Maggie missed her mother, thinking how Vivian would have been the life of the party. She would have joked about how Millie watched too much Martha Stewart because the table was perfectly set. She would have sympathized with pregnant Mitzi's swollen ankles and kidded George about delivering their baby at the animal clinic to save on hospital costs. Vivian could be delightful and funny without effort, a natural grace everyone envied and adored. She would have read an interesting article or knew the history of some famous family and shared it without boring her audience. When she was sober, her mind was sharp, clear and engaging. As a child, Maggie would admire her mother hosting a cocktail or dinner party, her hair always in place, and her make up perfectly set. With elegant pearls wrapped around her delicate neck, she could have been hosting the Kennedys or the Duponts. Vivian seemed the ideal woman. It was after the party, when the guests had gone, that plates would be thrown rather than cleared, and the polite talk would turn into anger fueled, alcohol induced rants.

Maggie tried to put those memories out of her mind as she sat here with the people she loved and had pushed out of her life. These were the people who had stayed with her mother until the end. They had shared in her last conversation, her last meal, and her last laugh. Had her mother been wonderful over the past couple of years? Had people seen her good side more than her bad? Maggie's hand felt for Marten's under the table as tears clouded her eyes. She squeezed him and looked away from everybody, feeling overwhelmed.

"You okay, Mags?" It was Mac who noticed her being quiet. Maggie nodded and tried not to look him in the eye, afraid the real tears might come. Then Maggie began to think about the stranger who was there the night of her mother's death. It was like fuel to her to keep going. Could it have been Mac? *No, he would have said something to me.* They never kept secrets from each other. It was the one policy Mac and Maggie adhered to because it was the only way to survive with Vivian. Vivian was never proud of her drinking and still, to the end, never spoke the truth about it. It was up to them to at least be open with each other.

Like the time she got a DUI while Maggie was away at college and then got a second one six months later. Vivian told Mac, *absolutely do not tell Maggie.* But he did anyway because Maggie caught on to the fact her mother stopped driving her car. And Maggie would tell Mac about the late night drunken phone calls she would receive from Vivian when he was away on writing trips. Mac was the only honest element that she ever had in her family and she adored him for it.

"I'm okay, Mac, really. I'll be fine. So how are you?" Maggie took a page out of the family rule book and was trying to not over-dramatize.

Mac nodded trying to fight his own tears, so Maggie quickly switched the subject. "I got the house," Maggie winked at him, "Now you know what that means, Bucko? Backgammon is back and will be taking place on that porch right there." Maggie pointed at his chest then at the her mother's porch.

Mac grinned. "I knew she was going to do that, We talked about it, I think it's perfect for you. And if you think you are going to win because it's your porch now, yeah right." They both laughed. Vivian had hated when they played backgammon outside because they were so loud, yelling and screaming profanities at every hit. Something about the game brought out the best and the worst in Mac and Maggie. Suddenly, Maggie could not wait to play again. But she would miss her mother opening up her second story window and shouting at them to *keep it down*.

Maggie then looked down the table and noticed Sarah chewing the inside of her lip, which was never a good sign. When Sarah fidgeted that usually meant she was upset, nervous, or uncomfortable with something. Maggie felt for her and understood there was a whole chapter of their family life with Mac of which Sarah was not a part. Sarah was roaming the country with God knows who doing Lord knows what during most of their mother's time with Mac. Those were the years that really separated Maggie from her sister. Occasionally she would get a postcard or a strange slurred phone call, but no constant relationship between them or Mac and Vivian.

Back then, when Sarah did come home for a few days at a time, she would be asking for money or running from some mess she had made. When she was not sleeping off the booze, Sarah would be arguing with Vivian. Now, Maggie was finding it hard to reconcile that version of her with the docile, polite person quietly chatting at the table. For days Maggie realized she had been avoiding Sarah, almost pushing it in her face that this was her house, her town, her friends and that Sarah was a stranger. Maggie did not mean to, but she wanted to make Sarah feel like she did not belong. She shoved her to the side the same way Sarah had shoved her to the side so many times when they were young. *Oh shit*, she thought. *I must be taking out revenge on Sarah for not paying enough attention to me and then leaving me with Mom.* Ugh, Maggie thought to herself, will this psycho babble stuff never end! She really could not deal with this right now. Had she really been unfair to Sarah? But, Sarah had been unfair to her, right?

Just then, as if on cue, Sarah says, "I have an announcement!" Immediately Maggie thought, *oh no, here it comes*. Whatever was going to come out of Sarah's mouth could not be good.

"I'm pregnant. Well, we are pregnant, David and I!" Sarah squealed like a little girl, which was so unlike her.

Maggie could not believe it. Here she was feeling sorry for Sarah, when all along it was still about Sarah. How could she twist their own mother's funeral and make it about her? Seriously, was this the time or the place to announce a baby? George immediately shot Maggie a look that said 'you have got to be kidding me, Sarah with a baby?' And right here, trumpeting it.

Millie choked on her tomato salad and Archie let out a chuckle. Mitzi forever the "Amy Vanderbilt Book of Etiquette" jumped up and said, "Isn't that terrific, isn't that terrific everybody!" Mac and Marten kept their heads down while Sarah and David beamed goofy grins at Maggie. Maggie was quick to recover but not very convincingly. "Gee, that's great Sis, can't believe it." Sarah's face quickly changed with Maggie's words. Apparently, it was not quite the reaction she was hoping for.

"What? Can't you believe that I, your great fucked up sister is doing something normal for a change? That I too could be like the beloved Maggie and have the perfect life?"

Sarah's tone had shifted and had become familiarly argumentative. She was challenging Maggie now, pushing her to say something, anything, so she could unleash an inner fury on her. *Where did twelve step, peace and love Sarah go? Uh oh*, Maggie kept thinking, *she really should have been nicer to her the past couple of days. Karma is a bitch.*

"Sar', really, I am very happy for you, just a little shocked because you announced it at Mom's funeral, that's all." Maggie could not help herself as she got the dig in about how inappropriate it was for Sarah to upstage Vivian's funeral.

"Well, you know Maggie, these things just happen and I thought that because everyone was all together you might be happy for me, for us, just once, and stop judging from that high horse of yours." Sarah began to huff like a kid who didn't get her way.

Thankfully Millie, who knew the girls better than anyone, realized where this would lead. She interjected, "Oh Sarah, we are all so happy for you. How wonderful to have a new addition to our little family! Maggie is just pleased as punch, you know that. It has been a long week that's all. Now Sarah, Sugar, why don't you come in and help me with the pie and tell me all about it."

Millie placed her hand on Sarah's back and practically forced her into the house. Everyone, wide-eyed, looked at Maggie.

"Were you expecting anything less, c'mon. We *are* the Atwoods, you know!" Maggie then got up in frustration from the table and stormed across the yard. She was edgy enough about the funeral, and now Sarah would be running around like Mary Madonna Pure as Snow tomorrow. Maggie could feel her irritation creep up the base of her spine.

"Hey, you okay?" It was Marten wrapping his arms from around behind her. "Yeah, that didn't even scratch the surface of the 'dark waters of Sarah and Maggie,' though. You just got a taste. Sorry." Maggie said turning to him.

"Hey, don't worry about me. I already prepared myself for, as you said many times, 'the family from hell.' But really, so far, I have been pretty disappointed. Everybody is great, and your sister is just a bit jealous of you, that's all."

"Yeah, but none of these people are blood related. The real show will be tomorrow. I don't know what to do about Sarah. It's like we are two sides to the same coin. We constantly see things from the opposite point of view. She thinks I am some sort of golden child because I didn't end up in rehab, and I think she bailed on the family, bailed on me, a long time ago. Wow, a baby. I never thought her the mother type." Maggie sighed.

"Well, maybe that's exactly who she needs to be, and then she could understand you and your Mum a bit more." Maggie agreed. Marten did have a point. Sarah, no longer the child but the parent, might make her more understanding. But Maggie would have to see it to believe it. Marten convinced her to let it go, at least for the sake of her mother, and rejoin the party. Maggie relented and together they walked back to the table.

For the rest of the evening, George lightened the mood by telling funny stories about Maggie as a child. Like the time she accidentally went to school with a pair of underwear stuck to the back of her pants. The static electricity in the laundry hamper caused them to hold up, unnoticed, all the way to school. Fortunately, it was only George who saw, but he never let her live it down. Sarah settled back down and talked about babies with Mitzi, while Mac and Marten sat like bookends silently supporting Maggie. The evening air began to get chilly, and all of them started to feel the burden of the next day.

Maggie had drunk a little too much, hiding it the best she could. She could not seem to fight how terrified she was anymore. Everyone was here, the troops had gathered, and tomorrow was the day. It seemed as if there would be some sort of finality to her mother that she was not ready to face. Would Maggie wake up after the funeral and get on with her life, never looking back? She thought of her mother's diaries, hidden safe beneath her bed, and was comforted.   There was her true mother, the one she would not dare let go this time.

THIRTEEN

The morning of the funeral, Maggie awoke with a foggy head and naked beneath the sheets. Spurred on by the wine, Maggie dove on Marten when they'd reached their room, not necessarily to connect with him, but more to disconnect from herself.

With Marten still soundly sleeping, Maggie slipped on a robe and realized it was early yet, just a little after six. She was out of aspirin for her pounding head and went down the hall to her mother's private bathroom. Maggie easily found bottles of Bayer lined up in neat rows next to bottles of Valium, Lexipro, and hormones. Poor Mom, thought Maggie, she tried so many ways to keep herself sane. She then walked back into Vivian's bedroom and found herself in front of the dressing table.

Vivian's lipsticks, perfume bottles, and pictures of Sarah and Maggie as children were perfectly placed. Maggie picked up her favorite black and white photograph of Sarah, her mother and her grandmother with her. Maggie must have been only five or six years old. The picture showed a bright summer day at the beach and Virginia and Vivian donning matching black bathing suits. Virginia looked like Jackie Kennedy in her large round black sunglasses and Vivian's pearls shown like tiny suns. Sarah was grabbing Vivian's leg while Maggie was grabbing her grandmother's other leg, and all four of them were laughing. Grandpa Jack must have taken the picture. There they were, three generations of crazy women without a care in the world. Placing the picture back, Maggie drew a deep breath. The past could be both comforting and maddening at the same time.

Maggie fingered her mother's finely polished sterling silver jewelry box. Her engraved initials VHM, the H for Virginia's mother, Hannah, looked worn and elegant. Inside she found her mother's two strands of pearls, one long and one short. Like the jewelry box, the short strand had been given to Vivian by her parents when she was young. It was the one she often wore because it did not catch in her reading glasses around her neck. Maggie did not recognize the longer strand. Maybe someone had bought them for her, maybe she bought them for herself. Pearls, her mother always said, should be off white, classic, and not too big, but not too small, and this strand was exactly that down to the perfect gold clasp. Maggie ran them against her teeth to feel the grit and slipped them over her head. Immediately, she felt the cool weight of the necklace on her chest. She slipped the shorter strand into her bathrobe pocket. She would give those to Sarah. They would be a peace offering and a reminder that this day should be about Vivian.

Maggie went downstairs to start the coffee and get the last of the orange juice to clear her head. As she turned the corner, she gave a little scream not expecting to see the back of a man standing there rifling through the mail on the table. "Shit, Uncle Johnny, what the hell are you doing here?"

"Magpie, Magpie, didn't mean to scare you. Just thought, you know, people would be up, getting ready, you know, for the..." He would not look her in the eye but sat down at the kitchen table to show he had no intention of leaving.

"It's 6:30 a.m., Uncle Johnny, the funeral isn't until noon. How did you get in house by the way? I thought I locked all the doors."

"Maggie, chill, you know the locks haven't been changed in fifty years." He was smiling as he jingled his key in front of her face. What an idiot, Maggie thought. Now she would immediately change the locks.

"What do you want, Uncle Johnny?" Maggie said with impatience as she began dumping coffee grounds in the pot filter.

"Well, now that you mention it, Magpie, I wanted to talk to you. You know you were always the reasonable one around here. You were never as dramatic as your mother or sister." Maggie knew he meant 'crazy', not dramatic. He was after something, and the idiot was trying to sweet-talk her. Johnny continued, "So here I am thinking about your mother and this house, and what is left of my family. It just gets me, you know…" and then he fist pumped his chest. If Maggie was not so irritated with him, she would have burst out laughing. She kept her mouth shut because she wanted to find out what he was after. "So anyway, Momma, your grandmother, when she passed, she left a lot of unfinished business that, you know, over the years Essie and I have had to deal with."

"Like what?" Maggie knew she was just egging him on because he could not answer that. Everything was perfectly in order when her grandmother died. There were no questions in the eyes of the law that all of Virginia's assets were complete.

"Well, in thinking about Momma and the house and Vivian, I remembered Momma used to hide her jewels in the house." Bingo, there it was. He was searching for hidden treasure. That is why he said 'Essie and I,' he probably had Essie believing there was a big stash of gold in the basement. Maggie did not interrupt him because she knew the more desperate and nervous he'd become, the more the he'd talk and the more she could find out. Maggie learned that from Marten, how to interrogate people as a lawyer- just let them talk.

"Well, as a kid I remembered this diamond brooch Momma used to wear that Daddy gave to her, a real eye-catcher. It was two sides, each with five one-carat diamonds on it. Do you remember it? Have you seen it, darlin'? Oh, and my mother used to always wear this yellow canary diamond cocktail ring, you must remember that sweetie, mmm? And the strand of diamonds and sapphires that Daddy gave her for their wedding anniversary? Have you seen any of these things, you know around the house, perhaps in your Momma's room? I mean, I certainly would not have want them to be hidden and never found. That would just be such a shame."

Johnny had become very animated as he was talking, waving his arms and a little sweat had beaded on his upper lip. What a greedy bastard, Maggie thought. Maggie had been leaning at the kitchen counter blowing on her coffee, when Sarah arrived. For once, Sarah had great timing.

"Ugh, I just threw up three times at the thought, just the damn thought of food," Sarah said as she walked through the door. Obviously, she expected Maggie to be alone in the kitchen and was surprised to see Uncle Johnny. Sarah turned and cocked her head towards Maggie, a gesture that said *What is this asshole doing here?*

"Morning sickness? Wow, I'm sorry. I've heard it sucks, sorry," Maggie said, truly being sympathetic. Then she decided to play with Uncle Johnny." Sarah's having a baby Uncle J, isn't that great?!" She turned to him with a big smirk.

"Wow, congratulations, Sarah," Uncle Johnny said a little more than shocked at the news. Both women watched him get flustered and loved it.

"So Sarah," Maggie said turning towards her and reached into her robe for the second strand of pearls. "I found these this morning and thought you should have them. They were Mom's strand that she always wore that Grandma and Grandpa had given her, and well, since you are having a baby, which could be a girl, you should have them. I found this second set so I will wear these today." Maggie opened up her robe a little at the top to show Sarah the pearls around her neck.

Out of the corner of her eye she could see Johnny sitting on the edge of his chair trying to get a look, and trying to figure out what else was in Vivian's jewelry box. "Thanks, Mags, these are great. That was a good idea, to wear Mom's pearls." Sarah teared up for a second, so Maggie switched the subject.

"So Sarah, you are probably wondering why Uncle J let himself into our house at 6 a.m.?" Maggie winked at Sarah to play along.

"Why, yes, Maggie the thought did occur to me," Sarah caught on.

"Well, it seems our wily mother had been holding out on the family. Apparently, there are jewels, lots and lots of 'family' jewels that our dear Uncle is very worried about this morning, the morning of our mother's funeral."

"Really? Uncle Johnny, is there gold bouillon we are unaware o? Perhaps, mmm some black opals hidden in a coffee tin somewhere?" Sarah said sarcastically.

"No, red emeralds! I bet that Grandpa had them hidden in his easy chair, and that's why he never got out of the damn thing!" Both women were in fits of giggles now.

"Nows, girls don't get your dander up. I was just asking is all. I'll let you guys go, and you and me can talk about this later." He pointed at Maggie like they were supposed to meet at the OK Corral at sundown.

After he left, Maggie turned to Sarah and said, "Dander, what the hell is our 'dander' anyway. I tell you, now that I know what he is after, I am sleeping with one eye open. Do you remember Grandma's diamond necklace and her yellow diamond ring?"

"Yeah, I do, but I don't know what happened to them. I wasn't in the best shape when Grandma died, you know." They both sat at the kitchen table and begun unknowingly to talk like sisters again.

"Well, he thinks Mom hid Grandma's jewelry from him and Essie. But she wouldn't do that, would she? I mean I haven't found anything. What was so funny though, I had gotten the pearls out this morning and was going to give them to you. But then Johnny showed up, and it was more fun to do it in front of him."

"Good call, I would have done the same thing. Listen, Mags, I wanted to apologize for last night. I shouldn't have, you know, gotten bitchy with you."

"Don't say it, Sarah. I should apologize too. I mean, since you have gotten here, I haven't been very nice. I have made you feel like a stranger here in your home, our home."

"Yeah, but I deserve it. Years ago I told everyone a big 'fuck you' and took off. I wasn't any better than

Uncle Johnny, but I was sick. Now with the hormones, and the funeral, and the baby, it's all messing with my head, making me think about the past all too much. You were right, I probably should not have announced the baby like that, but I didn't want it to be a secret any longer."

"I know, I know. I have been going back into the past myself and my head is spinning."

"Oh, Mags, I always loved you, probably more than I could ever show you. The problem with both Mom and me is we did not love ourselves enough. You just always seemed fine without us. We never worried about you because we were so stupidly focused on ourselves all the time. You were not messed up like we were, you were so loving and confident. Do you remember at boarding school when you won that national writing contest?"

Maggie had forgotten all about it. She had written a story about a mother and daughter stranded in a foreign country on vacation. The mother was an alcoholic and the daughter was responsible for getting them out of the country without them killing each other first. Maggie had submitted it to a teen writing contest and won. When they published it in a national women's magazine, Vivian was so proud she told anyone who would listen to buy the magazine, but she had neglected to read the story first. Of course, the main character was almost an exact sketch of Vivian and her drinking. While Vivian was immensely proud of Maggie, she also felt ashamed and humiliated. She would not return Maggie's phone calls from school for more than a month. When Maggie came home for school break, Mac informed Maggie if the story was never mentioned again then Vivian would return to normal. So Maggie disregarded the greatest achievement of her childhood for the sake of her mother.

"I think that was the worse thing you ever did to any of us, or at least, that is what Mom thought. Really you did nothing wrong at all. It was such an achievement too. But it was all about Mom, and well, we let it be all about Mom. We did not support you enough. Instead we worried about her feelings, her reactions. Oh, Mags, I should have stood up for you, showed you how proud I was of you."

"Sarah, that is in the past. I don't think about stuff like that. I shouldn't have used our private lives like that. Whatever." And Maggie waved her hands at the thought.

"Maggie, you have every right to use our lives. You had a voice, you had feelings, and we told you to shut up and take care of us. It wasn't fair."

Maggie was grateful for Sarah's acknowledgement, but saddened too. If Vivian and Sarah had supported her more, if she had not spent so much time worried about them, trying to hold them all together, would she have accomplished something with her life by now? Would she have books published? Would she still have a column in a newspaper or magazine?

In boarding school and college, Maggie spent many nights on the phone with her inebriated mother. Vivian would call after bingeing all day and Maggie, always terrified of what Vivian was capable of, would sit on the phone with her for hours until her mother passed out. In college, she spent more weekends at home than staying on campus. There was an invisible string from Maggie wherever she was, back to Haven. Even though Mac was there, Maggie felt she was the only one who understood Vivian, the only one smart enough to protect her. And with Sarah, Maggie was always trying to save her.

Maggie had given up on trying to stop Vivian from drinking but she always believed Sarah had a chance.

The last two times Sarah had gone to rehab, Maggie had arranged the interventions. In 1993, when Maggie was twenty, she had gone to see Sarah who was living in California at the time. The trip was horrific. Sarah never arrived at the airport to meet her, and when Maggie eventually found her apartment in Los Angeles, she discovered Sarah high and emaciated. Sarah was unresponsive, and Maggie immediately took her to the emergency room. For the next three days, Maggie was on the phone with Vivian arranging for Sarah to go to rehab for junkies in upstate New York. Maggie flew with Sarah, who was pumped full of hospital drugs, all the way to rehab to make sure Sarah was locked tightly away for the requisite twenty-eight days. Two years later, Maggie flew to Tucson and did the same thing all over again. It was Maggie who found the clinics, Maggie who championed and fought for Sarah. But each time, Sarah would thank her and love her for the first few months of sobriety. And then she would secretly begin to use again, ask Maggie for money and other things, abuse her kindness then disappear. That was why Maggie was so furious with her now because of the roller coaster of bullshit she had been riding with Sarah for years.

And now Sarah was right. When did they support her, encourage her? Who kicked her in the ass and told her to make something of her life? No one. Here she is, bitter, older and unaccomplished, just like them. When she ran away two years ago to New Orleans, she only became more like her mother and sister, not less. *Shit*, thought Maggie.

Both of them felt the weight of the day ahead so they left it at that. Sarah hugged Maggie, thanked her for the pearls and went to go throw up again. Here it was, only seven in the morning, and Maggie was exhausted already. She went out onto the front porch to have a smoke and a moment's peace before the rest of the house woke up. Seeing the lingering dew drops on the grass and smelling the edges of spring burning off the night air, Maggie missed her grandmother. Right now she could use Virginia's straight shooting, her level head and her icy emotions.

FOURTEEN

Maggie's grandmother, had a no-nonsense approach to life. Small talk was unnecessary and polite pleasantries should be kept to a minimum. She detested when people over explained things or took too long to tell a story. There was no room for gossip and idle chatter. She believed people had to give her a reason to like them, no one automatically earned Virginia's respect. Once, the garden club of Haven wanted to raise money to plant flowers around the city. One afternoon, two well-dressed housewives came to Grove Avenue to solicit money from Virginia. After obligatory tea and biscuits, Virginia asked 'Whose lives would these flower pots improve?' Virginia began to make them feel their request was silly and frivolous. Virginia felt all charitable money should benefit needy people. Lord knows, she did not need to look at another hydrangea in town square. By the time the two ladies left that afternoon, the garden club rededicated to helping under privileged families of Haven. The ladies also left with a starter check of $5000.

Her grandmother was very good at getting her way with people.

Grandpa Jack was content to let Virginia be the head of the household and rarely argued with her. They were not an affectionate couple, but Jack doted on her in a variety of ways. Every morning he brought her a cup of tea in bed, placed fresh flowers in the kitchen, or an occasional a jewelry box would appear out of nowhere. After that fateful trip to New York during one of Vivian's 'episodes', as her suicide attempts became known, they rarely left for weekend trips again. Maggie wondered about her grandparents' relationship. They had seemed content with each other over the years, yet there was an underlying strain between them. Maggie understood how difficult her grandmother could be with her staunch values. But in the end, were they happy?

For Virginia and Maggie, there was a special connection that made her see her grandmother differently than all the rest.

Virginia softened with Maggie. She taught her how to appreciate life, to look at the ocean and see the foam, the bits of sea glass, the caked sand, the broken shells, and to understand the world was connected within itself. Virginia and Maggie could walk as long as the shore would allow them, no preference for morning or afternoons, sun or clouds. Each part of the day brought a different slant of light, a varying tide. Virginia was always patient and kind with her wisdom. It was on those walks that Maggie felt close to her grandmother no matter what was going on in their lives.

"Maggie, dear, stand up straight," Virginia always would say, and Maggie would relax her shoulders and bring in her stomach, just like Virginia had taught her. All the while she explained to Maggie the science behind the fish the oceans, the trees on the shoreline, and how clouds moved through the sky. There was nothing her grandmother didn't have an opinion on. As Maggie got older, Virginia's teachings began to include literature. She would give Maggie books to read, such as *To Kill a Mockingbird* or *Lord of the Flies*, to discuss them on their walks. Virginia pushed Maggie to find the meaning in things. *Why did Boo Bradley save the children? Why did the characters hate Piggy? Why, why, why?* "Every problem has a solution," Virginia would say, developing Maggie's curiosity, teaching her how to reason with the world. Virginia confessed that if she had not been a mother, she would have been a teacher.

Maggie ravished the attention and admired the things her grandmother loved, wanting to please her. It was because of Virginia that Maggie began to write, and she wanted to publish a books someday to make her grandmother proud.

It was when Maggie would slip in questions about their family life that Virginia would turn cold. 'Why was her mother so sad?' 'What did Grandpa Jack think about when he stared at the ocean?' 'Why did Sarah and her mother fight so much?'

Virginia would shut down and tell Maggie not to be impolite, respect her elders, and honor others' privacy. Virginia danced and evaded her questions, convincing Maggie her curiosity was meant for the outside world and not for matters concerning the family.

When Grandpa Jack began to die, Virginia became more philosophical with Maggie.

"Margaret, dear, do you know what love is?" Maggie, as a teenager, had no idea how to answer.

"Well, Grandma, love is love…"

"Oh, child, love is so much more than love. It is sadness, and hatred, dread, and disappointment. It is all the emotions designed into one, shaping us, forcing us to make the decisions we make, good and bad." Virginia paused. Then abruptly, "You did not know my parents..." Virginia's voice trailed off.

"What about your parents?" Maggie was eager know more because they had passed away before she was born.

"Oh, my parents always loved me, always wanted the best for me, but I let them make decisions for me that ultimately changed my life. Never let people make decisions for you, Margaret, no matter how much you love them and they love you. I resented them afterward, I got angry at the people I loved the most."

Virginia was not making much sense, but Maggie knew enough not to interrupt her grandmother to ask questions.

"You see, there was a time in my life when all I knew was love, and I thought I was magical. Love was an illusion that I got to touch. I was special, my love was special. But then it disappeared, just like that. Gone from my life, leaving a memory stronger than the real thing." Virginia sighed and did not wait for a response from Maggie. "Do you know how much I love your Grandpa Jack? I did not know until now, until just now, how much I love him. He was a good man who loved the wrong woman. I should have loved him sooner, I should have loved him more, but I had forgotten what love was..."

Those words always stayed with Maggie, even though she never fully understood them. When Grandpa Jack died, Virginia ran his funeral with precision and grace, and any hint of emotion was silently forbidden. Something about her grandmother's stoicism only served to remind Maggie there was so much more she did not know. Her family remained a perpetual mystery, a question that no one would or wanted to answer. Her grandfather's funeral was the perfect metaphor for their family because Maggie could not recall if anyone even cried or was allowed to cry at the gravesite. How unnatural for death not to have grief. It amazed Maggie that for all the chaos and drama, the women in her family always arrived with their mascara applied and hair perfectly in place.

Excerpts from the Diary of Vivian Murphy Atwood March 1989

Even as I write these words, I don't believe them. How could Momma do this to me? How could I have done what I did? I have a million questions. I have poured myself a glass of wine. Eight months of sobriety down the drain, but I promise tomorrow I will go to a meeting. Just right now my nerves are so jangled and frayed I am afraid to go to bed. I must write all this down before I forget a single detail. I can't tell if Momma was being cruel...why did she do this to me????

I had gone on a date tonight with James Macdonald, the nice writer who I'd met a week ago in the bookstore. It was a nice enough evening but I was tired so I came home early. I found Momma in Daddy's chair staring out the window at the water. Lately, she had been drinking twice as much gin since Daddy's been gone but I wasn't about to point that out. It is just better to let Momma alone. Momma gets quiet and bitter when she drinks, me loud and terrible. So I just ignored her and slipped past her on up to my room, but she called me to come sit with her.

'Want a drink,' Momma asked slightly slurring her words.

'No, Momma, I'm fine.'

'Oh, that's right Miss High and Mighty isn't drinking. Well how long do you think that's gonna last?'

It was obvious Momma wanted to start an argument.

'Momma don't you think it is time for bed? We can talk in the morning.'

I was not in the mood for her to bite my head off about whatever was bothering her this time. But then she got real strange and quiet. I thought maybe she had fallen asleep right there in the chair but she slowly turned towards me and gave me the strangest look.

'You look like your father.' Her steely green eyes were pointed at me, and she spit this out with such venom my heart stopped a beat. I tried to be light and said, 'Now, Momma you know I look just like you, the red hair and green eyes, all you. Are you missing Daddy tonight? Is that why you are so upset?'

'Stupid child, you've always been a stupid child. No, your father, your real father. You have Stefan's face, the arch of his beautiful eyes, his stiff regal chin. Everyday you remind me of him, everyday, you remind me he is gone.'

'Who, Momma, who is gone? Who is Stefan? Jack is Daddy,'

I felt my heart start beating faster. I could not move my legs to get out of there. I said, 'What the hell are you talking about Momma?!' I waited, then slowly, she spoke like from a dream.

'Your father, my husband. My beautiful husband you took away from me. I suppose I'll be dead soon so I should tell you now. What's done is done.' Then Momma took a long pull from her drink and began.

'It was 1949, after the war. I lived with my parents in Boston in what is now known as the South End. We were middle class Irish Catholics, just ex-potato farmers who love their bibles. My parents had come over during the first war and settled in Boston. Papa worked for the Murphy insurance company, now our the insurance company. I had just turned eighteen and was going to start classes at Boston University. I didn't really know what I wanted to do. I thought maybe I would be a teacher someday at a university. Papa and Ma let me stay at home because I was their only child. How very un-Catholic, right? One child? They tried for years and I was the only one, unfortunate for them in so many ways.

'Well, anyway, it was after the war and America and the whole world was trying to rebuild itself. I still lived at home while I worked part time at a bakery, and Ma felt lonely at home with Dad and I working. My Ma, Hannah, your middle name, was such a good woman at heart. So she decided to help out the refugees that were flooding to America and that was when my world changed.

'When Stefan Schmitt walked into our house on a clear fall day she rented him a bedroom on the third floor. I still remember coming home from class and seeing him sitting in the kitchen helping shell peas. Ma had spent the afternoon getting to know his whole story. I blushed when she introduced us. He was so handsome and charming, with his fine German jaw and his blue eyes perfectly set apart. His blonde hair was combed over but kept fighting to stand on top of his head. His smile was wide and his strong arms immediately reached out to shake my hand. He had only been in America two weeks and was so grateful to be in our country. He was from Munich, and he had lost his entire family. He'd learned English during the war when he joined American soldiers to fight against Hitler. Now, 24, he seemed older beyond his years. He said he did not survive the Germans to let the rest of the world beat him down. He could hardly speak of his lost mother, brother and father, but he had he fought to live and live he would.

'Stefan slipped into our lives with energy and easy laughter. He and I fell in love so fast that I barely slept at night. Papa got him a job at the insurance company and he was a natural salesmen, making friends quickly. One of those friends was the owner's son, Jack Murphy. Jack was 28, and had fought in the war himself. Though Stefan was the more charismatic of the two, they admired each other and Stefan brought out the humor in Jack.

'Stefan and I were married at City Hall, and Jack was our best man. My parents overlooked the fact he wasn't Catholic. They loved him as much as I did. Stefan believed some people found God during the war and some people just lost him. He had clarity and decisiveness that we were all attracted to.

'When you came along, we named you after Stefan's French mother, Vivienne. I wanted to change the spelling just to make it easier for you. Stefan and I, we adored you. I stopped thinking about being a teacher and wanted to have baby after baby. We were so happy. He was doing well at the insurance company with Papa and Jack, and we could not imagine that anything bad would ever happen to us again.

'Then you did it, you took all of that away from us." Momma breathed deeply then let those words hang in the air like lightning bolts.

'Of course, you were a child and I couldn't blame you, but I could not look at you anymore. I saw Stefan's smile, his infection in you and I hated you. A hate that stayed in me like a gas always ready to explode. I suppose that is why you had such a hard time in life, you can blame me, the absent, hateful mother. I loved you, but I loved Stefan more and he was gone.

'Oh, don't look at me that way, Vivian. You know better than anyone that life happens and you can't do a damn thing about it. It was the simplest thing. You were in your high chair when he came home from work. I had been telling you not to throw your milk but you kept doing it anyway. You constantly wanted to defy me, even at three years old. I was so frustrated, I walked out of the kitchen and told Stefan to take care of you. Well, this is why I loved your father, he would laugh and never take me too seriously. Most men would have gotten frustrated but Stefan hugged and kissed me and told me to sit down for a while and he would take care of you. He loved you desperately, you know, having lost his whole family. You were slowly healing that hole in his heart. That is why I wanted to have more babies, to give him everything he gave me, life.

'Well, I guess you threw your milk on the floor again, and just like that Stefan slipped. When he fell, the back of his head hit the corner of the kitchen counter. At first, he stood and seemed to shake the pain off. But he quickly became disoriented. He held your milk cup and couldn't understand what it was, then he did not seem to recognize me. I called a neighbor to watch you then rushed Stefan to the hospital. By the time we got there, he was unconscious and I never spoke to him again. He slipped into a coma that night and two weeks later, stopped breathing. His brain had swollen and slowly suffocated his body. He survived Hitler, the war, but not you." Momma wouldn't look at me as she took another long pull from her gin. I watched speechlessly as she clicked the bitter liquid around her tongue.

'I was devastated, but Jack was by my side the whole time. For weeks, I wouldn't get out of bed and my parents had to take care of you. I saw nothing but blackness for my future, all my wonderful hopes were gone. And there was Jack, kind and thoughtful. He threw me a lifeline. He wanted to take care of us, he wanted to have a family - he loved Stefan too. He thought we could grieve together and find a future, even if not based on love, then common experience. My parents were worried about me and they were fond of Jack, so they quickly agreed. They encouraged, even pushed me, to marry Jack, and everyone-but me- decided we should leave Boston. Apparently, I should go where I had no memories of Stefan and start over. Jack had plenty of money from the company, so it was determined we should move to Haven. Everything was resolved for me. Maybe I was too stupid, or just too weak to protest. I did not want to be left alone with you, and I did not want to live with Ma and Papa because of the pity and sadness in their eyes. Jack said he already loved you like his own, so it was decided. It was when we gave you his name, when you became a Murphy, that broke my heart most of all.

'It was like everyone was so broken-hearted over Stefan's death that they wiped him clean away. I settled for compromise and security, and love and passion ceased to be in my vocabulary. I became the dutiful wife. I owed Jack that, he had tried to save me. I gave him two more children, but they weren't mine. The children I was to have with Stefan, those were the children I should have loved. Essie and Johnny, they were victims of my broken heart. You really can't blame them, since they were never really wanted or loved by me.

I suppose all of you children felt that, deep down. But maybe that's why you have so many issues, Vivi, because at one point I did love you. I loved you so very much and so did your father, both your fathers, but then I shut it off like a faucet. Gone. I ripped the rug out from under you and let you fly in the wind. I'm sorry, I am. I know you can never believe that. But, since your father, I mean Jack died, I have realized the damage I have done.

'Jack always wanted me to love him like I loved Stefan, but I couldn't. I was cold. And the poor man, he died cold, with a wife and children who never truly loved him. I'm rambling, I know. I am an old lady and a drunk one at that. It's just I always wanted to tell you that, that you look like him. That everyday you remind me of him.'

With that, Momma got up and walked out of the room. Too stunned, I sat there. I could not protest. I couldn't even ask her questions. That was it. The truth that had been lurking around the edge of my whole life, changing and shaping and eluding me. There it was, the heart of my disappointment, my sadness, my grief, everything I could never understand about my mother spelled out in one horrible story.

Even now, as I go over it again, I can't fathom this other man, Stefan. This true father who loved me and I probably loved as well, maybe that's the missing piece to my heart. Not Thomas. Thomas's death just added to my loss. But why was Momma so cold when Thomas died, shouldn't she have understood? Is that why she wanted me home? Why she never let me leave Haven? Never let me truly leave her? She says she hated seeing me, yet she always kept me around. Was it for me or the traces of Stefan she saw in me? Was she trying to help me or herself? I have already drunk too much writing this. Tomorrow, I will talk to Momma again.

April 1989

I am not handling this very well at all. Ever since Momma told me about Daddy and Stefan, my true father, and the whole lie we have been living under, I feel like I am drowning. There is not a soul I can tell about this and, even though Momma finally confessed to me, she won't talk any more about it. I try when we are alone but she calls me indecent and reminds me that Daddy just died and to leave well enough alone. Then why did she tell me?

Now I know why I've felt so out of place my whole life, like some bastard child. I represent everything that went wrong in Momma's life, and she blames me. She has kept me under her control to hurt me, to get back at me. How can she do that? Should I feel sorry for her, or maybe I should feel sorry for Daddy - I mean, Jack? But they both made their choices right?

I can remember clearly my sixteenth birthday, Mama and Daddy threw me a party on Grove Avenue. It was a time when girls wore dresses to parties and the boys wore coats. A beautiful affair. Momma put a tent on the front lawn and had it catered with lobsters for everyone. I felt so young and happy as I danced with the boys and laughed on the beach. It was when we cut the cake and opened presents that Momma and Daddy gave me my strand of pearls. I thought the necklace was the loveliest thing I had ever seen. I kissed each of them and was thinking this was the happiest day of my life. Then I heard Momma say, 'Well, they were your father's idea.' It was her tone I remember most. The disapproving edge that would forever signify the chasm between us. It was if in her eyes, I hadn't earned the pearls. I wasn't worthy enough, undeserving. Now when I look at my girls and feel the opposite, I want to give them everything. I don't want to deny them my love. I just somehow keep messing that up!

Now, Sarah has run away from me, and I feel I have ruined her the way Momma ruined me. I never was truly there for her. I was too young, too self absorbed. I did not know how to handle the loss of Thomas, how it must have felt for Sarah. Same as Momma, I suppose. I know Sarah is on the edge and I am terrified for her. But I can't control her like Momma controlled me, look how that turned out? Because I have failed, I will let Sarah make her own decisions, her own choices. Does that make me a coward? I don't know. Momma and I, we are confined to our fates, but I will give Sarah freedom, and maybe that will make a difference.

Maggie hovers like a hidden shadow around all of us now. Her instinct is good and she can sense we are all in trouble, she can feel it. I see it in her watchful eyes. Hurting, we roam through days like apparitions of ourselves. But I don't worry about Maggie. I see her go off on the sailboat and stick her face high in the wind. There is a fearlessness that we all admire in her. We need in her. I watch Momma grip to Maggie's innocence like a life boat. There is a quality about Maggie, and it is Thomas's nature I recognize, the thoughtful intelligence, the sincerity, the warmth. We selfishly keep Maggie close to us as our foghorn, our guidance in the dark waters. I think we all look at Maggie and know she will be okay. She has the best of us all, she will survive.

But I don't know how much longer I can keep going. I feel so tired again. I am tired of fighting for Momma's love, for Sarah, for myself. Now I know I never really had a chance from the start.

May 1989

That fucking bitch won't speak to me, how dare she! Every time I ask her about Stefan, she leaves the room. I called her a rotten whore and she slapped me. I feel like I am going crazy, my whole life has been her bidding. Precious Momma, her chest is filled with ice. Bitch. She called me a drunk, and I said I would rather be a drunk than a liar, at least that's honest. Oh my girls, I never have lied to my girls this way. But I did because I couldn't love them, because my mother couldn't love me. She handicapped me from the start. I did not kill Stefan, I was three!! How can you hate your child!!!

Momma could.

I don't hate my children. I love them but I am not good for them. I'm not good for anybody. I didn't matter enough, I shouldn't be here, Stefan should. She kept me around to remind her of him, but what if I go, what if I leave, for good. Then I will take away from her everything she took away from me...

FIFTEEN

The house finally began to stir with the expectations for the day, as David and Marten were making friendly conversation in the kitchen over rolls and coffee. Sarah's never-ending nausea had her trapped in the bathroom upstairs. And Maggie was showering before the caterers arrived.

Under the hot water, Maggie's mind was still curiously seeking the mystery man who had come to see her mother that night. Today, she needed to find him and understand what happened her mother. Maggie did not like the missing pieces to her mother's death. When in doubt, Marten told her to go over the facts and make a list. Fact one: Vivian was not legally intoxicated according to the autopsy. Fact two: She was aware enough to try and stop from from falling thus her broken wrists. Fact three: There was a man here sometime that night, who left on a bicycle. Then Uncle Johnny mentions the diamond jewelry. Could that have been a motive for murder? Could her mother have been pushed down the stairs? Lastly, there was her mother's diary. According to the last entries, Maggie was certain her mother had no intention of dying right now. So what really happened?

Toweling herself off, she talked to herself in the mirror. Should I tell someone? No, everyone will just think I'm crazy. I need proof, so today I will question every person at the funeral to find out where they were that night. Someone must know. Maggie felt good about that assumption and now had a purpose to the day, other than the real one.

When Maggie came downstairs, the caterers were setting up tables on the porch, and the bar had been laid out like an altar. Even though it was only 10 a.m., she made herself a screwdriver. She figured if it looked like orange juice no one would notice. Thankfully the weather was going to cooperate for the afternoon, but a storm was expected to blow in from the North for the next few days. Standing in the last of the sunshine she thought *yes, the sun should retire for the day*. Warmth and light seemed so inappropriate for a funeral. The thick layer of gray clouds would keep her mind steady and still for the day's events.

Marten came out onto the porch looking gorgeous. He brought his best Armani suit, and Maggie thought he looked perfect.

"Well, aren't we a pair, I'm in Dior." Maggie leaned up and kissed him to show her appreciation for being there.

"And you are into the booze, I see. I think I will join you myself. I really don't relish these days," Marten said with a wayward sigh. Maggie remembered he had already done this for his parents, and the memories would be painful as well.

"I'm sorry, honey, are you okay? " Marten put his arm around her. "Don't you worry about me. I'll have this fascinating family to watch and keep my mind occupied."

Maggie used that as an opening to tell him about Uncle Johnny's visit that morning. She hinted that the jewelry may be someone's motive to hurt to Vivian but Marten was not taking the bait. He stood there silently sipping his drink. Either he was clueless to Maggie's insinuations, or he was ignoring her craziness completely. Maggie figured it was the latter.

They were interrupted by Millie dragging Archie up the porch stairs. "Damn woman, I'm coming!" Archie hugged Maggie and shook Marten's hand. Archie was a gruff old fisherman without a mean bone in his body. He griped and complained about everything, but he was the first to hug and the last to let go. As a child, Maggie was fascinated by his calloused, gnarled hands worn by years of pulling a fishing line. Now she found herself reaching out to hold one, just to touch the weathering old man.

Archie obliged and, without words, conveyed he was there for her. Maggie's affection for the old salty dog ran deep inside her.

When banished to Millie and Archie's house, it was Archie who Maggie enjoyed playing with the most. Instead of Barbie dolls and Easy Bake ovens, Maggie preferred the Legos and car sets Archie bought her. Maggie was not a dress-up kind of girl and loved sitting on the floor with Archie building little plastic cities and running race cars around tracks. Millie never interrupted them knowing how Archie found immense joy in Maggie. Archie was never a talker but, what he did say, always had meaning.

Archie would say, "Maggie, you are in the salt, kid." It was an old fishing term that roughly meant you are in the thick of things. When a fisherman is out on the water, with the gritty salt in the air, the ocean can consume them. Every part of them holds and breaths and tastes the bitter sand of the sea. It was Archie's way of saying Maggie was in the rough of it but, hopefully soon, she would sail back to shore. The term for Maggie said it all.

"I'm in the salt, Arch." Maggie now turned and looked him in the eye. Her own eyes starting to glisten.

"I know you are, kid. I know you are." He understood and that was all Maggie needed. They both paused for a moment and let the truth of it stand.

"What are we drinking? Not too early for a snort, is it!" Archie said loud enough to reach Millie, who was ordering the caterers around. Millie turned and gave him a *don't you dare* look. Archie started chuckling and poured himself a snitch of scotch. "I assume I'm not drinking alone?" Archie winked at Maggie's and Marten's screwdrivers in their hands.

"No, sir. No, sir indeed." Marten answered and all three of them clinked their glasses.

"You know, Maggie, your mother was a helluva fisherwoman." Maggie had forgotten that her mother and Archie fished in Haven's yearly derby. Every September, after the tourists had waved goodbye for the summer, the town of Haven had a fishing derby for its residents. Archie and Vivian would hit the seas for two weeks of competitive fishing and, on occasion, won a division or two. It was after Grandpa Jack died that Vivian started fishing as a sort of homage to him. She'd once told Maggie that every time she reeled in a fish, she understood her father a little better. Through the solace of the ocean and the satisfaction of the catch, Vivian could find the same joy her father found.

"She really did love fishing with you, Archie, because it made her think about Grandpa Jack. But mostly, she said you guys spent the day laughing about everyone else out there."

"Yeah, well, she always brought a few good jokes and a box of eclairs. And real orange soda, none of that diet crap Millie makes me drink. " Maggie saw tears in his eyes and knew Archie was going to miss her mother more than others would realize. Vivian had that charm over people. She could connect with them, make them laugh. It was a charm she did not use often enough.

Sarah and David joined everyone downstairs and Maggie felt a little guilty about drinking. But hell, Sarah was a big girl, right? Maggie was just glad she had a drink in hand when Uncle Johnny returned with Aunt Essie.

"Hello everyone! Thought it best to join you if we are all walking to the church," Uncle Johnny bellowed. Maggie instantly became irritated. He was making a show of family and now was he trying to play the head of it? Everyone exchanged knowing glances, the consensus being to let Uncle Johnny act like an ass and just ignore him.

"This isn't New Orleans, Johnny, there is no marching band." Maggie could not help but quip.

"Yes, yes, but we should all be together." Uncle Johnny swirled his arms about in the air as if one for all, all for one.

Marten leaned over to Maggie and whispered, "If this is the first act, can't wait for the second." And Maggie elbowed him in the ribs as she did introductions of Marten and David to Johnny and Essie. Essie immediately cornered Marten and began regaling him with her tales of her one and only trip to Germany. It was a cruise, actually, and in total she spent maybe 6 hours in the Hamburg Harbor. But still it gave her enough to talk and talk and talk about. Maggie winked at him and refilled his glass.

Everything was falling into swing as Maggie began to feel a little buzzed from the vodka. There was still a few more minutes before they left for the church, so she went inside to check her make up. She had almost forgotten her mother's urn sitting on the table and picked it up on the way to the powder room. She decided Vivian was going to stay with her for the day. Again, Maggie began to think about her mother's mysterious death. Could it have been Archie? He lives next door and obviously adored her mother. No, that's crazy, Maggie thought. Besides, why would he bike to their house? Okay, not Archie. And what about Johnny? Would he have come over and attacked her mother for jewelry? He hated Vivian, no question, but could that have been a motive? Maggie held up her mother's urn and said, "Speak to me, Mom."

Outside George and Mitzi finally showed up, Mitzi looking like a little black teapot. All three of their children were in miniature dark blue blazers and khaki pants like George. It was typical of Mitzi to match all her boys. Actually, Maggie thought it was pretty cute. George came over and punched her arm.

"Ow, what are we ten, G'?" Maggie said rubbing her arm.

"What, you can't take it anymore, Little Red?" That was the Indian name he had given her when they were kids building teepees in the forest.

"Bite me. So did you notice the big red and yellow tent over the house because the circus is all here." Maggie waved her hand in front of all the people on the porch.

"It wouldn't be a party over here without the sign that said 'Freak show'" George snickered.

"Hey, G', do you know who came over the night, you know, the night when Mom fell?" Maggie asked. George was silent and took a swig of the beer he had opened. "George, we don't keep secrets from each other, so don't start now. If you know something…"

"Naw, Mags, I don't know anything. Mitz said something about someone being here the other day. But you know me, if I didn't see it with my own eyes, then I sure as shit should not be talking about it. I don't know what or who Mitzi saw, if there was anybody. But just let it be Mags. Today is about your Mom, and you need to focus on that."

Maggie stood swaying with a cocktail in one hand, urn in the other, and guessing he was only telling her half the truth. He may not have seen anything, but George knew something, and she was going to find out what. Just then, Uncle Johnny began commanding everyone to begin the walk to the church.

"That man is an asshole. He isn't speaking is he?" George asked.

"God no, I asked Mac to give the eulogy. Sarah and I decided we would be too much of a mess if we had to get up in front of everyone." Maggie knew that Mac would write something graceful and elegant, capturing the essence of her mother better than they could. They had never exactly been in love with their mother. Mac was, as usual, humbled by the honor. The ceremony would be simple with quick prayers, a couple of hymns, and Mac.

It was becoming a family tradition to have modest funerals, but Maggie had a little twist for today.

Grace Episcopal Church was a quaint New England building, cedar shingled, and only a story and half high. The Puritanism of early America echoed in the architecture, with stained glass windows and a discreet cross embedded over the door. If one did not look left while driving by, you would have never have known there was a church at all, or the sign for five dollar lobster rolls every Friday.

When Maggie arrived, she was surprised to see how many people were milling about. Immediately, she spotted Bill Getty in his impeccable three piece suit and Hermes orange tie. He was talking to a handsome, older man, also flawlessly dressed. Maggie recognized Peter, Vivian's second husband, with the same giddiness and affection she had for him when she was five years old.

Peter had made a fortune during the early development of the cellular phone technologies. He had transformed from an alcoholic to workaholic. He never married after Vivian but was known to have a string of actress and model type girlfriends. Nobody knew that Maggie had kept in touch with him occasionally over the years. Wherever she lived, whenever Peter blew into town he would take Maggie out to a fabulous dinner and ask a million questions about Vivian. Peter never stopped loving her, either one of them, but he could not live with Vivian's drinking. He was not the acquiescing type like Mac. He liked moving at his own pace, a little too focused on himself. But it made him a very successful and very rich man.

Maggie broke free from her family and hugged both Bill and Peter. She introduced them to Marten, and seeing the three of them together, so finely dressed, it looked like a meeting on Wall Street. Bill and Peter immediately looked down at the urn in Maggie's arms.

"What?! Don't you think Mom wants to join this party?" Maggie asked, making a mock face.

"No, your mother would never miss a party nor would I miss one for her," Peter said, kissing the top of Maggie's head and squeezing her shoulders. Maggie immediately began to tear up and all three of the men, terrified of her melting down, rushed her inside.

Walking up the aisle, Maggie could see Officer Lou Mayhew with his father, Chief Frank Mayhew. They were dressed in full uniform out of respect. Maggie also saw her mother's hairdresser Justin, Mrs. Hanes, and the other ladies from Garden Club and such charities, as well as the Atwoods' longtime gardener, Bart and his partner

T.K.. There were so many faces from her past. Vivian was more outgoing in Haven than Maggie's grandmother, and the locals found her charm infectious. These were the people who did not see her late at night, and if they did, never held it against her.

The front pews were taken up by George and Mitzi and their boys, Millie and Archie, and Peter and Bill. Essie and Johnny sat in the front row on one side with Mac, Maggie, Sarah, Marten and David on the other. Millie made sure to sit right behind Maggie and Sarah so she could hand them tissues throughout the service.

Maggie finally let go of the urn and placed it on the altar. The church was eerily silent. They started by singing *Amazing Grace,* and the Episcopalian priest led them in the Lord's prayer. Millie then read a psalm, and Mac proceeded to the altar to eulogize his true love.

Excerpts from the Diary of Vivian Murphy Atwood September 1991

I cannot believe I'm getting married again. The past two years have been so dark, and now there is a speck of light. I don't deserve Mac, he is kind and gentle and funny. He makes me laugh and laugh, and he is so unafraid of me or us, I should say - as I am still with Momma. Mac doesn't mind. He says he never had much of a family. His mother died young so he actually likes Momma. Again, fearless. Momma gave him a run for his money, too. For the first month she ignored him, the second she bitched at him, the third she absolutely adored him. Nothing phases Mac, even my little sob stories. And he isn't interested in our money, that's for sure; I tried to buy him new clothes and they are still in the boxes upstairs! I'll have some work to do on his appearance. He thinks he is Hemingway! Maggie likes him too, which is such a relief. I trust her judgement more than anyone. It appears they both like the same music and can spend hours discussing the same books. Maggie is past needing a father, but I feel she deserves something out of this, not more pain or sadness.

I lost her after my incident, that was my biggest regret. My incident, listen to me, even now I can't say what I did! But the hardest part of the whole situation was Maggie going to boarding school. We both had surrendered ourselves to the damage I had done and neither of us argued the decision. We both agreed that it was better for her to be away from me, but it still broke my heart. When I had to walk away from that cold, cement dorm room, her eyes terrified and resigned at the same time, it left me feeling so ashamed. I know how scared she was. She had never been away from home and yet she felt like it was her duty to leave. What have I done? I kept asking myself over and over, how could I have done this to my child? Something inside of me is so broken and crucified that there are times I just can't hide it any longer. I lash out with such tempest and terror. I would never hurt Maggie or Sarah but I do hurt myself. I am so embarrassed and mortified by what I have done to them.

That is why I could never go ahead with this marriage without Maggie's approval. Sarah has not met Mac and is uninterested or angry or both about the marriage. Unlike Maggie, who has learned how to move forward, I'm afraid Sarah has learned how to live in the past. She holds on to it like a scar she needs to show everyone, for attention and sympathy. I can't blame her, I just wish she could get past it for both our sakes. We all need a place to find some joy, some humor, some life. Mac does that for me, he will do so much for me and all of us. I just know it.

SIXTEEN

In 1989, when James 'Mac' Macdonald first saw Vivian in Haven's bookstore, he stared at her for quite a long time. At 38, not only was she lovely but had refinement and maturity most women her age felt the need to mask. Leafing through self-help books, Vivian's brow was furrowed and she tapped her manicured nails against her side as she pulled out book after book. What she was looking for did not seem to be on the shelves. Mac broke from his reverie and approached her.

"If you need something to read, try this," Mac said handing her his first novel.

"Oh, yes, I read that ages ago. It was a charming book. Thank you, but no," Vivian said politely and tried to turn away from him, but Mac persevered.

"Well, you certainly don't need to read self help books. I find they only make you feel worse about yourself. You read them and suddenly realize you are more disturbed than you actually thought. They are full of terrible lies, really." Vivian chuckled and nodded her head in agreement.

"Well, I suppose. But I have run out of answers to all my great life questions, and I thought all these knowledgeable doctors could help me."

"Well, you don't need them because I am a doctor - well I have a doctorate in literature anyway, so I suppose you could consider me knowledgeable as well," he said with his most charming smile.

When he introduced himself, she recognized the name of the author he was trying to peddle. Mac laughed and said, "Isn't dating shameless self-promotion anyway?"

With little coaxing, Vivian agreed to have dinner with him but afterward Mac did not hear from Vivian for days. He left her many messages and, when she finally returned his phone call, she politely explained she just was not emotionally in the right place to date. Vivian said she had just lost her father and needed to focus on her mother. Mac assured her his door was always open but he would not pry, although he felt his heart sink.

Mac and Vivian did not meet again until late 1990. It was by chance they were both at the same fundraiser, so Mac switched the place cards so they would be seated at the same table. The gentleman that he was, Mac did not push or pry into why Vivian never pursued their relation-ship, instead seeing this as an opportunity to try again. He had realized how easy Vivian was to lose and loved the challenge of persuading her to stay. But this time around, Vivian was much more open to a relationship and within six months, Mac found himself down on one knee, so old fashioned, asking her to marry him.

Vivian was honest with Mac about her drinking, to a point. She disclosed her visits to rehab, the loss of her first two husbands, and her daughter's drug abuse, but she glossed over the more scandalous details of her past, believing she had her moods under control. Mac, who was always in good humor, saw her as a woman who endured life's tragedies, and it was no surprise that she drank excessively now and again. At their age, who didn't? Maggie warned him on the eve of their wedding that her mother's drinking could get worse, a lot worse. But Mac thought she was being an over-protective daughter and told her he could handle it. Maggie laughed and said, 'We will see about that.'

For the first couple of years, Mac could handle it. They spent a great deal of time traveling while Mac wrote books about foreign cultures. And although they lived with Virginia, all three of them kept busy and everyone was relatively content. There would be nights when Mac worried about Vivian, finally noticing how easily she became angry and disoriented. Mac learned not to react but to calm her and get her to bed. Soon he reached out to Maggie, not so much for her help, but as a confidant. Maggie explained that this was just Vivian, vivacious and loving one day, dark and nebulous the next. Neither of them could coax Vivian to get help, so they monitored her the best they could, always vigilant that she did not harm herself. Mac and Maggie had assigned themselves the task of chaperones; it was the price of loving an alcoholic mother and wife. The first lesson in co-dependency, you can't save someone else, and you don't bother to save yourself.

Years passed and, like life, some times were better than others. Mac stayed true to Vivian and over time his love deepened. Every time Sarah was in trouble, Vivian would pull herself together and not touch a drop to drink. She would throw herself at saving her daughter, and Mac would feel such compassion and admiration for a mother so deeply lost with her daughter. Once, Mac wrote a book about a touching mother-daughter relationship, but Vivian asked him not to publish it. She told Mac that, while she was honored to be his muse, her story was her story and not for public amusement. People in Haven would know it was about her and Sarah. Mac again acquiesced to his love for her and shelved one of the most poetic books he had ever written.

Then Virginia's memory lapses became notice-able. Her usually sharp mind and tongue quieted. She no longer lashed out over the politics in the morning news-paper, and she forgot important events that required her presence. She withdrew to her room most days and drank her gin with abandon. Vivian blamed it on the alcohol, but Virginia was in the early stages of Alzheimer's dis-ease. Deep down she knew it. But Virginia did not share her fears and thought better if people excused her ab-sence of mind due to alcohol. Eventually, Mac and Vivian caught on and forced Virginia to see doctors.

Vivian decided Virginia should stay at home as long as she could and set up a mini private hospital at their house. Vivian hired nurses and moved a hospital bed into her room. But while Virginia received the best care the family money could buy, it could not stop the deterio-ration of her mind. Easily confused, Virginia began to mistake Mac for her long dead husband, Stefan. She would weep when Mac entered the room, or she con-stantly asked Vivian why Jack had not come to see her. Eventually, during those dark nights of comforting a con-fused Virginia, Vivian found herself slowly telling Mac more about her past, her true story, the one her mother had kept secret all those years.

Vivian told Mac what it meant to her to find out that Jack was not her real father, and that she'd believed she killed her biological father, Stefan. Vivian confessed to her suicide attempts and her constant struggle with her weaknesses. Mac, never judgmental, listened as the walls crumbled down between them. It was a somber time for Vivian, watching her mother's mind fade to dust. She was reflective and thoughtful and clung to Mac like the husband she had so desperately wanted all those years. Although the situation with Virginia was bleak, the closer Mac and Vivian became, the more they enjoyed each other. She doted on him and encouraged his writing and he remained by her side.

But there were nights that were long and dark for the two of them. Neither Virginia's living nor her dying eased Vivian's troubled mind. Days, weeks could pass when Vivian could remain sober but then Mac would find her locked in their room, lost in a haze of alcohol. As Virginia's health deteriorated so did Vivian's, and those were the nights Frank Mayhew would find her weaving along country roads, lost, angry, dangerous.

Six months after Virginia died, Vivian made a surprising announcement: she asked Mac to leave. Everyone was shocked but Mac. He had seen his beautiful wife disappear to places the mind should not go. Vivian explained she needed time alone. Vivian laughed at the irony because she had always felt detached and isolated when surrounded by people. But all those years, she never had the opportunity to disassemble herself from her mother or her children. Vivian was fifty-two years old and wanted to try life unsupported and unneeded, at least for a while. She hoped the independence would help her take control of her demons.

It took all the love in his heart for Mac to walk out of Grove Avenue. Every part of his character told him to stay, to care for Vivian, to watch and keep her out of harm's way but, like he had always done, Mac honored her wishes. And regretted it to this day.

"How do you write in the past tense about the woman you love?" Mac said to the crowded church, fighting back his emotions. "To all her knew her, Vivi was a woman of unique character - kind, polite gracious and caring, a beautiful woman in every way. But that was only part of the woman I married.

Vivian had a vulnerability that was honest and a sensitivity that was tragic. Some feel the world is never enough for them, for Vivian it was too much. She had such a magnificent capability for kindness but a heart-breaking blindness to affection. I watched her fly through this life like an injured butterfly, strong, determined but damaged. She never wished ill on anyone but herself. I wanted to turn and run away so many times, but the gravity of love was heavier. She had a light inside that entranced me, and I broke the rules to be with her. Why? Because when Vivian laughed, you heard it echo off the ocean. When she talked about her daughters, you heard sunshine. When she gave you something, it was big, like a piece of her heart she had wrapped just for you. Every summer her garden reflected what was beautiful and natural about her. And that was what we all saw in Vivian, her natural beauty inside and out. But it was her bitter frailty, her whispering sadness that I should have bartered for peace. But I didn't even try. It was who she was, why she laughed and loved and cried, why she cared so greatly about all those around her, why she loved me.

Vivian used to tell me, you're the world to me because you take me as I am and that cannot be easy. No, loving Vivian didn't come easy for any of us, but we did because touching the sun isn't easy. And now we must say goodbye to our beloved one, who taught us the only weapon against our own humanity is compassion,

compassion for ourselves, for each other, and mostly for our Vivi. I hope you know how much we loved you."

When Mac finished the eulogy, the silent reverence was palpable in the room. No one doubted Mac's love for Vivian nor Vivian's imprint on this world. Both Maggie and Sarah hugged Mac coming down from the pulpit. Those who were strong enough to hold their tears at first, quietly cried at the sight of the bereaved family. Maggie still had one special tribute for her mother.

From the side altar emerged three very large, very black gospel singers in bright blue and gold robes. There was a murmur throughout the church, as the trio of gospel singers was an unusual sight for the predominantly white Episcopalian funeral service. The women began to sing an acapella version of Ashford & Simpson's *Ain't No Mountain High Enough*.

Maggie beamed in the church pew as she recalled her most favorite memory. Mac and Vivian had thrown a twenty first birthday party for her on Grove Avenue, and it was a party to remember. It was a cold February night. George and her college friends were there and even Sarah, sober. As the the wind howled outside, the living room pulsed with Motown and Funk, keeping beat with dancing bodies. Even Virginia found herself being swung around the room by Mac to Ray Charles. Maggie had never laughed so hard at the sight.

Then her mother stopped the music, and Maggie had expected a cake of some sort, but Vivian, Sarah and Millie emerged from the kitchen donning gigantic black wigs and pink satin gloves. Doing her best Diana Ross impression, her mother was lip syncing *Ain't no Mountain High Enough*. Virginia, who'd originally refused to be a part of the trio, joined in as well. There they were, the supreme women of Maggie's life, belting out the words.

The light in Vivian's eyes that night was irreplaceable, the words they all sang were so true to their heart: *to keep me from you.*

Maggie had surprised everyone in the church with the musical tribute, especially Millie and Sarah who also remembered that night fondly. Hearing the music washed them of their tears and the service ended with everyone feeling satiated that Vivian had been loved and honored. Groups of mourners exited the church and began the short walk back to Grove Avenue. Maggie felt herself caught up in the tide while she greeted old friends of the family and thanked everyone for thoughtful condolences. People tried not to stare, but they could not help but notice the football hold on her mother's urn.

SEVENTEEN

The reception reached full swing with in minutes of everyone having a cocktail. Maggie and Sarah stood side by side greeting old friends and receiving their kindnesses. All the while Maggie scanned faces and looked hopefully for her mystery man. Lou and Frank Mayhew approached, and Maggie joked with Lou about his upcoming wedding to lighten the mood. Chief Mayhew hugged Maggie hard and surprisingly, said how fond he was of Vivian. Immediately, Maggie's instinct went up. Was her mother having an affair with Chief Mayhew? His wife Wendy, Lou's Mother, had passed away years ago from breast cancer. Maggie took the opportunity to hold onto the chief's arms.

"Chief Mayhew, did you have a soft spot for my mother?" Maggie would not let go of arms, waiting until he answered.

"Oh, yes. When Lou's mother was going through chemotherapy, Vivian came to the house almost everyday with vegetables from her garden or books for Wendy to read. And when Wendy lost all her energy, Vivian made sure a maid came to clean the house, and there was always food in the fridge. Your mother helped us out during the worst time in my life and, well, we were so grateful." Chief Mayhew saw the confused look on Maggie's face.

"I suppose your mother did it because she felt indebted to me, but really she shouldn't have. I guess I can tell you now, there were a few nights I found your mother driving on the road when she shouldn't have. You see, I grew up with your mother here in Haven and, well, I always had a crush on her. But everyone did. When we were in elementary school, your mother was the prettiest and funniest girl in school. I always had problems with English class, and your mother would help me write the essays. She was such a sweet girl. Wendy was in a class behind us, and we all remember Vivian. She had a light around her. We all thought she would grow up and be famous, do something beyond Haven. After Vivi left for boarding school, no one saw her until she returned to Grove Avenue with you two girls. Well, she was a changed woman, the world had done something to her. It was not just losing your Daddy, there was something sad inside her. So when your mother went on her "bouts", shall we say, those of us who knew her, we wanted to take care of her. And, from time to time, I would have to help her out with your sister as well. So I guess, when the problems started with Wendy, your mom saw it as an opportunity to return the favor. But she never had too. We loved her, we had always loved her."

Maggie was speechless. There seemed to be so many details about her mother she never knew. She'd rarely imagined her mother as a child before her father and Sarah. But she was a little girl who had grown up in Haven, and people knew and loved her. Maggie hugged Chief Mayhew again and let it linger. He had given her another piece of her mother. Of course, now she knew the Chief was not the one who came to the house that night. In million years, he would never hurt Vivian.

The receiving line broke up and Maggie was dying for a cigarette. Marten had kept her screwdriver filled so she was feeling a slight, pleasant buzz. Carrying the urn in one hand and a drink in the other, Maggie went to find Peter.

"Hey, old man, got a smoke for me?" Maggie asked of Peter.

"Sure kid, let's go over there. Are you going to carry your mother around all night?"

"Why not?" Maggie shrugged playfully. After they lit up, "Peter, can I ask you something?"

"Shoot, kid."

"When was the last time you talked to Mom?"

"Oh, let's see. It was after her trip to New York. She had called my apartment when, shall we say, she was a little more than distraught." Peter was being polite and not saying her mother was dead drunk.

"But I was in London and didn't get the message until later. Your mother never figured to call my cell phone. Ironic huh, since that was my line of work. Anyway, when I called her back a few weeks later she explained everything that happened between you two. I let her talk. She wanted me to listen but, like always, I never knew what to do for her."

"Yeah, well, I suppose she told you about our big fight. She showed up drunk to visit me, and I lost it. I haven't spoken to her since, and now look."

"Maggie, don't go there. You were in self-preservation mode. You know how much I loved Vivian, but her drinking turned her into another person: mean, angry, bitter. I did not want to spend my life being the backboard to her hits. Do I regret it? A little, but that's just the way life goes. You make your decisions and stand by the consequences."

"I suppose. I guess, now, I don't really have a choice." Maggie sighed.

"Nope, but I will personally kick your behind if you live the rest of your life beating yourself up over it." Peter squeezed her shoulder.

"So you have not seen Mom in the past couple of years, not at all?" Maggie pushed him a little further.

"Nope, I've been in London and Tokyo a lot. My company keeps splitting, merging all the time. All I know is that I've got a shit-load of money but gray hair to show for it." Peter and Maggie laughed at his little joke. They both wanted to get off the subject of Vivian. Maggie felt for sure Peter had not seen Vivian but she was running out of options of who was at the house that night.

"Peter, what did Mom ever tell you about Uncle Johnny? "

"Oh, your mother never had to tell me anything, I saw it all in person. Vivian and I used to laugh about Johnny, a real piece of work and, from the looks of it, still is. You know, when Vivian brought me home, your grandmother and grandfather liked me. I guess I was the man they had envisioned for their baby girl. And for awhile, if you can remember, it was good between all of us. Life was full of dinners and fishing trips, like a family. Well, Johnny became intensely jealous that your grandparents were paying so much attention to us. He was in his early twenties and should have been off seeing the world, but he still clung to his parents. Or more to their money, God forbid he go off and try to make his own.

Yeah, Johnny's insolence was written all over him, so I really had no time or respect for him, and there were a couple of run-ins between us. Johnny remembers, and that is likely why he hasn't said howdy to me today." Peter winked at her and gave her a smirk.

"Yeah, I never particularly cared for my uncle's company either. Since I have been home, he has been sniffing around here like a bloodhound on a scent. This morning I found him in the kitchen. He let himself in no less, asking me about Grandma's jewelry. He thinks Mom stashed diamonds somewhere."

"Can't say it surprises me," Peter affirmed.

"Well, do you think he would have ever hurt Mom?" Maggie raised her eyebrows at Peter.

"What? Like physically hurt her? Oh, no, Maggie. I don't think so. Your uncle is the most prostrate guy I know. He hides behind lawyers, not his fists. What? Do you think someone pushed your mother down the stairs?"

Maggie paused. She wasn't sure how to answer.

"Listen, Maggie, I know you are upset about everything, not speaking to your mother and now this, but really, I think it was accident. We all think your Uncle Johnny is a gigantic ass, but I don't think you should take it to the next level, okay kid?" Peter eyed her warily, and Maggie appeased him by nodding, still unconvinced. But her search was not over.

Maggie continued to move around the party and observe everyone. Sarah had been telling people she was pregnant and accepting congratulations. As much as Sarah has changed is as much she has stayed the same. No matter, she would search for a spotlight anywhere even though it was not meant for her. Millie was keeping the food flowing and everyone's drinks filled. Archie had the unsavory duty of keeping Aunt Essie company in the corner. He looked at Maggie, trapped and pleading, and Maggie managed to convince David to relieve Archie.

"Essie, how are you doing?" Maggie asked and

realized too late someone had given Essie a few gin and tonics. "Essie you feeling okay?"

"Jusstt fine, darrling," Essie slurred. "You know your Mama, everyone just loved your Mama. She was so sweet and good." Maggie sat David next to Essie and quickly removed herself before she was trapped into a long sentimental soliloquy. Maggie thought to herself, how did Mom turn into such a saint today? Vivian was a great person, but she also could be a real feisty bitch. Had everyone forgotten that? Maggie looked down at the urn she was still holding and said quietly laughing, "You don't fool me, Mom."

Archie thanked Maggie for the save, and she asked if he had seen Marten or George. Archie thought they had gone inside to hide, and he commented under his breath that they were smarter than he was.

"I heard that, " Maggie said as she headed into the house. Maggie was happy for the reprieve. With everyone outside, she heard voices in the kitchen and headed towards the doorway. But when she neared, she moved slowly. George and Marten were talking and instinct told her to stay back, a childhood habit of spying. She saw them drinking beers and eating deviled eggs off a tray at the kitchen table, so she quickly ducked back around the corner. She could hear George.

"How much has Mags told you about growing up here," George waved his arm in a circle, implying the house, Grove Avenue, and Haven itself.

"Honestly, not much. It seems like only what she had to, if you know what I mean." George nodded because he knew Maggie. She told people enough about her to make them feel a part of her life but, in reality, she only scratched the surface. Never details, she always said with a laugh, she would save those for the book.

"Maggie would kill me for 'over-sharing', as she says about people who talk too much, but I think you need to know a little more about how it was for her. I like you, and I think the consensus is that we all would like you to stick around. But you need to know a few things first, about Maggie and this family and why she has such a hard time talking about it." George paused, and they both looked at each other and nodded in an unspoken agreement. This conversation would be a secret from Maggie.

Maggie slid down the side of the hallway wall. As much as she hated them talking about her, she knew this had to happen. She wanted to tell Marten some of the more sordid details of her life but it was never the right time. Now George was going to do the dirty work, and Maggie sat with her head between her hands and listened to her own story.

"I will tell you about the one time I remember the most. I know it is one of the most painful memories of my childhood, so I can't imagine what it is for Maggie. It was May 1989, near the end of school, the best time of year. Maggie and I were fourteen, about to finish the eighth grade. We were scared to start high school but summer vacation was beginning and we could forget about everything for two blissful months. We were looking forward to swimming everyday, biking to town for ice cream, the stuff kids do before we were old enough to have summer jobs.

"Anyway, that day, when we got off the bus, Maggie was talking about going out sailing because a stiff spring wind was up. Of course, I had Little League practice then, so I was disappointed I couldn't join her. I still remember her laughing and saying something sarcastic about baseball and watching her swing her book bag down Grove Avenue. There is always one moment you remember right before your whole world changes. Mine is the picture of Maggie without a care in the world.

"It was just a few minutes later. My mother and I were about to get in the car to go to practice when we heard the screaming. It was the most horrible sound. Not even words. It was just a howling, over and over again. Mom and I both started running down the hill, by instinct we knew it was coming from Maggie's house. I saw the garage door open and, as soon as my eyes adjusted, I saw Maggie."

George stood and pointed to the two car garage off the kitchen, separate from the house like a little cottage decorated with hydrangeas. He grabbed two more beers and sat down again.

"It was the look on Maggie's face, so misshapen with fear and horror. I don't think I could ever know that much emotion unless perhaps I had lost one of my children." George took a long pull of beer before he resumed his story.

"Maggie was on her knees and frantically tugging at something in Vivian's Mercedes. The sound of that damn diesel engine was so loud that I was having a hard time understanding what I was looking at.

"The driver's side door was open, and Maggie was pulling at, what I finally realized, was her own mother. Vivian was slumped over and unconscious - all I saw was her red hair moving back and forth with Maggie's arms. My mother rushed forward and I just stood there, paralyzed. You have to understand, I was a fourteen year old boy from the all-American home. I just had no idea what was happening. It wasn't until later that day my mother explained suicide to me. But at that moment, all I felt was my gut turning with each of Maggie's screams."

George paused and shook his head at the memory. Maggie's screams always haunted him.

"My mom, Peggy, was the calm type and, if she was shaken, I don't remember. I watched amazed as she pulled Vivian out of the driver's side and put her in the back seat of the running car. Everything went from bad to worse as Vivian started throwing up on my mother and then Maggie. But at least then we knew she was alive. Mom grabbed Maggie by the shoulders and looked her in the eyes. And when she did, Maggie finally stopped screaming. Mom told her they were going to the hospital and Maggie needed to sit with her mother in the back seat to keep Vivian's head upright. I remember my Mom clearly saying, 'She could choke on her vomit' and then they were gone." George, again, shook his head trying to push the images away.

"It has taken me years to process that scene, much less understand what Maggie went through. I just can't. The smell of the gas haunts me. When I walk past that garage, I can still feel myself choking on it. I mean, how did Maggie know to go in the garage? We just figured she heard the car running, but what if she hadn't? What if just another hour had passed? What if she had gone straight to her sailboat? Why did Vivian time that with Maggie getting home, or maybe Maggie wasn't supposed to be home that early? I look at my 8 year old son and try to comprehend him going through something like that at fourteen. It is unimaginable to me. It is unimaginable that I would do that to him." George took another long pull on his beer as his thoughts deepened.

"What happened after that?" Marten asked.

"That night, Maggie didn't stay with Millie like usual but at our house. I think Mom needed to be with Maggie as much as Maggie needed to be with us. We had all survived something horrible together. As for the rest of them, Maggie's grandfather had already passed, and Virginia was out at bridge club that afternoon when it happened. My dad had to go find her and tell her what had happened."

"When Maggie came home from the hospital, Mom immediately put her in my room to sleep, so I didn't get to talk to her at first. I was so innocent. Mom and Dad had to explain to me what happened, what did I know about carbon monoxide poisoning? They told me how I had to be there for Maggie, support her, be her friend. I may not have understood what happened, but I knew I had to be right by her side. When Maggie woke up, she was so quiet, it scared me. I don't think I was three feet away from her all night. I wasn't going to let anything bad happen to her ever again, at fourteen, I thought I could protect her forever."

"Mom ordered pizza, which she never did, and let us stay up watching television. I still remember we watched the James Bond film *Goldfinger*. I can't ever see the movie without thinking of that day. Afterwards, Maggie and I slept in the same room, and then she finally spoke."

"Lying in the dark, she was able to tell me what happened at the hospital. She explained how my mom had talked her through the car ride, saying over and over that it would be okay, but Vivian just kept throwing up on her. Maggie said it felt like she couldn't breathe the whole way. She said all she could do was focus on the blur of the trees passing by, like time had stopped. When they reached the doors of the emergency room, my mom told Maggie to get out of the car and walk away for a bit. Mom would not allow Maggie to go inside the hospital. Maggie watched as doctors and nurses rushed out and put Vivian on a gurney and disappeared through the doors with her mother. All she could do was sit outside alone on the curb next to the car. She wondered if she would ever see her mother again. Finally, my mom came out and led her into the waiting room. Now that I am older, I understand what my mother did. She was trying to protect Maggie from seeing the doctors pump and resuscitate her mother, to save her from one more horror that day."

Maggie remembers that day exactly as George told it, only she relives the feel of her mother. Vivian felt limp and lifeless in her arms, heavy. Maggie had so much adrenaline pumping though her that the whole memory seems to have taken place in less than a minute in her mind.

"Maggie said her grandmother eventually showed up with my father, and she was angry, which shocked Maggie. Maggie had watched everyone else be too scared to be angry. Her grandmother grabbed her and hugged her and leaned right in her face, pointing at her chest saying, 'I love you, okay. I love you.' But then she stormed away, charging between the swinging doors like a general, looking for Vivian."

"The last thing I remember from that night was Maggie asking, 'George, why does she do this?' I didn't know and all these years later, I still can't answer her question. "

"You see, that's what eats at Maggie. She feels like they did all the hurtful things to her. She can't separate their actions from their love for her. Somehow, some way, she needs to answer that question for herself, the why."

Hearing George, Maggie nodded her head quietly in agreement.

"But what happened after that night?" Marten asked.

"A couple of weeks later, Virginia announced that Maggie would go to boarding school in the fall. It was strange. Usually Maggie was so outspoken about anything concerning Maggie and she just seemed to oblige. I knew she did not want to leave. Maggie felt responsible for 'saving' her mother, like something was going to happen to her mother if she wasn't around. My mom mentioned to me that Maggie had interceded her mother's suicides twice before. This wasn't the first time. I was horrified. So there Maggie was, 14 years old and feeling responsible for keeping her mother alive. Again, now that I have kids I could never, never imagine placing that burden on them. At 14, my biggest concern was getting a teenage girl down to the pier at night and, frankly, I want the same for my boys."

"So, I don't understand Maggie's grandmother in all this. Maggie talks about her like she was the greatest influence on her life, this tough old broad with a heart of gold. But their family was, well, so screwed up?" This time Marten got up and got two more beers.

Maggie was still sitting out in the hallway, picking at the edge of her dress.

"Oh yes, Jack and Virginia Murphy-quite frankly, they scared the shit out of me. All I knew about Jack was when he wasn't out fishing, he was sitting in that den out there drinking and watching the water. He rarely ever spoke to us kids, which was fine by me. I think he died not long before that incident with Vivian.

"Virginia was a tough old broad. She was the spitting image of Vivian and Maggie, same height, really skinny though. I always thought I could break her in half, but she radiated this strength, like a steel pipe. And just like Vivian, she dyed her hair its original reddish-blonde color and never went gray. Her and Vivian always wore this red lipstick. I used to joke with Maggie that they were actually twins and if she put on lipstick they could be triplets. If you noticed, Maggie never wears lipstick."

"Yeah, you're right." Marten nodded his head.

"Anyway, Virginia was pretty in her day, just as Vivian was, just as Maggie is-although Maggie never realizes it. But something must have gone sour for Virginia because she was not a sweet old woman like our neighbor Millie. When Virginia drank her gin, she could slice you in half. But she loved Maggie, I mean really loved her. They took these endless walks on the beach, and Virginia always encouraged her writing. She introduced her to authors in Boston, always talked to her about politics, the arts, et cetera. She really wanted Maggie to make something of herself. Virginia was the only one who could have talked Maggie into boarding school. But after Maggie left, well, we didn't see much of Virginia. Some people, when they get old, just seem to turn a corner and age really fast. But when Maggie went away, I didn't pay much attention to what was happening down the street."

"But where was Sarah during all this?"

"You have to remember Sarah is five years older than Maggie. When we were just kids, Sarah was already in high-school and left the house by the time Maggie was twelve. What I do remember of Sarah wasn't good. Hung out with a rough crowd and caused a lot of chaos in their house. Sometimes I'd look out my window and see a cop car bringing her home. They had tried to send her to boarding school, but she failed out her first year. And by the time she was seventeen, they sent her to rehab in Rhode Island. She wasn't around much after that. Again, at that age, Maggie didn't want to talk about anything going on in her house. We just went sailing, rode our bikes, stuff like that. Maggie always tried to be normal and, looking back, Maggie was the toughest of them all."

Maggie began to cry out in the hall and decided she could not listen to George and Marten anymore. She loved George so much for doing what she could not do, talk. And she loved Marten for listening, but it was all too much. She escaped back to the living room without them knowing she was ever there.

George spent the next hour telling Marten the stories he knew about Vivian and Virginia. George, never one to gossip, stuck to the facts and tried to paint an accurate picture for Marten. Marten started to understand how Maggie's home was filled with alcohol and drug abuse, which brought out the sadness in everyone. But there were some good times as well. Maggie had come from a world of extremes. George explained how one day her mother would be planning a party and the next, silently drinking herself to sleep in a locked room. Maggie lived with the uncertainty of every new day during her childhood and now was paying a price as an adult.

George said, "She's overly cautious and scared to death of anyone able to get close enough to hurt her again. She had trusted her family, loved them with everything she had, but she had to watch them die a little everyday by their own will."

"Yeah, I noticed." Marten said with deep sadness, thinking of the emotional gulf between him and Maggie.

"For example, my mom insisted Maggie stay home from school the day after the incident but she refused. Maggie was determined to get back to her normal life and that one night be just a a blip, a momentary unplanned event. Her mother was alive, everyone was fine, so they should get on with the show. Mom apparently called ahead to the school knowing there would be rumors around Haven, so Maggie was excused from homework and quizzes without question. Instead, Maggie found herself assuring her teachers she was fine and desperately wished they would not make a big deal of it in front of her classmates. She told me the principal, Mr. Montgomery, called her in with a pitying look on his face and that just angered Maggie more. Maggie wanted everyone to leave her alone and thought what went on at home was her private business. She learned that from her grandmother, as long as they could get up in the morning and put on their pants, they were fine."

"We wanted to help, and tried any way we could, but Maggie was always so stubborn. Her grandmother called it stoicism." George rolled his eyes in disapproval.

George and Marten agreed the pressure the family had placed on Maggie had done its damage. Though both of them admired her strength, her inability to accept help wore them both down.

Shaking old thoughts out of her head, Maggie left the boys in the kitchen and headed back outside to the bar. She had been talking to Bill Getty when they both heard the loud crash. Her and Bill looked at each other in surprise and immediately rushed into the house. It was almost the climatic moment Maggie had been waiting for when she saw two cowboy boots waving in the air at the bottom of the stairs. There was Uncle Johnny lying on his back. She assumed he had tripped down the stairs, but seconds later Peter appeared at the landing holding his fist in the air shouting, "You son of a bitch!" Bill Getty's arm shot out, holding Maggie back. Marten and George appeared from the kitchen, and others began to pile in through the porch door to check out the commotion.

"What are you doing, man! Hey, this is *my* house!" whimpered Uncle Johnny struggling to roll himself upright. Peter jumped the last two steps and grabbed the front of Johnny's shirt. Maggie assumed he was going to pull him up; instead, he held him at arms length and punched him full force in his face. Everyone gasped.

Uncle Johnny went down again as Peter towered over him holding his right hook in the air.

Bleeding from his nose, Johnny screamed like a girl, "You're gonna pay for that man! Chief Mayhew! Hey, Chief! Get your ass in here and arrest this jerk for assault and battery. I wanna press full charges!"

Chief Mayhew was already at the doorway and walked to the center of the room. "John Junior, looks like you took a nasty spill from those stairs. Careful now, that is why we are all here today. Millie, would you be a dear and get the man some ice for his nose."

Frank then paused and put his hands on his hips. Slowly, he scratched his face and turned to Peter, "Now, seems the starter on my car is not working quite right to-day. Peter would you mind coming outside with me and seeing to it?"

Everyone stood stone still in the living room and waited to see what would happen next. Eventually Peter lowered his fist, straightened his jacket, and stepped over Johnny to follow Chief Mayhew. "Sure, Chief, be glad to," Peter said casually as if nothing happened. As they walked past Maggie, whose mouth was wide open, Chief May-hew nodded and gave her a little wink. Peter kissed her on the top of her head and whispered to her, "I'll tell you later."

After they left, no one helped Johnny off the floor, and Millie threw him a bag of frozen peas for his nose. Johnny pointed to Maggie and shouted, "I need to see you!" She did not like how his crazy eyes honed in on her and his stubby finger waved in the air.

"Not without us," George bellowed from the oth-er side of the room as he hit Marten's arm in solidarity.

"It's okay, guys. Come on, Uncle J," Maggie led her uncle into the kitchen as a passing George whispered, "Stay close."

Maggie got herself a beer from the fridge. "What is it you really want Johnny?"

"I don't like that tone, missy. This was my house once upon a time, and this was my family long before you came along. You need to show some respect for me and my place. You and your freaky sister in there are hiding things from me and Essie just like your mother. Don't you think I know your game? Momma was always keeping secrets, and then Vivian and you girls had the run of the house. Something was up I tell you." Johnny had his head tilted back and nose plugged with a paper towel as he paced and ranted.

"What could we possible be hiding, Uncle J, really?" Maggie responded, detesting him more each second.

"See, that tone? That tone right there! You people have always been against me. I'm gonna find that damn jewelry, I tell you. You got my house, my childhood home, but you can't have everything. Oh, don't think we all didn't see you were Momma's favorite."

"Oh my God, have you ever seen a therapist?"

"You are a disrespectful little girl, you know that!?"

"And you are a grown man trying to steal money from his dead mother and sister. Hey, why were you up-stairs anyway?" Maggie pointed back at him.

"Never you mind that, missy. Some things are rightfully mine, and I am going to get them one way or another."

"Where were you the night Mom died, Johnny?" Maggie asked with her eyes baring down on him.

"What in Sam Hill do you mean by that!?" Johnny looked right back at her.

"Just what I said. Where were you? Like, for example, oh, let me see… did you let yourself in the house the night my mom died? *That* is what I mean."

"What the hell are you implying, Margaret? For your information I hadn't seen your mother in months, and she wouldn't take my phone calls either."

"That doesn't answer my question, Uncle Johnny. Were you here that night?"

"I'll tell you right now you little bitch.." Johnny was cut off when Bill Getty appeared.

"Your mother would be ashamed of you, John Murphy Junior. But then again, she often was, wasn't she?" Bill said as he strode into the room. He leaned back on the kitchen counter, crossed his arms and fixed his stare on Johnny.

"This is none of your business, Bill. This is between me and my niece."

"No, Johnny, this is my business. In fact, it has been my business for many years, and it has made me a very rich man, or didn't you notice? Now, let me tell you why it is my problem. Virginia and Jack made it my problem. Your parents decided a long time ago how, when, and in what form each of you got your share. And you got it, John, and there is nothing more for you. So I suggest you leave this house, and these people, alone."

"I'll leave when I am good and ready." Johnny puffed up his chest.

Maggie moved closer to him, pointing her finger. "You have never been good, Uncle Johnny but I can tell you this, you are damn well ready. This house is officially mine, and if you ever step foot in it again uninvited, I have a whole police force that would be more than happy to escort you off the premises."

"I think you heard the lady," Bill stood too and began to walk closer to Johnny. As he began to back out of the door way, George and Marten, who had been sentries just outside, blocked his exit. "Can I get your coat?" George said with a smirk.

Johnny huffed out of there like a steam train and all four of them had a laugh. They returned to the party without Uncle Johnny and focused on Aunt Essie, who had passed out next to David ages ago. Afraid to disturb her, David stayed trapped between Essie and the end of the couch and missed the whole show. Eventually, George, Marten and Archie managed to lift Essie and move her inside to the downstairs guest room.

Finally, Peter returned to the porch too, and he was quite jovial. The Chief beeped his siren a couple of times after dropping him off in the driveway.

Maggie looked at him, "Now what was that all about?"

"Kid, let's talk-but first pour the old man something because I am mourning the love of my life, " Peter said as he slumped on the outdoor sofa.

"You don't drink, Peter," Maggie said surprised.

"I know, you got soda water don't you?" He laughed at Maggie.

Peter leaned across the table to Mac, "Hope you don't mind me saying, Mac, but you were the lucky bastard who stuck around."

"Peter, you know I could never be jealous of a fool." Both men deeply laughed and Maggie thought, my God, was every man in love with my mother?

Maggie pulled up a club chair between the two of them after refreshing their drinks. She turned to Peter, "Begin from the beginning please."

The few who were left, Millie and Archie, Bill Getty, Marten, Sarah and David, and George all gathered to the couches, wanting to hear what had happened between Peter and Johnny. Everyone there was considered family, so Maggie encouraged Peter to share with all of them.

Peter addressed both Maggie and Sarah.

"There was a lot that happened in that short amount of time I was with your mother. You see, I don't know if you girls knew it, but I was desperately in love with your mother. Vivi was just the spunkiest, wittiest girl I had ever met. I wasn't from the nicest part of town, and I hadn't run into to many girls like her. Early on, I was determined to make something of myself. I had a few brain cells and made it to college on scholarship. But I had my demons and kept screwing myself up from the bottom of a bourbon bottle. I met your mother during my second trip to rehab."

"Well, she was the red in my gray world. All of her class and education, she was smart as a whip, I tell you. Women did not look like her where I had come from. She reminded me of Audrey Hepburn but acted like Katherine Hepburn. Your mother had this endearing fragility about her. She wanted so desperately to be loved and to give love. It was, well, intoxicating."

"I knew how wealthy your grandparents were and how they'd view me as a vulture. But I never took a dime from your grandfather, not for dinner, not even for fishing. I would even pay for the gas on his boat. If I came to the house for dinner, I brought Virginia her favorite gin and flowers. I never showed up here empty-handed."

"Well, your bottom-feeding uncle, who was seriously sponging off your grandparents at the time, did not look too kindly on me. Called me a show-off under his breath and started calculating right from the start how to discredit me. Johnny would whisper to Virginia how he could smell liquor on my breath, implying I shouldn't have been around you two girls. But my parents, just a school janitor and housekeeper, raised me with manners, and that's what your grandparents saw. God bless them.

"Whatever Johnny did, your grandparents ignored because they truly wanted Vivian and I to work out. And

I did too, so I dove into my work. I wanted to provide for your mom and you girls. I didn't want children of my own, but I liked you girls. You were ready made, and I could handle that.

"Vivi didn't like me being gone so much, and I tried to explain to her that I was working for all of us. But I guess she had been down that road with your Dad and well, Vivi wanted a husband. She wanted someone home at night to watch T.V. and mow the lawn on the weekends, and I wasn't that kind of guy. But I thought there could be a compromise between us. Maybe one day, I would be rich enough to give you all everything you wanted. Vivian wasn't buying it, she wanted immediate satisfaction. I thought I could handle your mom, make her see it my way, but then your Uncle Johnny got involved."

Everyone was captivated around the porch. Maggie and Sarah re-lived their own memories of that time.

"Well, every time I came to Haven, Johnny would magically appear at the house. He ratted Vivian out about her drinking, detailing to me her binges. Unfortunately, I already had my suspicions. But his disloyalty, the seediness of wanting to ruin his sister, always disgusted me. I tried my best to ignore Vivian's drinking, but I could not dismiss it. It just wasn't the life I wanted to lead. I could not weather any more bad times while waiting for the good. My company was on the verge of a breakthrough in cell phone technology and I had to see my own ambition through. It was my dream to honor my father and mother and never wear uniforms like they did. I wish Vivi could have understood that, but she didn't. So I let her go. She knew my door was always open if she was sober, truly sober. But I never got *that* call. Over the years, I would get other phone calls from her but only when she had been drinking, and it broke my heart.

Peter paused in sadness and continued.

"That piece of shit Johnny has never sat right with me. He wasn't what caused Vivian and I to break up; I won't give him have that credit. He never could do anything for anyone but himself." Everyone nodded in agreement.

"So tonight, sitting right here on this couch, I happened to see him go upstairs. And I thought to myself, now why would Johnny be going upstairs? So for shits and giggles, I followed him and found him in Maggie's room." Maggie's mouth dropped open because she thought Peter was going to say Johnny was in Vivian's room looking through her jewelry box. She was not expecting him to be in her room.

"Yeah, Maggie. Sorry to say, but it seems he has a bulls eye on you."

"Son of a bitch! What was he looking through?" Maggie all but screamed. She thought about the diaries under her bed.

"I found him on his hands and knees looking under your bed. He was about to pull something out when I grabbed him by the back of the shirt. Well, I guess all these years of pent up frustration got to me, and I got a couple of right hooks in. I know I shouldn't have but it was such a good opportunity. It just felt so good to slug him and know that I have enough money to hire every lawyer on the Eastern seaboard to defend myself," Peter said with a wink and a smile.

"But wait," Sarah interjected, "How come Chief Mayhew totally let you off without even a warning? I mean, I know the Haven police department isn't keen on Uncle Johnny but, seriously, you really did knock him out in front of everybody." Everyone was was wondering the same thing. Why did the Chief do such a huge favor for Peter?

"Well, again, it goes back to when I was married to your mother. Johnny was trying anyway to shame me in front of his parents and his attacks became idiotic. One day every one was out shopping or something, and I had work to do. I was in the house alone."

"Next thing I knew, Frank Mayhew, a patrol officer at the time, came screaming up to the house, sirens blasting. I came out to the front porch and see Johnny screaming 'That's him' and pointing to me. Johnny was holding up a diamond necklace of Virginia's saying he saw me putting it in my suitcase, which was bullshit, even Frank could see that. Problem was we could not get ahold of Jack or Virginia-this was before cell phones you know," Peter said with a wink.

"So Frank radioed the Chief of Police and asked him what to do with me. He said to arrest me. You girls know what kind of pull your grandmother's money had around this town, so they we not going to take any chances if I did happen to steal the necklace and Johnny was right. Frank pleaded with his chief on my behalf, as he did not want to give Johnny the satisfaction of seeing me in cuffs. There was not a single piece of evidence against me except Johnny's word. But I told Frank it was alright, and I let him cuff me and take me in. Frank thanked me for saving his butt with his boss but I wasn't worried. I knew Vivian would get me out of this mess. But Frank kept apologizing because he had to do what he was told."

"By later that day, Virginia had all but strung Johnny up by his you know what. She had me out of jail in seconds, and any paperwork that had been filed was destroyed. Virginia, embarrassed by her son's behavior, pretty much banished him from Grove Avenue. That's when he started bumping into me around town to tell me about Vivian's drinking. And well, you know the rest."

"So Frank Mayhew always said he owed me one. Well, tonight was a golden opportunity to return the favor, don't you think?" Peter looked around at everyone, looking deliciously satisfied with his revenge.

Nobody could believe what Uncle Johnny had done, so Maggie poured more drinks and toasted to her family's never ending crazy past. The funeral became a party and did not wind down for hours. They told stories about Vivian, about their childhood, they laughed and cried and drank. All night Maggie moved her mother's urn around the porch reminding everyone, in a good way, they would not have been gathered together if it a had not been for her.

Excerpts from the Diary of Vivian Murphy Atwood June 1993

Oh, how could we have done this to Maggie? That poor girl always gets the short end of the stick. Yesterday was her graduation day and I made the mistake of inviting everyone in the family. I was blinded by pride, I couldn't help myself.

It was a beautiful summer day, not a cloud in the sky as Momma, Mac and I drove to the graduation. Maggie's school was only a little more than an hour away on the coast of Rhode Island. The tall chapel looked majestic against the rolling green hills and the ocean just in the distance. White chairs were aligned in neat rows and the faculty roamed in austere robes. It looked like a movie set.

Momma and I had spent a week picking out our outfits. I had never seen Momma with such a spring in her step. For a month she could not stop telling everyone her grand-daughter was graduating with honors and was winning the English literature award. When Maggie was accepted into Tufts University, we'd both cried. She will be the first woman to go to college, really go to college since

Sarah did not graduate from her junior university. Maggie has everything we could ever want for her.

Maggie looked so beautiful. All the girls were in white dresses, and Maggie was such a the young woman now, it filled my heart. I could see how nervous she was, graduating, accepting the award, so Mac and I were trying to make her laugh. Even Momma was in the spirit with her big hat and heavy pearls. , I must say she looked like Queen Elizabeth on Derby day. All the parents and families were dressed to the nines, and even Mac picked out a new silk tie for himself.

Then as we gathered to get seats, it all came to a halt. Johnny came up the long tree lined school entrance with Essie, and I admit, at first I was so pleased to see them. I thought they had come to root Maggie on and hugged them each with joy. Essie was so sweet, carrying a bouquet of roses and was dressed in her finest silk dress. I felt for her because of the distance between her and her own daughter and immediately wanted to include her in our happiness. Johnny, on the other hand, in his damn jeans and cowboy boots, he looked like a reject from a country western band. I managed to put my annoyance aside for Maggie, but I have to say, I was nervous to have him around. Mac squeezed my hand constantly to let me know it would be alright. But Johnny started acting like he was the head of the family, ordering us where to sit and pushing other parents out of the aisle. I could feel my embarrassment grow. But Momma was pleased to have her family around, so I resigned myself to the situation, until Sarah showed up.

She never told me she was coming. Last I heard she was heading to California, so I guess she thought she would surprise us. Well, it was a surprise. My daughter looked as if she had just crawled out of a dumpster. Her clothes were dirty, torn and scant...I guess it's 'punk rock.' I don't know. She was wearing black eyeliner and her beautiful hair looked dirty. Oh! And the tattoos! Don't get me started! I don't know what she was on but it was more than booze. Plus, she brought a man with her who I would not have trusted with a child under ten years old. He looked that creepy-for lack of a better word. My heart fell. Yes, I am ashamed to say, I was embarrassed about my daughter but I was even more embarrassed for Maggie.

Luckily, she did not see Sarah before the ceremony. The whole mood for the day had changed, Mac and I went into survival mode. I missed Daddy so much at that moment. He would not have allowed anyone to act out. He would have kept Sarah and Johnny in line. Thank god for Mac who put Essie on one side of Momma and he sat on the other. Of course, it was my job to deal with Sarah, who acted like her skin was on fire. I swear her eyes were going into two different directions.

Well, we got through the ceremony. Thank God they don't serve booze at these things. We were quite a loud cheering section when Maggie went up both times to get her diploma and her award. Momma and I cried, ruining our mascara. Afterwards, Maggie beamed as we took pictures of her with her friends and us. I could see her hesitation when she came near Sarah, and I just became so mad at Sarah for doing this to Maggie. How selfish of her! We would have been proud of Sarah if she just even worked half as hard as Maggie. But Maggie was a trooper (again) and didn't acknowledge her sister's slurring and the strange date she dragged along. Then, we made the biggest mistake of all, we took everyone out to lunch.

Mac and I had made reservations at a nice seaside restaurant, thinking we were going to celebrate lunch with Maggie before she headed off for a week of parties with her friends. But it turned into Mac, Momma, Johnny, Essie, Sarah and what's-his-name, Maggie and myself having the worst luncheon in the history of luncheons.

Oh lord, I would be surprised if Maggie ever speaks to us again. First everyone began drinking, not a good idea after being in the hot sun all morning. Momma, in her diamond brooch, knocked back gin and tonics like a sailor. Essie stuck to wine, Johnny was pounding scotch, and Sarah and her date, drank God knows what. But the waiter kept coming back to their end of the table with more *rounds so, by the time the entrees landed in front of us, Johnny and Sarah were arguing about something impertinent, Momma was bitching at me to keep everyone in line, and Sarah's date was smoking at the table (which was not allowed and the waiter had to keep telling him so). Mac and Maggie were huddled at the other end, Mac desperately trying to help Maggie ignore the scene.*

Then Momma started in on Sarah telling her to pull herself together, clean herself up and scolding her date with the 'manners are for free young man' speech. Of course, Johnny jumped on the bandwagon and tried to play head of the family again, reprimanding Sarah, again, not a good idea when she has been drinking. Right before things really heated up, I made a toast to Maggie to help remind everyone why we were there. Thankfully, they all quieted down and Momma and I got excited because we had a wonderful gift for Maggie. Mac and I got Maggie a round trip ticket to Paris ,and Momma was going to give her a thousand dollars spending money so she could have the trip of a lifetime. Maggie had always wanted to go to Paris. She was so touched she actually burst into tears and Momma, Mac and I just felt so good. But we forgot who we were sitting with.

Sarah became absolutely unruly after that, and I can't say I behaved any better because I was so furious with her for even showing up. I heard her comment that I never gave her anything and that's when I blew up. I said I gave her exactly what she earned: a twenty-thousand dollar trip to rehab, and look at how much good that did her! Well, the cat fight started and even Johnny got in a few digs at me. It amazes me how he can be a part of something that is none of his business. He managed to spit out how, if I hadn't been a wreck myself, than maybe Sarah would not have turned out so badly.

Things went from bad to worse. Momma got up and went to go sit in the car. It didn't end until Maggie started screaming 'Stop! Stop!' and slamming her fist on the table. We all turned to look at her, and my God, I had never seen such fury and disgust in her eyes. Then she just said very controlled, "Someone get Aunt

Essie." Well, none of us had noticed that Essie was literally face down in her mashed potatoes. What horrible people we are.

Mac paid the bill and everyone left after that, and we drove Maggie back to campus. You could just feel her relief to get away from all of us. We hugged her and she thanked us for the trip to Paris. I tried to apologize, but I still could see that fire behind her eyes. We had ruined the most important day for her. We could not even give her one day, one day just for her. She said to me, "Just forget about it, Mom." And she turned and walked towards a life hopefully far away from us.

EIGHTEEN

Maggie's mouth was as dry as cotton and her head felt like shards of glass grinding together. It was nine a.m. already and the house was still quiet. Everyone was sleeping off the previous day and night. But every morning that week, there was yet again another surprise waiting for Maggie in the kitchen - Aunt Essie.

"Oh, Aunt Essie, I forgot you were still here. How do you feel?"

"Like how you look, little one, and that ain't saying much."

"Ouch, my head. It is like someone is pinching my brain. I need to remind myself never to mix vodka and funerals again."

"Oh, dear heart, none of us are ever going to learn that lesson. " Essie poured some orange juice in a glass for Maggie.

"I'm sure you want to get home, but I think I am still too intoxicated to drive a car."

"Oh, that's all right dear. I was just sitting here thinking back to days long gone. I like how your mother redecorated the kitchen. I see absolutely no traces of our childhood."

"Well, it's kind of a family tradition to obliterate the past, isn't it?" Essie chuckled at that, and Maggie started making some coffee. Millie came walking through the back door in very large black sunglasses.

"Good chitlins and gravy, what the hell was that?" Millie exhaled slumping down at the kitchen table. "I can't give blood for a week with the amount of Chardonnay in my system. I think I even, dear almighty, had sex with my husband last night!" All three of them burst out laughing at the thought of seventy-year old Archie and Millie going at it.

"What's so funny?" Sarah strolled in looking much better than the rest of them.

"Oh God, not much Sis. We just all have hangovers that are going to kill us and you look like you got sunshine up your ass. I'm jealous."

"Yeah, well, I have been doing my fair share of throwing up too this morning. This baby has it backwards, thinks I am supposed to lose weight."

"Oh, that will pass in a month or two and then you will eat through your hand, trust me." Essie had one estranged daughter, Samantha, who was a few years younger that Maggie. Everything about Samantha pointed to her being an outcast. She was a large unsentimental girl who immensely disliked her parents and felt no familial ties with any of them. At seventeen, Samantha joined the Peace Corps and never looked back at Haven. Now, she is running a lesbian guesthouse in Key West and has never invited Essie to visit.

After Maggie poured them all coffee, except Sarah who drank ginger tea for her stomach, Maggie asked a question she had always wondered about.

"Aunt Essie, do you know why Uncle Johnny hated my mom so much?"

"Yeah, Aunt Essie, what was up between the three of you anyway?" Sarah chimed in.

"Oh, children, I don't know if I can even begin to explain," Essie sighed.

"Well, Grandma's gone, and now Mom is gone. No one ever 'talked' about anything in this family." Maggie said.

"Well, you're right about that," Essie nodded in agreement. "Can't say we sat around and talked or hugged it out, no - can't say that at all. Well, we all know that Johnny is jealous of Vivi, has been since he was a kid. Why? I hate to disappoint you but that is not much of a story."

"It may sound simple, but I think Momma loved Vivi more. Maybe because she was her first child or because Vivi's life was so upside down, troubled...I don't know. Momma just was always comparing us to Vivian. Even when Vivi had gone to boarding school and then to Boston when she had you two girls, she was always a presence in this house. So it was really about how Momma treated each of us."

"Oh, Momma and Daddy took the best care of me that they knew how because I was sick all the time. But I guess being weak gave me a free pass from Momma's scrutiny. So Johnny, who was never even a very nice kid, would get in some sort of trouble and Momma always would say, 'Why can't you be more like Vivian?' Look at how strong Vivian was, how independent. Momma was especially proud when Vivian started writing in those Boston magazines. She had them scattered throughout the house like they were the original pages of Genesis. I mean, Vivian was never around most of our teenage years, so Johnny began to loathe even the idea of her. When Vivian had you, Sarah, or even when Thomas passed the bar, literally it was all Momma could talk about. Johnny never really knew your mother, so it was her hold on Momma that got to him."

"Wait, just wait," Maggie interrupted, "I thought Grandma was always disappointed with Mom. Mom always talked about how she wasn't good enough for her mother."

"Oh, well, yes. I can see that. Virginia could be proud but she would never show it. It was because Johnny and I lived at home that we witnessed it. But again, it was more in the twisted form of 'why can't you'. 'Why can't you be more like Vivi?' 'Why can't you be more independent?' 'Why can't you get along without the family's help like Vivi?' And so on. Your grandmother could really make us feel pretty small.

"Well, I guess I was somewhere in the purgatory of it all. I got used to everyone pitying me because of my health. No one ever really had great expectations for me, and, quite frankly, I did not have them for myself. That's why I married that prick, Roger, who really only married me for the family money. And I had my darling daughter, Sam, who now wants nothing to do with me. Maybe if Momma fought with me like she did Vivian, I might be better off, who knows."

"Back to Johnny, though. I remember when I knew he was really impaired. It was when your father, Thomas, died and your mother had that breakdown. Johnny was giddy with the idea that Vivi was locked up somewhere. His euphoria only lasted until Vivi brought home Peter, though. We all know that Peter outshone Johnny in every way. At that point Johnny realized he could never win when it came to Vivi. He hoped Virginia would somehow turn her back on Vivi when she had her breakdowns or something. Johnny was always hoping our parents would get fed up and toss her out on the street, but they never did. Vivi stayed by Momma's side until the end. Or vice versa.

"So, I think Momma just didn't like Johnny, and I think he knew it. But because she adored Vivian, Johnny just automatically hated Vivian. It was easier to direct his anger towards Vivi than to really see the truth. The truth is often a hard pill to swallow, as I think we all know."

The four women silently nodded in agreement. They'd sat without saying a word, digesting everything Essie had said. It explained why Johnny was so irrational about Vivian, attacking her any chance he could. He was hurt by this family, so he hurt others. It had become a familiar theme on Grove Avenue.

"Aunt Essie, do you think Uncle Johnny would ever, you know, physically hurt Mom?" Maggie asked with trepidation.

"No, little one, I think your Uncle Johnny might be mean-spirited but like we all saw last night, he is a coward at heart. He epitomizes a spoiled little boy who never grew up."

"What did you mean by that, sugar?" Millie asked Maggie skeptically, one eyebrow raised.

"Nothing, oh nothing, just forget about it. Silly thought, that's all." Maggie backtracked, although Millie kept her head cocked and staring at her. In order to change the subject, Maggie decided to be honest with everyone.

"Listen, I have a confession," Maggie said. All three women were immediately intrigued.

"Sarah, please don't get mad at me, let me explain first. The other day, I found some old diaries of Mom's."

"And you didn't tell me?!" Sarah's voice immediately shot at her, and Millie put her hand on Sarah's arm to calm her and whispered to let her finish.

"I know. I was going to tell you, but Friday night you announced you were pregnant, and then yesterday was the funeral. I was going to give them to you, I swear. Blood out, blood in, through sick and sin, I swear." That last phrase came flying out of Maggie's mouth, even though she had not spoken those words in years.

Somewhere in their childhood, Sarah and Maggie made up that saying. Neither one of them could remember when. It was born out of their sisterhood and the chaos around them. Whenever they endured the trials of Vivian or came together over Sarah's own disease, rather than through thick and thin, this was their battle cry-through sick and sin.

Sarah begrudgingly said, "Okay, Mags, I believe you."

"It was by accident that I found them, and I had to read them immediately. They have everything. Mom talking about when she had us, when Dad died, her whole life. It's crazy. But my point is…" Maggie paused for effect, "I found out the big family secret."

"Maggie, dear, what do you mean, 'the family secret,' " Essie said cautiously.

"Well, Grandma was Grandma for a reason, all the bitterness and drinking and the strange relationship with Grandpa. There was a reason. Are you sure you want to hear this, Essie?"

"Sure as shit, I do. Spill it child. If there is some explanation for this lunatic family, then I damn well have a right to know." Essie started wheezing and Millie got her a glass of water.

"Are you sure you want to do this, sugar?" Millie warned.

"Really, it can't hurt anyone now. But it tore apart Grandma, and I think Essie needs to know. But can we all promise not to tell Uncle Johnny?" They all nodded in agreement again and levitated out of their seats waiting for Maggie to spill it.

"Grandpa wasn't our grandpa, Sarah. Grandma was married to a German man named Stefan after the war, and that was Mom's real dad. Stefan worked for Grandpa Jack at the company, and all three of them were friends. Well, mom, when she was three years old, made a mess in the kitchen, or something. And Stefan, her real father, fell down and hit his head hard then died because of it. Grandma was devastated, and somehow everyone persuaded her to marry Jack. He adopted Vivian as his own daughter. They never talked about it again, and that is when they moved to Haven and had you, Essie, and then Uncle Johnny.

"So you see, Grandma was always heartbroken. I mean, she loved Grandpa but he wasn't her true love. And apparently, Mom was always a reminder of Stefan and Grandma blamed her for the death that changed their lives. So that explains why Grandma was always so focused on Mom, she loved and resented her at the same time."

"Are you kidding me!?" Sarah exclaimed immediately.

"Well, that does certainly resolves a bushel full!" Millie said ,getting up to grab the orange juice and a bottle of champagne, "I don't know about you kids but I need a drink for this one."

"When did Mom find out?" Sarah asked, her expression incredulous.

"According to the dates it was right after Grandpa died, that winter. It is the reason she, you know, she tried to kill herself in the garage. Mom was never to good at handling the truth."

"Oh, my Lord, that poor thing. Right across the lawn and I had no idea what was really going on over here!" Millie took a hefty swig of mimosa.

"Essie are you okay? Say something." Maggie leaned closer to her Aunt, who had a stunned, faraway look in her eye. She finally turned and looked Maggie in the eye.

"Thank you, honey. Maybe I should say thank you, Vivian. That was just about the best gift anyone could give an old woman," Essie said with tears in her eyes. "We lived with it everyday and never knew what it was... why our mother was not cruel but seemed so distant, mad, but not *at* us. It is hard to explain, but for our whole lives, we never could understand Virginia and it made it hard to understand ourselves. Does that make sense?"

"Yeah, it does, a lot of sense," Maggie agreed.

Millie began passing around mimosas and another tea for Sarah. They all started discussing the past again as Maggie went upstairs to get the diary with Virginia's story in it. When she did, she saw her mother's urn on the living room table and brought it in to be with them. Finally, Maggie did not feel right in keeping anymore secrets.

All morning, the four of them laughed and cried over Vivian's words until Marten and David came down and found three of four very tipsy women. Marten kissed Maggie and told her he was proud her. He had been urging her to open up with Sarah and her family, not to shoulder everything alone. Archie finally appeared, wearing a pair of Millie's large designer sunglasses, giving everyone a laugh. Even for a fisherman, the light was too bright for a hangover. Millie made more mimosas while the men made bacon and eggs. Sarah slipped away upstairs to read her mother's diaries from start to finish, and Maggie hung onto her mother's urn wishing she felt relieved.

NINETEEN

The funeral was over, but Maggie still found herself restless with unanswered questions. It was Monday and presumably life was going to somehow return to normal, but all signs led in the opposite direction. Marten postponed his return to New Orleans. Maggie was happy to have him by her side, he calmed her anxiousness. Sarah and David were packing to leave the next day. David needed to get back to his bicycle shop. Maggie guessed that Sarah hadn't yet informed him of her inheritance. She would have to ask her about that later.

Marten had gone off with George to see his animal hospital. Although he had little interest in animals, it was a good excuse get away from the house and have a little male bonding time. Maggie was happy to be alone to snoop once again through her mother's room for clues.

Maggie brought the ashes of Vivian upstairs with her. She knew it was not healthy to be clinging to an urn, but she found it amusing and comforting at the same time. She would talk to the urn saying, "Come with me, Mom" or "Did you forget to tell us something before you left?" Opening drawers and looking under the bed, Maggie was really searching the missing jewelry. It had been bothering her since Saturday and she wandered if her mother had hid her grandmother's valuables. Could her mother have been selfish like that? Maggie did not think so. Not once could she recall her mother ever hoarding or hiding things for herself, but Maggie could not explain where the jewelry had gone.

Then, while going through her mother's antique dressing table, she found an envelope with her name written in her mother's script. Sealed, Maggie ripped it open and found a tiny key. Then it dawned on Maggie, it was the key to her mother's safety deposit box. Maggie remembered the conversation she had with her mother over fifteen years ago. She was home from college, probably just for a weekend, and her sister was not doing well. Vivian was increasingly worried about Sarah's stability. Just for practical purposes, Vivian explained to Maggie that if something happened to her, she had put Maggie's name on her safety deposit box and left the key upstairs for her. And here it was, in her hand, the key. But Vivian had never told Maggie what was in the bank.

Immediately, Maggie ran downstairs and grabbed her coat and the keys to her grandmother's Mercedes. With Marten out and Sarah and David at an A.A. meeting, she did not have to explain to anyone where she was headed. The day was overcast again. A storm had stalled over the northeast, and the winds and rain had yet to reach the Massachusetts coast. She rolled down the window and inhaled the salt in the air, delivering the ocean right to her. Excited and eager to find out what was in the box, Maggie ran a stop sign. Immediately, she heard the siren.

Pulling her grandmother's Mercedes over, Maggie cursed as she attempted to look for a registration, which was probably long ago expired.

"Hiya, Mags," the officer said as he strolled up to her window.

"Dammit, Lou, you scared the crap out of me!" Maggie said, relieved it was only Lou.

"You ran the stop, Little Red," again with her nickname. "Want me to call Mr. Hoffman to give you driving lessons?" When they were kids, crazy Mr. Hoffman ran a driving school and was known for touching the girls legs as they were shifting.

"No! What happened to that freak?" Maggie asked.

"Running a strip joint in Jersey, kid you not." Maggie burst out laughing.

"So, you gonna give me ticket or what?"

"Naw, just kidding you, but pay attention, Mags, will ya? We can't keep saving your ass," Lou said with a wink referring to the funeral.

"Yeah, you and your Dad, you guys were great handling Johnny and Peter like that. I really appreciate it. Hey, but I have a question for you. Did you read my mother's autopsy report when you brought it over to me?"

"Yeah, I had to sign off on it. Why?" Lou looked at her quizzically.

"Did anything strike you as odd?"

"No, what are you getting at Mags?"

She hesitated.

"Well, Mom fell down the stairs like Mr. Keegan, right? But she had broken wrists because she tried to stop herself unlike him-and her blood alcohol wasn't as high as his."

"What? You think their was something funny about that? Let me tell you something, Mags, these accidents, they happen everyday, and each time in a different way. There is no formula to it. I saw the reports, I saw the scene, Maggie. Your mom had a bad spill."

"I know, I know, it just doesn't feel right to me."

"Mags, you just lost your mom. I know how it felt when I lost my mom. Nothing feels normal, okay? Now where you headed?" He derailed her questioning.

Maggie told him she was just running errands. Obviously Lou was not going to buy her theories either, and it was pissing her off that everyone kept thinking she was over-reacting. Maggie's instincts had gotten her pretty far in life, and she knew with certainty she should be listening to them this time. She promised Lou they would get together soon, meet his fiancee and have a beer, and then she headed on her way to the bank.

Maggie forgot what a small town Haven was until she parked on Main Street. Three different shop owners came out of their stores to give Maggie condolences. When you live your whole life in one town, everyone knows you one way or another. It was nice to be on the streets of Haven again. Living in cities, the buildings and people felt remote, like Maggie was a constant tourist. But here, the buildings were low and small and the people inviting. When she walked into the bank, Maggie walked right into the past.

Maggie opened her first bank account here when she was fifteen. She was home for the summer from boarding school and had gotten her first job at the gourmet deli. Five days a week, she sliced ham, turkey and roast beef and piled it high on sandwiches. At the end of each day, her legs ached, but she had fun with the other teenagers behind the counter and loved having her own paycheck at the end of the week. Not a summer went by when Maggie didn't have a job, as a waitress at the lobster shack by the docks, or behind the counter at Brickman's department store. It made her feel normal working with the other teenagers in town and forgetting about being a Murphy. Everyone knew her family and assumed Maggie would never have to work a day in her life, but she loved it, the hours, the exhaustion, the camaraderie, and her own money. Over the years, her little bank account grew and grew until she went to college. With the money she earned, she was able to buy herself her own car. Maggie had proved to herself and everyone else that she did not need to rely on her family.

Now, back in the bank as an adult all that childish hope came flooding back to her. All the old tellers she once knew were gone, so she went to the counter and explained her situation. Immediately a stout Irish woman, Mrs. Gallagher, came out and introduced herself. She held Maggie's hand and said how terribly sorry they were at the bank and how lovely Vivian was and what a loss to the community. Maggie thanked her and inquired about the box. Mrs. Gallagher, thankfully, did not talk Maggie's ear off and led her to the room with the safety deposit boxes. After placing a wide but thin tray in front her, Mrs. Gallagher patted her on the shoulder and said, "Let me know when you are done, dear, no hurry." *Such a nice bank*, Maggie thought.

Maggie then hesitated, she really had no clue what she would find. After the diaries, now what? She wasn't surprised to immediately see an envelope addressed to her, again in her mother's script. Hopefully, her mother had been thoughtful enough to explain everything this time. Underneath the first envelope were two large manilla folders and a small jewelry box. Maggie impatiently inspected the items. She did not read the letter addressed to her but opened the jewelry box first. And there it was, the canary yellow diamond cocktail ring her grandmother always wore. Virginia had never taken it off as long as Maggie had known her. Vivian must have kept it in the bank since Virginia died. But there was no other jewelry, no diamond sapphire necklace or diamond brooch. Maybe Grandma had given those things to Essie and she never told Johnny, Maggie thought. Who knows? Maggie opened the first folder and found the deed to the house, insurance papers, and divorce papers. Nothing unusual, just paperwork stored for safekeeping. The next folder was far more interesting, and Maggie let out a slight gasp after she opened the contents.

There were several 8 x 10 glossy photographs, each more shocking than the last. The first two were pictures of an unknown woman's face. She was young and attractive, black hair, dark skin, exotic looking-Brazilian, maybe. The shores of Massachusetts were populated with small enclaves of Brazilians who migrated to the U.S., working menial jobs in rich communities and then sending the money home to Brazil. This woman could be one of those migrants. It struck Maggie that she looked familiar but her memory was foggy. They were official police photographs capturing the image of the two large bruises encircling her swollen eyes. She also had a large bruise spreading across chin. Maggie was struck with how vacant her eyes were, a distance no camera could measure. Immediately, Maggie felt heartbroken for this young, hurt woman. When Maggie flipped to the last picture, she could not help but slam down her fist and yell, "Son of a bitch!" a little too loud. Mrs. Gallagher's head shot through the door, "Are you okay, dear?"

"Oh, sorry. Yes, ma'am, sorry, thank you," Maggie sputtered. "I know you have questions about my mother's accounts, but I have to go right now. I promise, I will be back soon to take care of it. Is that all right?" Maggie gathered the contents of the box and quickly shoved everything in her purse.

"That's alright, dear, we can do it another day. Is there anything else you need help with?" Mrs. Gallagher barely managed before Maggie raced past her and out the bank. She hurried back to the car, resisting heading to where she wanted to go, and swung the old Mercedes around back towards Grove Avenue. She could not afford to make any more mistakes and needed to think of a plan.

TWENTY

No one was home when Maggie arrived, although she wished Marten was there so she could show him. Instead, she poured herself a glass of wine and took everything upstairs to her mother's room and laid it out on the bed in front of her mother's urn on the dresser. Taking a few steady breaths, Maggie opened up the letter from her mother hoping it would tell her what to do.

Dear Maggie,

If you are reading this, I am so sorry that I am not there. Hopefully you are a very old woman and I have died a boring death drooling on myself in a nursing home. I also hope I didn't cause you any trouble or pain. I remember how hard Momma's last year was, and I just wouldn't have ever wished that on you or Sarah. Well, I don't want to get sentimental. If you are reading this you are probably having a hard enough time as it is...so I will get down to business.

First, I don't know if you ever knew this, but I kept a few journals over the years, even though I kept them a secret. I guess I wanted you to read them all along. I just could not be around when you did. They are in the back of a garage in a black box. You will find them, don't worry. Yes, they contain some hard truths but some good ones as well. They have all the things I could never say to you and Sarah. I hope if I have left you with questions, the journals answer them; otherwise, what you need to know is in your heart. I love you and, as sorry as I am for the many things I have done to you, I love you even more than that-remember that always. I love you.

You will recognize the ring as your grandmother's. Your grandfather, your real grandfather gave it to your grandmother and that is why she gave it to me, not Essie. Again, the diaries will ex-plain. I ask that you never sell this ring. I could not decide whether to leave it to you or your sister because, well, your sister could be in good or bad shape at the time you get this. I trust you to guard this ring and to decide where it should go. It is a symbol of love, know that.

Now, you are probably wondering about the photographs. The woman's name is Luciana Silva and she was a nurse here in Haven. She worked for us when Grandpa Jack was dying, coming in once a day to help take care of him. Luciana was only twenty one and such a sweetheart. She even warmed the heart of your Grandma! She took care of all of us, helped Momma cope with losing Daddy, helped me with taking care of everything in the house. You were just twelve so I don't know if you remember her. It was just a short time she was with us.

Well, after Daddy passed, things got a little chaotic around the house. Your grandmother was not taking Daddy's death well, and your Uncle Johnny was furious because Daddy did not leave him the company and, instead, sold everything out from under him. Plus, none of us got anything when Daddy died. We were going to have to wait for Momma to give us the family money, and well, that infuriated Johnny to no end. So with everyone so upset, I decided to keep Luciana on to help us out, mostly for you and me. Your sister was already gone and your grandmother just was not quite herself.

Your Uncle Johnny, being who he is, kept coming over and giving your grandmother and I a hard time.

So, one time he showed up while I was out and, as the story goes he was yelling at your grandmother about money and Luciana stepped in front of him to try and calm him. But Johnny had been drinking, and maybe doing some drugs. We were never sure, and he just blew up. He pushed Luciana so hard she fell sideways and hit that big end-table downstairs and then the floor. Well, I can't blame Luciana a bit for what she did next: ran like hell out of there. She went straight to the police station and nailed Johnny right away. By the time I got home, Frank Mayhew was leading Johnny away in cuffs. He was officially arrested as you can see by his mugshot.

After Luciana calmed down, Momma got to her with a huge check and Poof! the whole thing disappeared. I was sorry because I thought Johnny could use a little jail time to settle his soul. Momma could practice tough love but never that tough. I think because she was so shaken up by Daddy's death she just could not deal with anymore drama. She had her reasons, and I had to respect them.

I didn't know about the photographs until Momma was dying. In one of her last sane moments she gave them to me. I asked her why she hadn't destroyed them. She told me she loved her son but he was greedy, and greedy can make people do awful things. She said she wanted me to have them in order to keep Johnny inline. As long as I had something against him, he would be on his best behavior.

So now, I bequeath them to you. I don't know if you need them or not but it never hurts to have insurance. Johnny does not know where they are but just be careful all the same. Use them to your advantage. I just want you girls to be alright and not have him bothering you they way he always bothered me.

Well, that's it honey, I love you. Take care and go find those diaries before anyone else does...
Love love love, your mother

Maggie sat back, stunned to learn another family secret, but it was not surprising to see Uncle Johnny's true colors. Maggie held up the 8 x 10 glossy of his mugshot and snickered. He could have been looking for this in Maggie's room the night of the funeral. No wonder he was hanging around here so much. And it certainly gave him motive for wanting to hurt her mother. If the small town of Haven found out he hit a woman, no one would dare come near him again. People do not tolerate rich kids getting away with beating the help. And, Maggie thought, he *pushed* Luciana, so it is not such a far stretch to think he may have pushed Vivian. Maggie was starting to think Uncle's Johnny's cowardice was just an act. He might have had more gumption than anyone realized.

TWENTY ONE

Excerpts from the Diary of Vivian Murphy Atwood
July 1997

It is worse than we thought. Mac and I are noticing the little things, the forgetfulness, the confusion, but I just thought it was old age, or worse, dementia or senility. But we took Momma to Boston today and did test after test. Alzheimer's Disease, what a horrible and undignified sickness. As we sat there with the doctor listing symptoms like some sort of restaurant menu-memory loss, problems with language, decreased judgement, changes in mood and personality, disorientation-I have the pamphlet in my hand. A pamphlet, two little glossy folded pages to describe how our lives are going to change not just today but forever. How Momma's mind, which has always been strong and sharp, will crumble and disintegrate while we sleep in our beds and eat our breakfast and read our morning paper. Day after day will become a spiral downward. This isn't death; it is a nightmare.

Momma just sat there, steel-boned. I will never forget how rigid her back was, how her eyes went unblinking as she heard her fate. I think she knew already. It must have been months that she *had suspected, her instincts had known her destination. Poor Momma. When we came home, I tried to talk with her about it but she refused. She fixed herself a gin and called Maggie in New York. Maggie has just gotten back from Europe and has not come to visit yet. I heard Momma saying she would pay for her to take the train. I have never heard Momma ask for anyone to visit. But Maggie is our touchstone, our bridge to normalcy, sanity. Maggie was Momma's purpose in life, the daughter she never quite had, right? I am not jealous. Now that I know about my real father, I understand. It is his personality I have, not Momma's. That's why we don't see eye to eye. But Maggie, she is the one who likes the same things as her grandmother, sees the world the way she sees it. I am happy for both of them that they can share that, it is so rare.*

Maggie agreed to come home, which always makes me happy. Having her around, her youth, her humor will be good for all of us. But I suppose I should tell her, Lord knows Momma won't. I'll need her to get through this with me, isn't that selfish? Maybe as a mother I should shield her from things, but Maggie is a grown woman now and my only real friend aside from Millie and Mac. I'll call Sarah later, I can't handle her right now. Oh, and Essie and Johnny, what to do about them? Essie will help as much as she physically can, and I know I can count on her emotional support. Johnny, well, he just won't make this easy for any of us. Maybe I can just hide it from everyone, like Momma can, for a little while longer.

Excerpts from the Diary of Vivian Murphy Atwood April 1998

I have to laugh. What else do I do, cry? Momma can go from bad to worse to terrifying and all the money in the world can't save her. Ironic, huh? We are rich but poor! Money can't buy our way out of this mess. I know I shouldn't make jokes but it is Maggie's influence on me. She says sarcasm is better than booze, which I am trying so desperately to be better with, the booze and the sarcasm.

Maggie comes home often. She says she wants to get out the city and breathe the ocean. I remind her there is an ocean next to New York City as well. But, I think she can't separate from us, not when we are in trouble. She was always like that as a child, sitting outside of my door at night, watching over me, or Sarah. As the mother I should have stopped it, but I needed her there, just within my grasp. So now, she needs us just with in her grasp. She is wonderful with Virginia even on the days Momma doesn't recognize her. Maggie sits for hours reading to her from their favorite novels or from the New York Times. When Momma stresses about a new nurse-I now have nurses all the time-Maggie can calm her. What would I do without her?

Even though I talk with Maggie everyday, I wish I could be more honest with her, tell her about our past. But I just don't want to burden her with more of our pain and sadness. Sometimes Momma cries out Stefan's name-I am not used to hearing or saying my father's name, and I become paralyzed and don't know what to do. I finally told Mac the whole story and now he steps in to soothe her when her memories come. Mac has always been so kind but I wonder if he isn't too kind? He lets me get away with so much. When Maggie isn't around I have my bad nights. Something in me just snaps and I can't take the pressure anymore.

It is like my mind is full of these dark thoughts and they just keep crashing and colliding and all I can do is drink to numb myself. I get so tired of it all. Of course, I will keep helping Momma, but it is hard because Essie and Johnny don't do shit except cause me trouble. And Mac, he practically pours me the drinks so I calm down but then, once I do drink, I become this hideous monster. The other night Frank Mayhew had to bring me home again which was embarrassing. I don't know which is more embarrassing, though, Maggie knowing how bad I can get or everyone else knowing. But it really wasn't my fault this time. I could have controlled myself if my brother wasn't such a shit.

Johnny had come over to see Momma that day and usually I just leave them alone. I want him to deal with Momma's confusion, so he has a taste of what I go through everyday. Well, I just happened to be walking by and caught the sneak going through Momma's drawers. Of course, I walked in to ask him what he was looking for and he blew up at me. He accused me of stealing things from Momma, like her jewelry, and secretly using her bank account. Of course, I am using her bank account-how else would I pay for the nurses and the bills for Momma? Then he accused me of sponging off Momma all these years, never having a life of my own. Thank God Mac came in and got him to leave but, before Johnny left, he looked me right in the eyes and said, "I know about you." Shook me to my core. Did he know Momma's secret? I mean, even though I am not Daddy's biological daughter, he still adopted me so Johnny can't claim I am not a Murphy. But still, I don't trust him not to use it against me somehow. Lord knows, I don't want it to be him who tells Maggie or Sarah.

Well, after that, one glass of wine turned into several. I got into a nasty fight with Mac and threw his clothes on the front lawn. Now Millie is going to think I have lost it again. I must have left, but I can't remember where I was going. Sometimes I just need to drive. I think Mac called Frank to come find me. Dear old Frank, when I was a child I never knew he would be such a good friend. I owe him in so many ways.

Excerpts from the Diary of Vivian Murphy Atwood June 1998

Well, I'll be..isn't that what people say when they are amazed and bewildered at the same time? That's how I feel after today. Momma is always good for a surprise and today was no exception. I had gone into her room after the morning nurse had fed her and changed her clothes, and there was the old Momma. She was propped up in bed like the Queen of England who had business to do. Usually, I just change the flowers by her bedside and adjust the TV channel but there Momma sat alert and ready to talk. Well, I just almost fell over when she said "Vivian, sit for a minute please and stop your fussing." It was Momma alright, to the point.

And after months of her thinking I was some stranger, blow me over. So I sat and listened.

"Close your mouth, Vivian it is unattractive. I am not dead yet, am I?"

"No, Momma," I said but it sure felt like it.

"Now, Vivian, I don't know how long I have before, you know, I flutter away again. So listen to me. Bill Getty has all my arrangements. I did them a long time ago and as far as I can tell, I haven't changed my mind. I've lost my mind, but I haven't changed it. Oh, lighten up dear, that was a joke. But I have some other business. First, take my ring." Momma then pulled off the yellow diamond cocktail ring. "It is rightfully yours because it came from your father, Stefan. If the other two make a stink, well, I can't help them. The world just works out that way."

"Now, here take this folder. If you are wondering why you have never seen it, it is because I kept it between my mattresses. Don't laugh at me, just look inside. I don't know why I kept those photographs all these years but they seemed they might be useful if you know what I mean."

Momma handed me the photographs of Luciana and the mugshot of Johnny. I knew the story well, but I never knew there were photographs, let alone that Momma hid them all these years! That's what Johnny has probably been looking for! Momma continued.

"Now, Vivian, I know this has been hard on you, taking care of me. I certainly do not like that it turned out this way so I want you to know that this house is yours. Now, and after I am gone, you will be the sole owner. Essie has her house so I don't worry about her, and Johnny, well that son of mine can take care of himself because I have been doing it long enough. Now that you know it is yours, I want you to do one last thing for me, okay dear?"

Momma was looking at me with all the strength and vigor she had when she was young. I was sure that I could do whatever she asked of me but she told me, 'Put me away.'

'Vivian, I am an old bird now and it is just not going to get easier. We don't know how long this will take. I told Bill to make all the arrangements ages ago, and I think it is time. This house shouldn't smell of the dying, and I don't want to ruin our home, your home.'

Momma's head began to sink into the pillows again and she took a few deep breaths. I didn't know what to say, and I started to cry. I felt in an instant the world had changed, shifted. Momma would never be in this house again which is as close to death as I could imagine. I took Momma's hand and we sat there for a long time smelling the salty, summer breeze through the window. I could tell Momma was inhaling ocean air like her last breath, the last taste of her life, that she wanted to remember.

Tears rolled down my face as I understood then that I was without her. All these years, I let Momma pull my puppet strings, and now I was left limp and, discarded, no strength left in my limbs. Momma fell asleep after that and, when she awoke, she had forgotten who I was again.

Later, in the afternoon, I walked all the way into Haven to clear my head. I put the ring and the photographs safely in the bank so Johnny couldn't get his hands on either. When I got home, I called Maggie just to hear her voice, and I it was time for Momma to go into a nursing home. I didn't tell her about my conversation with Momma because I didn't want Maggie to get her hopes up and come home to try and talk to her. So I said it was my decision and Maggie agreed, she thought it was time as well. Thank God for Maggie's level head.

I have called the home and Momma will be moved in a couple of days. I called Essie to tell her, and she was supportive, but I could not bring myself to call Johnny. Essie, thankfully, agreed to *that. Now, at the end of the day, I don't feel as sad as I did before mostly relief. Maybe now I can sleep again.*

TWENTY TWO

Maggie was pacing the house by the time everyone came home. Sarah and David had bought groceries and were going to make dinner for everyone on their last night. George and Mitzi would come over later, after leaving the boys with Millie, so the six of them could relax. Marten had a great day bonding with George, and they were old buddies by the time George dropped him off. Maggie was eager to get Marten alone to show him what she had discovered. But Marten had had a couple of beers and was more focused on her body than anything else. The farthest thing from Maggie's mind was sex, so instantly she became annoyed with him.

"Honey, pay attention," Maggie kept saying as she lay the photographs on the bed.

"Maggie, sweetheart, I am and I have been, but I think you are just making more out of this than there is. Listen, your uncle is a creep. We all get that and, as far as

I can tell, the entire town of Haven gets that, so really why would these photographs make a difference to him? To anybody?" Marten was perhaps right in his logic but Maggie did not want to listen.

"But you saw Johnny, he thinks too highly of himself to let Mom or me have the upper hand over him. He had a serious vendetta against her for being close to Grandma and getting this house."

"Yeah, but Maggie, you are trying to imply the man *killed* her, and I just can't go there with you. Don't you think you are just trying to find a reason for your mom's death? It is completely understandable, everyone who grieves needs reasons. The reality is, it happened."

"Jesus, Marten, do you really think I am that big of an idiot? Just some stupid little girl with a crazy idea?" Maggie was starting to get upset. "I get that I am grieving, of course I am, but look at the facts - someone was here that night, and we don't know who it was, and no one is admitting it either. Now, with or without your help, I am going to find out who!" Maggie was breathing hard and glaring at him. She thought Marten would be the one to understand her.

"Okay, okay, I get it. I'll help you find out. Just promise me you won't blow this out of proportion. I know how you get when you're angry, and it's not pretty."

"Bite me, " Maggie said as she jumped off the bed and threw the photos in a drawer. Nothing about the conversation made her feel better. Marten was being logical and impassive. But when she turned around to keep talking with him, he was snoring.

Maggie went back downstairs in a foul mood. She was thankful to see George and Mitzi coming through the kitchen door so she did not have to endure Sarah and David's banter while they cooked dinner. All they could talk about was the baby: baby names, the baby's sex, the baby's due date, baby, baby, baby. Maggie's mind was about a thousand miles away cavorting with the ghosts of her grandmother and mother. She could not think about the impending new life when the old ones were not quite done. Her mother's urn sat on the kitchen counter reminding her to finish what she had started.

"Hey, George. Hey, Mitz," Maggie said as she jumped up to hug them.

"Where's the man?" George said

"What, I'm not good enough anymore? Like your new playmate better? He fell asleep, thanks to you," Maggie responded.

"I know, " Mitzi said, "when boys find a new friend, it is like they're dating. 'Did he call? Is he home yet?'"

"Aw, shut up," George said, a little embarrassed. "What did you do today, Mags?"

"Yeah, sister dear, we saw you pulled over by the police. Finally getting hauled in by Haven's finest? It's about time, I must say," Sarah chided.

George and Mitzi turned wide eyed at Maggie.

"Hey, you guys, it was Lou. What did ya' think?" Maggie threw up her hands.

"Does Officer Mayhew still have a crush on you, sis?"

"Sarah, he's getting married. No, I happened to run a stop sign."

"Finally, the bad girl in you is unleashing her fury."

"Ha. Ha. You guys think you are pretty funny?" Maggie sneered.

"I thought I saw you on Main Street today but I had the boys and couldn't catch up to you," Mitzi said pointing to her burgeoning belly.

"Yeah, I had to stop at the bank. I went to Mom's safety deposit box," Maggie said looking at Sarah over the rim of her wine glass, wary of her reaction.

"Oh, and what did our family detective find today?" Sarah had turned around and was looking at Maggie. Maggie could not tell if she was being funny or sarcastic. She decided to tread lightly.

"Well, I had found a key to it, so I just went, I didn't know if I should wait for you or not," *Lie, lie, lie,* Maggie thought. Why was she lying anyway? Because she did not want to hurt Sarah's feelings? But how many times had Sarah hurt hers? "I didn't think there would be much in there, and there was just some papers, deed to the house, insurance, no big deal." Maggie wavered and took another slug of wine. She had already had a little too much wine that afternoon and found her emotions a little itchy. It was an itch she should not necessarily scratch.

"And?" George said, sensing Maggie was holding back.

"And, there were some photographs," Maggie said. Now she had everyone's full attention and there was no going back.

"Photographs of what?" Mitzi ventured.

"Apparently our Uncle Johnny was a very bad boy after Grandpa died. He hit the nurse who was working for Mom and Grandma. Her name was Luciana, and she was helping out with Grandpa, and then stayed on to help with us after he died. Sarah do you remember her? Anyway, Grandma kept the pictures of Luciana's bruised face and Uncle Johnny's mugshot. No one ever found out about it because Grandma paid off Luciana so she would drop the charges. And the Haven police department buried the evidence because of Grandma."

Maggie was hoping someone might catch on to what she had been getting at.

"So when Uncle Johnny was rifling through my room the other night, I'll bet you that is what he was looking for. Don't you guys think it's weird how infatuated with Mom he is?" Maggie posed the question to the room.

"Mags, what are you driving at? Because it seems like you are getting a tad too obsessed with your uncle," George said in a slightly angry tone.

"George, don't you get it? Johnny hates Mom with a passion. He wants her house, the family jewelry, and someone was here the night she died..." Maggie began waving her arms in the air, waiting for someone else to put the pieces together.

"What do you mean, someone was here the night she died?" Sarah asked.

"Mitzi said she saw someone leaving on a bicycle, and we don't know who it was." Maggie was getting excited that everyone was listening.

"Now, Maggie, I don't know about that. Really, it could have been any one of your Mom's friends," Mitzi began backpedaling.

"Maggie, are you seriously implying that Uncle Johnny may have had something to do with Mom's accident?" Sarah looked at her incredulously.

"Well, think about it-Mom, according to the autopsy, was not legally drunk, and she had broken wrists. She tried to stop her fall meaning that she was cognizant and aware. So how could she just throw herself off the stairs? Hello! Doesn't the whole scenario sound a little odd to you!?" Maggie was getting worked up again while all four of them blankly stared at her.

"Maggie, I don't like this. I don't like this at all, just cut it out. You're worrying me," George said in a parental tone.

"Yeah, Mags, you are sounding a bit crazy on this one and you are the sane one in the family," Sarah joked, trying to soften the rising tension.

"So none of you believe me, none of you see what I see? Are you all unbelievably blind? I mean G', I know you live some sort of fairy tale life where nothing happens in your Pleasantville, but c'mon!" Maggie was furious with them and the wine had loosened all her frustration. She knew it was a low blow, and she immediately regretted it. George was her best friend, though, shouldn't he be backing her up on this one?

"Now, Maggie, we know you are hurt. George only has your best interest in mind," Mitzi tried interjecting but Maggie stopped her, "Mitzi what the hell do you know about my interests? My mother is dead and something doesn't smell right here in la-la-land." Maggie was getting too worked up and making a fool of herself.

"That is it, sister dear, out on the porch!" Sarah grabbed Maggie tightly by the upper arm and with surprising force pushed her out of the kitchen. It was the kind of act only an older sister could get away with.

Then Marten walked in saying, "Now, what did I miss?"

Out on the porch, Maggie sat down hard in a club chair and crossed her legs. With her arms folded across her chest, she looked like a defiant child. She refused to look at Sarah and stared out toward the ocean.

"What is wrong with you, talking to your best friends like that? I may be older and pregnant but I can still kick your ass, you know." Sarah stood pointing over her. "Listen, this little witch hunt of yours has got to stop. Really, you are worrying me. You don't get this angry, Maggie. You don't get this obsessive, it is not you. Mom died, that is it, end of the story. I have spent the past year going over all the insanity in this family and getting past it, and I won't go back there. And you shouldn't be going there either.

"Whatever Uncle Johnny is, whatever he has done, let it go. Do I think he killed Mom? No. Do I think he is a totally certifiable asshole? Yes. But that's none of our business, Mags. I've got a baby to worry about, and you've got this house and that great guy in there. And you need to start focusing on them."

"Jesus, Sarah, are you just going to run away again? You never could handle anything could you? You never could care about us enough to stick around. It is all about you. Well, this is about Mom, and I don't care if any of you listen to me or not, I don't need you, or any-one. Never have." Maggie was full blown angry now.

"Maggie, you are acting like a self-righteous bitch and I'm sick of it."

"You're sick of it?! How could you be, you are never around long enough! I was around, Sarah. I was around for every goddamn day of her drinking, her lamenting, her anger, and her crying. I cleaned up the broken plates and the clothes on the front lawn. I listened and held her hand when Peter left, when Grandpa and Grandma died. I got the phone calls when Johnny went after her. I was there for everything and, on top of it, I had to go scrape you off the side of the road a few times as well. Isn't that what everyone says, *I'm* the responsible one? You count on me to always do the right thing, clean up everyone's messes, make it all better? And now, when I see how broken everything is, how wrong it all ended, you are telling me to ignore it. You are *un*believable."

"Jesus, Maggie, you're right," Sarah said slowly and calmly. "It is broken around here but not in the way you think. Mom and Grandma, for as much as they loved you, they used you. We all used you to take care of us. We thought you were strong enough for all of us. And you put up with so much of my shit. Hell, maybe I used you as a mother too. We always wanted you to hold our hands and tell us it was all right. What I am trying to tell you is that it is all over now. You don't have to take care of Mom anymore. You don't have to take care of me either. You need to start focusing on yourself. You are angry at all of us, which you should be, but you need to think about letting that go."

Maggie knew deep down Sarah was speaking a truth, but she could not accept Sarah being rational and logical even though that is all she wanted her sister to be all these years, a sister. Now, Maggie was too fired up. She had lost control, and no one was listening to her.

Sarah went back inside and left her to stew on the porch. Maggie could hear the sounds of everyone in the kitchen, laughing and continuing on with dinner. None of them came out to check on her, not even Marten. Everyone inside had mutually decided Maggie needed to work things out on her own. Meanwhile, Maggie became more determined to prove them all wrong. She was not crazy and she was not making all of this up. Something happened the night her mother died and, if it was the last thing she did for her mother, she would find out.

TWENTY THREE

Maggie did not like to think back to the time when her grandmother died. The years leading up to it were the closest she had ever felt to her mother. Living in New York, Maggie was just getting started as a writer. Nothing was easy, each day was a struggle to get something written and noticed. Many days were spent in isolation, in her apartment, reading countless newspapers, trying to get a feel for what people wanted to read. New Yorkers prided themselves on their knowledge of all things cultural. '*The arts*' was a phrase used as often as '*Fifth Avenue*' or '*the subway*', you just could not talk about the city without using it. Maggie contacted her college friends to get into parties and social events as she tried to find her niche in the city. When it came to the end of the night, Maggie returned to her cold, cramped studio apartment alone. So many people in one city, and she always felt alone.

Every morning, Maggie welcomed her mother's phone call. The loneliness got to her, the silence in her own mind, so when she picked up the phone to her mother's incessant talk, it was a relief.

Vivian never started a conversation with "How are you?" or "What did you do last night?"- instead she launched into the morning tirade of what had happened to her. It was either the gardeners were late and cut the wrong bushes, but they gave her two extra tomato plants, the nurses were having a hard time with Virginia, or she thought Mac's hearing needed to be tested. Every morning Maggie listened and commented where appropriate. She constantly told her mother to relax and not get worked up over the small stuff. They would gossip about the women from garden club and laugh over the latest news. Then her mother would go into her worries over Sarah or Virginia. It usually took an hour to get through their agenda, but it helped Maggie feel connected with the world again and ready to write.

After the incident in high school when Maggie wrote about her mother, they never talked about Maggie's writing unless it was benign and outside of their emotional sphere. Like an article Maggie wrote about the White House intern, blaming her life's fiascos on her fashion choices. Maggie claimed when you dressed in a generic off-the-rack dress from the Gap, that was proof that one was "off-the-rack" as well. Fashion for New Yorkers was like religion, you worshipped and revered it. Vivian, who was always impeccably dressed, delighted in the article and passed it around to all the garden club ladies. Having the appraisal of her mother, as well as a few magazines in New York, caused Maggie to shelve any ideas for a novel based on her own experiences. Even Maggie was repelled by self-indulgent 'me' novels, the ordinary trying desperately to make themselves extraordinary. New Yorkers, like her mother, preferred witty commentary and insightful sarcasm. If that was what got her noticed, then she was going to do it. But the work was hard, and she easily got frustrated. Like every inspiring writer, she told herself she had years to write what she wanted.

In the years before Virginia died, Maggie had found comfort and refuge in going home to Haven. She would take the train up to Boston and be home in four hours. Since Maggie was working for herself, she could come and go as she pleased. Often, weekends turned into whole weeks on Grove Avenue. Mac, Vivian, and Maggie found a rhythm in the house together. When Virginia was still living there, Maggie would come to help her mother. She would step in with the nurses or spend hours calming her grandmother by reading to her. After Virginia went into the nursing home, Maggie would accompany Vivian on daily visits. It was easier to go together to the "drooling" home, as Maggie called it. It was tough enough seeing her grandmother so frail and senile.

Now that Maggie was an adult, she and Vivian began to enjoy each other as friends. If it was summer, they would pack sandwiches and head to the beach after seeing Virginia. If it was winter, they would go shopping in Haven and make big feasts for dinner. Mac usually stayed upstairs writing and working all day until he came down for a cocktail and a game of backgammon with Maggie. Mac enjoyed Maggie being home because they often talked about books and literature and laughed over many inside jokes. What is more important is that Vivian curbed her drinking when Maggie was around. Vivi managed to keep the edge out of her voice and go to bed before any scenes. In strange ways, those were the good old days for all of them.

The summer Virginia died, Maggie had come home in July and stayed until Labor Day in September. Nothing happens in New York in the summer and the doctors were making noises that Virginia did not have much longer to live. Vivian could not see the point of Maggie going back and forth to New York and urged her to stay through the summer. Maggie agreed. All of her New York friends were in the Hamptons, and that was about as foreign to her as the West coast.

During the time Virginia was in the nursing home, Maggie and Vivian became accustomed to the irregularities of Alzheimer's. Constantly, they would prepare themselves for Virginia not to recognize them or even to get upset with their presence, just as the doctors warned. Virginia never did follow the rules of others and challenged her own disease. There always appeared to be one kernel of familiarity behind her fierce green eyes. Either Virginia flat out would say one of their names or it was more subtle like her commenting "you know I don't like chicken salad." If you handed her lipstick in two different colors, she always picked the one Vivian had worn for years. It was in these indirect ways that Virginia was still there, still with them. At night, the phone would ring on Grove Avenue waking everyone. It was Virginia calling from her bedside, confused and disoriented whether it was day or night. Against all odds, she remembered their home telephone number. Vivian was Virginia's touchstone and needed to connect with her, so if Virginia's mind was powerful enough to remember their telephone number, then dammit, Vivian was going to answer no matter what time.

The years took their toll on Vivian, though, worrying and caring for Virginia. When Virginia stopped recognizing them, stopped fighting with the nurses, stopped calling, Vivian's dark moods returned. That summer, many nights were spent letting Vivian rage past twilight. Mac and Maggie would do what they could to calm her but, once she starting drinking, she could not be handled.

It took all the strength Maggie and Mac had not to argue with her as she hurled insults, threw objects and sat in her father's chair, eyes glistening with drunken tears.

The next day the house would be filled with remorse. Maggie and Mac would retreat to their writing as Vivian went about paying her penance with vases of fresh flowers and dinner on the table. They forgave her because she was losing her mother, but they resented her because she made it harder.

Excerpts from the Diary of Vivian Murphy Atwood July 1989

That SON OF A BITCH! Excuse my language but that screaming asshole! I am so furious right now, I can barely breath. I just told Mac to fuck off, but everyone can just fuck off. That's right, Vivian Murphy Atwood has said FUCK OFF. That low life brother of mine has crossed permanently over into the dark side or wherever the hell he came from, who the hell knows. Mac says I have to calm down, WHY!? Why do I have to put up with this shit? That creep has had it in for me from day one.

FIRST, we go to visit Momma on her birthday with Essie to have cake, cake that I ordered, presents that I bought, and that asshole doesn't show up. But what does he do? He breaks into my house! Mac and I caught him red-handed in our bedroom rifling through the drawers and through my things. I couldn't help myself, I completely lost control, I said, "You pig, what are you doing in my house!" Which started a colossal argument.

"Missy, it ain't your house. You walk around here like Queen of damn Sheba, but this isn't your house." Johnny replied.

"What the hell do you mean by that? Momma gave it to me and you know it," I shot back at him.

"Why? Because you're daddy's little girl or just a drunk like Momma? Oh, don't pretend you are so innocent, Vivian. I know all about Momma's first husband. Daddy just married her to save her reputation. Their whole marriage was a sham and we, the 'children', are like the antique furniture, thrown around just to make the place look nice. Momma, with her uppity airs was no better than anyone else in this world, she just had money. And let me tell you, that money is mine because I am the true heir to this little palace. I'm a true Murphy," Johnny spit.

Mac stepped in and got Johnny out of the house, thank god, before I hurt him. He doesn't go visit Momma, he has no idea what any of this is like for me, for her, but it is all about him. And how does he know about Momma's first marriage anyway? Now I know why she gave me those photographs, she knew there was some-thing wrong with him. I am the one making sure our mother is happy and taken care of. Hell, now I am stopping by Essie's house once a day to check on her, and what the hell does anyone do for me? What the hell does anyone do for ME!

Excerpts from the Diary of Vivian Murphy Atwood August 2003

I don't know how much more of this summer I can take, how much more of the heat I can take, how much more of anything I can take. My insides hurt and my bones feel like marble. I wonder why I bother to get out of bed in the morning? It is not like mother thanks me, ha, no thanks or gratitude for anything I do. My broth-er, what a piece of shit, he has been waiting to humiliate me his whole life. God knows why. Suing me? Give me a break! What was so terrible that happened to him? Really, what truly horrible thing has ever happened to him? I mean, he does not even have enough personality to be alcoholic or even a drug addict. At least the women of this family have that covered, personality and addiction!! Maybe if I were narcissistic like him, I could skate through life completely unaware of the people around me, totally focused on myself. Is that the key to life we are always searching for? The answer being, just fend for yourself and forget everyone else? If I could only be so lucky.

Maggie and Mac are downstairs "guarding" me. I hate that, they can be so damn needy. Why can't they just let me go do my own thing and they do theirs. I hate being watched, so what if I drive into a tree or fall off a cliff? That's my own damn business! What has ever been mine in this life? Momma controlled every damn thing! Maybe I didn't want to be a Murphy, maybe I wanted to be a Schmitt. Did I get the choice? Did I get the choice to stay in Boston? No, no choices for Vivian. I have to take care of mother, is that by choice? NO. She's made me.

And my children, are they mine? No! They don't belong to anyone, good for them. And there Mac is, like a goddamn basset hound at my feet. I wonder how they would feel if they knew how I truly felt, how I just want to scream, 'GO AWAY.' Maggie eyes every drink I have, the little bitch. Hey, I deserve something to get by, to put up with them. My drinking is none of their goddamn business.

Next day..

Did it again, but I just can't apologize for my behavior anymore. I may hurt Mac and Maggie but I don't mean to. I love them, but I don't have time to do penance. Mother is going to die, I can feel it. As she used to say I need to sit up straight and focus on the task at hand. Mac and Maggie will be all right, and now Johnny is in his place for the moment, so I need to focus on Momma.

The week Virginia died was one of the worst Maggie had ever endured on Grove Avenue. It was an unusually sultry August and the trees and flowers were as tired as Vivian and Maggie. All summer long they had watched Virginia disappear before their eyes. By July they were going to the home daily, but it was hopeless. Virginia's body had withered as much as her mind, and the visits were sad and tense for them all.

Maggie never realized she had said goodbye to her grandmother long before she passed. Somewhere in the lonely hours of reading to her, the words replaced the tears. Her eulogy was book after book, the books that had bound them long ago and now separated them. They were no longer teacher and student, grandmother and granddaughter, but simply the dying and the living. On those hot August days, Maggie would quietly brush her grandmother's hair, polish her nails, and prepare both of them for the inevitable. Maggie did not see her grandmother as she once was but as a spirit, tired and weary, crossing the finish line.

The chaos started two days before Virginia died when Vivian opened her door to a process server. The well-dressed young man handed Vivian a notice that her brother was contesting Vivian's medical proxy of their mother. Uncle Johnny was claiming Vivian was an unfit guardian due to her psychological history. Maggie and Mac were home and rushed to Vivian's side.

"Mom, what is it?" Maggie asked looking at her mother's pale stricken face.

"Well, dear," Vivian said through clenched teeth, "It seems my brother, my S.O.B. of a brother, has decided he should take care of your grandmother." Then Vivian threw down the envelope and stormed upstairs. Mac and Maggie were left in the open front door confused. As they read the papers thoroughly, they could not believe it. Mac ran upstairs and tried to talk to Vivian, but she had locked herself in her room. All they could hear were sobs on the other side. They felt helpless, whenever Vivian was truly hurt she closed herself off to them. That was never a good sign.

All afternoon, Mac and Maggie sat vigil downstairs. Neither one of them could get through to Vivian but they were not about to leave her alone. They had watched Vivian over the past four years care for Virginia with such love and devotion. It was Vivian who went to the home, Vivian who knew the nurses by name and the doctors schedules. Vivian who put fresh flowers by her mother once a week and bought her new robes and slippers, who sent cakes and pies for Sunday dessert and put photographs of the family up in the room. It was Vivian who hired hairdressers to do Virginia's hair and put real sheets on the bed. It was Vivian who had acted like a daughter when Johnny refused to act like a son.

Uncle Johnny's lawsuit was a slap in the face. The reality was, he could use any number of her personal trips to rehab or the hospital against her. How could she fight the truth? He would unearth the most intimate and shameful moments in her past and parade them around a court of law to get his way. He would embarrass her simply out of spite, and that is what hurt Vivian the most. Logically, they all knew Virginia did not have long. The doctors had been preparing them for months, so by the time this lawsuit went through the courts, Virginia would have already passed. It was the malice and animosity that Uncle Johnny directed towards Vivian that offended her deeply. There was no appreciation or love for what she had done all these years for their mother.

Mac called Bill Getty that afternoon, and Bill reassured him that the process would take too long for anything to happen to Vivian. He would make sure of it. Bill said there was no way in hell Virginia would ever leave her life in the hands of her son. Mac pleaded with Vivian through her bedroom door, but there was no answer.

When Vivian did emerge, the sun was setting and she was bitterly drunk. All it took was a bottle of wine for Vivian to be set off, and she must have snuck one up earlier. It was always a shock for Maggie to see her mother like this, hair ruffled, eye make-up gone, her movements slow like an elderly woman, a stark contrast to the strong woman that morning comforting her dying mother. Now Vivian was bumping into the walls as she all but crawled down the stairs. Mac rushed to her side and tried to help.

"Get your hands off me, Mac," Vivian said with a cold slurred voice.

"Mom, why don't you go back up to bed, let us bring you some dinner?" Maggie tried.

"Oh, such a good little girl aren't you, my dear daughter, trying to hide your old drunk mother away. Everyone just wants Vivian to go away, huh?" Vivian looked at Maggie through half opened eyes. She moved slowly, shuffling across the room towards the kitchen.

"Vivi, where are you going? I'll get whatever you need," Mac pleaded.

"Get what I need? You've never had what I need Mac. You don't have anything I need. I have everything *you* need, living in my house, using me. Everyone just using me." Vivian was in her enraged state, and they had to take the hits whether she made sense or not.

"Mom, c'mon, you are in no shape." Maggie approached and tried to turn her mother around.

"Get off me, you little bitch. Miss goody, goody, sticking your nose in everyone's business. You know, we were just fine here without you. We didn't need Saint Maggie to come watch over us."

"Vivian stop it now. You're drunk and you just need to sleep it off." Mac's tone was firm now, trying to stop Vivian from saying too many hurtful things to Maggie.

"I've been asleep, Mac. My whole god forsaken life, I have been asleep. Letting all of them control me, take over. No matter what I do, I am not allowed to be human. I can't care for someone without being hurt, so maybe I shouldn't care, huh? Not give any of you vultures anything." Vivian slurred. Mac and Maggie knew where this was going, Vivian could spend the whole evening yelling and biting at them with her self pity. They had heard these tirades before, and Vivian would only manage to get angrier and meaner as the night wore on, so Mac interjected.

"Okay, Viv', whatever you want. Maggie and I will be over here if you want us." Mac winked at Maggie as to say let's pull back and see what she does. They went to the far side of the room and sat in front of the living room TV while keeping an eye on her. Vivian held onto the wall as she lethargically made her way into the kitchen. Once inside, Mac and Maggie heard a crash but instead of jumping up to check on her, they waited. Like soldiers in a foxhole, they did not run to the danger but waited the war out strategizing. Vivian did emerge with another bottle of wine and appeared to be otherwise unharmed.

After she returned upstairs, Mac and Maggie investigated the kitchen, where the refrigerator door was open and most of the contents lay on the floor. Quietly, they cleaned up the mess. Mac made them a couple of sandwiches and told Maggie to pick out a movie to watch. Their vigil would continue through the night. After a few hours of silence from upstairs, Maggie went to bed only to be awoken awhile later by Mac in a panic.

"Mags, wake up, Mags. Sorry, honey, but your mother is gone." Mac's voice was shaky with fear. Mac had fallen asleep downstairs and, when he went up to bed, he found her mother's room empty. Mac and Maggie immediately began their search. They knew Vivian could not have driven away because they had hidden the car keys, but the garage was the first place Maggie looked anyway. Maggie, for the rest of her life, would always check the garage first. Both of them fueled by the horrible possibilities, they walked the beach, the yard, and Grove Avenue until the sun was peaking up over the ocean's horizon. Mac called Frank Mayhew, who offered to drive around and look for Vivian in his cruiser. After searching the neighborhood, helpless, they went inside to make coffee and wait.

Later that morning, they heard the gravel drive, and Maggie felt paralyzed with fear. Mac, sensing the possible danger, jumped up and looked out the kitchen window and said, "He's got her. Frank's got her."

Mac knew that was all Maggie needed to hear to breath again, that her mother was home.

When Frank brought her into the kitchen, Maggie was shocked to see her mother dressed and in make-up. The woman who had been too drunk to stand somehow pulled herself together to go out. Here before her was an entirely different woman from the night before, Vivian was herself again. The slur in her voice was gone, her movements young and quick, and her voice drained of venom. Quietly, Vivian poured herself a cup of coffee and offered some to Frank.

"I'm sorry, Mac, Maggie," Vivian said nodding in their direction. That was it. They waited but there was no further explanation of where she had been. Maggie expected more, wanted to see remorse or shame for what her mother had done to them, but Vivian was quiet. Maggie could not help the sarcasm in her voice when she said, "Quite all right, Mother," and stormed back upstairs.

Frank had found Vivian leaving Virginia's nursing home, and everyone assumed that Vivian had gone there for the night. Naturally, that was not the full story. Vivian did pass out for a while, but when she awoke in the night, her mind settled on one determination: to confront her brother. How dare he do this to her? The past four years had shown how little he cared for his own mother. He barely visited her, left all the details to Vivian, and had no responsibility what-so-ever. Now, just to hurt Vivian he was going to use Virginia as a pawn in a sick game? Vivian was not going to stand for it. She had sobered up some and decided that feeling sorry for herself was not going to get her anywhere. That is what her mother taught her, to get up and move on. Her mother had given her the means to do it, three glossy 8 x 10 photographs.

Vivian snuck out of the house past Mac after a futile search for the car keys. She had to give them credit for hiding them. So she set out on foot to her brother's house, who only lived two miles away. The night summer air felt good, and the exercise opened Vivian's eyes as her anger built and fueled her steps. By the time she arrived on his doorstep, her eyes were as clear as her rage.

Confused to see Vivian standing there at 4 a.m., Johnny let her in thinking maybe Vivian was delivering the news in person that their mother had passed. There was a slight glimmer in his eye when he thought about his possible inheritance, which would be worth giving up the lawsuit.

"Hello, John, Jr.," Vivian said being formal and cool with him. "May I come in?"

"Of course, Vivi, has anything happened?"

"Oh, yes ,I would say something has happened," Vivian said as she entered.

He offered her a seat but she declined. She liked the feeling of power she was now starting to feel and preferred to stay on her toes. She knew what he was expecting, but she was going to deliver something else.

"Is Momma okay?"

"Yes, sorry to disappoint you, but Mother is fine at the moment." Vivian smiled.

"Well, that's good. No, that is very good. We need to take care of her."

"Don't you mean *you* need to take care of her?" Vivian directed right at him.

"Well, yes, Vivi. I do think I should be the one taking care of her."

"Why is that John, Jr.? Because you have done such a spanky job until this point?"

"Now, don't get bitchy Vivi. It's just your condition."

"My 'condition', now what would my condition be?"

"Well, I know how upsetting all this can be for you, and we would not want you to have one of your breakdowns."

"One of my 'breakdowns'. Ah yes, I see," Vivian said as she kept her eyes cooly on him.

"I knew you would understand. You're like Essie, a little bit delicate and, well, all those papers and decisions concerning Momma should be left to me. I am head of this family and, well, I should start acting like it. So you know, no hard feelings Viv'. You understand."

"What I understand, John, Jr., is that our mother and father never trusted you with the business, the house, or even the family car, let alone trust you with their lives. I think the last person in the world Momma would want holding the plug would be you, John, Jr.."

"Now, listen to me, Vivi, I have put up with your high and mighty attitude long enough. Don't you dare talk about Daddy, because he wasn't your daddy. Your father was some German immigrant," Johnny said with a cunning sneer. "Don't you just love private detectives? They can find out so much about your own family."

"Since you are so clever, John, Jr., what do you think you know?" Vivian's blood ran still, as she wondered how much he had learned.

"I know he fell and hit his head, and Momma married Daddy just to save herself. She just wanted Daddy's money, anybody could see that. She used him just like you use people, Vivian. Both of you are the same. You think I don't see your game? Moving into the house, taking care of Momma, playing the poor Vivian act? Please, the two of you are such actors to get what you want."

"You are really sick, John, Jr.. You are truly disturbed." Vivian felt relief that he did not know the details of Stefan's death and could not hold it over her head.

"Don't talk to me about disturbed. I wasn't pulled out of a garage by my fourteen year old daughter."

"That's it. I won't stand for you to talk to me like that," Vivian ordered.

"Well, the way I see it Vivian, you don't have a choice," Johnny said smugly.

Vivian took a deep breath and a small smile crept across her face. "You never learned anything from Momma, did you, John? We always have choices. Like she used to say, 'with every problem there is a solution'. And it just so happens, I have the solution to my problem, which just so happens to be you. You think you can bully me, take over Momma, and humiliate me and my family publicly? For what? Your own personal enjoyment? Revenge? Revenge for what? I can't even possibly imagine what I ever did to you that caused you to hate me so much. Whatever it was, I don't care anymore. The only thing I care about is protecting my family, including Momma, so here's the deal." Vivian opened the large yellow envelope in her hand and waved the three photographs in front of Johnny. She never let them out of her hands for fear he would grab them.

"The deal is Johnny, you leave me and my family alone. You drop this asinine lawsuit, and you *never* tell a soul about Momma's past. If she had wanted you or anyone else to know, she would have told you. The irony is - guess who gave me these photos? Now, if you want to keep whatever reputation you have, you will keep your mouth shut because if these photos get out, no one, I swear to God, no one will come near you in this town again. I certainly would not want the whole Brazilian community watching my butt. Because that's what they do, that's what families do, they protect their own, Johnny. So you lay off, and these photos will never see the light of day again. If you try to take me down, I will sure as hell take you down with me."

Vivian stared at him and waited for his response. He finally nodded his head in agreement.

She put the photos back in the envelope and walked out. In those early dawn hours, Vivian should have felt victorious. She had gone to battle and won, but what did she win? Nothing that she cared for, Vivian understood she would never have freedom from her brother, freedom from the family secrets or lies, freedom from their feelings toward each other. Vivian felt exhausted to think about how she would have to watch and manage her brother for the rest of her life. She understood his hatred was dangerous, and he was unable to mask it anymore. Vivian still did not know why she deserved all of his venom, but she accepted it. Like accepting her mother's dying and accepting her own shortcomings, Vivian understood this was the way of her life. Everyone has burdens, regrets, secrets that you can either let destroy you or live inside you.

The call came the day after Vivian visited Johnny, Virginia's breathing was labored. The doctors cautioned that she did not have long. Vivian showered and put herself together, wearing her clothes and make up like armor. She vowed there would be no scenes of tragic grief, no bed-side wailing. She would behave just as her mother did so long ago by her father's side, graceful and accepting. Maggie and Mac had managed to put aside Vivian's tirade the day before and move on as they always did. There was no benefit to dwelling on the situation because Vivian could be remorseful but never truly apologetic. The underlying code was it was just the way things were, and they had to accept it.

When Maggie and Vivian got to Virginia's bedside, Uncle Johnny was already there. Maggie could feel her mother's irritation emanate from her. Mac had gone to pick up Aunt Essie, and Maggie wished he was there to referee. Maggie imagined there would be an explosion between the two, but Vivian and Johnny were unearthly quiet with each other. Vivian busied herself checking in with the doctor and pulling up a chair bedside with her needlepoint. On the other hand, Johnny paced and snapped orders to the nurses and rubbed forced tears from his eyes. Ignoring him, Maggie sat by her grandmother's side and patted her hand. Like her mother, Maggie felt there was no need for hysterics. Eventually, Mac returned with Essie, who followed Maggie and Vivian's lead, and retrieved her needle-point from her handbag.

"Maggie, dear, did you bring a book?" Vivian asked her.

"Umm, let me see, yes. It's a mystery, is that okay with everyone?" Maggie said as she opened the book.

"That's fine, dear. We will follow along," Essie said. Maggie began to read aloud, until moments, later when she was interrupted.

"Maggie, I'm sorry, but what the hell are you doing?" Johnny barked.

"She's reading to her grandmother, you twit. She always has, but that is something you would not know, now would you? Go on dear," Essie said and then burst into a coughing fit. Vivian remained quiet while she patted her sister's back and got her a glass of water. The tension between all three siblings was thick and impregnable. Maggie kept looking at Mac because they were like two civilians caught in a war again.

"I know that, Esther. I just don't think it's appropriate when our Momma is about to die. I think we should get a priest in here, and has someone called Bill?"

"Oh, for the love of God, John, Jr. Murphy, you sit down right now or else!" Essie mustered a shout.

"Or else what, Essie. Are you gonna cough on me?" Johnny snickered at her.

"Or else I am going to take a full size ad out in the paper saying that, even after you take Viagra, your penis is no bigger than the size of the pill itself," Essie shot back at him. Immediately, Vivian's hand shot up to her mouth, while Mac and Maggie fought to stifle their laughter. Essie's words hung in the air.

"Essie, I expected this from Vivian, but you?" Johnny said.

"What, I'm acting like a bitch? Still makes me far superior than whatever you are, Junior." All of them were not used to this clear headed, sober Essie, and they were immensely enjoying it. Essie just grinned and continued with her needlepoint. "Johnny, let me give you a little piece of advice," everyone was waiting to see what she would say next. "Shut up."

She waved her needle at Maggie, "Now go on dear." Johnny got up and stormed from the room like a dismissed child. Mac clapped his hands and said "bravo" while Vivian stared at her sister like a new person. Maggie began to read aloud again.

The next few hours were slow. They watched the sun move across the room as Maggie plowed through, chapter after chapter. Johnny would occasionally come in but, for the most part, he waited in an outer room. Finally, the monitors started beeping and all three women looked at each other. Putting down the book and their needlepoint, they gathered around the Virginia's bedside. Nobody bothered to call a nurse, the time had come. Johnny came and sat in the corner. Maggie started.

"Remember Grandma's flowered bathing cap?"

"The one she wore for fifty summers?" Essie chimed.

"I think she had a secret stash of them, that's why she was able to have one every summer," Vivian continued.

"They stopped making them didn't they?" Maggie asked. They kept their conversation going, remembering, laughing, talking about Virginia in the past. When the monitor did sound the final call, the long steady signal of death, the three women were lost in tales and memories about Virginia. When the nurse came in to turn off the machine, each of them took their turn to say goodbye. Johnny wailed and made a spectacle of himself, but he was the first to leave to make phone calls eliciting sympathy. Essie kissed her mother and said a prayer for her. Maggie recited Virginia's favorite lines from Robert Frost: *Two roads diverged in a yellow wood, and sorry I could not travel both, and be one traveler, long I stood.* Most people preferred the ending to Frost's famous poem, but Virginia was different. She loved the beginning, the idea of choice. Maggie then left her mother to say goodbye.

The final goodbye between mother and daughter was never to be known. The complicated and arduous relationship had come to a close. Everyone had respect for Vivian who handled the last years with her mother with immense love and devotion. No one would have known the fatigue Vivian felt when she thought back on the years of her mother's demands, criticism, and exhausting coldness. How her mother had orchestrated their lives because of one accident. Or the guilt Vivian felt for being the catalyst to her mother's deeply hidden sadness and disappointment.

TWENTY FOUR

Vivian began planning Virginia's funeral with precision the next day. It occupied all of their minds to set themselves to various tasks. Millie and Maggie received the multitude of flowers that came from every charitable organization Virginia had donated too, which was far more than anyone ever imagined. Mac took command of organizing the house for guests, while Vivian made endless phone calls and arrangements, overseeing every detail of the funeral. Essie helped Vivian with vigor, enjoying moments of closeness with her sister. They sat and composed thank-you notes together and laughed over how Virginia would have managed her own funeral. Without their mother around, their was a new-found ease between the two of them. No longer vying for Virginia's affection released them from an undiscovered weight. Uncle Johnny remained aloof, which was fine for everyone involved. He stayed clear of Grove Avenue helping-instead they heard tales of him going around Haven making a spectacle of his mourning. Uncle Johnny felt the need to personally tell people who'd known Virginia, further proving his desperate desire to be the center of attention.

Maggie, while she felt sad, understood this was the natural order of life. She would miss her grandmother but had the memory of her voice to comfort her. The Alzheimer's had taken away the shock of her death and had forced everyone to wish for it. Given the circumstances, Maggie felt reassured that her family would get through the funeral without discord or turmoil, but then the front door opened.

Sarah stormed in saying, "Hey Sis, guess the old bat's gone for good now. Wonder what she left us?"

The night before Virginia's funeral, the scene during dinner was predictable and unavoidable. Vivian, who looked as exhausted as she felt, had a short fuse that night, and the combination of mother and daughter was combustible. The fight between them was inevitable. Sarah's appearance was their first warning sign: she had cut off all her hair and dyed it a platinum blond. It would have looked good for a sci-fi movie or a music video but, standing there, Maggie and Vivian felt themselves cringe. The long leather boots and the torn jean jacket were the sad tell of hard life. Immediately, they could smell the booze on her breath, but they also wondered what else might be in her system. At first, Vivian and Maggie did their best to welcome Sarah and show their appreciation that she had come home but as, the night wore on, everyone's patience wore thin.

Mac had picked up Chinese food to alleviate any added stress of cooking, and Essie was coming to go over last minute arrangements for the service the next day. Maggie could feel the tension between Vivian and Sarah as closely as she could feel her own blood pump through her body. She truly felt for her mother, who was emotionally bankrupt and now had to deal with Sarah's crass and brutal attitude. Maggie attempted to assuage the conversation at the dinner table.

"So Sarah, what have you been up to?"

"Not much, Sis', you know, fucking up as usual," Sarah said flippantly.

"I didn't mean that, I meant you know, boyfriend? New job? What have you been up to?" Maggie said light-heartedly.

"Oh, you wanted to know the extent of which I have fucked up. Oh, yes, of course, so then we can all decide how fucked up, fucked-up-Sarah can really be."

"Sarah, there is no need to use that kind of language,." Vivian said through gritted teeth.

"Oh yes, Mother, I forgot how proper we all are around here." Sarah was determined to start an argument.

"Ease up on your Mother, Sarah, she has been through a lot this week," Essie uncharacteristically defended Vivian.

"Oh yes, Aunt Essie, let's all think about Vivian. We would not want to take the focus off her, now would we? No one else could possibly matter when it comes to Mother."

"You are not being fair, Sarah. Grandma just died yesterday and we are all exhausted. You just don't know what we went through," Maggie pleaded with Sarah to let it go.

"How could I know? No one called me, no one wanted me at the deathbed party. So you guys are the martyrs and as usual, I am the thoughtless granddaughter."

"Sarah, this isn't about you. It is about Grandma. I tried to ask about your life but, since you walked through the door, well, you've been a real bitch." Maggie almost screamed.

"Maggie, dear..." Essie said while shaking her head at Maggie.

"That's right, little Maggie dear, behave. Be the good one. Wouldn't want you to act like me." Sarah snarled.

"Stop it! Stop it right now, Sarah Atwood." Vivian pounded her fist against the table.

"What? Mother, you don't enjoy having me around?" Sarah sneered back at her.

"You are acting atrocious, Sarah. Whether you like it or not, I am your mother, this is my house and you will behave accordingly while at my table."

"Wow, who are you, Grandma now? We all have to behave *accordingly?*" Sarah said while pouring herself another glass on wine.

"Don't you think you've had enough?" Maggie stared hard at Sarah.

"Yeah, I've had enough, enough of the lies and bullshit. Look at you people, gathered over a woman who had a heart made of ice. You know what she used to tell me? She was embarrassed to call herself my grandmother. I humiliated her, can you believe that? Now, correct me if I am wrong, but I can't be the only one at this table who humiliated the great almighty Virginia."

Sarah stared right through Vivian as she spoke. Everyone remained silent and looked at Vivian hoping she would not explode at that last insinuation.

Calmly, Vivian wiped her mouth with her napkin, turned and smiled at Mac. Calmly, she focused her eyes on Sarah and began.

"Sarah, I love you. You may not believe that, but I do., I always have. My children mean everything thing to me. No, we have not always gotten along, and you have disagreed with many of my choices. But, in turn, you have made many choices of your own. It is called life,

Sarah. Now in retrospect, I am sorry I did not prepare you better for it.

"I know you don't, or should I say 'didn't', like your grandmother. It was not in the cards for the two of you to see eye to eye. No matter what you think of her, she was my mother and you will, while under this roof, honor that. It is obvious you do not have any respect for the relationship I had with her, so I will not try to explain it to you. In fact, I will say it is none of your business. You are a big girl now, Sarah, but you do not get to choose what we have to share with you. You need to earn it." Sarah listened to her mother with her head down, her hand moving a fork around her plate. Maggie could see Sarah chewing the inside of her lip in defiance.

"Sarah, listen to me, and listen carefully. When I said this is life, well, there is no other way to put it. People have childhoods where good and bad things happen. You are not the first to be knocked around, nor will you be the last. You had a lot more than others, a beautiful house, every need you had was met, and no, I wasn't perfect, but I was here. I never left you, I never stopped loving you. You could have done a lot worse and, until you remove that giant chip off your shoulder, you will never see what you have."

"Sarah, I say this with all my heart, you need to put aside your anger and see the people in your life with a little more compassion. My mother was not always the nicest or most affectionate person, but that does not mean she didn't love me or love you. Life happened to her, and she did the best she could. Instead of abandoning her, I loved her. No, I am not a martyr, but I have found peace with her. Now, you need to pull yourself together and find peace with the people in your life." Vivian gazed at Sarah, never taking her eyes off her, all the while pounding her index finger on the table. Sarah lifted her chin up and everyone held their breath waiting for her response. Then she did not look at anyone and got up from her chair. She lifted her wine glass and swallowed the last half in one big gulp. She went up stairs for less than a minute, came down with her jacket and marched out the front door.

"Well, that went well," Maggie said, trying to be humorous. Vivian excused herself and went straight to bed leaving Essie, Mac, and Maggie to clean up. Maggie turned to Essie and said, "Will this ever end?"

"I don't know, sweetheart. Let's hope so," Essie said as she hugged Maggie and said goodbye.

Maggie heard Sarah come in some time early morning. Vivian was ignoring Sarah, so Maggie had the task of getting her to the church, where she passed out half way through the service. No one commented on Sarah's state, politely not drawing attention to her. Instead, they focused on Uncle Johnny, who was making a shameful spectacle of himself weeping for his mother. Later, in the privacy of their own homes, people would ridicule and mimic him. He had disgraced the ever-graceful memory of Virginia, who mourners would remember for her sharpness, manners, and boundless charitable giving. At the reception on Grove Avenue, it was Vivian, Maggie, and Essie whom well-wishers approached and expressed their condolences. Sarah and Johnny were abandoned to their theatrics.

Maggie watched her mother, who had stood so stoic during the service and reception, begin to crumble bit by bit. It wasn't just the sadness that week, but the years of slowly losing her mother that had been hard on

Vivian, and no one was giving her room to breathe. Maggie noticed the wine glass in her hand and tried to not worry, but it was always empty then full again. Most of the mourners had left the reception by the time Vivian and Sarah were screaming at each other in the kitchen. Maggie tried not to listen as the rage and hurt of their family was broadcast for the remaining guests to hear. It was the same story between the two of them only the volume was turned up thanks to all the alcohol. They both accused each other of being selfish, spoiled and unloving. Both claimed they were victims of the others' mistakes and choices. Both of them yelled the same thing at each other and went around and around until something was broken or someone left.

Maggie felt unbelievably sad that night because there was more lost than just her grandmother dying. Over all the years that had passed, nothing and no one had changed. Sarah was more angry and lost than ever before, and the connection between them as sisters was gone. Her mother, who she had grown so close to over the past couple of years, had gone back to being her distant, unreachable self. Maggie felt helpless to save them, they not only dug their own holes but jumped right in. Around and around the three of them had gone for years, only to end up back in the same place. Maggie had always harbored the foolish hope that one day all of this grief and drama would have a movie-like ending. There would be closure to their past. She thought, if her grandmother was not around picking favorites anymore, everyone could relax. But none of them wanted what she wanted, none of them wanted a family, none of them wanted to be better. Did they even notice if Maggie was around? Did they even care about her? That night was the first night Maggie felt truly on her own.

Excerpts from the Diary of Vivian Murphy Atwood
September 2003

Everyone is gone, Maggie, Sarah, Momma...the house is so quiet with just Mac and me rambling about. I guess I got used to the chaos over the summer. As much as I wanted peace and quiet, the noise distracted me in a good way. Now, I sit here in my house, that will never truly be 'my' house, because somewhere Momma will be quietly judging me. Should I sell it? Wipe the slate clean? Start over? Admittedly, I am too afraid. Where would I go? Mac says we could get a nice apartment in Boston and enjoy our golden years going to the theater and out to dinner. I feel too old to go in reverse. That was a life I wanted so long ago, too long ago. Now, I need to hear the waves of the ocean lapping against my sleep. I need the humid air of summer filled with flowers and to be safe by the fire during the cold winter. As much as I fantasize about leaving Haven, at heart, I could never leave the only home I have ever known. Momma, for good or bad, chose this path for me, and now my shoes are too worn to leave it.

I have felt a subtle shift since Momma died, like I lost my favorite coat. I go to put it on, so worn and familiar, but it isn't there. I don't know how else to describe it. I feel disconnected. Mac has been patient, such a sweet man. He thinks if he fulfills every one of my needs, I will be happy and content. We both know that will never happen. Something is crooked deep inside me and I can't control it. Like Sarah, poor Sarah, what a mess. But I don't have the strength anymore to clean up her messes. She is old enough to do it on her own, but I do worry for her. She is so filled with anger. I understand, but she has nothing to balance it with, no softness. I have Mac and my garden, and my little projects around town to keep me somewhat centered when I fall off balance, but Sarah, she has nothing. My heart breaks for her. I hope she knows, if I could have one wish for her, I would bring Thomas back and fill that horrible hole in her heart that I could never fix.

Maggie, I was no comfort to her, either. She truly loved Momma in a way that none of us could understand. And what did we do? We turned grief into a three-ring circus. She is back in New York and I have not heard from her much. I miss her, but I think it is good for her to get out there and back on her own. I don't want her to regret never trying in life, like I do. So many regrets I have. Even if she fails, she will never look back and say she didn't try. I have wondered my whole life what other life I could have had....I would never wish that hell on Maggie.

Momma left me a letter with Bill Getty. It has been sitting here for three weeks staring at me, and I cannot muster the courage to open it. I just don't want to know anymore secrets about our past, and I don't know what else she could say to me from the grave.

July 1997
Dear Vivian,

I imagine you are reading this after my funeral. I hope it was a tasteful occasion without much fanfare, as they say. I do pray our family was on their best behavior. I could not stand for any un-necessary attention being drawn to us. I guess I am finally in a posi-tion where I can't do a damn thing about it! (that was a joke, Vivi)! I do regret I was not more humorous in life, but I guess can-not change that now! Now that I have this horrible diagnosis in my hand (Alzheimer's, what a ghastly name), I suppose I can lighten up a little. Most days I feel like my head is disconnected from the rest of me. So now, when I have a bit of sanity, I need to seize it. I know I am on a downhill spiral, and I am not foolish enough to believe that anything will get better from here on out. Instead, I fully expect that you will take the burden of my life on your shoulders. Johnny and Essie are both incapable of the work and sacrifice it will take to see me to the end. I will do this one last selfish act in my life, and it is horribly selfish, entrapping you, but I would like to tell you why. Of all my children, you care about life, about people, and you have the strength and resolve to make sure that I get whatever I need. I trust you, Vivian.

I am not sure you know how strong you are because you spend so much time doubting yourself. I am not criticizing, but I will say, you get in your own way, Darling. Maybe I did that to you, what can I say? I made some difficult decisions. I don't regret marrying Jack, but sometimes, many times, I questioned the choice. You undoubtedly absorbed my fears, my apprehension, my sadness and took them on as your own. That I do regret. I see you with your children, and you can understand the choices you make when you are a mother can be immense.

I know now I was wrong to blame you for Stefan's death, so terribly wrong. I was angry at the world, young and foolish. It was just fate-nothing more, nothing less. Now I am on the eve of a tomorrow that may never come, and I am scared. When I search my heart for what I need, it is you, Vivi. I want you by my side before I go. Considering how long it may take, it is unfair of me but try to forgive a spoiled old woman.

So this last letter is a thank you. I know in my heart you did not let me down, you never let me down. You are truly my daughter.

All my love,
Your Mother

TWENTY FIVE

After the dinner party went on without her, Maggie could not sleep that night. Frustrated, she made her way down to the kitchen to have a cigarette and quietly think. But two minutes after she had settled in, David appeared.

"Hey, we can't keep meeting like this!" David said jovially, irritating Maggie.

"Mmm, yup," she tried not to engage in conversation hoping he would go away. But again, he did the opposite, he sat down and lit up a smoke as well.

"I miss these. Can't smoke around Sarah now, and especially not after the bambino comes." Again Maggie did not respond, so David continued. "Listen, I don't think you are crazy. There might be something to this theory about your mother. Sarah has told me a bit about the family history and, I gotta say, you guys have a knack for some fucked up secrets." Maggie could not help herself and chuckled at the comment.

"Yeah, well, we have a flare for the dramatic," Maggie commented.

"So how are you gonna find out who was here the night your mother died?" David asked.

"I don't know, really. I am just going by a hunch. Something just doesn't make sense."

"Yeah, like Sarah and I having a baby. That doesn't make whole lot of sense either but, here we are, two ex-druggies valuing life. Kind of ironic huh?"

"Yeah, ironic."

"It just amazes me how people can change."

"Ah, the optimist," Maggie said a little too sarcastically. "David, a little advice, people don't really change. I don't mean to offend you, but I don't think you've been around long enough to understand. People just grow more 'themselves'. All that self-help-spiritual nonsense is just a band aid. It makes you feel like you are doing something about your pain, but underneath there is still a cut and then a scar."

"Wow, you're pretty cynical."

"It's what old people call 'wisdom'." Maggie took a long inhale of a cigarette.

"Then why are you obsessing over your mother's death if your pain is going to remain the same? What will really change for you?" David challenged.

"Imagine you did have a scar, a big one on your arm so you always see it. And say on days it rained, it hurt like hell but you have absolutely no idea how you got that scar. It just has been there your whole life, growing bigger, and there is nothing you can do about it. But at least for me, if I knew how and why I got that scar, I could rationalize it, put it in its place, understand it if you will."

"How is that any different from what Sarah and I do, going to A.A.. Going to therapy?"

"You are searching for someone or something to take your pain away, somehow erase all your horrible memories, and well, that is a crock of shit. The memories, the pain, will always be there, like scars. You don't notice or feel them everyday but they are always there. The best you can do is just understand them and move on."

"I see your point, but all of us aren't as objective as you."

"That's right, you are not like me, and I am not like you, and that is okay. I mean, you have to do what works for you to get by, and you don't have to listen to me. But also, you don't have to listen to what everyone else tells you all the time either. Sometimes you have to figure it out on your own."

"Like you."

"Yeah, like me," Maggie said.

"Well, that actually isn't bad advice, again a little cynical, but I will keep it in mind. I suppose you don't want to talk about your relationship with Sarah, either?"

"You supposed correctly," Maggie answered.

"She loves you."

"I love her too."

"She wants you in her life, in the baby's life."

"I know." Maggie put out her cigarette, got up and left without saying another word.

Tuesday Maggie awoke to a storm not only pounding on the windows but in her head. For days the sky had been threatening and now it was here, the wind, the rain and it was as uncontrolled as Maggie felt. Instead of thinking about Sarah leaving, she had an entirely different mission in mind. She shook Marten awake.

"Hey, you still asleep?" Maggie whispered.

"No, I am presently training little kitty cats for the circus," Marten said without opening his eyes.

"I have an errand to do, wanna come?" Maggie asked, not really intending for him to say yes.

"Maggie," Marten asked skeptically, "what are you up to? It doesn't involve hunting witches or bad uncles, does it?"

"Ha. Ha. Don't worry, I will get George to go with me so you can keep sleeping," Maggie cooed.

"Alright, as long as George is with you. I *trust* George."

Maggie kissed him goodbye and flew down the stairs before anyone could stop her. It was only seven a.m. but Maggie knew the Sherwood clan would be up getting ready for school. Maggie found her mother's rain jacket and boots and headed out into the squall.

"Maggie, girl, what are you doing out there?!" Mitzi said as she opened her kitchen door. All three boys were running in different directions, and Mitzi looked like she had slept under a train. "Sorry, can't talk hon. We already missed the bus and I gotta get the boys to school." Mitzi proceeded to wrangle each boy into a rain coat and kick them out the back door while leaving Maggie alone with George in the kitchen. He had on his reading glasses as he perused the sports section, largely ignoring her presence.

"Hi, G. Listen, I'm sorry for being rude last night." Maggie pleaded. George slowly turned a page of the newspaper and did not look at her.

"La la Land, huh? That's where we live? I never knew. Thank you so much for informing us Maggie."

"Awe, G, c'mon, don't be like that. You know what I meant."

"Yeah, but what you said was, 'Maggie is the only one on the planet with a grip on reality', Ha. Double.

Ha." George said as he flipped another page. Maggie could tell he was not really reading anymore.

"I'm sorry. It was out of line. Mitzi didn't seem mad at me."

"Mitzi doesn't get mad at anyone," George retorted.

"C'mon, let it go, let it go, let it rain let it snow.." Maggie began singing and dancing like an idiot until George finally looked at her.

"Dare I ask what you want from me?"

"For you to forgive me! And to go for a little, teeny tiny drive with me," Maggie said with a big sheepish grin pinching her fingers close together in front of his face.

"You have a car."

"Yes, but everyone recognizes my car. Who doesn't hear that old diesel machine coming?"

"Am I to assume you wish to sneak up on someone?"

"Naw. Well, sort of. Just a little surveillance, that's all."

"Really, now who pray tell would be your target?"

"John Murphy Junior."

"Oh, Maggie we are not going to follow your uncle around, that's ridiculous." George shook his head and took off his reading glasses to glare at her.

"You know, I will bug the shit out of you until you do this. Look at it this way, after I confirm that my Uncle Johnny is a complete benign turd on our planet, I promise I will drop any fantasies of flushing him away for good. I just need to spy on him a bit," Maggie said with a cheerful smile.

"A benign turd?"

"C'mon, you know what I mean. Get your coat, c'mon, c'mon," Maggie was dancing from foot to foot.

"You know I have a job to get to," George said still unmoving.

"Yeah, yeah, yeah, the little bunnies and puppies will miss you for a couple of hours. G, c'mon, I'll pay you for God's sake." With that George rose and grabbed his raincoat. Both of them knew all along he could not resist an adventure with Maggie. He had to admit something always happened when he is with her.

"I suppose someone has to keep an eye on you," George acquiesced.

As they were backing out of the driveway, Maggie turned and said, "Donuts, we need donuts and some coffee. I'll buy!" She was giddy about their impending stakeout and forced George to go into the local bakery for a dozen donuts and two black coffees. George would never admit that he was enjoying playing hooky with Maggie, and he could never resist a donut.

He pulled the Suburban onto Johnny's street and rolled to a stop with a clear view of Johnny's yellow Hummer in the driveway. Johnny also had a red 911 Porsche, but he kept that in the garage. Both cars made Maggie cringe. "Seriously, G, look at that car, truck, whatever the hell it is. I mean, c'mon. If he lived on a farm in Montana, maybe, or wanted to be spotted by satellite in the Sahara, but who the hell needs a car that size in Haven?" Maggie spewed powered donut bits out of her mouth. She had already eaten a cruller and was eyeing an old-fashioned next. George was working on his third raspberry jelly.

"You know what they say, big truck...big truck," George snickered.

They sat there for awhile as the wind blew by, laughing and eating donuts. Finally, when George was eating his fifth donut the front door opened of Johnny's house. Maggie was grateful the rain had subsided for the moment so she could get a clear view. They waited for Johnny to shut the door and get into his car, but he stopped on the front stoop. Finally a woman appeared. She was much shorter than Johnny, just barely over five feet and a little heavyset. Maggie could not see her face, only her long black hair and dark olive arms.

"G, who's that?"

"I don't know., I have never seen her before, but look, he is kissing her." Johnny had just planted a big messy kiss on the woman before he locked the front door and they both climbed into the Hummer. Maggie and George looked at each other at the same time and said, "Eeeeeewwe". George started up the Suburban and slowly pulled out behind them.

Uncle Johnny drove out of downtown Haven and inland down old country roads. After ten minutes of sparse suburbs, he pulled onto an unknown street lined with small block houses.

"G', where are we?"

"Oh, I think I think we are in Little Brazil."

"Huh?"

"You know about all the Brazilians and Portuguese who immigrated here, well, they live close together in neighborhoods outside of town. I had a receptionist who was Brazilian and lived here. Mostly because everyone prefers to speak Spanish."

"So do you think the woman is Brazilian?" Maggie eagerly said. Finally, the pieces were fitting together.

"Yeah, she looked it to me. Why Mags? Oh hey, Johnny is leaving. Should I keep following him?" George asked.

"Yes! Yes!" Maggie said banging her hands against the dashboard and spilling her coffee.

"What? Jeez, what is it?!" George asked.

"G, don't you see? He is in love with a Brazilian woman and I have photographs of him hitting a Brazilian woman. He would probably get his ass seriously kicked if she or her family found out, right? Doesn't it make sense?!" Maggie grinned at him wide eyed knowing he could not deny her triumph.

"Okay, Little Red, you got me on this one. Yep, makes sense, Johnny falls in love, or whatever he is capable of, with a woman who, probably your grandmother would not have approved of, sorry she was a snob at heart." Maggie nodded in agreement.

"But also, knowing your uncle, he is probably ashamed of it as well. He is a total 'turd' that way." Maggie kept nodding in agreement.

"And secondly, you just do not go into Little Brazil and dip your pen in their ink, if you know what I mean."

"Nicely put, G'," Maggie said with lighthearted sarcasm. "So now I know why he is so scared. I got him! See, now wasn't it worth missing the little bunnies this morning?" Maggie punched him the arm and was giddy with her discovery.

"Should we keep following him?"

"Yeah, let's just see where he goes next."

Johnny only went to the post office and the local diner on Main Street. After he went in, George convinced Maggie he had to go to work and was taking her home. As she got out of the car on Grove Avenue, Maggie said, "See, you have to admit, G', I'm not that crazy."

"I'm not admitting to anything." George smiled and shook his head. He said he would stop by after work, hopefully before she got into anymore trouble.

Excerpts from the Diary of Vivian Murphy Atwood August 2004

It has been a year since Momma died and I can't say we are any better for it. Twelve months of a blur, waking up doing what I am supposed to do, being what I am supposed to be. But what is that? A wife? A mother? I realize my whole life has been filled with safety nets and cushions. In A.A. they talk about rock bottom, have I ever hit it or have I been here all along? I am trying to control my drinking, my disease, as they say. I manage a month or two, and then I can't seem to make it any further. I need to make a change, and I fear it might be the worst mistake of my life.

Mac, my dear precious Mac, he wants to fix me, make it all better. He protects me too much from myself, never letting me feel too guilty for my actions. I could rip him apart, and he would still tell me it was okay. I admit, I want him to leave. He is always asking me what I need, and I need him to leave. It is so hard to confess my true feelings. The one thing I have never had in my life was being alone. Maggie and Sarah have that solitude even though they struggle against it. They are too young to realize what they are gaining from it: independence and confidence. Even though both of them are stubborn to a fault, they are each their own person, they can make decisions for themselves and stand by them. Momma made the decisions for me, the girls, Mac. I have never had a chance to prove myself, find some self worth. I love Mac, with all my heart, and this is not about finding another man. It is about finding me. I know no one will understand, but I also know Mac will. He will see the reason, the logic, because he wants me to be happy. His heart will be broken but he will never admit it because it might make me feel worse than I already do.

He will be fine but will I be? Finally, no babysitters, no guards at the gate, it is about time I grew up and took responsibility for just myself. Isn't that what they say in the program? Keep the focus on yourself, let go and let God?

TWENTY SIX

When Maggie walked in the house and stamped off her boots, she saw the suitcases. Again she was at a crossroads whether to tell her sister what she discovered considering Sarah bit her head off last night. Standing there, with seconds to decide, she knew her decision. Hearing someone in the kitchen, Maggie hung up her raincoat and went to go see who it was.

It was Marten fixing himself his usual fried egg on toast, "Hi, Honey! How are you?" Maggie said with too much glee.

"I think, my dear," Marten said while kissing her forehead, "I should ask, how are you? I detect a little gleam in your eye."

"Yeah, well, George and I discovered something."

"Did you find the keys to the magic kingdom? Were there lucky charms at the end of the rainbow?" Marten asked with a smile full of runny egg.

"You have been watching too much American television, mister. We followed Uncle Johnny this morning."

"Surprise, surprise," Marten dead panned.

"No, he has a girlfriend, a *Brazilian* girlfriend," Maggie said nodding her head in a 'you know' fashion.

"Yes, and you have a *German* boyfriend. Shall we have a Green card party?" Marten's sarcasm was on a roll.

"No, don't you ever listen to me?"

"Only every third word. I find it more efficient."

"Asshole. Okay, remember the pictures of Uncle Johnny being arrested because he beat up a Brazilian woman? And now is dating a Brazilian woman? Hello, you have got to see it!" Marten slowly finished chewing his breakfast, wiped his mouth and took a sip of coffee.

"Okay, yes, I see. Sordid uncle doesn't want sordid past to affect his sordid relationship. Very good, Perry Mason."

"I mean it, no more American television."

"So, sordid uncle could be looking for sordid pictures. Okay, man the doors, I am going to go buy a gun. Should I get a rifle or a shotgun? What do you Americans prefer in this kind of situation?"

"Okay, you're a funny guy. But now, I know what he is up to, and I am not going to let him bully me."

"Well, what are you going to do? I suppose my suggesting you let it go could not possibly be an option?" Marten leaned close to her and looked her in the eye.

"I'll make a deal with you, honey. I figure out this family mess and I am yours, completely yours, and no more craziness. No more drama, I promise."

"What if you don't find what you are looking for? Then what? Where does that leave us?" Marten was being dead serious now. Then they heard Sarah and David coming down the stairs. Maggie quickly leaned in and kissed Marten on the lips and whispered, "Don't worry. And don't tell Sarah anything."

David trailed Sarah down the stairs with their suitcases, and Maggie could not help but wonder what extra items from the house were hidden in them. Although she outwardly accepted all of Sarah's changes and reform, Maggie knew her sister at heart and guessed she would find some small, yet valuable, family heirlooms missing from the house later. It was in Sarah's nature to take what she wanted and in Maggie's to mistrust her.

"Hope you don't have a rain delay," Maggie said trying to convey false sincerity. In truth, she wanted to walk her sister right through Logan airport and onto the plane.

"Nope, we are fine, the real storm isn't coming until later. Can we talk a minute before I leave?" Sarah insisted of Maggie. Maggie cringed on the inside and dreaded more scolding from her sister.

They moved in to the kitchen leaving David and Marten to make small talk in the living room. Undoubtedly they had come up with a few inside jokes about the behavior of the two sisters over the past week. Maggie immediately busied herself with making a cup of coffee to avoid Sarah's chiding stare.

"Sit down Mags, and stop avoiding me," Sarah said.

"Whatever do you mean?" Maggie sat across from her at the kitchen table and stirred sugar into her coffee.

"Sarah, I know what you are going to say: drop this witch hunt, let Mom go, the past is the past, seek therapy, yadda yadda yadda., I get it. But here's a little news flash, I am not you, and I do things my own way."

"Yes, we have certainly all learned that."

"What's that supposed to mean?" Maggie shot back at her.

"Listen, I don't want to fight with you. Okay? Just do what you have to do to settle your issues, but don't get to crazy over it. Uncle Johnny's a creep, I'll back you up on that one. But Mom's death, no matter how, happened. And that really is the end of the story. Regardless of how insane you are, you are my sister, and I love you. I would like it if we could talk more and not disappear on each other again. This baby is going to need some form of family." Sarah said with a grin.

"Yeah, sure." Maggie hesitated but deep down she too did not want to argue with her sister anymore.

"C, mon Mags. Blood out, blood in, sisters through sick and sin, right?"

"Yeah, okay, we'll talk more. I promise. Are you taking Mom's diaries with you?"

"If you don't mind? I want to re-read them."

"No, just promise we will pass them back and forth when the other wants them. But what about the ashes?"

"Let's wait awhile on that one. I'm not ready, are you?" Sarah said.

"No. I'll keep her on the mantle so I won't lose her." Maggie said with an ironic smile.

They got up and hugged because there was nothing more that needed to be said. They were sisters again, tentatively. Each would have to try a little harder, make an effort and mind their manners with each other. Their grandmother would have been so proud.

The rain stayed at bay as Marten helped David load their rental car. Hugs and kisses and promises to talk soon were relayed back and forth. Marten put his arm around Maggie as they headed back into the house.

"Relieved?" Marten asked as they entered the house.

"Yes, am I awful?" Maggie replied.

"No, you have time to have a relationship with her. This isn't the movies, the credits aren't rolling." Maggie and Marten both sat on the living room couch and breathed in the silence. "How do you feel?" Marten looked at her sideways with concern.

"Tired." She knew he was asking more about her suspicion of Uncle Johnny, but she avoided the issue.

"I take it you didn't tell Sarah about your detective work this morning?"

"Nope." Again Maggie was trying not to go into it with Marten, afraid he might take up Sarah's cause of getting her to let the situation go. Luckily she was saved by a knock at the front door. Archie, it seemed, wanted to have his play time with Marten and offered to show him his fleet of fishing boats down at the harbor and a pint at the pub afterwards. Marten hesitated to leave Maggie since they were finally alone, but she convinced him she just wanted to take a nap that afternoon and they would have a quiet night later. Kissing her long and hard, Marten looked into her eyes and whispered "Be good" with a knowing wink. Maggie watched as two of her favorite men in matching yellow raincoats climbed laughing into Archie's old Chevy truck.

Maggie stayed at the window for few minutes watching the squall line over the horizon. Although it had rained all morning, she knew later the torrential downpours would come and hopefully drown out any noise in her head.

She did not know how long she had been napping upstairs, when she heard the heavy footsteps. It had been nice to have a quiet house and to fall asleep with the rain pattering against the window pane. Coming out of her fog, she assumed the weighty stomps were Marten's and did not bother to call out. Instead Maggie raised herself up and marveled at how the sky looked majestic with its low cloud cover and the cedar trees swaying. Putting on a heavy sweater and wool socks, she walked out into the hallway and screamed.

"You son of a bitch, I'm calling the police!" Maggie roared.

"Awe, Maga-doodle, calm down. I am just family, remember? I saw you were asleep and didn't want to wake you."

"This my house, Uncle Johnny, and you are trespassing again." She noticed he had a box full of stuff in his arms as he started going down the stairs, and she screamed "What the hell do you have?!" Maggie raced down after him and tried to get her hands on the box.

"Whoa, missy, these are some of my things that I am just taking back," Johnny said as he lifted the box over Maggie's head when they entered the living room. "You really are just like your Grandmother, you think everything is yours." Maggie's eyes had to adjust to the blue darkness radiating from the storm clouds filling the room. She felt a chill down her spine being alone in a dark house with Johnny, so she quickly began turning on the lights. She noticed on the wall clock it was only three in the afternoon and by the silence of the rest of the house, she knew Marten was not home with Archie yet. Standing by the far side of the room, she decided to go on the offensive with Johnny.

"Let me guess, Uncle Johnny, I bet you were looking for some photographs?" Maggie shot at him as she folded her arms over her chest. Maggie was going to stand her ground this time and confront him.

Pausing just slightly, Johnny then slowly put the box beside the couch and took a seat. Keeping his eyes on her, a sly smile began to spread across his face as he ran his fingers across his hair, smoothing his ponytail. "Forgive me, Maggie, I spoke too soon. You are exactly like your grandmother, as well as your mother." The sarcasm dripped off his tongue, but he still kept the grin plastered to his face.

"How did your search go?" Maggie said flippantly, knowing he did not find them since she had moved them under her mattress before she slept.

"What do you want, Maggie?" He said with venom. "You want to be like those other two bitches and keep me in line? Rule the family and control everyone?"

"Do I have to? I mean, certainly seems like it if you keep breaking into my house and taking my things."

"These are my things, and I earned them."

"Well, then why didn't Grandma give them to you or Mom let you have them? Mmm? Doesn't seem like after all this time whatever is in that box is really yours, does it? Did you find the family jewels? And here is my question to you, mister, how badly did you want them? Were you willing to hurt my mother for them?" Maggie began to slowly inch across the room to see what was in the box.

"Jesus, Maggie, for Christ sakes! It is just my mother's Limoges collection and my father's pocket watch and cuff links." Johnny then began to pull the little Limoges boxes out of the cardboard box and the gold pocket watch of her grandfather's. He also pulled out some photographs of him when he was younger. Virginia had collected the French porcelain boxes for years and had quite a large collection. Although the items were valuable,

Maggie admitted they were not much to get worked up over. She could understand why her mother would hang onto such things, but they did not mean that much to Maggie.

"Don't you want the photographs?" Maggie persisted, "Or, more importantly, how desperately do you want the photographs? Or the family jewelry for that matter?" Maggie raised one eyebrow and crossed her arms even tighter. She could hear the rain coming down harder as it got even darker inside the house.

Johnny kept cool and began picking his teeth with his pinkie nail. A habit, Maggie realized, he did when he was nervous. But she was disgusted all the same. Since he was not breaking his silence, Maggie broke her own rule and kept talking. Her nervous energy was getting the best of her, and the stress of the past week was fueling her questions.

"Who was that Brazilian woman at your house this morning? Is she why you need the photographs, afraid her *familia* might find out she is with a violent man, huh? A man who hits Brazilian women? And this brings me back to the question, considering how seriously you may want those photographs, and knowing my mother had them-oh yes, I know all about the 'arrangement' between you two-how far would you go to get them back?"

"And the jewelry? Who doesn't want jewelry, especially if they think a treasure trove is hidden right in front of them? So, Johnny, again my question is: how far would you go for such things? What would you do for them? Where were you the night my mother died? Were you in this house collecting what was yours?!!" Maggie was spitting and breathing so hard as the last few words came out of her mouth, she did not feel her own nails digging into her arms.

The tree branches clattered against the side of the house and the lights flickered slightly. Maggie's blood pumped anger as she stared as hard as she could at Johnny.

Johnny, on the other hand, looked away and gazed out at the descending night sky. She watched him as he slowly shook his head from side to side and then lifted his eyes up to hers. During her tirade, Maggie had been so focused on her words she had lost focus on him. Something had left him. The straightness in his spine was gone, his hands were clasped and relaxed on his lap and his leg had stopped swinging. The fight had gone out of him, and now Maggie was terribly confused.

"Is that what you think Maggie? I came here that night and…what? Shoved your Mother down a flight of stairs for some diamonds?" Johnny paused to shake his head from side to side some more.

"You know, I never really fit into this family, and now I just figured out why. I just don't think like any of you: my mother, your mother, my sister, your sister. I lack imagination, or insanity, or whatever you want to call it that all of you have. Sure, I've made mistakes and haven't been the most straight and honest guy, but murder? That's how you see me? My mother was a cold, stubborn, manipulative bitch, and… my sister? Well she was screwed up, and I got the pleasure of growing up in the shadow of that. So forgive me, if I don't speak so fondly of my childhood. "

"But Maggie, don't confuse insensitivity with evil. No matter what you may think you know or have learned about my past, you never lived in my shoes. I have my reasons for how I feel, same as you about your past, and at some point, you are going to have to respect that and let sleeping dogs lie."

"Yeah, but..." Maggie started, a little too desperate. Johnny just held up his hand to stop her.

"Maggie the night your mother died, I was nowhere near this house. I was home with the woman you saw me with this morning. Her name is Maria, and she is my wife. We have been married for five years and, yes, I have kept that a secret. Of course, I am embarrassed by what happened with Luciana. I admit, I screwed up. But that was a long time ago, and I am sick of it being held over my head, dammit. Yes, of course, I was looking for those photos, what do you think? Maria's father and three brothers would kick my ass if they found out. So I kept Maria from the family so Vivi would not have anymore ammunition against me. And, as for the jewelry, no I did not find or steal any, I just wondered what happened to these things. It is not like your mother and I talked a lot after Momma died and, well, Vivi seemed to get everything else from Momma, so I just figured she got those things as well."

Johnny's voice trailed off as he looked at his hands clasping and unclasping. Then he finally turned back to Maggie and said, "Ah, hell, Maggie. I see where you are coming from. You just lost your mother but as far as I know, Vivi was probably drunk again and fell down the stairs. Sorry, kiddo, but this family isn't known for its happy endings."

Maggie undid her arms and dropped down into a club chair. Now the fight had gone out of her as well. She forgot the golden rule of writing: every story has sides, and every side has a story. Uncle Johnny may be a creep but she believed him. He was a jaded adult who carried around his childhood grudges like badges of honor. They justified his arrogance and bad behavior. But like Peter said, Johnny was a coward at heart. He was a hurt little boy who could spin his tantrums like webs, and she just got caught up in them.

With that thought, Maggie got up and went upstairs. When she returned, she handed Johnny the photographs and said, "Stay out of my house, Uncle J. If you want to come in, you knock."

"Thanks, Magpie, I knew you were a good girl," he said, as he lifted his hand like a pistol and shot at her while winking at the same time. *What an idiot*, Maggie thought. Maggie leaned down and grabbed the cardboard box and handed it to him. She stepped out of the way hinting that it was time for him to leave but, right as he reached the front door, Maggie stopped him.

"Wait. I don't suppose you know if Mom was seeing anybody when she died? Or if you knew of anybody who might have been coming over here at night?" Johnny slowly turned and looked her in the eye.

"Sorry, kiddo. Again, your mother and I just did not know each other very well." Johnny turned and walked out into the rain. Maggie stared through the drops feeling defeated again. She finally got answers, but not the ones she wanted.

TWENTY SEVEN

Excerpts from the Diary of Vivian Murphy Atwood
January 2006

I am going to go see Maggie in New York in a few days and I regret scheduling the trip. I just signed the divorce papers with Mac, and I dread telling Maggie because I know how upset she will be. Ever since Mac moved out she has been distant and cold with me, and I can't blame her. I know she thinks this is another one of my monumentally bad decisions. She had been less patient with me this past year, but I really can't ask her for anymore understanding. I have forced her for years to look past my behavior, to love me unconditionally and now, when I need it the most, I fear I have used her up.

Mac and I are still friends, and see each other often. He has rented a little house just a mile from Grove. And when Maggie *does come home, which isn't often, she will see Mac spends more time over here. The whole situation has actually turned out for the best because, finally, I don't feel obligated. The pressure of marriage and motherhood has been lifted, is that awful to say? Everyone can be on their own. I have my own routine finally. I work in the garden and have lunch with friends. I make my own meals and clean up my own messes. Sometimes, I admit I have dark nights, not because I am alone but because I am sad, so very sad for the many things that have happened. I miss Thomas still, odd, after all these years to imagine loving a man whose face I can barely recall. Or maybe when I was with Thomas, that was the last time I felt myself. All these years of being in the Murphy shadow, living Momma's way, at least with Thomas I was somewhat on my own. I have to get back to that, find myself, my independence again. I know then Maggie and I will be close again. She will eventually understand, I know she will.*

Excerpts from the Diary of Vivian Murphy Atwood February 2006

I regret so deeply what I have done to my girls, the awful memories I have given them that I can't even begin to apologize for any of it. It has been three weeks since Maggie has spoken to me, and I feel my insides curling up and dying. What I did in New York was unforgivable, I know, and her silence is a constant reminder. Somehow, I got so nervous to see her, to tell her about Mac and everything going through my head. I just do not handle pressure very well. I can't even recall how many drinks I had on the train, and I don't even remember most of the night. God knows what I said or did to her. I do remember her hitting me, that animal look in her eye of fear and loathing. I keep thinking, I, her mother, did that to her. How could I be capable of hurting someone I love so deeply? How could I push her that far? So I have made a decision, I will let Maggie be. I know Momma would not agree. Momma would have to stick her nose in things and fix and change them to suit her. But, I will act differently. I will let Maggie be. I won't try to change her mind or guilt her into forgiving me. Maggie is decent at heart, and if I force her into holding my hand, then she would, whether she wants to or not. Because that is how I was with my mother, ever so obligated to her. No, I won't do that to Maggie. No matter what my problems are, I will have to handle them. And then I will prove to Maggie that I have changed and she will come back to me.

Excerpts from the Diary of Vivian Murphy Atwood February 2008

It is Maggie's birthday today and I can't say my heart isn't breaking. Two years have passed since we have spoken, and not a day goes by I don't think of her. Of course I got her a present, but I cannot bring myself to mail it to her. I will just save it and give it to her when I can see her face. I know she is with a man now. I hope he is the right one but I have learned that is not for me to decide. Maggie needs to do this on her own. I just wish I could tell her how proud I am of her. She has already broken the family cycle and will find all the things I never could in life. Sarah, too, is doing much better and I am proud of her as well. I hope she can stay sober for her sake, not mine. My girls deserve everything that I took away from them. My only wish is that someday the three of us will be here in this house again. I want to see my grandchildren. They may not believe it, but I know they will have beautiful children who will never know the horror of those dark dark nights. That is what keeps me going. Knowing in my heart that someday they will return, my own beautiful children as the women I always dreamed of being, and perhaps will be someday.

The April storm was blowing hard over the coast now, daring the sea to remain calm. The moored sailboats, waiting for summer's easy tides, swayed frantically in the rising wind. New England was always hard pressed to let go of its winters. Summer had to push and fight and usher itself in like a boxer taking the ring. As the skies pinched black at every corner, Maggie's mood lay silent and still and ready to pounce on anyone who questioned her. After Uncle Johnny left, she was determined to finish this story. She spent the rest of the afternoon putting in phone calls to Lou and Frank Mayhew, who were both unavailable due to the storm. Then Maggie grabbed her mother's phonebook and began calling everyone her mother knew, asking them if they had come over on a bicycle that fateful Saturday night. People apologized for knowing nothing and, again, expressed their condolences.

An hour later, Maggie paced the front porch smoking cigarettes and sipping on a gin and tonic still at a dead end. She welcomed the cool, salty wind and the chill that matched the one in her heart. She was desperate to solve this mystery. It was so simple for Maggie, why did George or Marten not understand? Her mother did not just die; there was a reason, an explanation. As the rain began to punch the side of the house, Maggie's thoughts collided with themselves.

If someone was in the house, did they fight with Vivian? Her mother was prone to slapping when she was drunk, did someone fight back? Did that someone think they could get her money? But they should have known everything was to go to her and Sarah? Every instinct in Maggie told her someone was not being honest with her. She was not crazy. Maggie always knew one thing, to trust her instincts. When Maggie was young and would ride the school bus home, she would get this feeling. Everyday after school, when the bus rounded this certain bend in the road she would get a premonition as to whether or not Vivian would be drunk when she got home. And she was almost always right. Since then, she always knew if she felt it in her gut, she should listen. Like when she met Marten, she knew he was the one, that she would be with him for the rest of her life.

Archie had dropped Marten back at home a few minutes before, and Maggie had sent a tirade of emotion in his direction. He had listened to her calmly as she told him about Uncle Johnny and all the phone calls she had made that afternoon. She could see the disappointment cloud his eyes at her frantic behavior. But instead of arguing with her to be reasonable or trying to calm her down, he simply said okay and retreated to the kitchen. Frustrated, Maggie went out on the porch to figure her next move.

When there was a knock at the front door, Maggie ran inside hoping it would be anybody willing to help or listen to her. Marten emerged from the kitchen as Millie was letting herself in. Under a gigantic, light blue umbrella with a matching rain coat, Millie looked straight into Maggie's eyes.

"What is going on with you, child?!" Taken aback by Millie's sternness, Maggie's mouth dropped open. "You have got this poor man worried to death about you," and pointed at Marten. "Yes, he called me and told me everything. And now you have got this whole town thinking that your mother has been murdered! I know you are upset, but have you completely lost your mind?" Maggie was not used to Millie being infuriated by her.

"I just had some questions, that's all," and even as Maggie spoke she knew how pathetic she sounded. She had completely forgotten how small Haven was and when you go around hunting the chief of police, you can be damn sure people are going to talk about it. "I'm sorry

Millie, I just.... Well, there was someone here the night Mom died, and I have to find out what happened." Maggie could hear the whine in her voice, she sounded like a stupid five year old again.

"Maggie, darling," Millie's voice was softer, kinder now, "you need to just forget all about that. Sugar, your mother had a terrible accident, plain and simple. She tripped coming down the stairs and that could happen to any one of us as we get on in years. Lord knows, I shouldn't wear my pumps anymore. Listen to me, Maggie, let well enough alone."

"Yeah, but Uncle Johnny was here searching for all of Grandma's jewelry. You remember Grandma's diamond brooch and necklace, don't you? Well, I can't find them and Johnny doesn't have them. So maybe someone robbed Mom last Saturday and hurt her, and here we are like a bunch of idiots pretending like it was an accident?!"

Millie looked questioningly at her and Maggie thought she had finally gotten through to someone. "Hang on, just a second dear. We will get to the bottom of this." Millie then turned and, in two strides, left the living room and was in the kitchen on the telephone. Maggie and Marten heard her speaking in low tones until she peered her head around the corner and said, "Maggie, hon, someone wants to talk to you."

Maggie went into the kitchen and grabbed the receiver to hear a male voice.

"Hello, Maggie? Millie said you had some questions about your grandmother's jewelry?" Maggie immediately recognized Bill Getty's voice. Of course, she dumbly thought, she should have asked him at the funeral.

"I am not sure if you knew or would remember Virginia giving away some money before she got sick? Well, I guess Virginia, being as smart as she was knew her time was up and had me sell all her jewelry. She did not want Essie, Vivi, or Johnny fighting over the pieces when she passed. She just gave the money to her favorite charities and causes because she thought they could use it more than her children. Remember when George received one of those donations for his animal hospital and Johnny tried to sue him get the money back? Well, I believe that was the diamond brooch," Bill said with a chuckle. "Sorry, Maggie, I am sure your grandmother never meant to disappoint you if you wanted those things."

"Oh, no Bill, it was nothing like that. It's just that Uncle Johnny made me think they were missing. Sorry to bother you. I just had the wrong idea."

"No worries. Maggie, you can bother me anytime."

"Thanks, Bill." And Maggie hung up the receiver and stared at the kitchen counter knowing Millie and Marten were behind her waiting.

Maggie could hear the cedar tree banging against the upstairs window and felt the banging in her heart. All three of them moved back into the living room where there was more light. Outside was pitch black and the torrents of rain blanketed them. Maggie explained to Millie and Marten what Bill had said, and they all agreed it made sense. "See, child, there is nothing to get yourself so worked up over. There was no plot against your Mama," Millie kept saying. But Maggie kept hearing the word 'no' resounding in her head. Millie did not understand. Her mother believed they would all be together someday. This accident could not just happen. Vivian would not have allowed it.

"Millie, something happened here that Saturday night, I know it did. You and Marten and George just think I am crazy, but I feel it in my heart. Why can't you have a little faith or trust in me that there is a cover up of some sort? Mom and Grandma kept so many damn secrets from me, and I can't let this be another one."

Just then George came storming through the front door, stomping his feet and shaking the water from his hair like a St. Bernard. "Jesus, Maggie, are you trying to give this town a heart attack? You know how many phone calls I've gotten about you today? What the hell are you doing!" Maggie was tired of being yelled at and yelled back.

"So I have all of you ganging up on me? That's just great! Silly me to think any of you would support me. George, you heard Mitzi, someone was here that night, and Mom was not that drunk! I mean, falling down the stairs, it is just crazy! As you said Millie, it is plain and simple!" Maggie felt herself starting to scream a little and tried to calm down.

"Honey," Marten started towards her, "it is not that. Sometimes you just have to accept the way things are and let them fade into the past. Of course we love you, but you will never get over this until you get past it." Maggie felt like Marten was coddling her, trying to talk her off the ledge. It pissed her off. She wanted to be angry, anger felt good to her like the battering rain outside. Maggie started.

"The whole story about Grandma being married before and never telling Mom, it's the perfect climax to our family. That is why they were all so screwed up, secrets! Her whole life, Mom knew something was wrong, that her mother was distant and angry with her, but Mom never knew why. No, let's all pretend we are one happy family until everyone is so twisted and sick. Mom knew there was a reason that kept Grandma from loving her. Grandma blamed her only daughter for killing the love of her life. If they had only talked about it, if they did not walk around like martyrs, so stoic and cold, then maybe this would have all turned out differently." Maggie swung her arms in large arcs around the room to encompass her point before she kept going.

"This family is about lies, the lies they told themselves, and the lies they told me. Well, it stops here. You think it's best for me to sit down and shut up? That's what they did for years and corked their mouths with what?! THIS!"

Maggie picked up her crystal tumbler full of gin, wound her arm back, and smashed it against the wall. Hearing the glass break was like a small spray of fireworks in the living room. Everyone was silent after that. Maggie could not stop staring at the spot where the glass had hit. Her heart was racing and she focused on the sound of the furious, whistling wind outside. Her cheeks grew red as she remembered the three pairs of eyes all focused on her. How could they understand her anger, her loneliness? The memories of her childhood had created a chasm between her and the rest of the world. She was filled with a rage and hurt that never went away. How could they understand?

Maggie felt her family had scarred her somewhere deep inside that she could not find or heal. Now that she had answers to why her Grandmother and her mother lived with caged hearts, she felt little satisfaction. She felt cheated at not being able to yell at them, to blame them. Maggie desperately wanted to see her mother. She wanted to hug her and tell her she understood, but also, she wanted to yell at her for treating her the same way Virginia treated her. If only I could talk to my mother,

Maggie thought, but 'if only' was gone now because someone took that chance away. It was no accident.

Without looking at Marten, George, or Millie, Maggie sat on the couch and slowly put her hands over her face. There was a feeling of black coming over her, wiping her mind free, turning her heart to stone. The heels of her feet rocked her shaking body. Only the ghosts in the room could understand her, and they were just ghosts, whispers of the past that would always haunt her. Nothing was real. Then she felt large arms envelope her, and she could smell Marten trying to warm life back into her. His aftershave was like flowers in the stale room. Maggie would never remember if it was a few moments or a few hours before there was another deep rapping on the front door.

Swiftly, George moved and answered it. Maggie looked up but Marten kept his arms anchoring her. She turned and saw Millie smile and nod her head toward the two men coming through the door. Millie seemed delighted all of a sudden and said, "Frank, Mac, very good timing. Come in, come in."

Maggie saw the chief of police but also her old stepfather, Mac. She remained silent trying to register what was going on.

"Maggie, sorry, I did not get back to you today, but I think everything you want to know, Mac here can explain. I hope we aren't disturbing anything," Chief Mayhew said as he noticed the tension in the room.

"No, no, come in and sit down. I will put on some coffee," Millie said bustling to the kitchen. George remained standing not knowing whether to stay or go.

Mac picked up on that. "It's okay George, you are a part of the family. Have a seat," Mac said as he took the club chair across from Maggie on the couch. Maggie almost forgot that this had been Mac's home for the better part of ten years. He was comfortable here, he knew it here. The lines of the ceiling, the lines of the fabric, they had once been his and Maggie had once been his step-daughter.

He sat across from her and smiled affectionately, as if he approved. Maggie could not understand what was going on and looked back at him, remembering those lost nights of laughing at each other across a backgammon table. She found comfort in his eyes not because he was a father figure but because he was family.

Sitting there staring eye to eye, Maggie felt the familiarity she had always had when Mac was around. Mac was the quiet pillar in the corner who held every-thing together. All he had done for Vivian, holding her hand those deteriorating nights, cleaning up the mess the next day, and never being fully appreciated. Virginia treat-ed him like Vivian's babysitter and, well, so did Vivian. They always expected him there to take care of her. But it was Vivian who asked him to leave, and he did so quietly. Until now, Maggie assumed that it was Mac who had got-ten sick of playing second fiddle to Vivian's drinking and had left himself. Maggie never understood why he had stayed all those years anyway.

Vivian did not want to be taken care of, not cod-dled by her family or anyone. Now that the truth had been revealed to Vivian, about her father and the acci-dent, everything in her had crumbled. Everything she had known or understood sat sideways and disheveled in her heart. The only way she could sort through her sixty years was to be alone. She loved Mac, but this time was not about Mac, it was finally about her. Vivian was 57 years old and needed to find out what she wanted from her life before it was too late. They parted amicably and Mac re-spected her wishes.

Mac crossed and laced his fingers and eyed Maggie, "Mags, sweetheart, I had put Vivi to bed just like old times. I thought she was asleep, you know, so I left. I swore, she was asleep. I didn't think in my heart she would get back up again, or I would have stayed with her. I should have stayed with her…if only I had stayed." Maggie took a few moments before her hand went flying to her mouth. Tears welled in her eyes, and she understood. It was Mac. Mac had been there that night, faithful loving Mac, just like when he was her husband. He had gently convinced her to go upstairs, undid her sweater and slipped off her loafers. He probably even talked to her a bit like he used too. Maggie could see the image in her mind, she had it embedded in her memory over and over.

"Mac, oh God, I didn't know.." Maggie trailed off because she understood the gravity of the situation. All of them, Virginia, Sarah, Maggie all had the fear that something would happen to Vivian on their watch. It was the nightmare of loving her mother, that you could be responsible, but you could also be the one who failed her. Maggie had lived with it everyday of her life. Just then, Maggie leapt off the couch and threw her arms around Mac.

"It is not your fault, Mac, you did not do this. You did not fail her or us or me. It was an accident, it just happened." Just the way they all feared, Maggie thought in her head. "But why were you at the house?"

"Well, you know I never stopped loving your mother even though I moved out. I understood why she asked me to leave, but sometimes that just don't make a person gone. On her bad nights, she would call me up and well, I would get on my bike and come over. I did not want anyone to see my car so they would not get the wrong impression about us. So I would just sit with her, get her to bed, and well, you know the drill. I know I should have said something to you a few days ago, but I just feel so guilty that I left that night. I should have been here Mags. If I was here then maybe this never would have happened. I would have stopped her from going down those stairs."

"Shut up, Mac, don't talk that way. I had know idea you still came over. I acted so foolishly because I feel that way too, I should have been here. I let her down too. I guess, my mind grabbed another explanation that if someone hurt Mom, or there was a reason for her death, then I would be absolved. I guess we both have to stop playing God and stop thinking we had the power to save her. There was no sin so we don't need absolution. Mac, you and I, we were watchmen and the clock stopped. It is as simple as that." As Maggie said the words out loud, it began to register with her. She finally could put an ending on her mother's story.

"I am sorry, Maggie, for everything. I did not mean to make you worry, but I just felt so horrible."

"Sshh, Mac. Now, I understand. Now, I under-stand everything."

"Did you know those were meant for you?" Mac asked as he pointed to the long strand of pearls around her neck. "Vivi bought them for your birthday last Feb-ruary, but I guess she did not have enough courage to send them to you. She was sorry, Maggie, so sorry for everything she put you through. She often said you were the best thing that ever happened to her. You were her best friend." Maggie's hand instinctually went to the pearls and felt their cool roundness between her fingers. Her mother knew she would never wear short pearls but she would love a long strand. Vivi knew Maggie like only a mother could and, with that thought, Maggie smiled through her uninterrupted tears. Silence hung in the room, and Maggie could feel herself coming back around. She saw George sitting at the edge of his seat, intent and focused on the scene. Marten kept his eyes on Maggie and was looking at her with all the love and worry in his heart. Chief Mayhew stayed back in respect twirling his cap in his hand. It had been Frank Mayhew who convinced Mac to confess. They were good friends and it was Frank who had told Mac about Vivian's death soon after she was discovered. Mac immediately admitted he had been with Vivi the night before, and they both thought it was best to keep it quiet so that Vivian could maintain a little dignity. Out of their love for Vivian, they did not want people to gossip about her drinking and thought it best to leave it just as it was, an accident.

"You knew, didn't you?" Maggie directed at Millie, who was quietly forcing coffee cups into everyone hands. Maggie didn't mean it as an accusation just the full reveal of the truth.

"Of course I did, dear. I live next door," and Millie winked. Maggie was not mad. It was not Millie's place to tell, she understood. Maggie got up and gave Mac a kiss on his old wrinkled forehead. The storm still raged outside and Maggie walked out onto the porch. Millie put her hand on Marten's shoulder to keep him where he was, they all understood Maggie needed to be alone.

Outside, the cold wind enveloped Maggie and the ocean's salty air mixed with the salt of her tears. Through the squall, she saw a light across the harbor and fixated on it. There she stood, still and calm, feeling the eye of the storm pass. She had survived the worst of it, she thought. It was over now. Instead of feeling an ending wash over her, she chose to renew her attention on tomorrow. Maggie did not want to look back anymore, but forward to something, anything. She knew in her heart it would be clear and sunny, perhaps the first true day of summer. That was good enough for her.

Maggie imagined the morning light in her bedroom to be clear and bright like when she was young. A time when she awoke to Vivian in the kitchen packing tuna fish sandwiches, cokes, and potato chips for the beach. Maggie could see her standing there, lovely, in a one piece black bathing suit and a pair of shorts, still in her pearls from the night before. Vivi would hustle Sarah and Maggie, and Virginia and Jack into the Mercedes along with chairs and towels and toys until they all fit. Cramped in the station wagon, they would wind along the coast for thirty minutes to the dune filled shore while smelling the fresh cut grass and rosa rugosa. The sea would be just along the left hand side and Maggie would squint at the bright sunlight that looked like gold cresting along the waves. When they got to the beach and unloaded their towels and baskets, Vivian would rub white zinc oxide on their noses to keep them from getting burned. The day would be filled with friends and neighbors parking blankets, chairs, and umbrellas next to theirs. Food and gossip would be shared amongst everyone. Maggie and Sarah would run in and out of the waves with the other children. Vivian stood vigilant at the shoreline with her hands on her hips, worrying as they crashed with each wave. She would wipe the sand off their fingers before they ate their lunch and think of games for them to play with each other. Grandpa Jack would build large sandcastles for all the children, and Virginia would sit with a book and look out every so often, smiling under a large sun hat. As their skin began to feel chilled and tanned, everyone would make noises about home and barbecues for dinner.

After a day of playing in the dunes, her mother would check them for ticks and pull fresh t-shirts over their heads to warm the goosebumps on their salty skin. They would laugh. Virginia and Vivian would discuss stopping at the store for lobsters for dinner. At the fish market, Maggie and Sarah would go to the ice cream stand and get vanilla chocolate chip cones that Virginia would make them eat before they got back into the car. Her mother would wink at them as she stole spoonfuls. Maggie would drift off to sleep as the car rolled the hills home, full. Tomorrow, Maggie thought, she would make tuna fish sandwiches and take Marten to the shore. To-morrow, Maggie thought, she would only remember the days at the beach and how beautiful her mother was just like a pearl in the sun.

TWENTY EIGHT

The next day, Maggie did take Marten to the shore. May had come and was ushering in summer in Haven with clear blue skies and bright sunshine. Millie and George left them alone, and they found themselves laughing outside in the sprinklers, reading on the porch, and having lobster dinners. After a week of pure bliss, Maggie awoke dreamily in her bed and found Marten standing over her.

"Do you know your mother only had a typewriter?" Marten said. Her mother never understood computers. Maggie laughed and nodded as he handed her a typed piece of paper. Written on it was Marten's resignation as a carpenter in New Orleans.

"Do you think we can find an actual fax machine in this town?"

Maggie nodded again and asked, "Are you sure? I was thinking maybe we should stay up here for the summer, but I wasn't sure how you felt. I mean, I was thinking maybe it was time we made some changes."

Marten cut her off, "Maybe it is time, as you

Americans say, that we settle down?" Then, he pointed to her hand laying on the bed sheet.

Maggie noticed this was not a question. And when she looked down at her hand, there, already placed on her ring finger, was the most beautiful antique diamond engagement ring. He had put it on her while she slept. Maybe she had always been asleep to this and she was finally waking up. The biggest smile she had ever felt grew across her face and, laughing, she pulled him down on top of her.

Maggie and Marten were married on a sunny Saturday in July. The day before, Sarah had flown in with David, and Maggie was surprised to see her round belly. Sarah's hair was its beautiful shade of brown again, and her face was glowing with pregnancy. Happy for Sarah and happy for herself, it was the first time in years there was no hidden feelings between them.

The night before the wedding, bathed in the late afternoon sun, Archie took just Sarah and Maggie out for a boat ride. They said little while Maggie and Sarah held Vivian's urn high in the air and released her ashes into the water. Silently, with grace and dignity, they each said their own goodbyes as tears flowed quietly into the salt air. Their grandmother would have been so proud.

The wedding was a small ceremony on the front lawn of the Atwood house, with Sarah and George standing up for Maggie and Marten. Everyone joked that George should have been standing up for Maggie, but she was just as happy to see his face right behind Marten's at the altar. George and Marten had become fast friends and even Mitzi was quickly growing on her. Mitzi was livid that she was seven months pregnant because she really did look like a beach ball in all the pictures. Sarah managed to stay focused on Maggie the whole weekend and not turn everyone's attention to her burgeoning belly. Millie and Archie sat up front during the ceremony, so everyone could hear Millie's sobbing and laughing her tears of joy. Mac walked Maggie up the aisle and teared up himself when he let her go. Aunt Essie wheezed and got buzzed on champagne before, during, and after the ceremony, and Frank Mayhew danced her around the porch too many times. Poor Lou had to drive both of them home. Uncle Johnny was invited but, instead of coming, he sent them a strange package of old table linens, until Maggie realized he must have stole them from the house and re-gifted them back to her.

Bill Getty came with his much younger bride and toasted them with a very old and expensive bottle of Dom Perignon, which he could afford, again thanks to their family. Peter was in Geneva but, that morning, Marten and Maggie woke to a two seater 1976 Mercedes 450 SL red convertible in the driveway. The note said, "You needed one of your own," and Maggie just laughed. For Maggie, it was truly a perfect day.

The party had gone on through the late hours so Maggie was surprised to see Mitzi bright and early bouncing in her kitchen the next day. "How ya' feel?" she asked with a delicious grin on her face.

"Uggh, I drank too much champagne, and my stomach is turning." Maggie responded.

"Yeah, champagne, sure," Mitzi giggled.

"Mitzi what are you talking about?" Maggie groaned through her hangover. Next thing Mitzi was handing her a home pregnancy test. "I buy these at Costco, got a dozen of them. Go on now...bathroom's right there," Mitzi pointed at the door. "I didn't want to tell you yesterday, because well, for the rest of your life you will only think about the baby. I thought you should have one last day of freedom."

Maggie looked at her like she was a complete alien and waved her hands like she had to be kidding. But she felt too awful to listen to Mitzi nag her, so she went into the bathroom. Maggie could not believe it, Mitzi was right. She was pregnant! There were lines and plusses all over the little stick within seconds. First came the biggest wave of fear she had ever felt and then, after, a gigantic burst of happiness. Okay, this was good, she thought.

When she came out of the bathroom, Mitzi screamed like a school girl, "I was right wasn't I? I'm always right!"

Maggie nodded and ran up the stairs yelling, "Marten, you are not going to believe this!!"

It was early September and Maggie's morning sickness was finally fading. The phone call came when she was upstairs writing at her new computer. Finally she had gotten back to work, but this time it was the story of her family. She wrote it for no other reason then to give her baby a piece of her history. When Maggie lifted the receiver, George screamed, "It's a girl!" She felt a surge of happiness for Mitzi and said, "Name, please."

"Peggy Peyton Sherwood"

"Oh you didn't! Does Mitzi know?"

"No, not yet. She just thought Peyton was pretty." What Mitzi may not have realized was that George took the name from Peyton Manning the football quarterback.

"You are really awful George, but I think Peggy was great idea. Your Mom was a great woman. Marten and I are coming right over."

Excited to go to the hospital, Maggie went running to tell Marten the news. Right as she reached the top of the stairs, all of a sudden, her big toe snagged on a quarter inch of the floorboard sticking up. Immediately, her arms went flailing before her and she began to go headfirst down the stairs. Just then she managed to reach around and grab the top of the railing with one arm and hold on. The weight of her body halted and slammed down hard on the riser. Maggie sat dazed and unable to move or let go of the railing as her heart raced at what might have just occurred.

Then Maggie realized what happened to her mother. Vivian must have tripped on that quarter inch of wood and was unable to catch herself going down the stairs. Maggie righted herself and steadied her breathing. For the baby, she needed to remain calm. Maggie thought, this was exactly how her mother had died.

Marten had heard the thud of her fall and had immediately come running. He raced up the stairs and held Maggie as she sat shaking with her realization. He kept asking where she was hurt, but she wasn't, not on the outside. The puzzle was complete. The last piece had slowly and quietly slipped into place. She cried because now she could finally put it all away.

Hugo Max Klein weighed nine pounds, two ounces and was born on a clear spring day in April. Marten was so animated that George had to drive them to the hospital. Mitzi proclaimed that Hugo would marry Peggy someday and live on Grove Avenue. Archie broke hospital rules and poured champagne, while Millie sobbed on the phone with Sarah. Everyone laughed and cried around this new life for all the right reasons.

And in the still of the hospital night, as Maggie held her son and watched her husband sleep in the chair beside her, she did not regret a thing. Her life had been molded by forces unseen, and she was not bitter or ungrateful for the bad times, the hardness that life had handed her. She could smell the ocean air coming in through the cracked window, and she knew that it was being in the salt that had made her.

The End

ACKNOWLEDGEMENTS:

Many thanks to: my first editor Julie Botteri, for her hard work, Alice Tasmin for encouragement, all my KW friends—thank you for just being so damn supportive, especially Victoria Scudder for her fabulous editing. To my German family: I could not have done this without being a Blinckmann, Danke. Tosh, thank you for 23 years of Delusions of Grandeur. For my dearest and ceaseless friends: Alisa Marie King, Kerry Ann Gallagher and Brooke Schmitt White for being my gladiators- in every way- with this script and in my life. Mom, you've been the wind behind me, and Dad, you've been my rock, without both, I would have been so boring. For my true loves, Jan, Hugo and Max, everything I do, I do for you.

ABOUT THE AUTHOR

Hays Trott Blinckmann is a writer, interior designer and painter. She has a Bachelor of Arts from Tufts University and a Bachelor of Fine Arts from the Museum School, both in Boston. She specializes in oil painting and has had several gallery shows in Florida and New England. Hays lives in Key West, FL with her husband and two young sons. *In The Salt* is her first novel. Please visit haysblinckmann.com for more information.

68719507R00201

Made in the USA
Middletown, DE
01 April 2018